Engaged to Die

ALSO BY CAROLYN HART

Death on Demand

Death on Demand
Design for Murder
Something Wicked
Honeymoon with Murder
A Little Class on Murder
Deadly Valentine
The Christie Caper
Southern Ghost
Mint Julep Murder
Yankee Doodle Dead
White Elephant Dead
Sugarplum Dead
April Fool Dead

Henrie O

Dead Man's Island
Scandal in Fair Haven
Death in Lover's Lane
Death in Paradise
Death on the River Walk
Resort to Murder

Engaged to Die

A DEATH ON DEMAND MYSTERY

Carolyn Hart

DOUBLEDAY LARGE PRINT HOME LIBRARY EDITION

WILLIAM MORROW

An Imprint of HarperCollinsPublishers

This Large Print Edition, prepared especially for Doubleday Large Print Home Library, contains the complete, unabridged text of the original Publisher's Edition.

ISBN 0-7394-3412-8

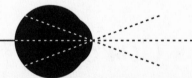

This Large Print Book carries the
Seal of Approval of N.A.V.H.

To Mary Price (aka Mary Lois)—When I was three and you were five, I took unlawful possession of your blue tricycle, the beginning of my life in crime and the beginning of our cherished friendship.

Love, Carolyn

Engaged to Die

· *One* ·

"We always go to Saint Thomas in January." Irene lifted a thin dark eyebrow. "If it weren't for Virginia, we'd be there now."

Carl stared into her amber eyes, looked quickly away. Those eyes—they reminded him uncomfortably of a cat watching a bird, remorseless, predatory, unfathomable. He focused on the coffeepot, a fine china one with pink roses twining around the spout. He watched the clear black stream of coffee, strong, hot, nerve-stretching, pour into his cup. Because of his diabetes he permitted himself only a half cup every morning, no cream, no sugar. He wished with a quick bitterness that he could as easily control his appetites in every sphere. Including Irene. But no matter how little she cared—and sometimes it seemed to him that she made her disdain for him more apparent every day—he knew he would never leave her, that he would do what she wished, when she wished. What was her fascination? It wasn't her beauty, though her dark hair had the sheen of midnight and her almond-shaped eyes and smooth creamy skin and sultry mouth inflamed him. Right this moment he wanted her with a hunger that was painful. But her attraction was more than beauty and passion. There was an aura of recklessness about her that held infinite allure. Funny, he'd always been such a cautious man. . . . He took a sip of coffee. The hot liquid burned his tongue.

"Wouldn't we?" It was a taunt. She held out one perfectly manicured hand, glanced at the shining red nails, turning her hand this way and that.

"Irene"—his tone was harsh—"I can't swing it this year."

Her gaze lifted from her hand. Cold eyes stared at him. "It's that bad?"

"You know what's been happening. The money's gone." He looked through the shining glass of their private upstairs sitting room at the magnificent sweep of the courtyard. Water bubbled cheerfully in both fountains. Winter-bare rosebushes filled the formal beds in the terrace. When Dad was alive and footing the bill, there'd been a full-time gardener. If no one trimmed and spruced, they'd have a burgeoning wilderness by summer. God, everything cost so much. Now he worried whether he could afford the taxes. He'd been pleased several years ago when his father decided to deed the house to him, on the proviso, of course, that Susan and Rusty would always have their own wing. Now, the huge Italian-style villa was as burdensome as trying to heft an elephant. Maybe Virginia . . . He didn't want to ask Virginia. Not if he could help it. The house was his, the only property actually in his name. Everything else, including the gallery, belonged to her. But the taxes . . . Beyond the terrace was the point, much of it screened by pines and palmettos. He couldn't see the ruins of the old fort from the window, but he knew that once conquering Union troops had bustled about, stood by their guns, ready to engage the Confederate forces trying to regain the island. So long ago. The island families that had created fortunes from sea cotton lost everything then. Their world changed. But the world was always changing. Battle, pestilence, and sudden death. Good Lord deliver us. . . .

"You aren't listening to me!" The words were flung toward him, sharp as barbs catching a bull's flank.

Carl felt the beginnings of a headache. He'd had a lot of headaches lately. Who wanted to buy paintings now? If he didn't come up with at least twenty thousand in a couple of weeks, the gallery would have to go into bankruptcy. It would have broken Dad's heart. Would Virginia help? Surely she would. But to Virginia twenty thousand dollars sounded like a fortune. She still had a substantial amount of cash. Dad had believed in cash. If she were fearful—and so many were fearful now—would she see it as throwing good money after bad? If she didn't help . . . Who would ever have believed that the Neville Gallery could go down? It was a solid business, catering to rich vacationers and to the well-heeled retirees who'd settled on the South Carolina sea island of Broward's Rock to escape harsh northern winters. They still had money, but the days of free spending for luxuries were gone. If only he'd been more cautious when times were good. He'd put all he earned from the gallery into stocks. He'd bought more on margin. Dad always warned against buying on margin.

Only a year ago, he and Irene had been rich enough to do anything, go anywhere. That was over. He'd had to borrow to make good. Money was due now on the notes. If Irene knew just how little money they had . . .

"I want to go to Saint Thomas." She tossed down her napkin, pushed back her chair. She rose gracefully, lithe and athletic, stopping at the breakfast room door to flash the enigmatic smile that had held him in thrall since the day they met. "You'll find a way, Carl. I know you will."

"Maybe we should tell Virginia to stick it. Just not show up. The damn gall of her having the damn party at the gallery at the same time as the Mackey opening." Rusty shoved a hand through his hair, now a faded red, nothing like the flaming thatch he'd had when Susan first met him. His charm had attracted her, and the Hollywood boy-next-door appeal of his broad open freckled face. And just like Hollywood, it was all show and no substance. Oh, he was charming still, but now there was often an undercurrent of petulance when they were alone. In public, he was always a pukka sahib, perfectly attired in a navy polo shirt, chinos, cordovan loafers, welcome at a country club, on a cruise ship, hail fellow well met.

Susan slid the letter opener into the envelope. She scanned its contents. "The usual appeal. For the Palmetto Fund. This time it's all about the importance of preserving sea turtles. You know, I like sea turtles as well as anyone but—"

"Susan, for God's sake, stop chattering about sea turtles." He paced across the study, his face stained by an ugly flush.

She put down the letter. "Rusty, the party's not just for Virginia. Anyway, how can we object? If she wants to announce her engagement then, that's her prerogative. We have to get along with her. And we have to keep Boston happy." Boston Mackey was the most successful Low

Country painter allied with the Neville Gallery. They didn't dare lose access to his paintings. It didn't bear thinking about. Susan was still unsure whether planning the party in conjunction with Mackey's opening was inspired malice on Virginia's part or simply another example of the woman's inability to do what was right and proper.

Rusty jammed his hands into his pockets. "Maybe if I talked to Boston—"

"No." The word was harsh, explosive. "Don't do it."

"Your dad should have left the gallery to you and Carl." His tone was querulous, like a ten-year-old called out even though he beat the throw to first. "Thank God Carl already had the house. The bitch would probably have booted us out by now"—he spread a tensed hand in a wide sweep—"if she'd inherited the house, too. She wouldn't give a damn that we've lived here for years. Your dad always wanted the whole family together. Now we're trapped with Virginia. If Carl had any guts, he'd toss her out. By God, I would."

Susan gave him a level, considering stare. "Would you? What do you suppose Virginia would do with her will? Right now everything comes back to Carl and me. Oh, Rusty, don't be a fool. We have to be nice to Virginia."

"The will." He gave an ugly, mirthless chuckle. "Yeah, let's talk about the will. And what do you suppose she'll do with it after she marries sonny boy?"

Just for an instant panic rose inside Susan. Virginia had them in her power. Susan looked around the lovely room, at all the beautiful pieces that she'd collected over the years, the nineteenth-century Chinese drum stool, the Gobelin landscape tapestry, the paintings by Albert Gleizes and Georges Valmier, the Louis XIV cabinet with boulle marquetry. She and Rusty couldn't afford the kind of house her possessions deserved.

"Have you thought about that?" His tone was malicious, derisive.

She gazed at him briefly. Why did she still care so much? He was shallow and selfish and spoiled. But she had loved him for so long. He was part of her life, just as this lovely room was part of her life. Nothing seemed permanent now. Not Rusty. Not her home. Not the gallery, though she and Carl worked as hard as they could. Lately her world seemed dark at the edges, like a nightmare with terror lurking behind everyday, commonplace images, a friend's face metamorphosing into a gargoyle, a placid moon transformed to a bubbling mass of poisonous sulfur. A sense of impending doom pressed against her, making her morose and snappish. Only yesterday she'd gotten into a shouting match with the caterer, and she'd known Tony Hasty all her life. They'd been such good customers she'd hoped Tony would consider lowering the cost of the party. Worst of all had been the moment when Tony loomed over her, his face an angry red, muscles bulging in his taut arms. For an instant she'd been frightened. Of Tony! Somehow she'd calmed them both, but she doubted they would ever treat each other quite the same. She had to get a grip on herself.

Stone-faced, she dropped the charity appeal, picked up the next letter, turned it in her hands. Her thoughts rocketed down another slope, not much more pleasant. An invitation to the Murrays' annual Valentine tea. Last year, Dad had come with them. They'd been pleased that he had a good time and his companion maneuvered his wheelchair so carefully. That's not all Virginia had been maneuvering as they'd discovered to their sorrow. Susan's memory of the picnic was clear enough about her father—ebullient, commanding, his intense love for life making him seem vigorous despite his frailty. Susan couldn't picture Virginia on that lovely spring day. Virginia had been an appendage, not quite a servant but definitely not included in the party, quiet, efficient, almost invisible. It was only since her father's death and Virginia's emergence as the heiress that Susan had ever really noticed Virginia. To Susan's surprise, Virginia was attractive, slender with a gentle prettiness. It was the nurse's uniform that had reduced her to a kind of invisibility. She was certainly not invisible now. Truth to tell, she had charm. Truth to tell . . . Susan wished angrily that she was not so quick to look with clear eyes at those around her. She could not honestly accuse Virginia of subterfuge or pettiness or greed. Just as she could not honestly ignore the truth about Rusty's character. Or lack of it. Susan placed the invitation in the pile to be dealt with.

Rusty paced back to Susan's desk, picked up the antique gun she used as a paperweight. He lifted the old piece, cocked the hammer. "I wish it were real. I'd like to blow her fool head off. Dammit, I won't go."

Susan opened her bank statement. Her lips parted, then closed. She didn't want to ask Rusty about the two thousand he'd drawn out. She didn't want to know how he'd spent the money. Money . . . "We have to go." Her tone was brittle.

His hand tightened on the gun's curved butt. "Sue, we aren't slaves."

She gave a mirthless laugh. "Slaves? We might as well be. And we're going to the party." She lifted her slender shoulders in an irritable shrug. "Unless you want us to start looking for jobs." She looked at him sardonically. "You know, work. You've heard of it, I'm sure. I think you actually had a job once. Before you married me. Let's see, I could sell antiques. Maybe you could—"

He slammed the gun onto the desk, turned, bulled toward the French doors.

She looked down at the gash in the cherry wood.

The French door opened, slammed shut.

Susan slid the bank statement into the envelope, her face ridged and hard.

Louise Neville always wore black. No one knew why. No one asked. She was rail thin with a pinched, dried-up face and a sharp gaze. She paused in the central hall and stared into the sun-splashed drawing room at her sister-in-law. Louise's dark eyes glinted. Virginia was a fool. But the world was populated by fools, fools and knaves. She'd warned Natty when she realized he was infatuated with Virginia. He ignored her. He always thought he knew best. Arrogant. Determined. Willful. But death awaits all men. Even Natty. She'd warned him.

And she'd warned Virginia. The poor woman might as well try to pick up a rattle-snake with a rake as attempt to placate the family. They all hated her. Hatred was wrong. The Bible said so. Woe to those who flout the laws of God.

Louise turned and moved away, unheard, unseen, unnoted.

Beth Kelly put down the phone. She walked blindly to the balcony door, stepped out into the chill gray mist. She placed her hands on the railing, stared out at the fog curling above the dark waters of the marsh, felt the burn of tears. Rusty wasn't coming. Another night by herself. She'd hurried home from work, bought a bottle of cabernet and fillets to grill, taken a shower, brushed her golden hair until it shone, put on a lime green dress that he loved, and now he wasn't coming.

She wrapped her arms across her front, cold as the winter-chilled water. Maybe it was time to demand that he leave Susan.

What if he said no?

Jake O'Neill walked out to the end of the pier, looking in every direction. But it was the middle of the day. The girl wouldn't be here. He placed his hands on the wooden railing, stared out at the wave-riffled water. Tall and slender, with thick dark curly hair and bright blue eyes, he attracted women. He knew that, enjoyed his power. He'd had a good thing going at the gallery in Atlanta, clerking and painting portraits. A lot of rich women liked for him to paint them. And sometimes to make love to them. He made them feel they were part of a bohemian world that existed only in their imaginations. Rich women were fascinated by a man who was the opposite of their cookie-cutter husbands in their dressy casual polo shirts and slacks. So he made sure he was different. Women remembered him. In summer he always wore a white suit. If Tom Wolfe could do it, so could he. For winter, he chose a wool cap and argyle sweater over a white Oxford shirt and gray slacks. The summer hat and winter cap might be an affectation, but those old boys had it right. A hat kept you cooler in summer, warmer in winter.

He reached up, touched his cap. Even Gail had loved his cap. Gail, so slim and golden, so perfect. He'd always been the one to love, then leave. Until Gail. When she'd dropped him for that doctor, he'd been shocked. She'd picked that pudgy, balding asshole over him? That's when he understood that money made all the difference. Painters didn't earn much, not unless they were big shots connected to a major gallery. That's what he'd hoped for in Atlanta. But when Gail dumped him, he'd piled everything in his car, driven to the coast with his big red setter in the passenger seat, and got on the ferry. He hadn't much of anything in mind, but it was summertime and he'd found a job at the island gallery. It was only six months ago, but what a difference the time had made. When he met Virginia Neville, he'd made an effort to charm her. She owned the gallery. But he'd never expected it to turn out the way it had. He'd known she was falling in love with him. And he'd thought, why not? He'd sworn that he would never open his heart again, be vulnerable to the pain he'd suffered because of Gail. Virginia wasn't really old. In her forties. She didn't want to say how old she was. She'd looked at him one night with a question in her eyes. So he told her that she was a woman and he was tired of girls. That pleased her. She was pretty and passionate, and she treated him like a god.

Now he wasn't sure. There was the girl he'd met on the pier in the fog. Last night when they stood at the end of the pier, she'd laughed and plucked the cap from him and perched it on her auburn curls. "Hey," he'd warned, his voice soft, "anyone who wears my cap has to give me a kiss." He bent and kissed her, a tender, lingering kiss. For an instant time stopped. He knew he'd never forget the taste of her lips, sweet and clean and

warm. Before that moment everything had
been clear and simple. If everything went as
planned, he'd be on easy street. He could
paint anything he wanted to and be certain
of exhibitions. But now . . .

Virginia Neville's hands trembled. She
clasped them tightly together. She hated
being unhappy. After all she'd done for
them, why couldn't they be nice to her? Virginia hadn't realized until after Nathaniel's
death that the gallery and all the land belonged to her, everything but the huge
house that had been home for all of them,
Nathaniel's children and their families.
Nathaniel was as generous as a man could
be. But everything belonged to him—the
gallery, the house, the boat. Of course Virginia expected them to stay in the house. It
was their home. Anyone would think they
would have been appreciative. She'd left
Carl in charge of the gallery even though
she owned it and she could do what she
pleased. But Carl's wife still looked at Virginia as though she were a servant who
didn't quite know how to behave. Virginia
had paid for their daughter's wedding be-

cause Mandy was Nathaniel's favorite grandchild. Who would believe a wedding could cost almost fifty thousand dollars! Fifty thousand dollars. That was more, much more, than Virginia had ever earned as a nurse/companion. It was funny, though. She'd liked Nathaniel. He'd appreciated her. And he'd married her and left her everything but the house! She'd not believed how much money there was, though now nothing was worth as much as it had been. She'd been so surprised. All she'd hoped for was enough money so that she didn't have to keep going into houses where death waited. It had never occurred to her that Nathaniel had left everything to her. He'd made a new will after they married and he'd not told anyone of the change. She understood why. When they planned to marry, everyone was clearly angry, though they'd been polite. Nathaniel was offended. He'd changed his will, but he'd never expected to die, not until those last few moments when he'd asked her to promise to take care of Carl and Susan and their families. Of course she'd agreed. At the time, she hadn't felt it meant much. She hadn't known she would inherit everything. That lawyer, the one with the metallic gray eyes and a mouth all twisted as though he tasted something bitter, had been mad as hops. He thought she was a fortune hunter and taking away what rightfully belonged to Nathaniel's children and grandchildren.

Virginia looked across the elegant library, past the Hepplewhite table and chairs, at the portraits in their heavy gold leaf ormolu frames above the Adam mantel. Nathaniel stared boldly into a future now done. He'd been very handsome, really. A craggy kind of face, piercing eyes, dark hair touched with silver.

She still felt an instant of shock when she looked at her own image, pale brown hair in coronet braids, her mild blue eyes wide with surprise and shyness, her thin face soft-ened by a faint flush on her cheeks. What a difference from her years in a uniform, slip-ping quietly to a bedside. In her portrait, she looked like a lady. Now she didn't have to work. Never again.

She smiled at the painting. She'd known it would shock Nathaniel's children when she moved his painting enough to make room for hers above the mantel, too. She'd known and not cared. The shock of

Nathaniel's death was fading, and she was beginning to take pleasure in her role as his widow. She'd thought it fitting to put her portrait there when the new young painter had asked to paint her. He'd asked! That was when her happiness began.

Jake had entitled the painting *The Chatelaine.* She'd not known the word, but she didn't tell Jake. After he'd left, the day he hung the painting, she'd gone to the dictionary. Chatelaine: the mistress of a household. That's how Jake saw her.

But not Nathaniel's children. A few days ago, she'd stood near the doorway to the library and heard Irene's light, cool, sardonic voice as she glanced up at the painting. *"The Chatelaine,"* Irene had drawled. "How about *The Usurper.* Or perhaps *The Bitch."* Each word was light and uninflected, even the last.

Virginia felt uplifted by the portrait. *Authenticated,* that was the word. That's what Nathaniel would say about a painting that was proved to be genuine. She looked as though she belonged in the room. The pale blue slubbed silk dress was exquisite. She'd never been able to afford beautiful dresses until now. She felt a surge of pleasure when she thought of the new dress hanging in her closet, a soft silver georgette with a flutter hem. Her sandals were silver, too. Jake said she looked like winter moonlight, clear and clean and cool, impossible to grasp. She'd felt enchanted when she slipped into the dress. There had been a sense of wonder ever since she met Jake. Jake had helped her pick out diamond earrings and a necklace with diamonds speckling the wings of a silver butterfly. Jake told her she always reminded him of a butterfly, quiet and gentle and beautiful.

Jake . . . Her lips curved in a triumphant smile. Tomorrow night at the gallery, they would announce their engagement. She wanted to use the gallery because that's where she'd met Jake. If Carl and Susan didn't like it, that was just too bad. Boston had been sweet as could be when she'd asked if he minded. He had given that great booming laugh of his and told her the bigger the party, the better, and it was time for her to have some fun.

Fun. Yes, it would be fun. She'd never had a party for herself before. Never. The wedding would be simple, of course. Virginia stared at the painting. Chatelaine.

That's who she was now. Whether They liked it or not. She wasn't going to let Them (that's how she lumped them together now, Carl and Irene and Susan and Rusty) ruin the party. They were cruel and selfish and didn't want her to be happy, even though she'd always made it clear that everything would come to them. She felt a moment's unease. There was less and less money, and Carl kept telling her the gallery was in trouble. But she had quite a bit of cash, and she could do with it what she wished. Of course, eventually everything would go to Nathaniel's children. They had every right.

She had rights, too.

The thought pierced her like a shaft of sunlight spearing into a dungeon.

She had a right to be happy. And happiness was so near. For the first time in her life, she knew about love. She'd never thought it could be this way, her heart pounding when he came near, taking pleasure in the way his hair curled, in the touch of his hand, in his smell. The phone rang. She whirled to run toward it. Jake always called in the morning. . . .

———

Annie Darling wished she hadn't forgotten her muffler. Maybe she was getting soft. The high would be in the forties this afternoon, and that surely wasn't bad for January. To her it seemed as cold as the Arctic because of the drizzle and the cutting wind that swept across the water and the fact that the temperature had hit seventy only a week ago. However, in comparison with the biting cold and sleet-encrusted streets of Amarillo in January, the South Carolina sea island of Broward's Rock was almost balmy. Thinking about winter in her hometown should have helped, but the foggy dampness still made her shiver.

Annie glanced toward the dark window of Confidential Commissions. When Max had opened his business, he'd insisted he wasn't running a private inquiry agency. However, anyone who read the advertisement in *The Island Gazette* might think differently:

CONFIDENTIAL COMMISSIONS
17 Harbor Walk
Curious, Troubled, Problems?
Ask Max
Call Today—321-HELP

He'd solved some interesting problems. But no one had so much as rung the phone since the week before Christmas. He'd given his secretary a couple of weeks off and announced that he would be at Annie's disposal. Honestly, did anyone ever have a more fun husband? Of course, his idea of fun was to stay home and make love. But she couldn't just close up shop, as she'd pointed out this morning, slithering free of his admittedly tantalizing embrace and murmuring, "Later, honey." She prided herself on keeping Death on Demand open unless there was an evacuation order for a hurricane. The category-3 storm in October had been a big scare. They'd boarded over the windows, moved the books on bottom shelves to tall stacks on the coffee bar. At the last minute, the eye of the storm veered north and east. A near escape. She was determined to keep her regular hours at the store today despite Max's gleaming eyes. She needed to check with Chloe on the progress of the inventory. January was always a slow month, so it was a good time to be sure of her stock. And she'd drop by the hospital to see Ingrid, who was recovering from hip surgery after a nasty fall on the slick boardwalk last week. Thank heaven for Chloe. She'd been a fixture at the store during the Christmas season for the past few years, and this holiday she'd been a huge help. Chloe and her mother had spent Christmas on the island with her mother's stepsister until her mother's death last December. Annie had missed seeing Chloe then. But this year, she came on her own over her college break and once again was a willing clerk during the last-minute rush. Chloe was terrific with customers. She really knew her mysteries—her favorite authors were Janet Evanovich and Sarah Strohmeyer—and she was as bubbly as vintage champagne.

Annie was smiling as she reached for the doorknob. She admired the gilt lettering— DEATH ON DEMAND—on the front window. What a clever name. There was, of course, some competition for the best-named mystery bookstore: Remember the Alibi in San Antonio, Texas; Mystery Lovers Bookshop in Oakmont, Pennsylvania; Foul Play in Westerville, Ohio; Coffee, Tea and Mystery in Westminster, California; Book 'em in South Pasadena, California; The Poisoned Pen in Scottsdale, Arizona; The Black Orchid in New York City, and Something Wicked in Evanston, Illinois.

As she turned the knob, Annie took an instant to admire the front window display. These five books were guaranteed to transport readers to warmer, if not necessarily more hospitable, climes: *The House Without a Key,* the first Earl Derr Biggers's Charlie Chan novel set in lovely, long-ago Honolulu; *Death Comes as the End,* Agatha Christie's brilliant evocation of unbridled family passions in ancient Egypt; *The Key to Rebecca,* Ken Follett's absorbing World War II novel set in Africa, which opens with this compelling sentence: "The last camel died at noon"; Elspeth Huxley's *The African Poison Murders,* which was made memorable by the stunning denouement deep in the jungle, and current author Kate Grilley's compulsively readable *Death Dances to a Reggae Beat,* the first in a Caribbean island setting.

The sleigh bells dangling from the door merrily jangled. Annie gave a little skip—her own version of Sammy Sosa's home run leap—as she stepped inside, welcoming the wonderful, familiar smell of books, the bright lights that illuminated the dark feathers of Edgar, the stuffed raven who watched over the glass-encased collectibles, and the cheerful pop and crackle of the fire in the fireplace near the coffee bar.

"Chloe?" Annie slipped off her raincoat, hung it on the coat tree, and popped the umbrella into a jade green stand decorated with gargoyles. Glancing in the mirror near the children's books, she smoothed her thick, wavy blond hair, straightened her crimson sweater, and brushed raindrops from her black slacks.

"Annie"—Chloe erupted up the central aisle—"oh, Annie, you won't believe it!" She skittered to a stop only a foot away, her gamin face alight with delight. Her thin, irregular features were punctuated by sparkling green eyes and a wide, generous mouth. Dark red hair, spangled by the mist, bunched in irregular curls. "Annie, I'm in love." She reached out, grabbed Annie's hands, and pulled her into a rollicking schottische, caroling, "I'm in love, I'm in love, I'm in love," all the way to the coffee area. They careened to a stop by the coffee bar. "Annie, he was there again last night. Can you believe it!"

"I can believe it. But I don't think Agatha's

convinced." Annie pointed at the sleek black cat crouched atop the coffee bar, eyeing them balefully. Laughing, Annie reached out to smooth Agatha's cashmere soft fur. "Relax, Agatha. Chloe's just a little enthusiastic."

Chloe darted behind the coffee bar. "I'll fix us cappuccino. With caramel." She measured and poured, words spurting. "Anyway, I still don't know his name—"

Annie looked at her sharply.

"—but maybe that's even better. I mean, he doesn't know who I am either. We just met that night on the pier in the fog. I was out at the end and I heard footsteps and I couldn't see anyone, and then he was there. He and his dog, this gorgeous red setter. I knew it was all right because of his dog." She looked deep into Annie's eyes. "You can tell when people have dogs."

"Tell what?" Annie moved her wrist just in time to avoid Agatha's fangs. She moved to the end of the coffee bar, opened a cupboard, and got out a bag of cat food.

Agatha's expression didn't change. Her tail flicked.

Annie understood. In Agatha's view, dietary dry food sucked. Annie poured out the pellets, keeping well out of range of Agatha's swift paw. "The better for your slim body."

Agatha ignored the pleasantry, jumped down, ate, growled, ate.

". . . Well, he's a dog person. His dog's named Alexandre. After—"

Annie had seen the latest remake of *The Three Musketeers.* "Dumas?"

"Yes. Annie, you're so clever." The machine rumbled and fizzed. Chloe filled two mugs from the collection on glass shelves opposite the coffee bar, added a mound of whipped cream, and shook out chocolate shavings. She handed a mug to Annie.

"Thanks." Annie welcomed the warmth of the pottery. Each mug was emblazoned with the name of a famous mystery. Her title was *Grey Mask* by Patricia Wentworth, and Chloe's was *Run Jane Run* by Maureen Tan.

Chloe planted her elbows on the shiny wood and beamed at Annie. "Isn't that terrific?"

"The Three Musketeers?" Annie sipped, then happily licked away her whipped-cream mustache, avoiding Agatha's gaze.

"Oh, Annie. Just think. He named his dog after Alexandre Dumas. What does that tell you about him?" Chloe's green eyes were as brilliant as emeralds.

"That he's a good sight more free," Annie said dryly, "with his dog's name than with his own."

Chloe puffed out her thin cheeks. "Oh, Annie—"

Annie held up a hand. "Wait a minute, Chloe. Open your ears and shake the stardust out of your eyes. You met this guy when? Last week?"

"Thursday night. Just before midnight. A week ago tonight." Chloe's voice was dreamy. "It had to be fate. I couldn't sleep and I decided to take a walk. My aunt and uncle keep their house hotter than the Equator. And it's just about as boring." She paused, shook her head. "That's mean. Oh, Annie, I wish I liked them better. Frances was my mother's stepsister, and sometimes I don't even think she liked Mom, and I sure don't think she likes me. They always ask me for holidays, and I come because I don't have anywhere else to go, but it isn't any fun." Her face was forlorn.

Annie understood the tremor in Chloe's voice. Annie's mom had died when Annie was in college, and her uncle, who lived on the island, had welcomed her for every holiday. But nothing ever takes the place of home. Annie had a sudden quick memory of their plain wooden house in Amarillo and how she felt when she walked in that door. There would never—not even here on Broward's Rock in the house she and Max had built and loved—be the same sense of belonging.

"Anyway"—Chloe took a deep, quick breath—"they live close to the harbor. It was foggy as could be. I walked along the boardwalk to the pier and out to the end. I could hear the water and it was like being in a cool gray cocoon. And then"—her face glowed—"I heard footsteps. I was scared for a minute. It was almost midnight. A dog barked—a kind of cheerful woof—and this really nice voice shushed him and there they were, coming out of the fog, this guy with his dog. We started talking. About everything. Fog. And loving nighttime. And travel. Neither of us has been much of anywhere. He wants to go to the Galápagos Islands, and I want to drink a gin and tonic at Raffles Hotel in Singapore. He thinks *The X-Files* are cool and he never misses Buffy. He says Britney Spears gets better and better. He likes jazz, real jazz, George Schering and Gerry Mulligan. He thinks the TV people have made the Olympics sappy. And he saw Tiger Woods at the Masters."

"But he didn't tell you his name? Or where he's from? Or anything?" Annie knew she sounded like a maiden aunt. But Chloe had no one to care for her, perhaps to warn her. Annie had a gut-deep sense that a guy who had no name probably had something to hide. Why else be so secretive?

"Someday he'll tell me." Chloe's tone was utterly confident. "I go to the pier at midnight every night and he comes. That's all I need to know—"

The sleigh bells jangled.

Chloe abruptly sank out of sight behind the coffee bar. "If it's for me, please get rid of him," she hissed.

Annie raised an eyebrow. Shades of a Shakespearean comedy. Was there a first lover and a second lover? She gave a little shrug and turned toward the front of the store. Certainly life hadn't been boring since Chloe had come to Death on Demand over the holiday. Not that Annie ever found life boring. There were so many books to read, so many people to know, so much life to live, so much love to give. She moved quickly, ready to call out Max's name. He should be arriving any minute with the paintings.

But it wasn't Max. She looked up. And up. A basketball player? No, he was too thin and unfinished looking, his shoulders rounded from a habitual stoop, his long arms dangling. Water glistened on a khaki jacket that wasn't quite large enough, showing his wrists. He looked over Annie, his eyes behind thick glasses scanning the store. He had a nice face, though his long nose was crooked, most likely from a long-ago break.

Annie smiled. "May I help you?" Any customer on a rainy January morning was to be cosseted.

"Is Chloe here?" His voice was deep but diffident.

Annie restrained herself from asking brightly if he was Lover Two. Hmm, Chloe obviously had a talent. But she had asked Annie to get rid of this caller. "I'll be glad to help you." Annie half turned, waved her hand. "Classics are on the south wall, used books on the north. Mysteries are shelved by category, Christies, thrillers, and romantic suspense to my right, true crime, caper/comedy and—"

He took a step forward, his long face flushing. "I'm sorry. I just want to see Chloe."

"I wish I could help you." Annie reached to the cash desk, picked up a pad and pen. "May I give her your name?"

"Oh. I thought she'd be here." He sounded forlorn. "Her aunt said—well, anyway, tell her Bob came by."

Annie wrote, held the pen poised. "Bob?"

"Bob Winslow. She knows me." His eyes looked hurt and puzzled.

And you don't mind giving your name. Annie didn't say it aloud, but she wrote Winslow with a flourish. "Any message?"

He hesitated, his face furrowed. A shock of dark hair hung almost to the top of his glasses. "No. I guess not." He turned away. In two long strides, he was at the door. He pulled it open. As the bells jangled, he looked back, said abruptly, "Tell her . . . tell her I've been looking everywhere for her." Cool air and a dash of mist swirled inside as the door closed behind him.

Holding the pad, Annie marched determinedly down the central aisle.

Chloe was perched on a coffee stool. Before Annie could say a word, she held up her hand. "Nope. I know. He's honest, worthy, kind to animals, helps old ladies cross the street—and he's just deadly dull. I mean"—she crossed her arms—"Aunt Frances trotted out Bob the last time I was here. Before Mom died. And he was the first person she had over this Christmas. He's a lawyer. Probate and wills." Chloe yawned. "His father and Uncle Hal bowl together. Anyway, Bob follows me around with big eyes, hat in hand—" Her eyes lighted. "Bob doesn't really wear a hat. He doesn't have enough style. This guy, the one on the pier, wears a cap. You know, the kind golfers used to wear years ago. Annie, have you ever seen a really good-looking guy, curly dark hair and blue eyes and a golfer's cap, anyplace on the island?" She looked at Annie as though she might hold the secret to her dreams.

Slowly Annie shook her head. "Cap . . . hmm, I don't think so. But I don't know everyone on the island, honey. Why, at the last census we had ten thousand residents. We're darn near a metropolis anymore."

"Oh." Chloe's disappointment was clear.

Then she brightened. "But he'll be there to-night. Oh, Annie, he is so cool."

Annie waggled the pad. "Mr. Mystery Man may be cool. But I think I'd go for Bob Winslow. As in, he has a name and uses it."

"Oh, Annie, don't you have any imagination? Do you remember"—Chloe's eyes were suddenly serious—"when you met Max?"

The store was damp with the cool undercurrent of layers of moist air chilled by January wind. The flames in the fireplace added cheer and coziness but did little to warm the long room. Memories warmed Annie. Her lips curved into a smile. It wasn't that long ago when she'd looked across a crowded room at a tall blond man whose blue eyes met hers. They'd moved toward each other, a slender young woman with an eager face and a tall man who loved to laugh. They skirted other people, shook off greetings that might have slowed them. They came together and were quiet, their eyes meeting, oblivious to the noise and smoke and music, and both had known their lives were changed forever. "I remember." Annie's voice was soft: merry blue eyes, wiry blond hair, intelligence and charm and grace in his face, strength and power in his every move. That instant of attraction led to a whirlwind of days together, enchanted, magical, wondrous days, until she decided they were too different: He was rich, she was poor; he'd grown up with every advantage, she'd worked hard for her future; he was laid back, she was hard charging; he saw life as sport, she saw life as a challenge. She'd left him behind, returned to this South Carolina sea island, set to work in the bookstore she'd inherited from her uncle. But Max had come after her. And now . . .

Annie's eyes were still soft, but her voice was firm. "Yes, I remember. But, Chloe, he told me his name—"

The bells at the front door jangled. "Annie, we're here." Max's shout was ebullient. "Got the paintings. Boston's with me."

Annie laughed. Trust Max already to be on a first-name basis with the distinguished artist. Max and Will Rogers—and apparently Chloe, also—never met a stranger. Annie waggled her hand at Chloe. "Quick. Get those easels from the storeroom. I should have had them ready. . . ."

Annie pushed a table farther from the coffee bar. There was just room enough for five easels. What a coup for Death on Demand! When she'd heard in late summer that the Charleston artist was to be featured in a January show at the Neville Gallery, she'd called Mackey. After all, he'd bought mysteries from her by e-mail for several years. And he was a collector. He'd paid five thousand and sixty dollars for a signed very fine first edition in dust wrapper of Graham Greene's *Ministry of Fear: An Entertainment* (Heinemann, London, 1943). When Annie told him about her mystery contest—every month she hung five paintings by a local artist, each representing a famous mystery, and the first person to name the authors and titles received a free book (not a collectible) and coffee for a month—Boston Mackey boomed, "You can't afford my paintings." Annie had said quickly, "A crayon would do." His exuberant bellow of laughter forced her to hold the phone away, but he agreed to dash off watercolors. "Just one catch, young lady." "Yes?" "I get to pick the books."

As far as Annie was concerned, he could pick the mystery of Miss Muffett's tuffet as long as he produced. She'd wasted no time getting the word out across the island, and with Boston Mackey's approval, the watercolors would be auctioned in February to benefit the island's literacy program. Of course, the auction would be at Death on Demand. As Annie pointed out smugly to Max, "It just goes to show that it never hurts to ask." Max smiled agreeably, though obviously it didn't occur to him to apply the moral of the story. Not that Annie had any firm ideas about what Max should ask and of whom. But still . . .

Carrying a large portfolio, Max strode into the coffee area. As always when they met, whether an hour or days had passed, his eyes held a special light just for her. He gestured toward his burly companion. "We've got the goods." As he bent forward, there came an eager whisper for her ears alone. "That means you can take the afternoon off." To Mackey, he announced, "My wife, Annie, and her assistant, Chloe Martin."

Annie grinned, shot Max a cheerful but ambiguous look, and stepped past him. She held out her hand. "Mr. Mackey, I'm absolutely thrilled that you are creating this month's mystery contest. Everyone is very excited."

The artist beamed, enfolded her hand in a firm grip, vigorously pumped. "Mrs. Darling. Miss Martin." His dark eyes, bright and quick as a curious monkey's, swept the bookshelves and the collection of mugs behind the coffee bar. "I've wanted to see this store ever since I found you on the Internet." His tone turned casual. "By the way, I noticed a very fine copy of *The Moonstone* in your collectible display."

The locked glass case stood just inside the front door. Annie had recently added several treasures, first editions of Wilkie Collins's *The Moonstone,* E. Phillips Oppenheim's *The Double Traitor,* John Buchan's *The Thirty-Nine Steps,* and Eric Ambler's *Epitaph for a Spy.*

"We may have to have a little chat about it." Merry brown eyes peered from beneath bristly gray brows. Mackey seemed to take up most of the room in the coffee area, a huge man with flowing silver hair captured in a bushy ponytail, a massive face, close-cropped white beard, and a chest that rolled over onto a bulging stomach. His brown tweed jacket hung open and probably hadn't buttoned in a decade of good dinners. "Now"—he was suddenly busi-

nesslike—"those easels are too close together."

In a flurry of action, with Chloe and Max
and Annie responding to his directions,
Mackey had the watercolors placed to his
liking: One by the cash register. One by the
coffee bar. Numbers three and five on either
side of the fireplace. Number four near the
long line of bookcases holding hard-boiled
mysteries.

He led the way to the first painting and
looked at Annie. "You got 'em figured,
haven't you? I did them in order of publication, of course."

Annie looked at each painting in turn.

The first: A man's body, its bearded face
rigid with horror, lay in a dirty unfurnished
room. Splashes of blood surrounded the
victim who, however, appeared unmarked
by wounds. Three men stared at the fourth,
who knelt by the corpse. The first observer
was tall, white-faced, and flaxen-haired.
The second was a sallow, rat-faced fellow
with beady eyes. The third had a military
bearing though he was sadly emaciated
and held his left arm in a stiff and unnatural
manner. Oddly, his haggard face was
tanned nut-brown though he wore a thick

overcoat. The kneeling detective, his eyes sharp and piercing, was distinguished by a thin hawklike nose and prominent square chin. He was excessively lean, and the hands that examined the victim were blotted with ink and stained by chemicals.

The second: A dignified man with an egg-shaped head, dandified mustache, and glowing green eyes stood by a rumpled bed, observing the overturned bedside table and the debris lying on the floor—a reading lamp broken into two pieces, some books, matches, a bunch of keys, and the crushed fragments of a coffee cup.

The third: Two teenage boys clambered up the rickety ladder, several rungs missing or dangling, of an abandoned water tower near the railroad tracks. Their faces were determined, excited, eager. The boy near the top of the tower had straight dark hair, dark eyes, and a serious face. Close behind, pulling himself over the broken rungs, came a muscular, blue-eyed blond, who looked ready for any adventure.

The fourth: Light filtered through drawn blinds. A stocky man lay on the dining room floor, his right arm outstretched, his right hand folded around the blue-and-white handle of an ice pick that was embedded in the left breast of a dead woman. She lay on her back, her coarse brown hair fluffed around her face, her long muscular legs in line with the kitchen door. Her right stocking was laddered with a run.

The fifth: Inside a moving van filled with furniture and rugs and lamps, a slim, blue-eyed blond girl pointed her flashlight at an old-fashioned clock that lay on a blanket atop a table. A crescent decorated the top of the clock above the square face.

The images were tantalizing. Of course she knew these books. In just a moment— almost any instant—she'd be able to rattle off all five titles. Number one was easy. And number two. But the others—oh, the answers were certainly on the tip of her tongue. Well, maybe lurking at the back of her mind, to be honest. She was a mystery expert. She could talk about mystery writers from Delano Ames to Margaret Tayler Yates. She knew titles from *The A.B.C. Murders* to *The Zebra-Striped Hearse*. But maybe she'd never realized how challenging it was for her customers to look at a drawing or a painting and come up with the title and the author. She said hopefully,

"Your watercolors are lovely, so full of movement—"

Max's eyes glinted with amusement. He leaned against the coffee bar. "Tell us about tonight's exhibition, Boston."

The phone rang. Gratefully, Annie reached for it.

"Annie." The cheerful familiar voice was eager.

Annie smiled. "Hi, Henny."

Henny Brawley was definitely the best customer of Death on Demand. She knew, loved, absorbed, and inhaled mysteries, everything from the toughest to the most genteel. Her dark hair was silvered, her eyes wise with age, and her mind always on a quest. Henny had been young during World War II, and she'd never met a challenge she didn't take. One of her main aims in life was to demonstrate with panache and finality that she indeed knew mysteries better than anyone, including Annie. Her latest pleasure was flinging a name or place at Annie and awaiting the mystery connection. "Hepzibah."

Annie managed not to crow. She replied casually, "Maud Silver's middle name."

"Hmm. More anon." The phone clicked off.

Chloe darted toward the coffee bar. "A cappuccino, Mr. Mackey? Max? Or espresso?"

"Espresso," the artist boomed.

Annie was still smiling as she studied the paintings. Her panic began to subside. Oh, of course. Sure. She knew one and two. But the third, fourth, and fifth . . .

The coffeemaker bubbled and hissed.

The artist pulled a crumpled brochure from his pocket. "It's going to be quite a party. Of course"—his tone was wry—"Virginia is celebrating more than my paintings. But that's all right." His smile was magnanimous. "Why not celebrate romance? The more people who come to the party, the merrier. Who knows? Maybe somebody who comes for scandal will have a pocket full of cash and the wit to recognize true worth in art." He smiled admiringly at Chloe as he accepted the tiny espresso cup. He breathed deeply, inhaling the rich dark coffee aroma.

"Cream or milk, Max?" Chloe opened the door of the small refrigerator.

"Skim, please." Max winked at Annie.

Annie knew she should admire such character. In fact, she found Max's restraint odious. She moved to the coffee bar, reached for the whipped cream can, added a double shot to her mug, and winked back.

Chloe expertly moved the levers. "Scandal?" She turned, swiftly selected a mug. As she held it under the spout, the title was clearly visible: *The Scandal-Monger* by William Le Queux.

Max waved away whipped cream.

Mackey gulped down the espresso, shuddered. "Ahhh." He placed the cup on the coffee bar, overflowed onto a stool, and folded his big arms across his paunch. "Now, I like the Nevilles."

Annie and Max exchanged amused glances. Mackey's noun quivered with import. He was getting ready to dish out gossip with gusto despite his assertion. Annie knew all of the family except the late-come second Mrs. Neville. Irene played tennis of the smash-it-in-your-face-if-you-try-the-net sort. Carl was a good customer, especially fond of cerebral mysteries by writers such as Michael Innes. Susan was an assistant director of the Altar Guild. Rusty had his own table in the card room at the club and was reputed to be a man to watch at poker. Louise drifted through the Neville Gallery, her cold, watchful gaze keeping careful track of visitors.

"Good art people," Mackey boomed. "I was worried for a while after Natty died. But Virginia's left things pretty much up to Carl and Susan. Virginia inherited everything but the house. Hell, that's a crime, really. A man's supposed to take care of his family. You can bet I've made a will, and my kids get everything. I don't blame Natty for marrying Virginia. I mean, she's a sweet lady and she was good to him. By all accounts, she's been damn decent, left the running of the gallery to Carl and Susan, made a will leaving everything to them, that sort of thing. But now the fat's in the fire." He flung out his mammoth hands. "Sex and money. They cause trouble every time. I wouldn't think Virginia would be such a fool, marrying somebody half her age." Suddenly his bristly eyebrows arched, his mouth curved into an O, and he burst into raucous laughter. "By God, what's sauce for the gander."

Mackey became aware of three sets of eyes regarding him blankly. He turned his hands palms up. "Come to think of it, I've been married four times and each bride was younger than the last. And each one dumped me faster than her predecessor." His full lips spread in a huge smile. "But I can't say I didn't enjoy the hell out of each one for the duration. So more power to Virginia. Like I say, if she wants to announce her engagement to this young guy at my party, hey, that's all right. Of course, the family's not happy. To put it mildly." He heaved himself to his feet. "Anyway, be sure and come. Seven o'clock tomorrow night. Neville Gallery. Get a ringside seat." He whopped a big fist into an open palm. "Pow. Pow. Pow."

· *Two* ·

Fog pressed against the windows. The Tiffany shade of the brass lamp near the bed glowed like Tower of London jewels. Flames danced in the fireplace.

Annie smiled into the softness of dark blue eyes. Max's thick blond hair was mussed, his regular features relaxed and contented. He lifted her hand, drew it to his lips, gently kissed her palm. Annie turned her hand, squeezed his fingers, then sat bolt upright, tugging the sheet to her bare shoulders. Even with a fire, the bedroom was chilly. Her mind raced. There were books to unpack, customers to call. She should be at the store. After all, it was the middle of the afternoon.

Max didn't move. His eyes admired her, understood her. "The store will keep." He gave a satisfied sigh. "I knew today was going to be a good day. A very good day."

Annie laughed and reached for her robe.

The phone rang.

"Let it ring." His voice was drowsy. "Check the caller ID. Probably a mortgage company or a sweepstakes pitch. We don't need anything. Or anybody. Just you and me on a January afternoon . . ."

Annie reached for the phone. She glanced at the caller ID. Unknown. But it might be an important call. She grabbed the receiver. "Hello."

"Annie, Denise Abbott. I'm sorry to bother you at home—"

Annie pulled her robe shut.

"—but there wasn't any answer at Max's office. So I called your store and the clerk said you were taking the afternoon off. I guess it's slow as molasses there. Listen, I need some help. If you and Max could do me a favor, I'd really appreciate it." Denise's words rattled like seeds in a shaken pod, edgy, hollow, distant. "I don't know if you know about Dave—"

Annie had always liked Denise Abbott, an

elegant ash blond who loved turquoise and always dripped with beads. She'd managed the Vibrant Woman dress shop on the harbor boardwalk until her husband, Dave, was diagnosed with liver cancer. Nothing had worked, and they'd gone to Mexico in search of a holistic cure. "—but he's lots worse. I'm calling from a pay phone at the gas mart. We're staying at Dave's sister's home in Fresno. He's real sick, Annie."

The cheer and happiness of the room faded. "Denise, I'm so sor—"

"That's not the reason I called." Her tone was thin. "Except that's why I can't come back to the island. I've got this problem and I didn't know who to call, and then I thought about Max."

Annie covered the receiver. "Max," her call was soft. Then she spoke to Denise. "Max is here. Do you want to talk to him?"

Max was on his feet, pulling on his shorts. He came around the bed, sat beside her.

Denise spoke fast. "That's okay. I can tell you, Annie. And maybe this is better. I don't know if a man would understand. Anyway, do you remember my grandmother, Twila Foster?"

Annie recalled a tiny old woman with

deep-set dark eyes in a wrinkled parchment face. She crocheted afghans and sold them through the Proud Pelican gift shop a few doors down from Death on Demand. Annie had bought one as a Christmas present for Max's mother. "Does she still make those beautiful afghans?"

"Oh, I wish. But she can barely see now." A quick indrawn breath. "Macular degeneration. She doesn't even watch TV anymore. She's living in a retirement place called Snug Harbor. Do you know it?"

"Yes. It's really nice, isn't it?" Annie knew the building, a red brick hexagon. The unusual design offered a central recreation and dining room with residents living in the five remaining segments that angled from the entrance. Each room faced out with a view of the marsh or maritime forest. It was the island's newest retirement home, designed for people who were able to function without assistance.

"I guess." Denise's tone was doubtful. "They acted like everything would be taken care of for Gran. You know, all her meals provided and her room kept tidy and her laundry done and lots of activities. It costs . . ." A sigh. "The manager's all bright and perky. Her name's Stephanie. She burbles on and on about how much fun they have. I guess some of them do. They play bridge and bingo and have people come and speak. Annie, I thought it was swell. Anyway, Gran's been there almost a year now. I call her once a week. At least, I try to, but things have been"—just for an instant Denise's voice quivered—"real hard. I called last night and Gran sounded funny. I've been thinking for a while that she wasn't like herself. I asked her what was wrong, and real quick she told me everything was fine, she was just a little tired. But I know her voice. Gran has a real sweet voice, like children singing. I swear she sounded"—a thoughtful pause—"oh, God, I think she sounded scared. Now what could she be scared about? Anyway, she whispered that she was all right and she had to go. She hung up on me. I thought about it, and it didn't seem right to me. But this morning Dave was really hurting. I just got a minute to get away. I called Grandma's doctor and they kind of gave me the runaround, but they said she'd been in for a regular checkup a few weeks ago and she was just fine. I started to call Grandma, then I thought it wouldn't do any good. Maybe she's just blue and lonely and doesn't want me to know because of Dave. But if you could go and see about her, make sure she's all right, I'd really appreciate it. She's in room seventeen. I don't know how much Max charges, but one of these days I'll get back to work, and I can sign a note—"

"You won't do any such thing." Annie was crisp. "Of course I'll go see your grandma. It will be fun for me. You aren't to say a word about money—or you'll make me mad. And I'm ferocious as a tiger when I get going." She made a deep-throated growling noise.

Denise's laughter was shaky, but she laughed. "Oh, Annie, thank you."

The headlights scarcely pierced the tufts of cottony fog. Annie drove slowly, peering at the dimly seen glisten of the asphalt road, almost indistinguishable from the dusk-shrouded trees. Winter's early sunset combined with the fog to alter the landscape, hide familiar vistas.

A shiny white sign to her right marked the entrance to St. Mary's by the Sea. Annie's grip on the wheel eased. She was almost there. Around this bend . . . She strained to see, made a sharp turn at the last minute. She'd not realized that Snug Harbor was so remote from island traffic. Not that Broward's Rock teemed with vehicles even at the height of the tourist season. Accessible only by ferry, the island was just right, Annie thought with satisfaction. Not too big, not too little. Broward's Rock would never suffer the bumper-to-bumper congestion of Hilton Head.

The road ended in a circular drive that curved beneath a porte cochere at the entrance to Snug Harbor. Annie pulled into a parking lot to the right. She didn't bother to lock her car. Another advantage of island living. When she reached the entrance, she pulled on the door. It didn't budge.

Annie glanced at a sign posted next to a doorbell:

Main door locked after business hours
9 to 5, M–F; 9 to noon weekends

Business hours? People lived here. Did they get to see visitors only in the daytime? She glanced at her watch. It was a few minutes after five. Annie pushed the bell, held it for several seconds. She waited a moment, rang again.

The door swung open. "Coming, coming." The overhead lighting in the entryway was muted, casting a bluish light. A moon face stared down at her, ghostly in the dim illumination. Overlong black hair flowed onto his shoulders. He filled the doorway, a hulking figure in a wool plaid shirt, bright swaths of red against black, and baggy gray trousers. "Yeah?" The single word was faintly insolent. Dark eyes stared at her. The big face offered no welcome.

Annie smiled, the kind of smile automatic in common social interchange. "Hello. I'm Annie Darling. I'm here to visit a resident."

He didn't move. "It's almost time for their dinner." His voice was uncommonly high and soft. "You plan to stay for dinner? You have to have a reservation."

"No. This is a surprise visit to an old friend. I'll just pop right in and right out." She took a step forward, almost butting up against his chest.

Grudgingly, he stepped back.

Annie stepped into an oval reception area with shining parquet floors and a machine-made Oriental rug. Red and green balls glistened on a huge artificial Christmas tree. Silver swags festooned the branches. Hallways opened to the left and right. Straight ahead was a commons area with several sofas and easy chairs occupied by a half dozen old women and one bent and wizened man. Their wrinkled faces passive and weary, most silently watched the images flickering on an oversize television screen. Small Christmas trees decorated with popcorn balls and handmade paper chains dotted the room. Beyond the commons was a large dining room. White cloths covered round tables. Place settings gleamed in the lights of two chandeliers. Murals of the Low Country covered interior walls: sea myrtle blossoming with a November mantle of feathery ivory flowers, swarms of fiddler crabs crossing steamy mud flats, the rotting weathered wood of a bateau abandoned on a marsh hummock, a majestic purplish blue Louisiana heron in a willow swamp.

The only sounds were the muted murmur of the television, the thunk of a cane on the parquet, the rattle of dishes behind a service doorway into the dining area, and piped-in music from a recording of "Begin the Beguine" by Tommy Dorsey.

Annie skirted the big man, glancing to her right and left, trying to determine which way to turn to find room 17. She didn't want to ask directions of this oaf.

"Lady." His high voice was sharp, like the shriek of wind in telephone lines.

Annie looked back.

A meaty hand pointed toward a curved reception desk. "You got to sign in."

Annie gave him stare for stare. But rules were rules, even if she didn't like his attitude. Annie walked to the desk. A ledger lay open, the ruled columns labeled: Visitor, Resident, Time In, Time Out, Date.

Annie wrote her name. She hesitated for a moment, then scrawled an indecipherable squiggle in the Resident slot. It most certainly did not read Twila Foster. What business was it of moon face whom Annie visited? She flipped the cover shut and veered to her left into a broad hall. She felt eyes following her. She walked briskly as if she knew her way. The room numbers in this hall were in the fifties. Annie did some quick figuring. Each segment of the hexagon held ten rooms. She passed a cross hall and glimpsed the dining room to her right. As she walked, the numbers lessened. She

found room 17 on the far side of the building. It would have been much quicker had
she turned to her right from the main entry.

She looked behind her. The corridor was
empty. Quickly she stepped to the door,
knocked softly.

In a moment, it opened. A tiny woman
peered through thick glasses, her gaze uncertain. A soft cashmere shawl hung from
thin shoulders. Her green silk dress was
shabby but had once been lovely. A cameo
broach was pinned, a little lopsidedly, to the
bodice.

"Mrs. Foster? Do you remember me?"
Annie held out her hands, clasped cold,
clawlike fingers. "I'm Annie Darling, a friend
of Denise's. I've come to—"

A gong sounded, once, twice, three times.

Doors opened, up and down the hallway.
Old people, some leaning on canes and
walkers, a few in wheelchairs, moved slowly
toward the nearest cross hall.

Mrs. Foster fumbled near the door,
picked up an aluminum cane. "Oh, I wish I
could stop and see you," she said breath-
lessly. "But I have to get to dinner. I mustn't
be late." And she was out in the hall with
Annie, pulling shut her door. She stopped,

looked up at Annie. "I'm sorry. I really am. But I mustn't be late."

Annie was puzzled. She'd had a most casual acquaintance with Denise's grandmother, scarcely more than saying hello in passing. Annie understood that old people in retirement homes look forward to their meals. Meals punctuate days reduced to aimless conversation and bouts of bingo and sing-alongs and long somnolent hours perhaps filled with happy memories, perhaps not. But there was no eagerness in Twila Foster's soft voice. There was fear.

They stood in the hall amid the lemming-like movement toward the cross hall and stared at each other.

Twila Foster's old face suddenly crumpled. "I'm sorry." A hand plucked at the lace collar at her throat. "You must think I'm rude. But I mustn't be late." She ducked her head and followed the others.

"I'll walk with you." Annie kept slow pace. She bent over and said softly, "I'm just here to check on you. Denise is worried that something's wrong."

The old lady stumbled to a stop. "Oh, no. Please. Tell her everything is all right. Please." It was almost a sob. A trembling hand clutched at Annie's arm. Her head poked forward as she looked toward the dining room. "You didn't tell him, did you?"

"Him?" Annie, too, looked toward the dining room.

Mrs. Foster's words were hurried, desperate. "He's in charge at night. Please don't tell him. Please." And she lurched away from Annie.

Annie placed her cup and saucer on the mantel, held out her hands to the fire, but the cheerful warmth didn't touch the core of coldness in her mind. Despite a wonderful dinner—Max loved to cook, and tonight's beef fillets with stuffed artichokes had been spectacular—Annie felt hollow. She stepped away from the fire, began to pace. "I'm going over there tomorrow and find out what's what."

Max frowned. "We need more information, Annie. Why don't you call Mrs. Foster? That protects her from anyone knowing she's spoken to you. It seems pretty clear she's scared of the guy who's there at night. Let me get the number." He strode to the breakfast room, reached for the telephone book drawer.

Annie picked up the cordless phone.

Max scanned the directory. "Okay." He read off the numbers. Dorothy L., her white fur winter-thick, jumped up on the kitchen counter, batted at Max's fingers. He picked up the chunky white cat, nuzzled her ruff.

Annie punched the phone. It rang twice, then a faint voice answered, "Hello."

"Mrs. Foster?" Annie spoke fast. "This is Annie Darling, Denise's friend. Tomorrow I'm going to talk to the people in charge there—"

Max cradled Dorothy L. in his arms, listened.

"No." The cry was so sharp, Annie held the phone away. She reached down, clicked on the speaker, and the frightened voice spilled into the peaceful room. "Please, Mrs. Darling, don't do that. Tonight after dinner, he demanded to know who you came to see. No one answered. He said that when he found out"—her voice broke—"he'd have a little talk with that person. When anybody does anything he doesn't like, he comes to your room late at night. No one knows he's there and—oh, it's so awful. Don't do that to me. Please."

Annie held the receiver so tightly her fingers hurt. "Mrs. Foster, that's dreadful. He can't get away with hurting you."

"You don't understand. He doesn't hurt anyone. But he talks"—there was a shudder in her voice—"and he makes you listen. One night I went to dinner and I forgot my key. I had to ask him to open my door. You see, he has a master key. He can go in any room whenever he wants. I knew what would happen, but I had to ask. I didn't have anywhere to go. When I asked him, he waited and waited, and then he said in this awful voice that he'd open my door, but I had to stop being so careless. He walked with me back to the room and he held onto my arm"—there was a sob in her voice—"and I hated the feel of his hot fingers, tight on my skin. He came into my room and closed the door and he started talking. He said I must apologize. I did, and he said I had to say I was sorry again. And he made me go stand in a corner, and he kept talking in that soft voice, and he said I was nothing but trouble, that I'd been trouble ever since I moved there, and people who caused trouble, sometimes they died in their sleep. And he rattled his chain with the keys, and he said he could come in my room any time. When he left, I couldn't stop shaking." There was a choking sob. "Don't you see, there's nothing to be done. It doesn't sound like anything, but you don't know how he acts or hear his voice. Sometimes I wake up in the night and he's standing there at the foot of my bed. Once I screamed, and the next morning they told me I'd had a nightmare. There's nothing anyone can do. Please leave me alone. Don't tell anyone what I told you. Especially not Stephanie. She'd ask him about me. And it will be night again. . . ." She hung up.

Annie juggled the folder under her arm as she unlocked the front door of Death on Demand. She reached out, flicked on the lights, welcomed the cheery bright colors of book jackets, heard Agatha's irritated yowl.

"Okay, okay. Coming." She moved down the center aisle, heading for the coffee bar. Where was Chloe? She should have opened the store an hour ago. She certainly couldn't have picked a worse morning to be late. Annie plopped the green folder on the coffee bar. Agatha jumped up, spat out a series of querulous meows.

"Sweetheart, I'm sorry." Damn Chloe. Annie shook her head. To be fair, she hadn't called the store to report she was running late. Annie filled Agatha's bowl, and the imperious black cat, still meowing, leaped to the floor, hunched over the food, and began to eat in a fury of impatience.

"Chloe?" Annie didn't try to keep the irritation from her voice. There was no answer. Annie grabbed the phone, hesitated, loosened her hold. Max would be glad to take over, but he was busy. For her. She touched the folder. It was amazing how much information about Snug Harbor, its owners, employees, and residents he'd retrieved on the Internet from government records and articles that had appeared in *The Island Gazette.* If Chloe didn't show up, Annie would simply hang out the Closed sign. She had no intention of being late for her appointment at Snug Harbor.

The phone rang.

Annie snatched up the receiver. Chloe better have a good excuse. "Death on—"

"He was known to have written a novel over the weekend." Henny sounded as satisfied as if she were sipping a Singapore sling created especially for her by Madeline Bean, Jerrilyn Farmer's sleuth in *Dim Sum*

Dead, a catering mystery featuring a Chinese New Year banquet.

Annie's reply was equally smooth. "Oh, sure. Edgar Wallace."

"Oh. Yes. Right—" Call waiting clicked.

"Talk to you later." Annie ended Henny's call, took the incoming call. "Death on Demand, the best—"

"Annie." Chloe's husky voice dragged. "I'm sorry. I'll be there as soon as I can. I overslept."

Annie frowned. "Can you hurry? I've got an important appointment at eleven." Annie glanced at her watch. A quarter after ten.

"Yes." Chloe's voice sounded as if she were at the far end of a cellar. "I'll be right there." The connection ended.

Annie glared at the phone. Up to now, Chloe had been utterly dependable. Of course, anyone could oversleep. . . .

As Annie brewed her favorite smooth Kona, she opened Max's folder and began to read the information Max had gathered:

Snug Harbor

Opened three years ago, the Broward's Rock retirement home is a franchise granted by Warman Corporation of Atlanta, Miami, and Chicago, a holding company for retirement, assisted living, and nursing homes, which operates in eleven states. The local franchise is held by Crispus Markham of Charleston. Markham visited the island when the community opened. The local manager is Stephanie Hammond. Snug Harbor has twenty-four employees, including a cook, kitchen help, custodians, and aides.

Annie highlighted the name of the manager. She scanned the text impatiently. Ahh. Here's what she wanted:

Joseph J. Brown, 62, is a resident assistant in charge of the premises after hours.

Brown was the big moon-faced jerk. Annie was impressed. Max had certainly found out buckets about the retirement home's bad apple, proving once again that the Internet, assiduously searched, could provide more than most people would want revealed about their lives.

Brown, 62, is a native of Butte, Montana. Married three times. Each marriage ended in divorce. No children. Has lived in Washington, Texas, California, Alaska, Illinois, Michigan, and Florida. Work history includes stints as a stevedore, night watchman, photographer, radio ad salesman, nurseryman, trucker, and bartender. Has lived on Broward's Rock for two years. Was employed by Morgan's Diner until accepting the position as night manager of Snug Harbor. Free room and meals and a small salary in exchange for overnight supervision of the facility. Snug Harbor brochures emphasize that guests are assured of security because assistance is available twenty-four hours a day.

In the margin, Max had written, "Got a call out to the owner of Morgan's Diner, but he's down in Cozumel scuba diving. I'll see what else I can dig up."

Annie's gaze moved to the paragraph on Stephanie Hammond. In the margin, Max's red pencil had noted, "See photo on next page." Annie lifted the sheet. Stephanie

Hammond beamed from the color photograph, blue eyes bright, lips curved in a cheerful smile. Tawny hair in stylish tangles bushed to a crest. She looked wholesome and forthright, energetic and eager. In a postscript, Max had added, "Got this from their web site. Full color. Fancy. Everybody looked happy."

Annie sipped her coffee, turned back to the manager's bio.

Stephanie Hammond, 24, a native of Charleston. Master's degree in sociology. Single. Worked for the state in nursing home inspections division until accepting the assistant to the manager position at Snug Harbor. Was named interim manager when Leah Carew, an army reservist, was called to active duty. . . .

The dangling bells at the front door jangled.

"Annie, I'm here." Chloe came down the central aisle, moving as if every muscle ached. Her auburn hair was unevenly brushed. She wore no makeup. Freckles stood out against pale skin. Her eyes were tired and mournful. A violet turtleneck clashed with orange slacks.

Annie took a last gulp of coffee, closed the file. She was on her feet, heading for the door, car keys in hand. It wouldn't hurt to get to Snug Harbor a little before her appointment. "Chloe, I'm not sure when I'll be back. I doubt we'll have many customers today unless there's a business conference at the Buccaneer." The resort hotel offered guests a map of the island that included a thumbnail description of the businesses on the boardwalk by the marina.

She was almost to the door when Chloe called out. "Annie . . ."

Annie wanted to dash out the door, but she couldn't ignore the appeal in Chloe's voice. Annie paused, looked back.

Chloe's mournful face drooped like an iris beaten down by heavy rain. "I can't work the whole day." Chloe squeezed her hands into fists, pressed them against her cheeks. Her lips quivered.

Annie moved toward her. "What's wrong?" There was no doubt that Chloe was upset. But of all mornings . . .

"I stayed on the pier all night." She

choked back a sob. "He didn't come." Her hands dropped. Her fists opened.

Annie's first instinct was to ask what Chloe had expected. After all, if the guy wouldn't even give his name . . . The pain in Chloe's face stilled the words. Annie remembered her so clearly as a bouncy happy teenager talking about Harrison Ford and how someday she'd find a man like him. Maybe Chloe's hunger for romance had begun so long ago, was so deep that nothing Annie said would help. "I'm sorry, honey. Maybe . . ." Car trouble? Not on an island. No matter where he lived, it wouldn't take long to walk to the pier. Sick? Oh, sure. Struck down by a mysterious pox known as cold feet. The fact was that Chloe's mystery romance had ended in a whimper, not a bang. Annie looked at the grandfather clock near the fireplace. Fifteen to eleven. Okay, she could be at Snug Harbor in five minutes. But she wanted time to look around during visiting hours.

Chloe burst into frantic speech. "Annie, I didn't tell you before. He said he loved me, that he knew we would always be together, that we were perfect for each other. We made love there on the pier"—her gaze was defiant—"and it wasn't just any old one-night stand. I know it wasn't. It didn't matter that it was cold and damp. Nothing mattered but being together. I have to find him." Her breathing was quick and shallow. "I've been thinking. He has to work somewhere. It can't be here on the boardwalk or I would have seen him. I'm going to make a list of all the businesses on the island and go to each one. Annie, will you help me?"

Annie gripped her car keys. "Chloe, give it up. If he wants to find you—"

"He doesn't know my name." It was a stricken wail. "Annie, I have to find him. I've never met anyone like him. Never. If you'd ever seen him, you'd remember him. His face is kind of uneven. High cheekbones and a long jaw and sharp chin. He looks like one of those courtiers you see in fifteenth-century French paintings. I told him he should wear a ruffled shirt and brandish a sword and he laughed. But he was pleased. Annie, he was different." Her voice quivered with eagerness. "I've got to find him."

A sword? Annie wasn't impressed. "Chloe, I've got to go." She dashed toward the front door, paused only long enough to call, "I'll keep on the lookout."

Chloe touched the top of her dark red head. "He always wears a cap, one of those round tweedy kind that are soft. Like golfers wear. And an argyle sweater."

The door closed and Annie broke into a run. How could Chloe be such a passionate idiot? Annie had a sudden cold thought of how she would have felt if Max had walked out of her life without a word. Funny, when she thought about it. She'd tried to run away from Max, but Max had come to the island, looking for her. That was different. He darn sure knew her name and she his. Well, she didn't have time to worry about Chloe. She had to do something about Denise's grandmother.

Max Darling flicked off his computer. Amazing what could be found when a name was typed into a search engine on the Internet: charitable donations, bank accounts, work records, real estate transactions, and on and on. Max tilted his red leather chair, punching on the heater and massage unit. Annie had been pleased at the effort he'd made to gather information about the retirement center. Dear Annie, his serious, intense, hardworking, and, bless her, genuinely kind wife. He gazed at the silver-framed photograph on the corner of his desk, flyaway blond hair, steady gray eyes, kissable lips curved in an irresistible smile. He smiled in return. "Go get 'em," he murmured. Annie would set everything right for Mrs. Foster.

Max poked the chair upright, got to his feet. The appointment at Snug Harbor shouldn't take long. He'd call Annie in a little while, see if she wanted to have lunch at Parotti's. In winter, Annie loved the mungy old restaurant's homemade chili topped with grated cheese, steamed corn kernels, and sliced Vidalia onions. After lunch, they might take a long walk on the winter beach, maybe catch a flight of cormorants, check out the flotsam that had washed in from the nor'easter just before Christmas. Tonight the Boston Mackey exhibition opened at the Neville Gallery. Max grinned. A fun day. Most fun of all, there would surely be time enough this afternoon for him and Annie to go home. Ah, a winter afternoon and the woman he loved. Omar could keep the wine and verse. First things first.

———

Stephanie Hammond bounced toward the door, hand outstretched. A candy cane appliqué sparkled against the thick red fuzz of her pullover sweater. "Mrs. Darling, I'm delighted to welcome you to Snug Harbor." She waved Annie toward a chintz-upholstered overstuffed chair. Instead of taking her place behind the walnut desk, the manager took an armchair opposite Annie and leaned forward, her gaze eager. "What can I do for you?" She appeared genuinely delighted to greet her visitor. "Do you have an elderly family member who might be interested in living with us? I'd love to show you everything." She gestured toward the community area. "Perhaps you can join us for lunch. We have our larger meal at noon and sandwiches and soup in the evening. I think I can say that no one on the island has better food than we do. Today we're having meat loaf and mashed potatoes and green beans and lemon meringue pie."

Her words evoked a sense of ease and comfort, warming as a soft shawl or a crackling fire.

Patricia Wentworth's Miss Silver always espoused the truth. Miss Silver often quoted Alfred Lord Tennyson. There was a verse from *The Idylls of the King:* Live pure, speak true, right wrong. . . . And Alice Tilton's Leonidas Witherall was fond of exhorting Meredith schoolboys to tell the truth and fear no man. However, Leonidas (aka Bill Shakespeare) was wont to fudge a bit when enmeshed in the long tentacles of the octopus of fate.

Because truth once offered could not be retracted. Burning in Annie's memory was the quavery voice of an old and dreadfully frightened woman. Annie temporized. "Miss Hammond, I—"

"Oh, please, call me Stephanie. We're on a first-name basis here." The manager smoothed back a glossy curl. Her gaze was earnest. "I want everyone to feel that we are all friends. Buddies. Calling people mister and missus is rather off-putting, don't you think?"

Annie's home state was free and easy Texas, where first names were almost invariable, except when addressing the elderly. Formal address offered a certain dignity. You didn't call someone's grandfather Al unless invited to do so. "I'm glad you care about the residents."

Those wide blue eyes blinked. "Care? Of

course we care." Her well-modulated voice held a hint of surprise.

Annie wished she knew Stephanie Hammond. If only they'd played tennis together (Would she call the lines right? Did she drill an opponent at the net?) or gone to an oyster roast (Would she complain about the no-see-ums? Did she get easily frustrated trying to gouge open the shells?) or worked on a committee (Did she do her part? Was she dependable or all show and no substance?). The manager appeared good-humored and cheerful and committed to her job. Did she know what was happening on her watch?

"A good deal depends upon your staff, I would assume." Did Joseph J. Brown present one face to his boss, another to the residents?

Stephanie leaned forward, eyes glowing. "I have the world's best staff. I can promise you that. We have a registered nurse on the premises—Bonita Esperanza—and everyone loves her. Mary Harris is our program director and she's always coming up with something fun for everyone. Harry Thomas is our dietician. Jane Crandall is our chef. And we have—"

Annie flung out his name. "Joseph J. Brown?"

The manager's smile faded at Annie's crisp tone. "Why do you ask?"

Annie met her gaze. "Have you ever received any complaints about him?"

Stephanie frowned, her effervescence gone. She gave a sigh. "I suppose you mean old General Priddy. You have to understand"—she was reassuring and patient—"that when you deal with old people, they can get strange fancies. They can confuse the present and the past and imagine"—a tinkling laugh—"the most bizarre situations. One old lady is sure that Martians have a pipeline to Snug Harbor and listen to every word we say. And"—her eyes glinted—"a general is used to being in charge. I told his daughter that the general was reliving those war years, shouting in the night. But she wasn't at all reasonable and she moved him out." Stephanie snapped her fingers. "She talked to me that morning, and that afternoon he was gone."

Annie smoothed a wrinkle from her cream wool slacks. She said pleasantly, "Didn't that make you wonder a little?"

"Wonder?" The director sounded puzzled.

"About the validity of the general's complaint." Into the sudden, resistant silence, Annie demanded, "What was his complaint?"

The manager fingered a candy cane earring. "Oh, it was just crazy. He didn't like J. J., that's what it came down to. He told his daughter—and I swear, she should have been a general—"

Annie kept her expression pleasant and welcoming and mentally applauded the combative general's daughter.

"—that he—the general—had accidentally bumped J. J. from behind with his wheelchair, and then, according to the general, J. J. took his wheelchair and swung him around and rolled him to his room and—" She broke off, shook her head impatiently, her tawny hair rippling. "It's too absurd." Her eyes flashed. "I need to know why you are asking these questions."

"Because another resident has been abused by Mr. Brown. That resident"—Annie spoke carefully—"lives in terror of him. And I'm here to see about it."

The manager clamped her hands on the chair arms. There was no smile now. "That is a very serious accusation, Mrs. Darling. Who is making this claim?"

"An old woman." Annie remembered the shuddering voice: he makes you listen. "A helpless old woman who is terrified for darkness to come. He has a key that opens every door. Once he came to her room in the middle of the night and was standing at the foot of her bed when she awakened. She screamed. The next day everyone told her she'd had a nightmare."

The manager was indignant. "Old people often have nightmares!"

Annie folded her arms. "Miss Hammond"—no, they weren't buddies, not now—"you don't stay here at night, do you?"

Her silence answered.

"Then please listen to me. The man you've hired is cruel. He delights in frightening old people. I don't doubt there are many who've had no problem with him. He would seek out those who are vulnerable."

Stephanie Hammond surged to her feet, her face ridged. "You must give me the name of the person involved. And the circumstances."

Annie remembered Twila Foster's soft uncertain eyes and thin face and the clawlike fingers plucking at her lace collar and the fear, the demeaning, dreadful, terrible fear. Annie rose and the two women faced each other, wary antagonists. "What will you do?"

The manager gestured toward the door. "Why, I'll talk to J. J. and see—"

"What he has to say? What do you think he will say?" Annie spread out her hands. "Of course he'll deny everything. A nightmare." She was sardonic. "Or she's imagining persecution. Or confused. It's easy to say an old person is imagining things. If you tell him her name, he'll whisper to her late at night in that soft high voice. He'll tell her she will have to pay. He told her once that she'd been nothing but trouble ever since she came."

"This is all unsubstantiated. You can't expect me to take action against an employee without some kind of proof." A flush stained her smooth cheeks.

Annie remembered the wrinkled parchment face of Twila Foster and the tremor in her old voice. "There is one way to get proof." Annie's throat ached. Please, God, help us now. She spoke fast.

When she was done, Stephanie Hammond paced back and forth across the small room, her face furrowed in thought. Finally, she stopped, stared hard at Annie. "All right. I'll do it."

Annie leaned against the cool plastered wall. The interior door between the manager's office and the adjacent room was open a sliver, just enough to permit a line of light. This space had been Stephanie's office before she was named interim manager. Now the office was unused. It was chilly and smelled faintly dusty. The drapes were drawn, shutting out the thin winter light. Annie wondered if the heating vents were closed. She felt cold as ice. She folded her arms tight across her front, suppressed a shiver. If her scheme was unsuccessful . . .

A door squeaked. "I'll just take a moment of your time, Mrs. Foster. Here, please take this chair. It's the most comfortable."

Annie edged to the line of light. She could see very little, a portion of Mrs. Foster's aluminum cane and worn black shoes that laced. But she could hear every word.

Mrs. Foster's voice was uncertain. "Stephanie, I'm sure Denise paid my rent—"

"Oh, everything's fine. Well"—the manager paused—"actually, I do have a concern. But I'll wait until J. J. gets here before—"

The cane quivered as the old woman's hand shook. "J. J.?" Twila Foster drew her breath in sharply. The cane poked forward and her thin arm came in sight. "No, I don't want to—" She broke off.

"Stephanie." The high soft voice rolled across the room, thick as spreading oil.

"Yes. Come in, J. J. Close the door, please." Stephanie was brisk.

The door clicked shut. He walked across the room, briefly in Annie's sight, greasy black hair curling on the shoulders of the red-and-black plaid shirt, fat hands hanging loose at his sides, dark moccasins noiseless on the parquet floor.

There was not a breath of sound from the old woman.

"Thanks, J. J. Now, I've had a complaint that you have spoken sharply to Mrs. Foster." Stephanie cleared her throat. "Twila, I'd like to hear what you have to say."

"No. I didn't say anything." Her thin voice rose and cracked. "I swear I didn't. Please, I want to go back to my room."

Annie gripped the door jamb, rested her head against the wood. Oh, God. Anyone could hear the terror in Mrs. Foster's voice. Annie blinked back tears. This was dreadful, dreadful. . . .

"Twila," Stephanie was impatient, "I have to—"

The door opened. "Stephanie"—a woman's voice was urgent—"we've got a problem outside. Somebody's blocking the drive and I can't get them to move. Can you please come?"

"Oh. I'm busy right now." An exasperated breath. "But all right. J. J., stay here. I want to see about this." There were brisk steps. "I'll be right back." The door closed.

There was silence.

To Annie it was a hideous silence, heavy with menace. She stood there rigid, sick with apprehension. A faint squeak sounded. Annie's head jerked toward the hall. The door opened and Stephanie slipped inside. She pulled the door slowly shut behind her and tiptoed across the cold room. Annie pulled back to give Stephanie room to see through the sliver of space.

Twila's quavering voice rose. "I didn't say anything to Stephanie. I swear I didn't."

"Oh, but you must have, Twila." There was no sound from the moccasins, but he moved closer and closer until he stood over the seated woman. "You made a mistake. Now, you'll have to tell Stephanie you were having a bad dream. If you don't—"

Annie hated his high soft voice. It threatened menace deadly as the pinch of poison in a Borgia ring.

Stephanie bent nearer to the line of light. Annie smelled her gingery perfume.

"—it will be too bad. Do you like bats, Twila? Perhaps there will be bats in your room at night. That might happen. It might even happen tonight. You can dream about it when you go to sleep. Bats have tiny sharp teeth. Sometimes they're rabid. I wonder what will happen when a bat is dropped into your bed? It takes almost a year for rabies to develop, and all the while you can wonder if that's how you'll die, rigid as a corpse, frothing at the mouth."

"I won't tell her. I won't." Twila was sobbing now, hiccuping and crying.

"Or a spider might get into one of your drawers. It could be a daddy longlegs. But it might be a brown recluse."

Her hand shaking, Stephanie reached

out, banged against the door, yanked it open. She strode into her office, thrusting out her hand. "Give me your keys, J. J. You're fired."

J. J. whirled toward them, his brown eyes feral. His glance moved past Stephanie, settled on Annie.

Annie hated the look. It was as nasty as flipping over a flagstone and seeing slugs.

"Your keys." Stephanie held out her hand, her face set and determined.

Slowly, like a snake easing over a bank, his hand went into his pocket. He pulled out the ring of keys. Snakes can jump, fast. His arm flashed and the keys flew toward Annie.

Her hand rose. The keys, sharp and hard and painful, struck her arm.

Brown took a step toward the connecting office, his big hands clamped into fists.

"Get out. Or I'll call the police." Stephanie strode to her desk, grabbed up the phone.

Brown rocked back and forth on his feet and stared toward the open door to the connecting office, the open door and Annie standing there. His moon face was heavy with fury. The words to Annie were a high silky whisper. "You're going to pay, lady."

· *Three* ·

Annie took a deep breath, delighting in the swirl of fumes from beer on tap, sawdust-sprinkled wooden floors, live bait bobbing in salt-crusted barrels, chicken necks in battered coolers, and hot grease. Annie loved Parotti's, the island's oldest restaurant and bait shop, a combination unsettling to squeamish tourists. Since Ben Parotti's marriage, the restaurant wasn't quite as down home as it used to be, though live bait was still available. The menu now included quiche as well as chitterlings, the decor chintz curtains as well as sawdust. Ben was close-shaven and natty in a blue blazer and flannel slacks, a far cry

from his former bristly cheeks, long under-
wear top, and stained corduroy trousers.
Annie never ceased to marvel at the power
of a woman. Or maybe it was more accurate to applaud the power of love. In the
earlier days, Ben might have looked like a
grouchy leprechaun, but actually he was a
man waiting to fall in love with the right
woman. In a moment, Ben himself would
serve their table, bringing Annie a superde-
luxe bowl of chili and Max an equally big
bowl of catfish stew. Jalapeños and corn
kernels studded the faintly sweet corn
muffins. Annie picked up a muffin, warm
from the oven, slathered it with real butter,
and took a big bite. "Hmmm." Sparks
danced among the logs burning in the huge
stone fireplace. Only a few tables were
taken, and all the customers were islanders.
Not many vacationers came to Broward's
Rock in January, and the windswept
beaches and chill mornings were a time of
peace and renewal.

Max sat across the initial-scarred
wooden plank table, his eyes soft when he
looked at her. Dear Max. His wavy blond
hair curled a little more tightly in the winter
mist. She thought him the handsomest man

she'd ever known. And yes, he had strong and regular features and a stalwart chin and fjord blue eyes, but what made him handsome in her view was the character that shaped his face, the honor and steadfastness and courage and goodness.

He grinned. "Love you, too."

She grinned in return. How wonderful to be able to look across a table without guile or caution or reserve. How wonderful to be loved. Annie reached out, grabbed his hand. "Oh, Max." And she burst into tears.

In an instant, he was around the table and beside her in the booth, his arm warm on her shoulders. "It's okay, honey. Mrs. Foster's okay now."

"Max," tears edged down her cheeks, "it was hideous. She was terrified, sick with fear. It was awful."

Max's arm tightened. "You got rid of Brown. He's out of there. The locks are being changed right now. Stephanie Hammond's not taking any chances. And all because of you." He pulled out his handkerchief, gently wiped away the tears. "Come on, Annie"—he looked to his right—"Ben's here and he's got the best chili in the world."

She sniffed, took the handkerchief, scrubbed her eyes. "Outside of Texas."

As Max returned to his place, Ben slid the bowls across the planks, murmured to Max, "The missus under the weather?"

Annie scooted out of the booth, hugged a startled Ben. "I'm fine, Ben. Coming here is the best tonic in the world."

"Always glad to have you." Ben refilled Annie's iced tea, which southerners drink all year round, and looked at Max's tall frosted glass. "Another Bud Light?"

"Sure." Max added a dollop of hot sauce to the stew.

Annie slid back into her seat and stirred the topping of grated cheese and steamed corn kernels into her chili. "Peace and quiet," she said indistinctly through a big mouthful of chili. "That's what I need. And happy faces. I've had enough drama to last me all year." She brightened. "Rachel will be home pretty soon. I can't believe how much I've missed her." Annie's teenage stepsister was in Florida with a friend and her family. "And Pudge gets back next week." Annie's father was making the island his home but he was often off island for a pleasure trip. His latest was a jaunt to Rio.

"We'll have a party. As far as I'm concerned, no more winter blahs."

Max laughed. "Annie, it's only January."

"I'm not kidding." Her tone was determined. "No more misery. When we get home, I'm going to read the latest Mary Daheim and laugh my head off and take a hot bath—"

"And sundry other pleasures," he murmured. He nodded thanks to Ben for the cold beer. Ben started to turn away.

"—and I'm not going to let anything upset me. Or anybody." She banged the table for emphasis and Ben swung back.

"But if someone called, like Denise—" Max suddenly frowned, broke off.

"No way, José. I'm going to have a happy afternoon and go to a champagne gala tonight in a beautiful new dress—oh, Max, you'll love it—it doesn't have a back—and I am going to have fun, fun, fun. No more angst." Annie held up both hands, palms forward.

Ben peered at them, shrugged, moved away.

Annie picked up another muffin. "Poor Ben. I have him thoroughly confused."

"Calls," Max muttered. He began to pat his pockets. "Damn, where'd I put it?"

Annie's knife was poised above the butter. "What's wrong?"

Max found a crumpled note in the inner pocket of his jacket, pulled it out. "I forgot to tell you about the phone calls from Chloe."

"Chloe? Speaking of angst"—Annie said wearily—"what now?"

Max unfolded the sheet. "Three calls. In the first one, she apologizes for shutting down the store—"

Annie's head jerked up. On Friday afternoon? She looked around the big, sparsely occupied café. Okay, it was January. No big deal. Henny Brawley wouldn't be pleased to find the store closed. Henny had planned to drop by this afternoon to pick up her latest order, Kathy Lynn Emerson's *Face Down Beneath the Eleanor Cross,* Marlys Millhiser's *Killer Commute,* and Katherine Hall Page's *The Body in the Cast.* She'd call Henny and promise to bring the titles to the art exhibition tonight. Henny never missed a good party.

"—but she said she had to hunt for him."

Max raised a blond brow. "She didn't give a name, just said 'him.' "

Annie welcomed a jolt of the strong iced tea. "She doesn't know his name."

"No name, but apparently she has a description. In her second call, she was excited, saying somebody told her they'd seen a guy in a golfer's cap and argyle sweater out on Black Duck Road. I'm sorry to report"—Max's tone was amused—"that the sighting apparently did not lead to her quarry. In the last call, she was discouraged, lots of sighs and sniffs and sad laments. She perked up at the end and said she'd see you tonight. She said she'd decided to come to the reception at the gallery because Mr. Mackey was so nice and besides you'd said most everybody on the island came to a free party and maybe he—with hopeful insistence on the pronoun—would be there, and besides the gallery was on Black Duck Road. She asked you to call her if you had any idea what she should do."

"Lordy," Annie murmured.

"What's so special about this guy?" Max poured the Bud Light.

"Oh, he's some mysterious Lothario she

met in the fog on the harbor pier at midnight. She fell for him and thought they were having a great love affair. Most romantic of all"—Annie's tone was dry—"they never gave each other their names. What price he's married?" Annie spooned more chili. "Anyway, he didn't show up last night and she's trying to find him. I'd call and tell her to give it up, but she's pretty determined. You'd think she would realize he can't really be interested in her or he'd tell her who he is! Maybe she'll be a little savvier the next time she meets a romantic stranger." Annie pushed away the memory of Chloe's young, unhappy face. Chloe might have fallen in love with the idea of falling in love, but that didn't lessen the hurt. Annie almost reached for her cell phone, then steeled her resolve. She simply wasn't going to listen to Chloe moan. The episode at Snug Harbor had definitely exceeded Annie's daily quota for misery. If it weren't for that, she'd almost certainly look for Chloe, help her in her search. But, darn it, it was time Chloe grew up a little bit. Mr. No-Name was clearly bad news. Besides, she'd see Chloe tonight at the gallery. Annie would make a special point to introduce her around. It would be an elegant party. Surely that would lift Chloe's spirits.

The house was almost two hundred years old. The two-story tabby structure, with wide verandahs on both the first and second floors, sat high on stuccoed brick arches. Nathaniel Neville had transformed it into an elegant art gallery. As his fortunes prospered in the heyday of the nineties, when the rich got infinitely richer and many of them chose to invest great sums in art works, Neville had built a huge and elegant Italian villa that was less than a five-minute walk through a live oak forest from the gallery.

Max curved into the circular drive. "There probably isn't a spot this close, but we'll give it a try."

Japanese lanterns decorated both verandahs and dangled from the live oak trees. The lanterns were soft smudges of color in the fog. Through the uncurtained bay windows, Annie glimpsed men in tuxedos and women in winter gowns of silver lamé or black velvet or sparkling sequins on silk. The lighted windows were brilliant in the winter night, a welcome contrast to the patches of fog that hovered like dimly seen ghosts.

Annie wriggled in anticipation. "Oh, Max, it looks like a great party. Mr. Mackey will be pleased." She doubted the artist would be surprised at the success of the exhibition. Mackey had an air of confidence.

Max eased his crimson Maserati around a parked SUV that bulged into the narrow road. Some people thought they could park any damn place they wanted. Max prided himself upon his live-and-let-live, equable manner—except for hogs who didn't care whether their tasteless monstrosities of vehicles posed a hazard to others. He winced as his right fender cleared the back bumper of the SUV by perhaps a thousandth of an inch.

Without a word, Annie patted the tensed back of his hand soothingly.

He took a deep breath as the car eased past. "I'll drop you off and go back and park."

"Golly, everybody on the island must have come if the big lot over that way"— she gestured to her left—"is already full. Let's go back to the main road. There was a side entrance just before we got to the circular driveway." Annie peered out into the fog.

Max regained the main road and retraced their path.

Annie held up a hand. "Slow down a little. Okay, turn here."

Max swung to the left behind a grove of pines. The serpentine lane angled away from the massive trees. Abruptly, they left behind the sound and glow of the party. He drove slowly. "Are you sure?" The road meandered, curving back in the direction of the gallery.

"This comes out near the kitchen of the gallery. The Friends of the Library had a luncheon here over Christmas, and I helped set up the tables." She pointed ahead. "There. We can park by the catering van." There were only a few cars parked in the lot, and they probably belonged to the caterer's wait staff.

Annie popped out of the car and pointed at a flagstone path. "That goes along the side of the house to the sidewalk in front." She led the way. Max carried the book bag with the titles for Henny. They passed windows blazing with light, and once again there were the sounds of a party, voices and music. They reached the front yard and turned to their right, hurried up the moist wooden steps of the front porch, and stepped inside to noise and movement and color. A huge Christmas tree still glittered in the center of the spacious hallway. Great ropes of evergreen with huge red bows scalloped the cornices. Light cascaded from two magnificent chandeliers, one in the entry hall, one beyond a keystone arch that separated the entryway from the stair hall. A string quartet on the landing of the mahogany staircase played Pachelbel's Canon in D. Rush matting was laid to protect the heart pine floors. Paintings hung in the hallway and in the rooms that opened to either side.

Carl Neville stood just inside the door. Smiling, he welcomed guests with a quick handshake and an expansive wave toward the exhibition rooms and the stairway leading upstairs. He wasn't as imposing a man as his late father. Nathaniel Neville, hawk-faced and pencil thin, had dominated almost all gatherings. Slightly built Carl, his features pleasant but indeterminate, his manner diffident, scarcely made an impact

on the guests sweeping inside. "Annie,
Max. Good to see you. Great turnout tonight. Boston's paintings are displayed
down here and upstairs, too. And there's a
buffet. . . ." He looked over Annie's shoulder. "Hello, Vince. Great to see you. . . ."

Max turned to shake hands with Vince Ellis, editor and publisher of *The Island
Gazette.*

Annie gave a happy sigh. "I'll take the
books, Max, and see if I can find Henny."
She grabbed the book bag and plunged
into the crowd. Everywhere there was
color—the women's dresses, the paintings,
the richness of crimson draperies. Annie
caught a glimpse of herself in a long silver-
framed mirror. Her black velvet dress with a
plunging V neck and no back and cutout
sides was surely one of the more dramatic
dresses at the party. Was it too much? She
straightened a rhinestone strap and smiled.
Max liked it. She wandered from room to
room where the paintings were displayed,
greeting old friends, keeping an eye out for
Henny, and admiring Boston Mackey's bold
talent. The paintings were superb, sunflow-
ers that were outbursts of gold, a shadowy
lagoon bounded by cypress, a time-black-

ened tombstone in an abandoned grave-yard, old women plaiting baskets in the shade of live oaks, children laughing as sea foam swirled around a crumbling sand castle, a beautiful woman with an enigmatic smile, an oyster roast in high summer, geese in a magnificent V against a lowering fall sky, murky water swirling around a rotting pier.

It was hard to hear over the roar of conversation. Annie had lost track of Max when he appeared at her elbow with a glass of wine. "Henny's upstairs. I'll take the books to her, then we'll do the buffet. There's chicken liver mousse and curried lamb balls. Be right back," he shouted. Annie found a peaceful spot in an alcove and sipped the fruity chardonnay as she scanned the crowd. Carl Neville was still near the front door, welcoming guests. Boston Mackey, brown eyes gleaming, plump cheeks flaming, silver ponytail draped over one shoulder of his tuxedo, bent close to a beautiful young woman. Annie raised an amused eyebrow. Ah, the power of sex—

A sardonic voice hissed in her ear. "You can sure spot the sore losers."

Annie jerked to face Edith Cummings. The island's canny research librarian, who had a sharp eye for human foibles and a tongue to match, waggled a shrimp toward the cluster of people near the painting of a woman in white kneeling by a bed of crimson poppies. "Talk about looking daggers!" Edith's dark eyes glinted with mischief.

Annie knew that Edith wasn't describing the figure in the painting, whose cool gaze was pensive and remote. A shaft of light from a wall sconce cast a bright swath over Irene Neville, elegant in a white lace jacket and white satin trousers, and her sister-in-law, Susan Neville Brandt, equally striking in an off-the-shoulder full-skirted dazzling red georgette. Irene's compelling oval face made her husband, Carl, look even more ineffectual in comparison. At the moment, her beauty was marred by narrowed eyes and a scowl that drew her black brows into a straight line. Susan, her fine-boned face uneasy, watched her sister-in-law. Susan looked much like Carl, smooth fair hair, severe features, weedy frame, but she held her head high. No one would term her ineffectual.

Edith munched a celery stick. "Irene's forgotten that pretty is as pretty does. Susan's afraid Irene may dash the family's hopes by telling Virginia to her face what a fool she is. It may happen," Edith said hopefully. "Irene may let loose right here and now. Susan knows they'd better handle Virginia carefully. If they really offend her, she may spend all the money on her new husband." Edith chortled. "What if Irene's face freezes like that! Hmm. Maybe that would wake Carl up to the dangers of cuddling with an adder. Adders, yes. Also known as common vipers, though harboring a viper has always seemed highly uncommon to me. . . ."

Annie half listened to Edith's malicious nonsense. She felt a chill. Not so much from Edith's chatter, but from the reality of the repressed anger emanating from Irene Neville and Susan Brandt. Poor Virginia Neville. Annie didn't know the woman, but she felt sorry for her.

". . . and Susan's husband looks like a boiled pig about to explode. . . ."

Annie pressed her lips together to suppress a giggle. Edith didn't need any encouragement, but her image certainly described Rusty Brandt's choleric appearance, faded red hair, flushed cheeks, heavy frown. Either Rusty had drunk too much champagne, had rampant hypertension, or was teetering on the verge of a temper tantrum.

". . . Rusty's a real jerk. I've always liked Susan. You have to wonder"—Edith bent closer to Annie, dropping her voice—"if she knows he's screwing around on her. I've seen him out with Beth Kelly. She teaches at the middle school. She's really pretty, a creamy complexion and a sweet smile. Divorced. You'd think Beth would have better sense. But hey, women are always fools for men, and who knows that better than I? Speaking of fools, here's Virginia now. Fur's going to fly."

Annie didn't need Edith's excited pronouncement. All she had to do was follow the gazes of Irene and Susan as they stared at the slender woman framed in the doorway. Annie scarcely recognized Virginia Neville as the somber widow in black who had stood quite alone at Nathaniel Neville's graveside while the rest of his family—son Carl, daughter-in-law Irene, daughter Susan, son-in-law Rusty, sister Louise, and grandchildren—gathered at the other end of the bier. At the funeral, Virginia had been an indistinct wraith. Tonight she sparkled, seed pearls twined in her coronet braids, her delicate face eager and happy, her pale cheeks tinged with pink. Her dress—a swirling silver georgette—was artfully cut to give her thin form unexpected fullness. She swung toward Irene and Susan. For an instant, her glow dimmed. Then, lifting her chin, she swept toward a group of guests, pausing to receive enthusiastic accolades with the grace of a queen.

Edith finished the celery stick. "To the manor born. Not. But a pretty good imitation. Wonder if she's been watching old Di film clips?"

"Don't be mean, Edith." Annie spoke lightly, but she meant every word.

Edith gave a whoop. "Honey, I'm always mean. That's what—oh, hey, here comes lover boy. Wouldn't Irene like to scratch his eyes out. Or worse. Susan looks pretty grim, too. Even Carl isn't a happy camper. To see the family fortune scooped out of your grasping hands would turn most people nasty. Of course, Virginia may not leave everything to her new husband—when and if the wedding occurs—but I think by law, he'll get some of it when she kicks off."

As soon as Virginia Neville turned, the georgette dress rippling like a silver cloud, Annie understood. The older woman and her young lover. This was what Boston Mackey had told them about, the April-September love affair. Bright lights aren't flattering to older women, even a slender woman in a beautiful dress. The brilliance spilling down from the chandelier made clear her age, possibly in her late forties. She was attractive, and happiness added an aura of youthfulness. But she was youngish, not young. Opposite her, the focus of her unashamed adoration, was a very handsome and very young man with dark curly hair, chiseled features, and a flair for elegance. He bent toward Virginia with a smile, completely at ease in a beautifully cut tuxedo with a dramatic green paisley cummerbund. She looked old enough to be his mother. Well, maybe not quite. But old enough to be a big sister or an aunt. Annie pushed the thought away. Okay, society thought it was fine when older men married very young women, often younger than the children they'd fathered in a first marriage. Why shouldn't Virginia Neville choose a younger man for a husband? April-September marriages, including those of young men to much older women, sometimes succeeded fabulously, witness Agatha Christie's marriage to a man fourteen years her junior. But Virginia Neville was more than likely twenty years older than the man she planned to marry.

Edith popped a glazed pecan into her mouth. "Annie, the pecans are scrumptious." She wiped her lips with a red paper napkin, flapped it toward Virginia and her young lover. "Quite the dandy, isn't he? Of course, it's hard to recognize him without his cap. If I had gorgeous hair like Jake's— look at those curls—I wouldn't always hide it under a cap. But he's not satisfied with drop-dead good looks. He must think he's a modern Beau Brummell. He dresses like a matinee idol from the thirties, a white suit and panama hat in the summer and an argyll sweater and a golf cap in the winter. Not your usual good old—"

Annie stared at the doorway and remembered Chloe's husky, eager, love-struck voice: ". . . wears a cap. You know, the kind golfers used to wear years ago."

Annie reached out, grabbed Edith's thin arm. "Who is he?"

Edith raised a quizzical eyebrow. "My, my, should I warn Max that you too are smitten by the undeniable charm—"

"Edith, knock it off. Who is he?" Annie's voice was grim.

Edith's eyes narrowed. "Do I detect a decided interest in the young man since the mention of his headgear?"

Annie gritted her teeth. Nobody ever said Edith was slow. Maddening, yes. Slow, no.

"Okay, okay, simmer down, Annie." Edith was brisk. "His name is Jake O'Neill. He works for the Neville Gallery and he's a so-so artist. Actually, he does good portraits. He did one of Ken"—Edith's voice softened as she mentioned her teenage son—"and it's wonderful. Anyway, Jake arrived on the island last summer, and Virginia fell for him when he did her portrait. As you can imagine, the Neville family is less than thrilled. I understand they really have their collective nose out of joint since Virginia's combining the announcement of her engagement to Jake with Boston's reception tonight." Edith smoothed out the crumpled red napkin and held it out to Annie. "See?"

Annie glanced at the fire engine red napkin. At the top in green letters was the name: Neville Gallery. Below the name was an outline in green of the antebellum house. Down one side in gold letters were the names Virginia and Jake. Below the names were two gold rings intertwined. Down the other side in silver letters was Boston Mackey's name. Below his name glittered a silver artist's palette.

"Gaudy as hell." Edith's fingers closed around the napkin, reducing it to a tight red ball. "The Nevilles pride themselves above all on tastefulness. Maybe they're afraid Virginia will start putting out knickknacks for sale. Little ceramic porpoises or a miniature of Parotti's Bar and Grill."

Annie didn't, at the moment, give a damn about the Neville family's concerns. She scanned the dining room and the visible portion of the central hallway. Was Chloe here? "Edith, have you seen Chloe Martin tonight?"

Edith blinked. "The girl who works for you over the holidays? Nope. But I haven't been looking."

"If you see her..." Annie broke off, shook her head. "Never mind." She swung away, left Edith staring after her in surprise.

In the central hallway, admirers crowded

around Boston Mackey. His arm was firmly draped around the bare shoulders of a young woman who gazed up at him with heavy lidded eyes and a sleepy smile. People drifted up and down the stairway, easing past the musicians on the landing. In the drawing room, the tall windows were open to the cool January air, but the high-ceilinged room was warm, loud, and crowded. Annie, smiling, called out quick hellos, but she kept moving and looking. Near the buffet line in the library, Annie resorted to several quick jumps into the air to see over the heads and shoulders of taller persons.

"Ballet?" a husky voice inquired. "Or perhaps a version of perpetual motion. Oh dear, I hope not indigestion, though the holidays are notorious for challenging delicate systems."

Annie smiled at her mother-in-law, who, as always, looked beautiful and elegant, her patrician features quite classically lovely, her ice blue gown a perfect foil for Nordic blue eyes and spun gold hair. "Laurel, I grew up eating lamb fries."

"The prospect appalls." Husky laughter gurgled.

"Have you seen Chloe?" Laurel and Chloe had enjoyed discussing authors at the store Christmas party.

"No." Laurel touched Annie's arm lightly. "You look worried. Is there anything I can do?" Her blue eyes, which often were spacey and sometimes impudent, were filled with kindness.

Annie found her mother-in-law unnerving, fascinating, and dear. She gave her a swift hug. "If you see Chloe, tell her I need to talk to her."

"Of course." As Annie slipped past, Laurel called after her, "If you discover perpetual motion, my dear, do please share."

In the hallway, more guests were arriving. Annie frowned. Chloe could be anywhere, upstairs or down. They could have passed each other in the crowd. Annie debated stationing herself on the front verandah, decided instead to survey the second floor.

She was stepping onto the second floor porch when Max found her. "Hey, I've been looking everywhere. Ma pointed me upstairs." He looked puzzled. "She murmured something about jeté and her pleasure at your grace and agility. What was she talking about?"

"Darling, if you don't know your mother by now . . ." It was a familiar—and effective—response. Max's mother was prone to sudden enthusiasms, ranging from communing with the saints to night vision photography. Some pastimes resulted in situations Max found unnerving, and he remained vigilant to monitor Laurel's more peculiar pursuits.

Max was not quite defensive. "Well, she seemed perfectly . . ." he paused.

"Normal?" Annie inquired sweetly. Then felt ashamed. After all, it wasn't Laurel who'd been hopping about making a spectacle of herself. Quickly, Annie explained. ". . . and the guy Chloe met on the pier is the same one Virginia Neville's going to marry. If Chloe shows up and sees him, it will be dreadful for her. Oh, Max, I wish I'd called her this afternoon."

He shrugged. "Even if you had, you probably wouldn't have found the guy."

But Annie couldn't shake the feeling she'd let Chloe down. She knew how much Chloe had invested in those romantic meetings on the pier. She should have been willing to help in the search. If she had, quite possibly Chloe would not have come tonight. Annie had a deep sense of foreboding. She looked anxiously at Max. "Did you see Chloe when you were hunting for me?"

"Nope. Maybe she changed her mind about the party. Come on, let's get some food." He glanced at his watch. "It's already half past eight. There's a program at nine."

"Program?" Annie looked around. "Where?"

He waved his arm in the general direction of outdoors. "There's a big tent set up in the north parking lot. That's why everybody parked up and down the road."

Annie shivered. The night air had to be in the low forties. "Outside?"

"It's okay. I poked my head into the tent when I was looking for you and there are heaters. It smells kind of oily"—he wrinkled his nose—"but it's pretty warm. Anyway, there's a platform and chairs for an audience and a dance floor. Somebody said Boston's going to give a painting away and then Virginia is going to thank everyone for coming and announce her engagement. The tent company will pick up the chairs and a band will play and everybody will dance. So let's go get some food."

Annie was always interested in food. She

loved to graze buffets. Who knew? There might be salmon caviar or mushrooms stuffed with snails or pears with curried crab filling or smothered alligator. She stepped inside. The buffet beckoned. They were almost to the stairs when she stopped. "No. I'll stay on the porch, keep a lookout for Chloe. Will you get us some plates? Anything will do."

Max reached gentle fingers to touch her face, as if to smooth away her frown. "Annie, she has to find out about him sooner or later."

"I know." Her voice was sad. "But Chloe thought he was wonderful. Obviously, he's not. If I see her, at least I can keep her from finding out right in the middle of a crowded room."

Max bent down, kissed her lightly. "It will work out." His voice was hearty. "After all, she's lucky to find out his ratlike qualities before it's too late. You return to your post, and I'll get the food." As she moved toward the porch, he called out, "Carrot sticks?"

She grinned. "Only if slathered with cream cheese." Her smile faded as she walked to the edge of the porch, leaned on the balustrade to look down at the circular drive. She was still there, though shivering, when Max returned. She nodded her approval at the coconut-fried frog legs, crab cakes, salmon strips, chilies rellenos, and pistachio-stuffed mushrooms. Nary a carrot stick in sight.

Annie kept her gaze on the drive as they ate and tried to ignore the damp cold of the night. She waved the coconut-encrusted frog leg. "Max, this is divine."

"Not for the frog," he murmured.

She paused in mid-munch. "Let us not put this on a personal level." She dropped the half-eaten leg and speared a salmon strip. After all, salmon in her mind were fuzzily somewhere far distant in Washington State rivers, while there were platoons of lusty—Max was always admiring of their passion for the ladies—deep-throated frogs who inhabited the lagoon behind their house.

The food was excellent, and Max had brought coffee, which helped against the chill. When they finished eating, Max pointed at his watch. Almost time for the program. Annie hesitated, then nodded. As they stepped into the upstairs room—a lovely room with faded green walls and dark green drapes and the lovely glow of Mackey's muted yet warm Low Country paintings—she felt relaxed. Chloe hadn't appeared. It looked more and more likely that she'd decided not to come. Tomorrow Annie would have to tell her. That wasn't a pleasant prospect. But Annie was inclined to let tomorrow take care of itself.

There was a general movement toward the stairs. Annie took Max's arm, smiled up at him. The program might be interesting, and later there would be a band. She and Max did a polished tango. Okay, maybe their performance was just this side of campy, but they had loads of fun and always ended to a round of applause from onlookers. If Max had a thin black mustache and she had a rose to grip in her teeth . . . Annie was smiling as they reached the stairs, merging into the thick stream of guests beginning to descend.

Henny, elegant in a high-necked black chiffon, waved a black lace handkerchief. Over the crowd, she called, "I know this is too easy for you, Annie. Red-haired, loves the ladies, photographic memory, his boss's answer to physical effort."

Annie was casual. "Archie Goodwin."

Nero Wolfe's office assistant added great charm to the Rex Stout novels.

Henny laughed and moved on down the stairs.

"Annie!" Edith Cummings was on the landing. "I've been looking everywhere for you. I thought you'd want to know. Chloe Martin's here. I saw her a little while ago. She's really pretty with that dark red hair." Edith's tone was admiring. "Looks like polished mahogany in the sun. And what a dress! Kelly green taffeta, low cut, but with this gorgeous matching stole. Shades of Tara. And talk about drama—I was only a few feet behind her when she came face-to-face with Jake O'Neill."

Annie took a deep breath. "What happened?"

Edith's eyes glistened. "Big-time shock, I'd say. His face froze. He gulped. She ran up to him, excited as could be. He looked around, and then he took her by the arm and pulled her into the study. I'd love to have been a mouse with big ears on the scene."

The stairs were packed. The crowd moved slowly. On the ground floor, Annie once again made little leaps to scan the surroundings. Max, too, was searching.

A throaty voice called out, "Still leaping. Dear Annie, how marvelous to know you have such spirit, such élan, such indefatigability."

Annie grinned at her mother-in-law. "Practice makes perfect." But her smile slipped away as she poked her head into the study. Nope. Neither Chloe nor Jake were present. Annie backed into the hall, took Max's arm. They spilled out with the crowd onto the back porch. Annie gazed out into the foggy night. Was Chloe out there somewhere with her midnight lover? The guests were simply dark forms, indistinguishable in the pale smudges of color from the Japanese lanterns. Anyone could be part of that mass of guests moving slowly toward the tent.

The tent was set up to the left of the back porch in the north parking lot. The path was marked by luminarias. Straight ahead lay the gardens, famous for crimson azaleas in the spring. The land stretched away to the ocean, hidden now by the fog. Strings of tiny white bulbs sparkled in the nearby live oak trees, little glimmers of soft light in the fog.

Running footsteps sounded to the right. A dimly seen figure burst out of the foggy darkness and veered away from the house to disappear behind the pines that screened the service area from the gardens.

Annie gripped Max's arm. "Was that Chloe?"

He swung around, but the figure was gone, disappearing around the end of the house.

"Max, we'd better see." Annie hurried down the steps. She knew the area fairly well. The gallery was a popular site for teas and meetings. Oyster-shell paths went in several directions. Tonight the fog hung damp and thick near the house, but Annie knew that one path led along the back of the house to the north parking lot where the tent had been erected. Straight ahead was another path. As Annie recalled, this path curved in a lazy figure eight among banks of azaleas and ponds. To the right, another path curved toward a grove of pines, ending ultimately at the ruins of the Civil War fort that overlooked the ocean. The girl Annie had glimpsed—the girl in a green dress—was running toward the house on the fort path, but she veered away near the kitchen and disappeared behind the pines that screened the service area.

"Come on, Max." Annie hurried toward the kitchen area. She and Max moved against the stream of guests heading toward the tent. Slams and bangs from the kitchen signaled the cleanup of the buffet. They followed a twisting path through the pines and reached the service area. The pines threw dark shadows over much of the blacktop, but the back end of the caterer's van was open and its interior light flared over a burly man shoving closed bins in place. Annie recognized him. Tony Hasty was one of the premier caterers on the island. Annie picked up speed and skidded to a stop beside him. "Tony, did you see a girl just now?"

He swung around, stared at Annie. Close-cropped iron gray hair covered a blunt head with a light fuzz. Yellowish eyes glowed in a mashed-up face that suggested contact sports or barroom brawls. "What the hell's going on?" His voice was deep and brusque.

"A girl in a green dress came this way.

Did you see her?" Annie looked past him, but there was no one else in the area.

He slapped big hands on his hips, poked his head forward. "What's up, Annie? You're the second woman to run this way. Somebody bothering you?" His massive shoulders tensed as he looked past her at Max, his face disdainful of any man who couldn't protect his woman.

"No. I'm okay." She realized Tony had never met Max. "Tony, this is my husband, Max. We're hunting for that girl." Annie looked around the shadowy service area. Only a few cars were parked there. "Was she wearing a green dress?"

"Yeah. What's the problem?" He used the back of his hand to rub a heavy jowl. "She was crying. I asked her—just like you—if something was wrong." He tugged at the bunched front of a stained apron. "She kept on running and didn't say a word."

Annie swung toward the path to the front of the house. "Did she go that way?"

"Yeah. What's the deal?" He looked ready for action.

Annie didn't want to embarrass Chloe. Besides, she was probably long gone. She must have parked along the road leading to the gallery. "Oh," she said vaguely, "a lovers' quarrel, I'm afraid. We'll find her and see what we can do."

The tension eased out of his big body. "Okay. Let me know if you need any help." He turned back to his cart, hefted a bin.

Annie walked toward the front of the house, calling out, "Chloe? Chloe, where are you?"

Max pulled out his car keys. "I'll get a flashlight from the car."

Annie was halfway down the front drive, calling Chloe's name and pausing to listen, when Max caught up with her. They stopped at the foot of the drive.

Max swung the light back and forth, but silvery fog swathed the trees, turned the night to cotton. "Annie, if she's out there, she doesn't want to see us. She's probably halfway home right now. I don't think there's anything you can do tonight." The beam danced against cars, poked into low-hanging fog in the live oak branches, startled a raccoon who jerked his masked face toward them.

Annie felt stymied. But maybe this was best. Chloe obviously had discovered the perfidy of her romantic stranger. Let her run away and deal with her hurt in private. Annie turned back toward the house. "I'd like to punch him in the nose."

"Oh, what goes around comes around." Max's voice was easy. "Hey, I hear trumpets." He glanced at the luminous dial of his watch. "It's ten after. I'll bet the program's started. Let's put this"—he waggled the flashlight—"back in the car and go see."

The sweet scent of evergreen filled the tent. The swags made a deep green contrast to the strings of red and pink and yellow lights. Almost every chair was taken. Despite the dim lighting, the contrast between black tuxedos and vivid gowns was dramatic. Sharp white spotlights threw the low stage at the far end of the tent into bright relief. A beaming Boston Mackey stood by an easel. The painting on display glowed with color, splashes of orange and lime and red. Carl Neville, his thin cheeks flushed with excitement, hurried toward the platform and up the steps. At a podium, he grabbed the microphone. "Ladies and gentlemen, welcome to the Neville Gallery's celebration of the work of our wonderful Low Country artist Boston Mackey."

Cheers and applause. Mackey puffed like a pleased pouter pigeon.

Carl's pale face was tinged with pink. "This is an honor both to our island and to the Neville Gallery. Please welcome Boston Mackey."

Applause boomed. Neville handed the microphone to the artist, then stood to one side, clapping vigorously. As Mackey moved forward, Neville joined his wife beside the platform.

The artist looked like a man who had enjoyed the party, hair mussed, tie undone, jacket hanging open.

Annie stood on tiptoe and whispered to Max. "Is that confetti in his beard? Or lipstick?"

Max laughed. "I doubt it's confetti."

Oblivious to the pink smudge in his close-cropped white beard, Mackey stood at the edge of the platform. His voice rolled out to the audience. "Ladies and gentlemen, it is a pleasure to be with you tonight. . . ."

Ranged in a semicircle behind the platform were some members of the Neville

family. Irene Neville, laughing, held a champagne glass aloft. Susan Brandt's fair hair
rippled as she pumped her fists in excitement. A thin, dark-haired woman nodded,
her solemn face softened by a smile. Annie
plucked a name from memory: Louise Neville, old Nathaniel's sister. Louise's smile
slipped away as Virginia Neville hurried to
her side and tugged on her sleeve. Virginia
bent close, whispered. Louise shook her
head, held a finger to her lips, and nodded
toward the platform as if reminding Virginia
that their guest was speaking and Virginia's
attention was required. Virginia clasped her
hands, stared at Mackey, but every so often, as if she were a puppet jerked by a
string, her head swung toward the back entrance to the tent. She looked forlorn, like a
child invited to a party only to find the door
barred.

". . . hope all of you filled out a slip for the
drawing. Before our gracious hostess"—
Mackey waved the microphone toward Virginia—"pulls out the winner, I want to introduce Harrison Beaumont. Everyone on the
island knows Dr. Beaumont, but I want to
take this opportunity to let you show your
appreciation for his generosity to the

Broward's Rock Art Museum. Dr. Beaumont . . ."

Virginia Neville took a final desperate look at the back entrance, then slowly turned back to the platform. Her face held no trace of the joy that had transformed the gentle features earlier in the evening, adding a saucy flush to her thin cheeks. She looked irresolute, uncertain. One hand plucked at the silver diamond-studded butterfly that hung from an ornate silver chain. She kept glancing toward the flap. Once, she shaded her eyes from the stark light on the platform and looked out at the crowd, her gaze searching.

". . . know you want to give a rousing cheer for Dr. Beaumont in gratitude for his gift of my great blue heron mural to the museum."

The response was thunderous—clapping, cheers, whistles.

Dr. Beaumont, an orthopedic surgeon with a cue ball head and a pianist's hands, thudded on stage. "My pleasure. Now everyone on the island can enjoy your work. . . ."

The flap to the back entrance moved. Virginia Neville's face lighted. She bent forward eagerly when a tuxedo-clad arm appeared. The flap was thrust aside. Rusty Brandt stepped inside. He looked warily toward his wife and sister-in-law, but both seemed absorbed in Dr. Beaumont's accolade to Boston Mackey. Brandt hurried toward the back of the platform. Virginia Neville's face sagged in disappointment.

On stage the two big men clapped each other heartily on the shoulders, exchanged shouts, and Dr. Beaumont bounded off the stage.

Annie scarcely heard the huzzahs and hurrahs. She was still watching Virginia Neville. The older woman's hands twined together, twisting, twisting.

"And now"—Boston's cheerful face glistened with sweat and glowed with bonhomie—"it is a delight to me and to everyone here to call forth our lovely hostess—Virginia Neville. Virginia stands now at the helm of the good ship Neville Gallery and she is carrying on in the fine tradition. . . ."

Annie was not, she always insisted, prone to presentiments, that convenient foreboding so beloved of gothic authors from Mary Roberts Rinehart to Mary Stewart, but she could read the writing on the wall as fast as anybody. In a flash she mixed it all to-gether—the planned announcement of Virginia Neville's engagement to Jake O'Neill, Chloe's arrival at the gallery, her distraught departure from the gallery gardens, Virginia's questing glances—and exclaimed, "Max, Jake O'Neill hasn't shown up. He's supposed to be here." Annie flung out her hand. "I don't see him anywhere."

Annie continued to look, but every second that passed made her surer than ever that O'Neill was standing up Virginia Neville. How could he do such a cruel thing? But how could he make love to Chloe in the fog when he was engaged to another woman?

Annie's heart went out to the slender woman walking up the platform steps, one hand holding the skirt of her lovely silver dress, the dress she'd bought to wear on the night her engagement was to be announced. Virginia moved as if her legs were heavy. She paused, gave one more sweeping glance the length of the tent. Her shoulders slumped, but she held her head high and came onto the stage. She tried to smile as she reached for the microphone. The effect was ghastly, the misery in her face only made more apparent.

"Thank you, Boston." Her voice wavered. "I want to welcome everyone to the Neville Gallery's celebration of Boston Mackey's wonderful paintings. I want to thank Boston"—her voice steadied, grew a little stronger—"for his generosity." She bent her head toward the vivid painting on the easel.

Boston Mackey gave a modest aw-shucks shrug, tugged at an ear lobe. He never looked toward Virginia.

Carl Neville hurried up the steps, holding a rounded fish bowl filled with pieces of paper. He bustled to Virginia. "Here are the slips."

Virginia plunged one hand deep into the mound, brought up a pink slip. "Our winner tonight"—her voice was thin and stiff—"is Sally Morrison." She held the slip high.

An excited squeal came from a row near the front and a heavyset woman in orange clambered to her feet. "I won. I won!"

Virginia handed the microphone to Carl. The gallery director's face creased into a puzzled frown as his father's widow walked away.

The artist picked up the painting, carried it forward. After helping the winner to her seat, the painting cradled in her arms,

Boston returned to the platform. He stopped beside Carl. "Hey, it's time for the big announcement. Where's Virginia going?" He turned toward the audience, face cheery, voice booming. "Don't go way, folks. The show's just beginning." He strode after Virginia. "Come on, Virginia. It's no time to be shy. Everybody loves lovers. This is your big moment. Where's Jake?" His big head swung around. "Come on, Jake. Get up here."

Annie gripped Max's arm. "Oh, God, he's so full of himself. If he'd just look at her . . ." Mackey's every word was a blow to Virginia Neville. She stood frozen at the platform steps.

Still smiling, self-absorbed, a sponge for attention, Boston grabbed Virginia and pulled her to the center of the stage. "Okay, now." He looked out at the audience. "Where's Jake?"

"Jake." Virginia spoke his name in a whisper. She licked her lips. "He's . . . he'll be here in a few minutes. I know he will. And then we'll—" She looked small and defenseless. "But for now, please, it's time to dance. Come on, everyone." She gestured toward the crowd. "If you'll move toward the walls of the tent, the staff will pick up the chairs. The band is almost ready to play." Behind her on the platform, the musicians were setting up. "Please, everyone have a good time."

Annie grabbed Max's hand and pulled him outside. She exploded. "Max, we're going to find that jerk and drag him here by the scruff of his neck."

"Annie." Max combined warning, understanding, admiration, and exasperation.

Annie threw up her hands. She knew her threat was nonsense. She had no place in Virginia Neville's heartbreak. She scarcely knew the woman. But she knew Chloe, who had gripped her hands and pulled her into a rollicking dance because she was in love. All right. O'Neill was a stranger to Annie, and there was no reason he should care a whit what Annie thought or said. So that was that. But the party was over as far as Annie was concerned. How could she and Max whirl around a dance floor (and, oh, how Max loved to dance, especially a slow foxtrot. Annie knew music wasn't the attraction, but hey, it was nice to be wanted) having fun, happy and in love, always and ever in love, and know that within arm's reach was a broken-hearted woman waiting for a man who wasn't coming? Nope, Annie wanted to go home and leave behind the memory of Virginia Neville's stricken face. "Come on, Max. Let's go." She swung away and headed out into the foggy night. Max caught up with her. "Stardust" lilted from the tent.

They were almost to the gallery when a siren wailed. The sound rose, increased, filled the night. Abruptly, the shrill shriek cut off. Whirling red lights flickered from the service area behind the pines.

Annie stared at the irregular pattern made by the lights. Okay, there'd been a siren. Sirens were designed to capture attention. They didn't always signal disaster. Maybe it was too many shocks in one day, but Annie felt a sharp flicker of fear. She started to run.

· *Four* ·

Headlights from the police cruiser illuminated the service area. In the harsh glare, the chunky tough-faced caterer gestured wildly to the island's acting police chief. Billy Cameron leaned forward, one hand resting on the butt of his holstered gun, the other gripping a powerful flashlight. Billy had been part of the island police force ever since Annie moved to the island. He'd worked for Chief Saulter until Saulter's retirement and served as a sergeant to the island's new chief, Pete Garrett. When Pete's reserve unit was called up, Billy was named interim chief. He was well liked, a home-town boy familiar to most islanders from

school or sports or church. Big, athletic, energetic, and good-hearted, Billy took his
new duties very seriously. He listened in-
tently, though his eyes checked out the
shadows, as the caterer talked fast and
pointed toward the pines and the path leading to the gardens. The whirling red light
atop the cruiser continued to flash.

"The body's down by the old fort, Billy. I
can show you the way." Tony's voice was
high and excited and he gulped for breath.
"Lots of blood. The back of his head's
bashed in. I may have seen the woman who
did it. Come on." He turned but came to a
stop when he saw Annie and Max. He
pointed at Annie. "Hey, Annie came running
this way, too. Three women raced this way
tonight. Annie said the first girl was running
from some kind of lovers' bust-up. I thought
it sounded fishy." His glance at Annie was
questioning. "Anyway, the last one—Beth
Kelly, she teaches at the middle school—
ran past me a few minutes ago. I thought,
what the hell, something's going on out
there. I decided to take a look. I grabbed a
flashlight from the van"—he held up a large
black flashlight, the beam pointed skyward—"and hustled." He glared at Max.

"Women running for help and nobody giving them the time of day. Yeah, Annie was one of them."

Billy strode up to Annie and Max. They blinked against the glare of his flashlight. Billy's thatch of blond hair looked hastily combed. He'd dressed hurriedly and his uniform shirt was misbuttoned. "What's going on here?" He lowered the flashlight so they weren't blinded, but he had a good look at them. His glance at Max was puzzled. "Somebody bother Annie?"

"No." Max's answer was crisp. "We heard the siren and came to see what was happening. Earlier, Annie saw a girl coming this way and we tried to catch her."

Billy's face furrowed. "You don't know anything about a body?"

Behind them came a sharp gasp. "A body? Dear God, what has happened?" Virginia Neville's voice was sharp and worried. She looked anxiously at Billy. "Officer, I came to the house and someone told me they'd heard a siren. We looked out and I saw the flashing light." She gave a trembling sigh. "What else can go wrong tonight? This is the most dreadful night I've ever . . ." Her voice trailed away. She folded her thin hands into tight fists. "I hope it's not a fire. But there's no smoke. . . ." She glanced toward the police car. "You said there's a body. Has someone been hurt? Has an ambulance been called? Please, what is the matter?"

Billy looked harried. "Ma'am, I'm responding to a nine-one-one. If you and these folks"—he jerked his head toward Annie and Max—"will wait inside, I'll investigate."

"Where is the person? Who is it?" Virginia Neville swung toward the front of the house. "Is it a car accident? Oh, dear heaven, was someone struck by a car?" She pressed her hands against her cheeks. "Nathaniel always worried about evening events. People don't see well at night, and they drive too fast."

The caterer moved heavily toward her. "Mrs. Neville, you better go inside like Captain Cameron said. I'll take him down to the point. That's where the body is. And an ambulance won't do no good. He's dead as can be. His head's bashed in. And there's been women," he said darkly, "running here and there all night."

Virginia said uncertainly, "Tony, are you

sure there's been a death? Maybe someone's hurt. Strange things happen at the
point. We've heard that people buy drugs
there late at night. I wish we could put up a
fence, but it's a historic site. I suppose
someone had a fight down there. Anyway"—her relief was evident—"it can't have
anything to do with us." Her mouth opened
in a round O. "Oh, officer, I'm sorry. I don't
mean to sound callous. But none of our
guests would have any reason to go down
there. The reception was in the house, and
our program is in a tent in the north parking
lot. It's too chilly and foggy for a walk. I
don't mean to hold you up. I'll go in the
house and wait, as you suggested." She
tried to smile at Annie and Max. "Would you
like to come with me? We don't want to de-
lay the officer." She turned toward the walkway, her voice faint and querulous. "I'm
sure I don't know what to do. If only Jake
were here . . . I'd better find Carl. It's always
better to have a man." She stumbled to a
stop, flung out her hand toward several
cars. "Oh, look, look!"

There was an instant of shocked silence.
The caterer swung his big flashlight toward
the cars. Billy pounded to her side, unsnap-

ping his holster, flashlight beam bouncing. "What's wrong, ma'am?"

Hands outstretched, Virginia walked toward a battered black VW, an old one with running boards. Her fingers tangled in a raccoon tail that hung from the radio antenna. "Jake's car. I thought he'd left. How can his car be here and I can't find him anywhere?" Slowly, she turned and walked toward the caterer. She reached out, gripped one massive forearm. "Tony," her voice wobbled, "I know I'm being silly. It can't be anyone I know. I'm just upset. You see"— her voice was high and thin—"I've looked everywhere for Jake. But not down there. There'd be no reason for him to go down there. Oh, God, Tony, it isn't Jake, is it? You'd have said if it was Jake." Her voice cracked. "It can't be Jake. He got sick. That's what happened. He got sick and went home and he'll call me. . . . But his car's here. Somebody could have taken him home. Tony, tell me!"

The caterer's heavy brows knotted in a frown. "Mrs. Neville, I don't know who it is. All I saw was a guy sprawled facedown, the back of his head cracked in. That's all I saw." He rubbed his cheek with his fist. "But he had on a tuxedo."

"A tuxedo." Virginia wavered on her feet. "Someone who was here tonight . . ."

Annie took two quick steps, slipped her arm around shaking shoulders. "Let's go inside." Annie tried to turn the thin, trembling body toward the house.

Virginia Neville went rigid as a hard, thin strip of steel, then jerked away from Annie. With a sob she yanked the flashlight from the caterer's hand and began to run, her pace erratic and uneven.

"Ma'am. Ma'am." Billy, his big flashlight bobbing up and down, caught up with her, blocked her way. "Please, ma'am. All we have is an unverified report of a death. There's no need for you to be upset."

"Unverified, hell." The caterer's deep voice was a bellow. "Billy, you know damn well I don't make things up." He strode past Billy and Mrs. Neville. "I'll show you." He headed toward the pines.

Billy looked overwhelmed. He said urgently to Mrs. Neville, "Please wait in the house, ma'am. I'll check this out."

Max bent toward Annie. "I'd better get my flashlight." He moved swiftly to the

Maserati, unlocked it, picked up the light from the seat.

Virginia Neville darted around Billy and ran after the caterer. "I have to see. And I'm"—her voice was shrill—"I'm Virginia Neville. The gallery is mine and all the land, and you can't make me stay here."

"Hold up, people." Billy's usually pleasant voice was harsh.

Virginia Neville kept going. Hasty stopped and waited, but she was almost out of sight.

Billy came even with the caterer. "Come on, Tony." He hurried after the gallery owner, caught up with her, passed her. "Ma'am, stay behind me."

Max bent near Annie. "We'd better follow them. Billy may need help with Mrs. Neville if . . ." He didn't finish.

Annie squeezed his hand. She'd never had any intention of remaining behind. Tony Hasty had already lumped the running women—herself included—with the discovery of the body. Annie was almost sure the first running figure had been Chloe Martin. Why had Chloe run? What had she been running from? Billy would ask a lot of questions and he would continue to ask until Annie answered to his satisfaction. There was no way Annie could avoid telling him about Chloe. If Billy got it in his head that Chloe had run from the dead man, Chloe was in trouble. Especially if the dead man turned out to be her mysterious lover on the pier. Surely not. But why was Jake O'Neill's car in this lot and Jake nowhere to be found?

The lights from the house didn't pierce the gloom of the foggy garden, but the strands in the live oaks cast a faint radiance on the oyster-shell path. The flashlight beams bounced along the walk, briefly touching the live oak limbs and dangling Spanish moss and dark mounds of shrubbery. Fog eddied and swirled like silver chiffon scarves in a ghostly dance. Their shoes crunching on the oyster shells, they curved around a pond, the water dark as velvet. The hiss and slap of the incoming sea became louder and louder as they neared the bluffs.

"I checked everything out. There's a gazebo"—the caterer pointed at the white wooden structure, strung with lights like the trees—"but nobody was there. Then I thought about the fort. If there's anywhere a guy could take a girl and nobody see them, that's the spot. That's how come I found him. I'd come along this way, just checking things out. If some bas— If some guy was out here bothering women, I'd give him something to think about. Though any girl with sense ought to know something about a guy if she's going to come out to a place like this with him. I know all about the ruins. They hump up where the guns used to be. You can go up some steps to an overlook or go down to a platform built out over the rocks. There are a couple of benches there."

The path changed from crushed oyster shells to hard-packed dirt as they left the Neville property. On the historic site, there were reminders of the recent nor'easter. Cracked and broken limbs from live oaks and magnolias littered the area. Big waves had flung ashore huge logs as well as bricks eroded from old plantations. The beam of Billy's flashlight swung over the debris and the white wooden sign erected by the Broward's Rock Historical Society: FORT LOOMIS, SITE OF CONFEDERATE GUN EMPLACEMENT. CAPTURED BY UNION FORCES 1861. Small letters at the bottom warned: RE-

MOVAL OF ARTIFACTS PROHIBITED BY LAW AND PUNISHABLE BY $1,000 FINE.

The path ended in a paved circle near a clump of palmetto palms. Steps led up to a wooden overlook and down to a platform. The body lay on the uneven brick circle, facedown, hands outflung, shocking in the sharp brightness of Billy's flashlight.

The caterer pointed at the dead man, the outstretched hands shockingly white against the red brick. "You can see the back of his head's stove in." The dark head was misshapen, the force of the blow depressing the skull.

Annie stared at bunched green taffeta poking out from beneath the body, Kelly green taffeta stained with blood.

"Jake . . ." Virginia Neville's cry was high and piteous, unbelieving, sick with horror. She dropped the caterer's flashlight as if her hands had no strength. She stood rigid for a moment, then sobbed and tried to get past Billy. "We have to get help. Hurry. Call for help."

"Don't move, Mrs. Neville." There was no defying Billy's order.

The stricken woman wavered unsteadily, her breath coming in quick harsh gasps.

Annie hurried to her side, gripped her arm. Virginia's body trembled like high limbs in a gusting wind.

Billy picked his way over the shattered branches and palm fronds, the beam of light held close to the ground. Since the storm, the wind had laid down a carpet of dried pine needles over the bricks. Billy knelt by the body, slipped his fingers around an exposed wrist.

They waited in silence, the slap of the water the only sound.

Slowly Billy stood. He swung his flashlight in a wide arc, the beam sweeping the bricks, the ground beyond, and the thick bank of fog that masked the farther distance.

The caterer stepped toward Annie and Mrs. Neville to retrieve his flashlight. He added his beam to Billy's.

Annie supposed Billy was looking for a weapon, something that could have caused that brutal wound. There were pieces of wood, some of them hard and strong, and lumps of old brick everywhere the light touched.

Billy turned toward them, careful to retrace his steps, and stood near the trembling woman. "He's dead, ma'am. We have a homicide here." He was unbuckling the cell phone from his belt. "Can you identify the body?"

"Jake . . ." Virginia Neville swayed. "I couldn't find him. I looked everywhere. I never thought to come down here."

Annie slipped an arm around her shoulders. "Billy, she's in shock. Let me take her back to the gallery. His name is Jake O'Neill. He and Mrs. Neville were going to announce their engagement tonight."

Billy punched a number into the cell phone. "Yeah? But he got killed first. Okay, I'll check it all out." He jerked his head at Annie. "You can take the lady up to the gallery."

Tony Hasty pulled at the dangling earring in a cauliflower ear. "Listen, the girl that was running, the first one, she had on a green dress." He pointed at the taffeta crushed beneath the body.

"What girl? Who was running? Where?" Virginia's voice was sharp.

Billy held up a hand. "We'll get into all of this later. I've got a crime scene to secure. You folks go on up to the gallery. Annie, tell everybody there to stay put—" Billy broke off, spoke into the phone. "Mavis, we got a homicide. Get on the horn." Mavis was Billy's wife, and she also served as dispatcher for the Broward's Rock police. "Round up Lou and Doc Burford. Body's at the Fort Loomis ruins." Billy's forehead wrinkled. "Listen, there's a big party up at the Neville Gallery. I'm gonna need some help. See if Frank can come." He flicked a glance toward Max. "And maybe I can deputize Max Darling. You bring out the crime van." He clicked off the cell phone, turned toward Max. "You got any connection with the dead man?"

Annie looked sharply at Billy. For the first time, she considered the fact that the Broward's Rock Police Department had no female employees unless you counted Billy's wife. Annie didn't, much as she liked Mavis. The department had been understaffed ever since Pete Garrett and Joe Tyndall's reserve units were called up. That left Billy as acting chief and Lou Pirelli as his only full-time officer. No wonder Billy was looking for assistance. Frank Saulter, the former chief, would surely be willing to help out. But why had Billy asked Max and not her? Was it because Tony Hasty had lumped her with the other women who'd run through the parking lot? Or did Billy see investigations as the prerogative of men? Maybe she should pick a pack of books for his education, beginning with P. D. James's *An Unsuitable Job for a Woman.*

Max looked somberly at the body. "I've never met him, Billy."

Annie held her breath. Surely Max wasn't going to mention Chloe.

Max hesitated, but only for an instant. "He may have been a friend of the girl who's been working for Annie over Christmas, but I didn't know him. I'll be glad to help."

"Thanks, Max." Billy was pleased. "I can sure use a hand."

Annie frowned at Max.

Max's steady gaze was unfazed. And determined.

Annie understood. She didn't agree, but she understood. Max might be a light-hearted, easygoing dabbler, but he took his oath as a lawyer seriously. He was an officer of the court. But dammit, he had never even practiced law. She could imagine his eventual response. He would speak to her with reason and restraint, emphasizing that the truth never injured the innocent. She would point out with equal reason, if not re-straint, that Erle Stanley Gardner, famed as the creator of Perry Mason, created the Court of Last Resort to combat miscar-riages of justice. Hadn't Max ever heard of the dangers of circumstantial evidence?

"Miss, miss . . ." The whisper was ragged.

Annie bent close to Virginia Neville. Her breathing still shallow, Virginia demanded, "What girl are they talking about? Did some girl hurt Jake?"

"Nobody knows what happened." Annie had no intention of telling Virginia Neville about Chloe Martin. Oh, dear heaven, where was Chloe? Why had she run from the grounds tonight? And there could be no doubt that she'd been down here at the point. The green stole made her presence clear. Somehow Annie must get in touch with her. But Annie didn't have her cell phone with her. She didn't carry it in an evening bag. Max, of course, had his, either in the car or in his pocket. Could she call Chloe? Maybe not. Such a call might be considered interfering with a murder inves-tigation. But Chloe was not an official sus-pect. Not yet.

Max took a step toward Billy. "What do you want me to do?"

Billy cast a worried glance across the gardens. The fog hid the big tent and the party, but they could faintly hear the sounds of Big Band music. "Why don't you—"

Annie interrupted. "We can both help." At the very least, Annie could assure Billy that Chloe Martin might be volatile but she wasn't violent, and she couldn't have had anything to do with Jake O'Neill's murder even if her green taffeta stole was crumpled beneath his body. Circumstantial evidence . . .

Billy gave Annie a perfunctory smile. "You go on up to the house, Annie."

She felt excluded, diminished. Why was Billy dismissing her? "Billy, listen—"

The rumble of an old car overrode her voice.

Billy turned away. "That'll be the doc." Dr. Burford wore many medical hats on the island, including that of medical examiner. He was irascible, impatient, and took wrongful death as a personal affront. Headlights poked through the low limbs of a live oak. A car door slammed. A stocky figure carrying a satchel marched across the uneven ground.

A siren wailed, came nearer, and rose to a shrill squeal as a van bumped off the road, rolling to a stop not five feet away. The door opened, framing a slim figure. "Lou's on his way, Billy. And Frank, too." Mavis Cameron jumped to the ground. Her hair was caught back in a bun, her long face bare of makeup. She'd pulled on a navy sweatshirt, blue jeans, and sneakers. She hurried to her husband. "I loaded the videocam with night film."

"Thanks. String the crime scene tape, Mavis. Hey, Doc"—Billy pointed toward the corpse as the doctor stomped into the light—"see what you can tell me." Billy's tenor voice was brisk and his gestures decided as he set the investigation into motion. He waved a hand at Annie. "Annie, please take Mrs. Neville and Mr. Hasty up to the gallery."

Annie wanted to stay there, see what was going to happen. But someone had to help this distraught woman. Virginia Neville stood a few feet away, her head bent, her hands tightly clasped, a figure of mourning and despair.

"And Max, go up to the party. Find who-ever's in charge, and round up the people who knew this guy."

As Max ducked inside the rear entrance to the tent, a trumpet shrieked the "Beal Street Blues." Red, gold, and blue spots swept the dancers. Beyond the dance floor, guests milled, drinks in hand, or clumped in bois-terous groups. The roar of conversation al-most matched the blare of the music. Boston Mackey had shed his jacket. He danced, ponytail swinging, with a girl in a gold top, black silk trousers, and rhine-stone-studded boots. Max spotted Carl Neville and his wife standing near the dance floor. Carl's ascetic face was flushed with pleasure. He was snapping his fingers in time with the music. Irene flung back her shimmering dark hair and laughed as she raised a glass of champagne. Max threaded his way between the band and the dancers, his eyes scanning the crowd. Susan Brandt and her husband were deep in conversation near the front entrance. Max's stride checked. Susan's features were sharp and rigid. She bent toward her husband, talking fast. Rusty's reddish face looked stubborn and sulky. He stared toward the doorway, avoiding his wife's demanding gaze. Max's eyes narrowed. He swerved toward the Brandts. Rusty abruptly turned away from his wife, almost bowling over an old lady as he blundered toward the exit. Susan, anger evident in the hunch of her thin shoulders, hurried after him.

Max plunged across the dance floor. Smiling his apologies—"Sorry, sorry. Excuse me"—he wormed his way through the chattering crowd. He was grateful to step out into the cool, misty air. And the quiet. He hadn't realized the noise level inside the tent until he escaped it. He looked in every direction. Bright spotlights shone on the entrance to the tent, but the path curved into gloom between the tent and the gallery. The fog transformed the landscape and the house, smudging outlines, turning the lights from the old house pale and ghostly, muting the twinkle of the strands draped in the live oaks.

Max began to feel foolish. So the Brandts were having a quarrel. Married people did. He'd heard a few rumors about that marriage. But there had been an intensity about the exchange between them that caught his attention. Anything out of the ordinary might be worthy of exploring on the night of a murder. Max hesitated, uncertain where they'd gone. Most likely they'd taken the dark path to the house. He moved out of the light at the entrance, stepped onto the grass alongside the path to avoid the crushed oyster shells. He came around a curve.

". . . don't lie to me." Susan Brandt's cultivated voice was so harsh as to be almost unrecognizable. The Brandts stood near a bench that overlooked a lagoon.

Max eased quietly into the dark shadows of a pine, kept his balance on the slick needles, moved nearer.

"Rusty, for God's sake, what's happened? Don't try to tell me nothing's wrong. I know you." There was a catch in her voice. "Oh, God, how well I know you. You were late for the program. When you came in, your face was sweaty. Almost like you were sick. A few minutes ago, you looked down at your jacket and you touched it. A minute later you took your champagne glass and spilled it on your sleeve. You spilled it deliberately. That's crazy. Why did you do it?"

A siren shrilled.

Rusty grabbed his wife's arm.

She gasped. "Rusty, you're hurting me."

"Susan, shut your mouth. Do you hear me? Shut your mouth." His voice was rough with desperation. The siren choked off. He took a deep breath. "Listen, everything's fine. All you have to do is tell everybody I was with you all night. And I was. I went back to the gallery once to go to the john. That's all. Now come on, let's get back to the party." He pushed her ahead of him.

In the sharp light outside the entrance to the tent, Susan's face was empty of expression, but her wide, staring eyes were fixed on her husband as they stepped into the tent.

Max followed the Brandts. The siren probably signaled the arrival of Lou Pirelli. Billy would have the crime scene investigation in high gear. It was time for Max to get his job done. Billy wanted Max to corral everyone who knew the murdered man and bring them to the gallery. As soon as Billy finished with the crime scene, he'd come up to the gallery to question them. Billy had added one further request. He wanted Max to take special notice of their reactions to the news of Jake O'Neill's murder.

Inside the tent, the band was playing "Smoke Gets in Your Eyes." The Brandts were dancing. Not cheek to cheek. Max moved past. If ever a man looked like he'd had a shock, it was Rusty Brandt. He was going to get a bigger shock when Billy Cameron asked for the jacket to his tuxedo. That should loosen his tongue. Or his wife's.

Carl Neville stood next to the dance floor, his party mask gone. In place of the earlier high flush and ebullient smile, he gazed at the dancers with a pensive, almost forlorn, look.

Max followed his gaze. Boston Mackey, moving with grace for so big a man, was dancing with Irene Neville, his big hand heavy on her back, one meaty finger twined in her tar-black hair. Carl's wife leaned back in his embrace, her face sultry and inviting.

When Max reached Carl, the gallery director pulled his gaze away from the couple, forced a smile. "Hi, Max. Having fun?"

Max was abrupt. "Carl, I need to speak with you privately for a moment. In fact, I need to speak to everyone in the family. I'm authorized by Police Chief Cameron. There's been a crime. Will you bring your wife outside? I'll wait for you there." He swung around, ignoring Carl's shocked call. Max wanted to see the members of the Neville family in a bright sharp light when they were told of the murder of the young man Virginia Neville had planned to marry.

He walked a few feet away from the dance floor. Louise Neville sat in a chair, tapping the toe of one shoe in time with the music. She was, as always, in black, but silver beadwork adorned the neckline and cuffs of her silk dress. Max stopped in front of her. "Miss Neville, I'm Max Darling—"

"I know you. Your mother"—there was a sudden smile on her wrinkled face—"thinks the world of you." There was a dry note of amusement in her slow drawl.

Max smiled. "I can always count on my mother." It wasn't appropriate to inform Miss Neville that Max knew he could always count on Laurel to complicate any given situation, often reordering quite ordinary circumstances into a surreal landscape. His laughter faded. "Miss Neville, I'm asking the members of the family to step outside for a moment. There's been a serious incident.

The police are here. I'd appreciate it if you would come with me. I've already spoken to Carl."

The old woman's eyes narrowed. She gathered her black cashmere shawl over her shoulders and rose. She studied him for an instant, her brows drawn into a frown, then gave a slight nod and turned toward the exit.

Max moved toward the Brandts. He reached them as the music ended. Leaning forward, he said quietly, "Susan, Rusty, will you come outside? I must speak with you about a serious matter."

Annie poured Scotch into a tumbler. Not too much. That would be no help. Perhaps a quarter inch. She carried the glass with the shiny amber whisky across the small room. Despite the circumstances—Virginia Neville's quivering distress, the occasional far-away wail of a siren, the slam of doors—this small room, originally a library and now the office of the Neville Gallery, exuded peace, comfort, and welcome. The cypress-paneled walls were a rich tan, mellow as the glow of a banked fire. Everywhere there was elegance joined with practicality: an eighteenth-century slant-top desk perfect to display an unframed painting, a Sheraton corner stand topped by a fax machine. A mahogany secretary contained books that looked as though they'd been behind the thick greenish glass panes since the piece was new in the early eighteen hundreds. Always the bookseller, the thought darted through Annie's mind that there might be a first edition of the two volumes of Samuel Johnson's dictionary. She'd have to check and see. Deep rose damask curtains framed the two windows. Virginia Neville huddled at one end of a long Grecian couch, clutching a lumpy and faded red velvet bolster. The curved maple ends of the sofa reminded Annie of a sleigh.

Annie knelt beside the couch, held out the glass. "Mrs. Neville"—Annie spoke softly as she would at the bedside of a seriously ill person—"I've brought you some whisky. If you could drink some . . ."

Virginia Neville shuddered. She propped the bolster beneath her elbow and reached for the glass. She held it with both hands, but she didn't drink. She stared at the shimmering liquid, her ravaged face drooping. "I didn't want to leave Jake down there." Slowly she lifted her gaze. "It's so cold. He's lying there. . . ." Tears seeped unchecked down her ashen cheeks. "Did you know we were going to get married?"

Annie blinked back tears. "Yes, Mrs. Neville, I'm so sorry."

Irene Neville stared imperiously at Max, her lovely face marred by a scowl. Shivering, she folded her arms, pulling the white lace jacket tight, emphasizing the deep plunge of the V-shaped neckline. Her white satin trousers were dazzling in the glare of the spotlights focused on the entrance to the tent. She was as beautiful as a caged snow leopard and she exuded the same aura of danger. "If you've called us out here for a lecture on fire hazards, get it done. It's damned cold."

"It's more serious than that." Max looked at each in turn. Irene was impatient, irritated, ready to turn nasty. Carl, his faded eyes puzzled, his straw-colored hair ruffled, hunched forward like a startled heron. Susan Brandt's thin face sharpened. She touched the gold necklace at her throat.

Rusty Brandt, always loud and profane on the golf course, didn't say a word. He stood with his head down, hands jammed in his trouser pockets. Louise Neville's wrinkled face was bleak, her dark eyes stern.

Louise stepped forward. She was small and old, but she was in charge. "What's happened?"

"A body has been discovered down at the point near the ruins." Max waved his hand toward the garden.

Irene looked surprised, then excited. Carl held out his hands as if to ward away the words. Susan, eyes wide, pressed her fingers against her cheeks. Rusty Brandt's face was unchanged. Louise drew her breath in sharply.

Irene took a step toward Max. "A body? Is it Virginia?" There was a grisly eagerness in her tone. "I haven't seen her since lover boy was a no-show. Did she slit her wrists?"

"Irene." Carl's voice was choked. He reached out, grabbed his wife's arm.

She shook him off. "Well, who else would it be? And where is she?" She waved her hand. "All of us are here. Everyone but Virginia." Irene looked at Max, spoke fast. "A woman about forty-five. Wearing a silver dress that made her look like a refugee from a graveyard. Is that the one?"

Max kept his expression unchanged, but he felt cold inside. What a bitch. "The victim is male and has been identified as Jake O'Neill."

Max looked swiftly from face to face. All looked blank with shock. Except Rusty. His face was carefully, determinedly expressionless.

"Jake? I don't believe it. He was fine this evening." Susan Brandt's voice shook. "What happened to him?"

"Jake. Dead?" Irene's eyebrows rose. Just for an instant there was the merest suggestion of a smile.

"Murder." His voice was uninflected, but the stark word was shocking.

Susan's hands dropped to her throat as if breath were hard to find.

Rusty, his face still expressionless, folded his arms across his chest.

Irene's mobile features reflected shock and curiosity.

Carl winced, shook his head. "That's impossible."

Louise Neville's old face hardened into an unreadable mask. "What happened?"

"Someone struck him from behind. The blow killed him." Max gestured toward the foggy garden. "The police are there. They are investigating. I don't have any information as to the weapon used or suspects who are being sought. The identification was made by Virginia Neville."

"Oh, God." Carl's gentle face squeezed in horror. "God, that's awful. That must be why he didn't show up for the program. Who's taking care of Virginia?" He looked around as if seeking help.

Max said quickly, "My wife is with her. They're at the gallery now. The police want to interview everyone who spoke to him this evening. They also need to know who attended the reception tonight." Max looked at Carl. "Do you have a list of the guests?"

"Not really." Carl looked bewildered. "We sent out a lot of invitations. But you know how it is. Most people never RSVP. We always estimate we'll get around a hundred. I'm sure we had that many tonight. But there's no accurate list of those who came."

Louise cleared her throat. "There's an easy way to identify most of the guests. The drawing." She gestured toward the tent. "Carl, go get that bowl. I think it's tucked on the ground behind the platform."

"The drawing?" Carl repeated.

Max understood. "Sure. Almost everyone here tonight probably dropped a slip into the bowl. Here's what we'll do. . . ."

"We were going to have an April wedding. April is the most beautiful month on the island. . . ." Virginia's voice trailed away. She placed the untasted glass on a Hepplewhite side table, pushed away the bolster, sat up straight and stiff. "What are the police doing?"

Annie knew police procedure, how a crime scene is secured, the careful survey, the drawings and photographs and filming of the site, the medical examiner's preliminary findings, the removal of the body, the collection of evidence. She had a brief, vivid, sickening recollection of the crumpled green taffeta stole stained with the dead man's blood. After the wrap was photographed, gloved hands would carefully slip it into a labeled plastic bag. "The police are looking for information, anything that will lead them to the murderer. They'll ask everyone when they last saw Jake, what he was doing."

Virginia's face was piteous, her eyes brimming again with tears. "He was here. We were having fun. Oh, it was so lovely, everyone happy and everything going so well. The night was such a success. Then I sent him away."

Annie looked at her sharply. Had there been a quarrel?

Virginia clasped her hands together, held them against one cheek. "Oh, if only I'd kept him near. But I wanted him to take his place as he will—as he would when he was my husband. I wanted him to greet people and talk to our guests."

There was a knock at the door. The door swung in. Max stepped inside. There was a muted sound of voices and movement in the hallway behind him. "Here you are." His voice was warm. His eyes lingered for an instant on Annie, making sure she was all right. "Everything's under control. Carl made an announcement. He's set up a table by the front entrance to the tent. He's getting the names of those who didn't enter the drawing. Anyone with information about

Jake has been asked to come here. I'll go down and report to Billy. He asked me to round up anyone who might be able to help. He'll come up and interview them pretty soon. Will you take charge until he comes?"

So Max was returning to the crime scene and she was stuck up here, completely out of the loop. But the witnesses—everyone who had any contact with the victim—were going to gather at the gallery. Maybe there was more to be learned here than there. Annie nodded. "I'll take care of everything."

"Good." Max turned away.

Annie called out, "Max!"

He paused in the doorway.

"You might point out to Billy that the tide is coming in. Maybe you'd better take a look over the edge of the bluff for the weapon." That kind of search would take time. Annie intended to utilize every possible moment.

"Okay. I'll tell Billy." He stepped into the hall.

As soon as the door closed, Annie pointed at the desk. "Mrs. Neville, could you find some notepads or sheets of paper and some pens?"

Virginia pushed back a strand of hair, stared at the desk as if it and everything in the room were foreign. She gave a little shake of her head. "Paper . . ." She moved to the desk, pulled out a drawer, began to fumble inside, then blinked at Annie. "Why do you want paper?"

"To gather information for the police." Annie was brisk and confident and hopeful that the crime scene investigation would keep Billy away from the gallery for a good long while. "This is one way for you to help the investigation. We can take paper and pens out to the drawing room and ask everyone to write down what they know about tonight. Who Jake talked to. Where he was from the time he came into the gallery until he left to go down to the fort. We'll ask them to try to remember what time it was when they spoke to him or saw him. Why, we may find out exactly what the police need to know."

Annie felt virtuous. She was simply aiding the investigation, even though she wasn't included on the official team, and possibly, just possibly, there might be information that pointed at someone other than a running girl in a green dress.

· *Five* ·

The strobes set up at the corners of the crime scene blazed with penetrating brilliance, creating a stark rectangle to frame the body slumped in death. A heavy-duty orange extension cord snaked over uneven ground to the crime van. The rumble of the van motor melded with the slosh and slap of the incoming tide. Lou Pirelli, his curly dark hair damp with mist, his round face intent, moved carefully around the perimeter of the bricked oval, snapping one picture after another, noting the number and location in a notebook. Dr. Burford brushed pine needles from his knees. "Damn things are everywhere. Look, there's where the murderer skidded." He pointed at a streak in the carpet of pine needles. "See where it goes?" Three loblolly pines towered over a thicket of cane. The natural growth edged up the side of the grassy irregular mound that marked the remnants of the fort. "Probably came out from behind the cane."

Max studied the streak in the pine needles. If Dr. Burford was right—and he usually was—the killer had plunged across the needle-strewn pavement, coming up behind O'Neill. Max's face squeezed in thought. "You mean somebody was hidden back there?" He waved at the cane, the tips rustling in the nighttime offshore breeze.

Burford rubbed his florid face, scowled. "Looks like it to me. Anyway, it seems pretty clear somebody skidded across the needles fast to have made that trail. Why the hurry?"

Billy Cameron spread out his hands as if measuring the distance between the cane and the body. "If O'Neill and the killer were talking face-to-face"—Billy's face wrinkled in thought—"there wouldn't have been any need to hurry. Whoever killed him could have raised up the weapon and slammed him when he turned away. But if the killer"—Billy looked at the thicket—"was way over there and wanted to catch him, they'd have to rush. Hey, Frank"—Billy turned to the former police chief—"what do you think?"

"I think Doc's a damn smart man." Frank Saulter was leaner and stringier than when Annie and Max first met him, his dark hair speckled with gray, his saturnine face ridged with lines, but he still looked tough as a spiny lobster. "I'd bet the killer came out from behind the cane. But maybe O'Neill did, too."

Max squinted at the thicket. "Why would anybody go behind the cane?"

"Didn't want to be seen." Saulter's reply was laconic.

Max grinned. "Out of the mouths of old cops . . ."

Saulter's lips quirked. "Usually it's plain as the nose on your face, Max. You know I love to buy the good old books—Hammett and Chandler—from Annie, but most crimes don't take much figuring. The way I see it"—his eyes narrowed—"the dead guy came down here with somebody. The only reason to leave the party and come down here was to talk to somebody without being seen. It's not the kind of night to take a stroll to enjoy the weather." Saulter rubbed his arms. "Should have brought a jacket. Anyway, behind those canes is about as private as you could get. So maybe O'Neill's back there with someone, they quarrel, he leaves, the other person comes after him. Maybe the killer didn't start after him for a minute, then had to hurry."

Lou Pirelli lowered the camera, looked toward them. "Maybe O'Neill came here with somebody and they went"—his head swiveled around—"down those steps." He pointed to the edge of the bluff. "There are some benches on that platform, and it's darn private. Maybe somebody followed them and hid behind the cane."

"How many people would come down here on a night like this?" Billy's question was clearly rhetorical. "Nope, I think Frank's on the right track." Billy pulled a notebook out of his pocket. "O'Neill and the killer came down here for a talk. They went behind the cane. They quarreled. O'Neill left, and the murderer came after him." Billy glanced toward Max. "Maybe that girl the caterer told us about, the first one. What's her name, Max?"

Max had a vision of Annie's expressive face, dismay mingling with concern. But he had agreed to assist Billy. Chloe should have no fear of the law if she was innocent. Max kept his voice casual. "Chloe Martin. She's a college girl, and she's been working at the store over the holidays. Annie thinks a lot of her."

"If she was wearing a green dress . . ." Billy muttered, looking toward the blood-stained taffeta bunched beneath the dead man's chest.

Frank Saulter's brows bunched in a tight frown. "If so, she's got some explaining to do."

Max waved his hand in the direction of the gallery. "There are a bunch of people waiting up there, family members and others who believe they can be helpful. Maybe somebody can tell us what time O'Neill left the party." Clearly O'Neill didn't come to this isolated spot by himself. And it seemed obvious Chloe Martin must have been with him.

"Time." Billy glanced at the body. "Yeah. Doc, you got any idea how long he's been dead?"

Dr. Burford shot Billy a look of disgust. "I

don't have a crystal ball. Nobody can pin down the time of death any closer unless they saw it happen. He's been dead anywhere from a half hour to a couple of hours. I can do better on cause of death. I don't need an autopsy to figure this one. Blunt trauma to the head. Massive hemorrhaging. The weapon"—he squinted—"probably a tree limb. I think I spotted bits of bark in the wound. I can tell better when we get him to the morgue. But"—he spread his hand at the storm debris—"it would be easy enough to grab up a big stick, something pretty stout, and whack away. Have you found anything like that?"

Billy shook his head. "Nothing yet. We can take a better look tomorrow when it's light."

Dr. Burford glanced toward the bluffs. "If the murderer had any brains, he probably tossed it in the water. Even if you find a likely limb, there probably won't be any traces of hair or flesh left."

Max remembered Annie's advice. He glanced toward the darkness of the water. "The tide's coming in, Billy. Do you want Frank and me to take a look?"

Virginia Neville stepped into the drawing
room. Every face turned toward her. The
beautiful chiffon dress seemed incongruous
with the look of misery on her thin face.
However, Annie was certain the elegant
room with its pale cream walls, bois-de-
rose silk hangings, and old, well-worn furniture—Chippendale, Hepplewhite, and Sheraton—was no stranger to sorrow. In the
long history of the house that now served
as an art gallery, there had been gatherings
of all kinds, merry wedding guests, bereft
families, joyful christenings, hard-eyed po-
litical conspirators, weary war refugees. In
its two centuries of existence, the house
had known days of riches when cotton was
king and years of deprivation when carpet-
baggers swarmed the broken South. But
Annie doubted there had been many moments more dramatic than this.

The family members ranged in a semicircle near the fireplace. Carl Neville rubbed
his temple. Irene Neville's lovely face was
expressionless, but her golden eyes
watched avidly. Susan Brandt, pale and
grim, clutched at her throat. Rusty Brandt,

reddish face strained, tugged at his collar, pulling his bow tie askew. Louise Neville, her black shawl trailing over one arm onto the floor, was as still and stiff as the Sèvres figurine of a soldier of Napoleon's army on the white marble mantel.

Tony Hasty, his caterer's apron sagging, leaned against a wing chair. An unlit cigar stuck from the side of his mouth. It wobbled as he worked it with his teeth. Edith Cummings, her gamin face squeezed in commiseration, hunched forward on a settee. She looked solemnly toward Virginia, but she waggled her fingers in a clandestine greeting to Annie. Serious, intense, hardworking Pamela Potts sat primly in a Sheraton chair. Her blue brocade evening dress was high-necked, long, and generally shapeless. Pamela was active in almost every charitable endeavor on the island and quite often recruited Annie as a volunteer. Pamela made little bleating sounds and her huge blue eyes filled with tears. Henny Brawley, still carrying the book bag with the new titles, was as attentive as a raccoon and, Annie knew, just as inquisitive. Annie wondered cynically whether Henny, who claimed to read a mystery a day, actually knew anything that might be helpful to the police or whether she had been unable to resist the temptation to be in on a murder investigation.

Carl stepped forward, his manner diffident, his gentle face pained. "Virginia, I'm terribly sorry. We're shocked, all of us. If there's anything we can do—anything I can do . . ." His voice trailed away.

Virginia brushed back a drooping strand of hair. "No one knows what happened." Her voice was dull. The blush on her cheeks stood out against her paleness. "Someone"—she looked vaguely toward Tony Hasty—"said some girl came running up from the ruins." She pressed trembling fingers against her lips, struggled, managed to speak. "The police want us to help them." She glanced at Annie. "If you will tell them . . ." She turned away, walked blindly to a chair near the fireplace, sank onto a hand-crocheted throw.

Annie held up a clutch of pens in one hand and white sheets of printer paper in the other. "The police have requested that everyone describe their evening, what they did, who they talked to, and especially any contact with Jake O'Neill. Try to estimate the time when you saw or spoke to him. If there is any other information that might aid the investigation—any personal knowledge of Jake O'Neill—please include it in the statement."

Pamela Potts raised her hand, her eyes wide.

Annie was not surprised that Pamela had a question. "Yes?"

"Annie, I wish it to be clear that I am not aware of anything that pertains directly to Mr. O'Neill's activities this evening. Oh, he was really so nice." Pamela's voice was soft. "He did a portrait of my dog, Whistler, and you can see that Whistler is smiling."

Annie moved from person to person, handing out pen and paper. Annie's memory of Pamela's dog was of a yapping terrier who seemed to be all eyes and teeth and had about as much charm as a piranha.

Pamela gave a mournful sigh. "To see the end of so much talent . . ." She wiped away a tear. "But Max asked that anyone with information that might suggest something of Mr. O'Neill's involvements with—"

"Write it down, Pamela," Annie said gently.

Irene's eyes narrowed. She glanced at

the grandfather clock near the wide doorway to the hall. "Jake got here a few minutes after seven. I saw him with Virginia.
Then, like a good boy"—her tone was sardonic—"he started schmoozing the guests.
I expect Virginia had given him his orders."

Virginia's face twisted in anguish. "I
asked him to assume his proper role. After
all, as my husband . . ." She lifted a handkerchief to her lips. "If only I'd kept him near
me. But he loved talking with people. That's
the last I saw of him. He was smiling and
laughing. Everyone liked Jake."

"Whatever anyone saw of him will be
helpful," Annie said quickly. "Or if anyone
knows why he went down to the point . . ."
She looked inquiringly from face to face.
When no one spoke, she said firmly, "Let's
get started. The police should be up soon."

There was the scratching of pens on paper, an occasional cough or rustle. Annie
stared at her sheet. Ultimately she would
have to tell Billy Cameron about Chloe and
Jake. But there was so much more to Chloe
than her romantic interlude with a stranger
on the pier. How could Annie make Billy see
the vibrant girl who loved to laugh, who
held children spellbound when she read

aloud at the Saturday morning children's mystery program? Annie was certain that the Chloe she knew, the Chloe with whom she'd laughed and talked and worked, would no more strike down a living person than would Annie herself. Annie sighed. There was not space enough on the sheet of paper or time enough to tell Billy what she knew about Chloe. She was tempted to write down how Chloe helped at the Christmas party at The Haven, the island's recreation center for children and teenagers. When a little girl came late and hesitated in the hall, not wanting to come in because she didn't have a present to put under the tree, Chloe had slipped off a turquoise bracelet and insisted the girl take it and wrap it in Chloe's scarf and come in to the party. But if she told about that Chloe, wasn't she duty bound to tell about the Chloe who had fallen in love with a stranger in the fog?

Annie decided to stick to a brief description of what she had seen tonight. That wasn't much, a briefly glimpsed running figure that may have come from the point. Annie's hand tightened on the pen. Why had Chloe run? If only she knew the answer. To

run implies urgency or fear or—undeni-
ably—an effort to escape. Chloe. Where
was she? Annie took a deep breath, laid
down her paper and pen. She quietly
stepped toward Virginia Neville, bent down
and whispered, "I'll be right back."

On shore, Frank Saulter played the beam
from his heavy-duty flashlight over the edge
of the bluff, illuminating the big chunks of
reddish rock that littered the coast.

Max shielded his eyes from the light and
balanced atop a wide concrete barrier, now
crusted with oyster shells. The barrier had
been put in place in hopes of preventing
further erosion, but the cliffs continued to
crumble, a foot or so every year. Seawater
lapped near the top of the barrier, surged
around boulders, splashed against the base
of the fifteen-foot bluff. Max yelled over the
sound of the incoming tide, "If somebody
threw the weapon down here, we'll have a
hell of a time finding it."

Above him, Frank picked up a chunky
stick. He lifted his arm, threw. A geyser of
foam lifted as the branch struck the dark
water and disappeared.

Max looked, didn't even see a ripple marking the spot where the stick had disappeared. He walked back along the barrier, reached up, and climbed back onto the observation platform to join Frank. Max glanced toward the body. Lou was slow and careful. He hadn't found anything that appeared to have been used as a weapon. A search of the gardens in daylight might turn up something, but Dr. Burford had probably made a good guess. After striking O'Neill, the killer could easily have tossed the weapon into the water. With the tide coming in, the stick would be washed clean.

Max jammed his hands in his trousers. "A thick branch." His tone was thoughtful. "There are plenty of them left over from the last storm. Lots of them a foot or a foot and a half in length. Like staves. Perfectly good weapons right here at hand. But hey"—his voice was eager—"grabbing up a branch and striking out means the murder wasn't planned."

Frank swung the beam of light back to the body. "So we have to find out what the guy could have said or done that made somebody grab a branch and smash him in the back of the head."

Footsteps scuffed pine needles, clattered down the steps to the deck. Billy reached them, notebook in hand. "Okay, Max, fill me in on this girl Annie saw. A friend of Annie's?"

In the library, Annie found the telephone directory. Chloe was staying with her aunt and uncle. Smith? Smithers? Smitt? No, Schmidt. Annie flipped to the Ss. There it was: Harold and Frances Schmidt. Annie glanced at the Dresden clock on a side table near the sofa. Almost eleven. Was it too late to call? Perhaps so, if it were an ordinary evening. This was not an ordinary evening. She reached for the receiver, paused. Slowly, her hand dropped. She couldn't pretend ignorance. Billy Cameron may not have deputized her as he had Max, but Annie knew police procedure. Billy would want to talk to Chloe without warning. It was important for him to do so.

Annie traced a finger across the top of the telephone receiver. She couldn't call Chloe. If Chloe was innocent, as Annie felt certain she was, it would be better that she learn of O'Neill's murder from the police. In fact, if Chloe was forewarned, her reaction as an innocent person would be lost. But Annie hated thinking of the terrible shock that awaited Chloe. It was dreadful to know that she would soon receive devastating news and not to be able to help her.

Billy Cameron or perhaps Lou Pirelli might be on the way right this minute to speak to Chloe. There wasn't anything Annie could do about that. Okay. Morning would come. She'd call Chloe first thing, let her know that Annie was her champion.

Annie cast a final regretful look at the telephone, then turned away and opened the door into the hall. Her footsteps seemed inordinately loud on the heart pine floor of the foyer, but no one gave her any notice when she stepped into the drawing room.

She picked up her sheet of paper from the end table near Virginia. She stared at the paper, then wrote quickly. She'd barely finished when Max came in. As always, Annie thought him the most attractive man in the room, even though his hair was mussed by the ocean breeze and his tuxedo trousers damp and mud-smeared. He carried a plastic bag in his hand and scanned

the room until he found Rusty Brandt. He
hesitated, then veered toward Annie.

Max glanced around, spoke softly. "What
are they doing?"

"Statements. Where they were, what they
saw, any information about O'Neill." Annie
spoke with quiet pride.

"That's a good idea." His tone was admiring. "When they finish, gather them up for
Billy. He's going to be up here pretty soon.
He's in a hurry to track down Chloe. Do you
have a number for her?" He listened as she
gave him the name of the aunt and uncle
and repeated them to be certain. "Okay. I'll
tell him." He looked around again. "I'd stay
and take up the statements, but you can
handle this."

Annie pressed her lips together. Why yes,
she thought she could, even though she
wasn't a deputy, thank you very much.

Max wasn't through. "I've got a little job
to take care of, then I have to get back to
the crime van." He patted her on the shoulder.

In her heart Annie knew Max didn't intend
to be condescending, but to Annie's sensi-
bility his comment had a definite aura of the
old-timer commending the neophyte. As he

turned away, Annie drew the rear end of a donkey on her sheet of paper. Above it, she neatly printed in all caps: OFFICIOUS.

Max walked across the room to Rusty Brandt.

Brandt looked up. Abruptly, his face went rigid, his hand folded in a fist around his pen.

Max looked at him somberly. "As part of the investigation into the death of Jake O'Neill, Chief Cameron is requesting your jacket so that it may undergo forensic tests."

Brandt stumbled to his feet. "What the hell are you talking about?"

"Your tuxedo jacket." Max's face was hard and unyielding. "I'll give you a receipt for it." Max held up the plastic bag. "The coat goes in here. I seal the bag." He pulled a roll of tape from his pocket. "I tag it and deliver it to the crime lab."

"Rusty . . ." His wife was at his side. She clutched at his arm, then jerked her hand away.

"Dammit, Susan, I spilled champagne on it." His voice was deep and husky. "That's all. Champagne."

"Then it won't be a problem, will it?" Max spread open the bag.

Dragging footsteps sounded. Virginia stopped beside Susan. "I don't understand. Why do they want Rusty's jacket?"

Susan wrapped her arms tightly across the front of her crimson dress. "I don't know." Her voice was thin.

"Or you can come with me, Brandt." Max was brisk. "I am authorized to take you into custody as a material witness. Once you're in jail, Chief Cameron can contact the judge for a search warrant and the jacket can be impounded."

Slowly, his face grim, Rusty shrugged out of the tuxedo coat. He pulled a slender wallet from an interior pocket before handing the jacket to Max. He frowned at the billfold, stuffed it in a back pocket of his trousers.

Max folded the jacket and slid it into the plastic bag. He filled out a label, slipped it inside, sealed the bag, and taped it shut. He handed a receipt to Brandt, who crumpled it in his hand.

"As you can see"—Max addressed the room at large—"the investigation into the murder of Jake O'Neill is progressing. The chief has requested that there be no public discussion of the evening's events. Please complete your statements as to your whereabouts this evening and your contact with the victim as well as any information about O'Neill's friends or enemies or any known quarrels or disagreements and turn them in to my wife. Chief Cameron will be here shortly to receive the statements and speak with you. Thank you."

On his way out, Max hesitated, then whispered to Annie, "The statements are a great idea, Annie. I'll tell Billy you're responsible." Max looked at her searchingly. "I'm sure you realize the statements will be part of the official investigation." It wasn't quite a question.

Annie resisted the impulse to reply that she'd had no idea such was the case and had believed them to be destined for recitation on the local news station. She made an indeterminate sound. It might have been a breathy oh yes. It might have been a more earthy expletive.

He held her gaze. "Annie, promise me you won't read them."

"Who, me?" Definitely breathy.

"Annie." His blue eyes were stern.

She held up her right hand. "I do solemnly promise that I shall gather them up—and I shall not read them . . ."

He grinned. "Good girl."

As he turned away, she added in her mind a qualifying phrase, ". . . right now."

Billy reached out for the plastic bag containing the tuxedo jacket. "Good work, Max." He swung around. "Mavis?"

His wife poked her head from the back of the crime van. "Yo."

Billy took the bag to her. "Mark this jacket to be tested for bloodstains and cross-checked with the victim's blood." He kneaded the side of his face with his knuckles. "That wraps up the physical evidence." He glanced at the techs easing the body onto a gurney. "Frank, anything else you can think of?"

The former chief carefully surveyed the scene. "Nope. You've done everything you can until tomorrow. I'll come out and get some daytime photos, free you up to question witnesses."

"Good." Billy looked toward his wife. "Mavis, you and Lou can leave now. Take the van back to the station." He frowned. "I know it's late, but you better take the exhibits inside, lock 'em up."

Max knew he was remembering an episode when the island's crime van was torched.

"I'll take care of everything, Billy." Lou clapped shut his notebook. "Mavis can go on home."

Mavis touched her husband's arm. "Are you coming?"

Billy shook his head. "Not for a while. Got to check out that girl. Chloe Martin."

Edith, of course, finished first. She looked up, flapped her sheet of paper at Annie.

Annie sped across the drawing room. "Thanks, Edith." Annie spoke loudly, hoping to prod the others. It reminded Annie of finals and the proctor eager to grab up the blue books. Sure enough, as soon as she took Edith's statement, the others began to finish. In a moment, she had a full stack except for Virginia Neville, who huddled in a wing chair, staring blindly at the sheet of paper.

Annie spoke gently. "Mrs. Neville, the

chief will especially appreciate your help. If you could try . . ."

Virginia opened her hands, palms up. "I can't. I'm sorry. I can't think. All I can do is remember. . . ." She shuddered.

Carl rubbed his fingers over his bristly mustache. "Listen, Annie, Virginia shouldn't have to be here, waiting to talk to the police." He began with a mumble, then his voice strengthened. "Look at her. She's devastated. She needs to be in bed. I'm going to call our doctor, get her a sedative. After all, what more can be done tonight? The police can talk to her tomorrow."

Henny Brawley rose, picked up her book bag. "Carl's right. I for one am going home. I'll talk to Billy tomorrow. You can explain, Annie. Everyone's too tired to do any more tonight. Billy will understand. And obviously, no one here"—she glanced briefly at Rusty Brandt—"knows anything critical."

There was a flurry of movement toward the door.

Annie didn't try to stop them. It was after eleven. And she had their statements. But she angled across the room to intercept Henny. Annie whispered, "May I have the book bag. You can carry the books."

Henny gave her a sharp, inquiring glance. "Sure." She slipped the books free, handed the bag to Annie, but held on to it for an instant. "Providing you tell me why tomorrow. I'll give you a ring."

As soon as the front door slammed and there was quiet, except for the heavy steps of the caterer as he strode toward the back of the gallery, Annie whirled about, the book bag in one hand and the statements in the other. She darted across the hall and into the library. It took only a moment to feed the sheets into the fax machine. The fax paper, soft and limp and silent, oozed out. Annie took the copies, slipped them into the book bag.

"Annie? Where are you? Where is everybody?" Max's voice boomed in the hallway.

Annie tossed the book bag onto a Louis XIV chair. Moving fast, she reached the desk just as the door opened. She held up the statements. "I was looking for a folder to put them in. When they were done, everyone wanted to go home. I hope that's okay with Billy. But he'll have these." She waggled the sheets. "He'll be prepared when he sees everyone tomorrow. Oh, Max, I feel so sorry for Virginia Neville. She looked like a wax doll that had been left out in the sun. Carl took her home. Anyway, I don't know where they keep things." She opened a cupboard behind the desk. "Here they are." She picked up a bright orange folder from a stack and slid the sheets inside. "All present and accounted for. Except for Virginia. She wasn't up to it." Annie held out the folder to Max. "Unread, as promised."

Max took the folder, slid it under his arm. "Annie, I knew we could count on you." He pulled his car keys out of his pocket, handed them to her. "I'm going with Billy to talk to Chloe Martin. See you later."

Dorothy L., green eyes bright, paced along the back of the sofa.

Annie reached out for the fluffy white cat, but Dorothy L. eluded her grasp, flowing to the floor. Her claws clicked on the floor as she moved toward the hallway. She stopped, sat, stared.

"Your hero isn't here." Annie tried not to sound peevish. After all, just because it was Annie who had rescued Dorothy L. when she was abandoned as a helpless kitten in

the alleyway behind Death on Demand and
Annie who brought her home to be queen
of the Darling household (and free from the
unrelenting hostility of Agatha, the sleek
black cat who had no doubt as to the true
ownership of the bookstore) was no reason
for Annie to have her feelings hurt because
Dorothy L. adored Max. "Your hero," Annie's voice was cool, "is an officious ass."

Dorothy L. flicked her tail.

"Sorry to be the one to break it to you,
Dorothy L. I know you think he's quite perfect." Annie felt her lips curve in a smile. "I
have to admit he means well. He's just trying to help Billy, but he's taking himself very
seriously. Oh, I know," she said to the cat,
as if hearing an unspoken rebuke, "I'm always exhorting him to be serious, and now
when he's serious, I'm critical. Sure, I'm in
the wrong." Annie pulled the afghan over
her legs. Despite her toasty candy-cane-
pattern flannel pajamas and the crackling
fire, she felt cold. Usually she and Max
ended their winter evenings together on the
sofa with thick, sweet, dark hot chocolate
and half-finished sentences and gurgles of
laughter, then arm in arm, still laughing,
climbed the stairs to bed and the love poets

dream about. Annie enjoyed the study, the beauty of the golden tan cypress panels, the bright jackets of books, the comfort of the downy blue sofa. But tonight the study was cheerless and the cocoa tasteless. She set the mug on a side table. She wanted to pop up and hurry into the kitchen. She'd dropped the book bag on a counter near the garage door, handy for her to pick up on her way to Death on Demand in the morning. She knew she'd better wait until tomorrow to read the copies of the statements. Tonight she could honestly meet Max's questioning gaze. Of course she hadn't read the statements. How could he even think it?

Dorothy L. tilted her head, then rose, stretched, and trotted toward Annie. She jumped onto the sofa and plopped in Annie's lap.

Annie looked down. "Don't think you're fooling me. I know it's just the afghan. If Max walked in—" She broke off. She knew and Dorothy L. knew that Max was Da Man. Annie smiled, even though the room was chilly and her thoughts grim.

Her smile faded. Were Billy and Max talking now to Chloe? Poor Chloe, who had fallen in love with love only to discover that her knight of the night was a sham. Annie picked up Dorothy L., burrowed her face into the thick ruff. "I don't care how mad she was at him"—Annie knew Chloe well enough to expect that her volatile clerk had erupted like a pent-up volcano when she realized her lover's perfidy—"but she'll be devastated to know he's dead." To know the lips she had tasted were forever stilled. To know the body that had been so warm was now forever cold. "Dorothy L., I feel awful. I should have called her. Well, no, I couldn't. But I should have insisted on going with Max. She's my friend and I'm not there. She doesn't have anybody—"

The phone rang.

Annie grabbed up the portable phone, punched it on. "Hello."

"Annie." His voice was pleased.

All right, Max was an officious ass. But he was her officious ass. He must have realized she was desperately worried about Chloe. Annie was suffused with forgiving warmth. "Oh, Max, I'm so glad you called. How is Chloe? Is there anyone with her? Was Billy—"

Max cut in quickly. "We need some help. This is an official call—"

She sat bolt upright. Dorothy L. gave a startled mew and leaped to the floor. "Is Chloe all right? Max, what's happened?"

". . . information as to her whereabouts."

"Max"—Annie popped to her feet, tossing the afghan aside—"what are you talking about?"

"Chloe's not here." In the background, a car door slammed. "Apparently she came home around ten-thirty. Her aunt heard Chloe in her room and thought she was in for the night. Later, oh maybe a half hour or so, her aunt heard Chloe's car leave. Mrs. Schmidt got worried and checked Chloe's room. The bed was still made. A drawer or two were pulled open. Her high heels were kicked into a corner. Her slip was on a chair. Mrs. Schmidt was willing to let Billy and me take a look. We didn't find that green dress anywhere. You said Edith described it as bright green?"

Annie felt numb, but she replied, "That's right. Kelly green."

"Yeah, well there wasn't a green evening dress of any kind in her closet. Billy didn't touch anything, but he looked around. Her aunt's pretty sure Chloe changed clothes before she went out again. She says Chloe's heavy pea jacket is gone from the coat tree in the front hall. She doesn't have any idea where Chloe may have gone. She says Chloe doesn't have any friends on the island. Billy wondered if you had any idea where she could be."

The Aztec blue pottery clock on the mantel chimed. Midnight. Midnight . . . Annie shivered. "Maybe . . ."

Max spoke away from the receiver. "Yeah, Billy. Annie's thinking." He boomed in her ear. "Where do you think?"

Annie remembered the gleam in Chloe's green eyes and the eager words tumbling out so fast: "I go to the pier at midnight every night and he comes."

"Annie?"

The clock finished chiming.

"I have an idea. I'll meet you and Billy at the police station in ten minutes." She snapped off the phone. It was ringing by the time she reached the stairs. This time she didn't answer. She ignored the peals while she dressed. In less than five minutes, she was out the door and on her way.

Annie drove with the cell phone turned

off. She had no doubt it would ring if she turned it on. She drove as fast as she dared on the dark, foggy roads, alert for deer and raccoons. She slowed as she passed the gate of the residential preserve and waved at the retired marine who was on duty at night.

The island's small downtown was dark. Even Parotti's was closed, the facade dark, the red neon turned off. Annie pulled up behind the police car parked in front of the station. The one-story station overlooked the harbor. Tonight the fog hid the water. As she turned off her lights, Billy and Max piled out of the cruiser and strode toward her.

Annie rolled down her window and folded her arms.

"Now look, Annie"—Billy was tired, irritable, and peremptory—"if you know where she is, tell me. You didn't need to come down here."

"Yes, I did." Annie looked up at him. "I may be wrong, but I have an idea where she might be. Billy, let me come with you. I won't say a word until you've told her. But she has a right to have somebody there when she finds out he's dead. Billy, she thought she was in love with him."

Billy moved his head around on his neck, trying to ease tight muscles. "Annie, she may be a murder suspect."

Annie reached out, turned the key. The motor roared. "You and Max look for her. And so will I. If I find her . . ."

"Wait a minute, wait a minute." He gave an exasperated sigh. "Okay. But you have to keep your mouth shut."

The headlights diffused into a glow that was swallowed up by the fog. There was nothing ahead or behind but thick grayness. Annie nosed her car up to the concrete stanchion at the edge of the harbor. She grabbed her flashlight. When she got out of the car, it was as though nothing existed but impenetrable grayness.

Annie heard the slam of car doors. In a moment, Max and Billy were there beside her.

Billy was puzzled. "Why would she come here?" And suspicious. "Annie, this better not be some kind of joke. Nobody's around. Everything's closed down."

"The pier." She led the way. They missed

it once, going too far and ending up on the ferry boat dock. They backtracked.

Annie stepped onto the old wooden planks. She kept close to the railing, moving slowly. She swept the flashlight back and forth into cottony grayness that absorbed all light. The pier seemed endless in the fog. The hollow echo of their footsteps, the warning cry of the foghorn and the slap of water against the pilings merged into a mournful dirge. Annie shivered and knew the cold went deeper than the sodden January night. They came burdened by death to the place where life and blood had exulted in joy. At the end of the pier, Annie's light touched a huddled figure.

Chloe held up a hand to shield her eyes from the sharp white beam. Her freckled face was pale and strained, her eyes blurred by tears, her features flattened by fatigue, her dark red hair dampened by the mist. Suddenly her face lighted, disbelief warring with hope. She peered toward the lights. "Is it you?" She scrambled to her feet. The old navy pea coat looked heavy on her slim figure.

"Miss Martin." Billy's voice was as somber as the night. He strode up to her, a big man who looked even bigger in contrast to the slender girl in the bulky coat. "I'm Billy Cameron, acting chief of police. You were at the Neville Gallery tonight. I have to ask you for an account of your evening."

"My evening?" Her voice was dull and tired, bewildered. She bent to look past him. "Annie? Is that you?"

Annie stepped forward. "Chloe, I—"

"Annie." Billy's tone was stern, unrelenting.

Max slipped an arm around her shoulders, murmured, "Hold up. Billy's got a job to do."

Annie took a deep breath, spread out her hands.

Chloe smoothed back a tangle of damp red hair. She stared at Billy, her face puzzled and uneasy. "I don't understand. The police? What do you want with me?"

Billy was a foot from her. He lifted his flashlight and the beam struck Chloe squarely in the face. As she squinted against the glare, he threw out the words, sharp as knives cutting in a barroom brawl. "I am investigating the murder of Jacob Hendricks O'Neill."

Chloe looked utterly blank. "Jacob O'Neill?" Her tone was puzzled.

Jacob Hendricks O'Neill . . . The name came from his driver's license, no doubt. Billy would have checked the dead man's pockets, taken his wallet.

Annie stared at the girl and understood. "Oh, Chloe." Annie tried to steel her voice. She had to tell Chloe, tell her the handsome young man in the golfer's cap was dead. "Jake O'Neill, he's the one you met here. On the pier."

Chloe's pale face crumpled before their eyes.

Annie tried to think about little facts, the smell of the ocean, the slap of water against the pilings, nonessential, unimportant information that didn't stab her to the heart. Anything to avoid grappling with Chloe Martin's pain.

Chloe clutched at her throat, tried to speak, wavered unsteadily.

Annie brushed past Billy, ignoring his call. She embraced Chloe, felt her tremble even through the heavy coat. "Chloe, oh, Chloe, I'm so sorry."

Chloe pulled free, lunged toward Billy. She grabbed his arm. "What did you say?

You don't mean him? You can't. Not him. He can't be dead."

Billy had on his cop face, suspicious, watchful, measuring. "You went down to the point with him tonight. You quarreled."

Chloe's hand dropped. She stepped back until she pressed against the railing, her eyes wide and staring. She didn't answer.

"You were seen running away." Billy kept the light on her face. "Why did you run?"

"What happened to him?" Chloe's voice was thin but steady.

Billy hesitated, his face suspicious.

"Tell me." Her voice rose. "I have a right to know. What happened to him?" Her lips trembled. Tears spilled down her pale cheeks.

Billy frowned. "The deceased died from blunt trauma. A blow to the head."

"Where was he . . . killed?" She pressed her fingers against her cheeks, bent forward to hear.

"The body was found near the ruins of the old fort." Billy was brisk, almost impatient. "Is that where you left him?"

Her hands dropped. She lifted her head, stared at him.

When she didn't answer, Billy said

sharply, "I want an accounting of your actions, Miss Martin, from the time you arrived at the Neville Gallery to the present moment."

"Why?" The word was a whisper of sound.

Billy's face was determined. "I understand you had"—there was a pause—"a romantic attachment—"

Chloe looked at Annie. Her eyes accused. Her gaze held heartbreak and disappointment and recognition of betrayal.

"—to Mr. O'Neill. I understand you did not know that his engagement to Mrs. Neville was to be announced at the party. I understand you came to the gallery and sought out Mr. O'Neill and that you and Mr. O'Neill left the gallery." Billy looked grim. "You were next seen fleeing from the property. I must know what happened between you and Mr. O'Neill."

Chloe turned up the collar of the pea coat, held the rough wool against her cheek. "We went down to the point. I couldn't believe it when he told me he was going to marry that woman. Why, she's a lot older. I don't know what I said. I was so angry, I turned and ran away. He called after me." Her voice could scarcely be heard. "I heard him call, but it was too late." The tears came fast now. "It was me he cared for. I knew it. But I couldn't go back. He'd ruined everything. It was all over. I went home and took off my dress. I realized he had my stole but I didn't care, not anymore."

"O'Neill had the stole." Billy's voice was gruff. "How come?"

Annie knew the bloodstained taffeta was nestling inside a plastic bag and by now had been locked in the evidence room of the police station.

Chloe struggled not to sob. "What difference does it make? Oh, who hit him? I don't understand. He was fine when I left. I was so mad. . . ."

"Why were you mad?" Billy held up his notebook, his pen poised.

Chloe pressed her fingers against her cheeks. "Maybe if I'd stayed . . . But he was going to marry her. How could he? That's what I asked him. He said he had to, he'd promised. He said she was nice and they had fun together and he couldn't just not show up. He said if he married her, he'd be set for life with a place for his paintings and lots of money. That's when I turned and ran away. He grabbed at me, caught hold of my stole. I heard him call my name. But I kept on running."

The beam of Billy's flashlight didn't waver on her face. "Where's the dress?"

She stared at him blankly, coming back from her memory of the moment when her romantic dream had turned to ashes. Her lips trembled. "It was my happy dress. My best dress. I wore it because I had a feeling—oh, I was so sure—that I was going to find him at the party and that everything would be wonderful and he would be excited to see me. And then I found out." She rocked back and forth, her face empty. "I ran away and went home. I took off my dress and I knew I'd never wear it again. I came here and I threw it into the water. I never wanted to see it again. Never, never, never."

"You threw it in the water." Billy slapped shut his notebook. "Miss Martin, I'm taking you into custody as a material witness—"

"Custody?" Her voice rose. Both hands gripped the lapels of her coat. "Do you mean you'll put me in jail? Lock me up?"

Terror twisted her face, bubbled in her voice. "I haven't done anything."

Billy shoved his notebook into his pocket. "You were in the company of the deceased shortly before his death. The stole to your dress was found beneath his body, stained with his blood. You have admitted throwing the dress into the ocean. A thorough search will be made at daylight for the dress. A microscopic examination of fibers will determine if it is stained. You admit quarreling with O'Neill. There is sufficient evidence to hold you as a material witness. You will be permitted to make one telephone call. Tomorrow, when you are represented by counsel, I will formally interview you."

"No. Oh, no." She backed up, pressed against the railing. "Don't lock me up. I can't bear to be locked up." Hysteria lifted her voice, made it shrill. Her thin face looked like old pudding.

"Billy, please don't do this." Annie's voice shook. "There isn't any need. She can't leave the island."

"Chief"—Max stepped close to Billy— "there's no ferry until morning. The fog's too thick for a boat."

Annie wanted to cry out. She knew Billy's

decision hung in the balance. But he couldn't be pushed. Not Billy. Surely he saw how desperately upset Chloe was. How could Billy believe even for a moment that this distraught girl had battered a man to death?

"Don't lock me up." Chloe shuddered. "Please."

Water slapped against the pilings, as insistent and unremitting as the thoughts Annie wished she could dismiss. Chloe admitted coming to the pier and throwing away her dress. No wonder Billy believed the worst. Yet Annie had no difficulty imagining how Chloe—dramatic, vulnerable, emotional Chloe—might focus her misery on a dress and determine to get rid of it. A woman would understand. But Billy would believe Chloe threw away the dress to hide bloodstains.

As for the dress, had it been sucked away by the current or snagged on a boat or a log? Had it sunk to the harbor floor? Was it floating, a sodden mass of once beautiful taffeta, waiting for grappling hooks to haul it onto a boat and from there to a laboratory for testing? If there was blood on the dress . . .

Max said briskly, "You can interview her tomorrow."

Billy rubbed his face. "Yeah." He sounded uncertain. It was late. He'd have to roust Mavis from their house to serve as a matron at the jail. "All right. Miss Martin, I'll see you at nine o'clock in the morning at the police station. You are not to leave the island."

Chloe put fingers to her trembling lips and nodded jerkily. She started up the pier. She came even with Annie, stopped for an instant, her splotchy face slack and stricken. "I thought"—her voice quivered— "you were my friend." And then she bolted into the fog, the sound of her running steps echoing back to them.

· *Six* ·

Annie stepped out of the shower. She reached for the fluffy oversize towel, warm from the heated rack. Normally she preferred a leisurely bath with bubbles that fascinated Dorothy L. This morning she was in a hurry, though she was trying to appear casual and relaxed, as if this were any old day and she was going to the store with nothing more in mind than completing inventory.

Max whisked the razor through shaving cream. His eyes met hers in the steamy mirror, then dropped to take a leisurely inventory. "Hmm, nice."

She grinned. "Thank you." Max could always be counted on . . .

"Annie"—he carefully curved the blade around his chin—"you won't do anything . . ." He finished shaving, scooped up a hot wet washcloth, patted his cheeks and turned, blue eyes intent. ". . . rash."

So much for her attempt to pretend it was business as usual. She tossed the towel on the tile counter and slipped into a bra and panties. "I don't know what you mean by rash." She made an effort to sound reasonable. After all, she was reasonable. She hadn't read the statements she'd gathered up last night. Yet. "If you're asking whether I intend to see what I can find out about Jake O'Neill, well, sure." She placed her hands on her hips. "I have to do what I can. You heard Chloe last night." Annie's voice wobbled. "She thinks I betrayed her. She said she'd thought I was her friend. Well, I am her friend. If Billy arrests her today, he's making a big mistake. When we got to the pier, just for a minute I'm sure she thought it might be Jake."

Max pulled on his T-shirt. "Or she was putting on a good show."

Annie grabbed the hair dryer. She flicked it on high and blew her blond curls into a flyaway mop, a hairstyle that made her feel ready for a Himalayan trek. And the noise drowned out Max. As soon as she finished, she swiped her hair with a brush and hurried into the bedroom.

Max was almost dressed. He slipped on a V-neck navy sweater. "Annie, you need to butt out. It won't help Chloe for you to get crossways with Billy."

Annie selected a peach velour pullover, a nice contrast to her gray wool slacks. She slipped it on, looked at him with suddenly mournful eyes. "What will help Chloe?"

He was at the door. His answer was quick, forceful. "The truth." His look was skeptical. "If she's innocent."

"Okay." Annie stepped into gray suede loafers. "That's a deal. You look for the truth. So will I."

"Chloe?" Annie stepped inside Death on Demand, closed the door. There was no sound but the click of Agatha's claws as the black cat trotted up the center aisle. Annie flicked on the lights. The store still glistened in its holiday finery, evergreen swags along the walls, holly garlands and bunches of mistletoe on every end cap. Potpourri scented the air with the smells of roasting apples and cinnamon. In the chill January morning, the store had a frowsy feel of spent expectations like discarded wrappings crumpled for throwaway. Instead of her usual flare of cheer, Annie felt let down. Of course, she'd not really expected that Chloe would answer. Chloe was due at the police station at nine o'clock. Last night on the pier, she'd made clear her disappointment in Annie. She probably wouldn't come back to work even if she wasn't arrested. But Annie intended to make sure that Chloe knew she could count on Annie's friendship. Surely Chloe would understand that, painful as it was, it was absolutely essential that she not be forewarned of Jake's death.

Annie had a sudden quick memory of a Christmas several years ago and Chloe's present to her, offered diffidently as if it weren't worthy enough. Annie had unwrapped the little package to find a slim tan book, no more than five and a half by eight inches in size, a slender twenty-five pages in length. Chloe had murmured, "I don't know if you'll like it. I found it last summer at a garage sale." Annie had looked at the title in faded gold: *Writing Is Work,* by Mary

Roberts Rinehart. Annie still had the book, the exposition of how and why the famed queen of crime created her books, a straightforward, unpretentious, and fascinating essay. Annie had not known the little volume existed, but Chloe had found it among castaways and kept it to bring to her friend half a year later. Annie had taken to heart so many of Rinehart's observations. There was a favorite, which she often shared with visiting authors, "Of one thing the reader can be certain: the more easily anything reads, the harder it has been to write."

Agatha meowed sharply.

Annie reached down, scooped up the elegant cat. "Agatha, I've got to help Chloe. She thinks I've abandoned her."

Agatha squirmed against Annie's grasp, twisted free, and loped away, claws clicking loudly in the silent store.

Annie hurried to the coffee bar. Agatha was hungry. If thwarted, she'd begin to nip, and her incisors were sharp as a razor. Annie placed the book bag containing the statements on the coffee bar. She opened the cabinet and picked up a box of dry cat food. "Sweetie, stop fussing. I'm getting your bowl ready as fast as I can." Was Chloe frightened to go see Billy? Would her aunt go with her?

Agatha crouched, tail flipping.

Over the rattle of pellets, Annie said glumly, "I've never felt so rejected. Billy Cameron needs help and I am suddenly invisible. Max warns me not to be rash. Chloe looks at me like I'm Benedict Arnold." She measured coffee, frowned. "Benedictine Arnold? Anyway"—she turned on the coffee machine— "as far as Chloe is concerned, I'm a louse, a rat, a turncoat. Agatha, I feel awful."

Agatha hunched over her food bowl.

Annie reached for the book bag. Her mind was made up. She was going to read the statements from last night. Max would be appalled, but Annie promised her frowning conscience that she would be exceedingly careful not to compromise Billy's efforts. There should be no conflict if she sought the truth. Annie slid the soft sheets of fax paper onto the counter of the coffee bar and counted nine statements. Virginia Neville hadn't written one, and Annie hadn't made a copy of her own. Which should she read first? That was easy. Start with unbiased information. Quickly Annie sorted the sheets. She poured coffee into a mug—*Unfinished Crime* by Helen McCloy—and slipped onto a stool at the coffee bar. She began to read:

Edith Cummings

Jake O'Neill came into the drawing room about seven-thirty. He kissed Virginia Neville's cheek. Assorted members of the Neville family looked as though they were contemplating puking on the spot, but good manners prevailed. In fact, Susan Brandt chatted with the betrothed couple, and pretty soon everybody was smiling. Sort of. Virginia and Jake visited with some people. She stayed in the drawing room, holding court, and he left. I saw him in the main hallway about eight-thirty. I was two feet from him when Chloe Martin came in the front door. Wow. When she saw him, she fizzed like a Fourth of July sparkler. Incandescent. He looked like he'd run into a wall. Dazed. His head swiveled in every direction. It didn't take an astrophysicist to figure out he was checking for

Virginia. He rushed up to Chloe and grabbed her hand. They hurried down the hall and ducked into the study. I looked around downstairs for Annie Darling. She'd been hunting for Chloe earlier. I didn't find Annie and I decided to look upstairs. She was there. I told Annie what had happened. I didn't see Jake O'Neill—or Chloe Martin—again.

Annie put down Edith's statement. The times might matter. Annie hurried to the storeroom and found a fresh yellow notepad and pen. Back at the coffee bar, she wrote on her pad:

TIMETABLE
All times approximate

7:30 P.M. Jake in drawing room.

8:30 P.M. Jake in main hall.

8:30 P.M. Chloe arrives, sees Jake in hallway.

8:35 P.M. Jake and Chloe in study.

Annie recalled her own search for Chloe. She had looked upstairs and down, then taken up a post on the second-floor porch and left the porch only briefly. In any event,

Annie hadn't seen Chloe arrive. She sighed, wondering if it would have made any difference if she'd seen Chloe and hurried downstairs. She picked up another sheet.

Henny Brawley

Jake O'Neill painted my portrait last summer. It is customary for past presidents of the Women's Club to sit for a portrait when their term is finished. The paintings are displayed in the Women's Club building. The painting was done at my house. The first day he came, he walked around the living area and looked at everything. My house is really one long room with windows that overlook the marsh. There are bookcases everywhere. One row of bookcases marks off my bedroom. In the living area, there are many framed photographs and inexpensive knickknacks that are meaningful to me. No silver, no crystal. Wildflowers in a pottery vase. Finally he turned and said, "You don't have stuff." I said, "No. No stuff." "Why not?" he asked. I said, "Stuff doesn't matter." Just for an instant, he looked bitter and angry. "It does to most women. I knew a girl once. . . ." He turned away and started putting up his easel. I heard him mutter, "She married for money. But two can play that game." It was a few weeks later that he became engaged to Virginia Neville. I thought at the time it was a recipe for disaster. But I also thought it was Virginia who would suffer. As for tonight, I was getting my wrap from the cloakroom about ten to nine when he went through the back door. I didn't see him again.

Annie added a line to her pad:

8:50 P.M. Jake goes out back door of gallery.

Pamela Potts

I would never wish to embroil anyone in a police investigation. However, the request has been made for all who have any knowledge of Mr. O'Neill to come forward, and I have always endeavored to do my duty. I certainly want to make it clear that I never participate in gos-

sip. In fact, I only have this information
because I was personally involved. . . .

Annie sipped her coffee, brisk, dark, perfect Colombian, and skimmed over the rest
of the paragraph, which was vintage
Pamela, serious, humorless, well-meaning,
and repetitious. Ah, here was the meat.

. . . and I feel that I must report what
Elaine Hasty said about Jake O'Neill. I
truly regret having to repeat such
shocking words, but I am afraid her
remarks indicated extreme hostility.
However, this kind of information may
help the authorities as they seek to determine the character of Mr. O'Neill.
Elaine works for her father, and I have
often had contact with her when arranging banquets, such as the Celebration of Candles and the Low Country Wine Tasting and the Ladies of the
Leaf Christmas Tea. Most women in island organizations know Elaine.

Annie nodded. Elaine had been part of the
staff when the Friends of the Library had its
Christmas luncheon at the Neville Gallery.

Elaine pitches for the island women's softball league. I believe she is still in school, going part-time and working on a hospitality degree at the technical college. She is a pretty girl with dark hair and a most interesting face. Arresting, actually. Dark eyebrows, flashing green eyes. High cheekbones. Thin coral lips. In fact, she has almost the look of a cat—

Annie felt the softness of sleek black fur against her arm. She looked into enigmatic golden eyes, heard a throaty purr.

"No, Agatha. Pamela's not writing about you. But you know what? She's right." Elaine did have a look of wildness and the exotic beauty of a feline. Annie felt a quiver of excitement. She recalled seeing Elaine replenishing the buffet last night. But Elaine was not among those who responded to the request for information about the dead man. Maybe, just maybe, Pamela in her dogged, serious way was onto something.

—but she's really very nice. However, at the Ladies of the Leaf Christmas Tea Elaine was slamming plates about in the kitchen and she broke one and cut her hand. I took her to Melba's sewing room. The tea was at the home of Melba Wintersmith. Melba is . . .

Annie skimmed. She slid over Pamela's painstaking description of Melba, Melba's house, the party, Elaine's injury, and Pamela's expert ministrations.

. . . and I was shocked when Elaine sobbed and said she wished she could cut Jake O'Neill to pieces. She wished his heart would spurt blood just like her hand. She said he didn't deserve to live, that she hated him. He'd said he loved her, but that was all a lie. As soon as I finished the bandage, she ran out of the room and banged out of the house.

Of course, that is a very extravagant manner of speaking. Oh dear, I am tempted not to bring this to the attention of the authorities. However, I am here, and it would be quite odd if I didn't turn in a statement. At times one almost has to believe in fate. I had not planned to attend this evening, and then the fog prevented my taking the

ferry to the mainland. As you know, the
ferry doesn't run when the fog . . .

Annie dismissed Pamela's consideration
of fate and searched through the remaining
sheets for Tony Hasty's statement.

Tony Hasty

You got to remember the layout of the
gallery. Of course, it wasn't always an
art gallery. It used to belong to the Graham family, even before the war. They
say Matilda Graham played hostess to
the Yankees when they occupied the island and that's how come the place
didn't get burned down. Anyway, it's an
old place and the stand of pines between the parking lot and the garden
has been there forever. You can't see a
thing through those pines, but there's a
path from the garden that comes out in
the kitchen parking lot. It's a back way
from the garden to the front road. I was
loading up dishes around nine o'clock
when this redheaded girl in a green
dress comes running along the path.
She must have come within ten feet of

me. She was crying. Well, it didn't look right to me. I mean she was real upset. I called out and asked her what was wrong. She didn't slow down and she didn't answer. I almost followed her, but I thought, well, whatever it was, she's on her way out of here, so I let it go. I mean she didn't look like anybody'd hurt her. Her dress wasn't torn. I sure would have done something if I'd thought some-body had hurt her. Then Annie Darling—she owns that bookstore on the board-walk—came flying into the lot and she wanted to know about the other girl. I started to wonder what the hell was go-ing on. Annie said it was some kind of lovers' quarrel and she and her husband went out front, I guess to hunt for the girl in green. I kept on loading up and about ten minutes after that, here came Beth Kelly. She's a teacher at the middle school. She looked scared to death. I yelled out to ask what was happening, but she ducked her head like she didn't want me to see her and kept on going. That's when I decided to take a look. I got a flashlight out of the van and went through the pines. The garden was dark except for the lights in the trees. Of course the fog was pretty thick, but the lights in the trees kind of glowed and helped you keep to the path. And I had my flashlight. I wasn't sure which way to go. But there were plenty of people heading for the tent in the north parking lot. I figured if anything funny was going on it would be where there weren't any people. I decided to take the path to the point because it's damn private down there. I didn't see anybody or hear anybody. There wasn't any sound except for the ocean. I almost didn't go all the way down to the point. There wasn't a soul around and it was quiet as a grave-yard. But once I start something, I finish it. I kept going, swinging my flashlight back and forth. That's how come I found O'Neill. Not that I knew who it was then. I mean, I didn't touch him. I didn't know it was him until Mrs. Neville saw him and screamed. Poor lady. At the time all I saw was this guy in a tuxedo sprawled on his face with the back of his head stove in. I knew he was dead. I saw a lot of dead guys in Nam. So I ran back to my van and used my cell phone to call the cops. I looked at my watch. It was fourteen minutes after nine. I didn't see anybody coming or going.

Annie added to her timetable:

> **9 P.M.** Chloe runs through kitchen parking lot.
> **9:10 P.M.** Beth Kelly runs past Tony Hasty.
> **9:14 P.M.** Hasty finds body.

Annie rubbed her nose. Interesting. Hasty claimed he didn't know the identity of the victim until the police arrived. Hasty didn't say a word about his daughter Elaine, who obviously knew O'Neill very well indeed.

Annie returned Hasty's statement to her pile, plucked another.

Irene Neville

So here I am, within shouting distance of a murder, and damned if I didn't miss it all. I didn't even hear the sirens when the cops came. I guess there were sirens. We didn't know anything was wrong until Max Darling came and got us. Everybody's going to want a blow-by-blow and I must have been on my way back from the tent when somebody bopped Jake. I'd been up there fussing at Gene Hammer, the bandleader. Honestly, if Gene didn't have the only dance band this side of Hilton Head, he'd have to be a damn sight more charming to get gigs. But we're stuck with him. If you hire somebody off island, you have to pray there's no fog. Anyway, I'd promised Carl I'd sweet-talk Gene into playing something besides swing, but Gene is stuck in the forties. He wasn't even born then. I don't understand his time warp. We have an old crowd, but not that old! Gene and I started negotiating about eight-thirty. Finally, he grudgingly agreed to play some Beatles. As for anything circa the nineties, forget it. Maybe I could buy the man some sheet music from the current century. Anyway, I got that straightened out, then I went back down to the gallery to find Carl. I knew it was about time for the program to start. I ran into Carl on the path and he'd brought me a glass of champagne. I'd earned it. We went inside the tent and watched Boston who was loving every minute of his own performance. Virginia sidled in and she was obviously looking for lover boy. She wandered around, looking puzzled, and then she left. I guess she went to check the gallery. When she came back, he wasn't with her. By this time she really looked upset. I got excited, thinking Jake had come to his senses and was going to dump her. But I knew Jake had his eye on the dollar and Virginia's got the dollars. He never showed up. Now it turns out somebody killed him. I can't say I'm sorry. He was an arrogant, greedy, spoiled jerk. If he'd married Virginia, you can bet he'd have managed to get his grasping hands on our money. But don't cast one of us as first murderer. After all, if we wanted the money, it would make more sense to kill Virginia. Anyway, the Neville clan doesn't go in for murder. But I'm sorry I missed the show.

Annie doodled on her pad an iceberg jutting from the ocean. Beneath it she wrote:

Irene. She raised an eyebrow. Irene's attitude would certainly rankle Billy Cameron if
he looked beyond Chloe for a suspect. Irene
seemed to be accounting for her time—Annie studied her timetable—between eight
forty-five and nine fifteen. But in the noise
and confusion, she could have finished her
session with the bandleader and returned to
the house in time to see Jake Neville and follow him to the point. No, Irene couldn't be
considered the possessor of a cast-iron alibi. Irene's point—that killing Virginia, not
Jake, would be the sensible way to assure
the return of the family fortune to the
Nevilles—was undoubtedly valid. However,
she certainly was belaboring the existence
of her purported alibi. Thoughtfully, Annie
reached for Carl Neville's statement.

Carl Neville

Jake's murder can't be connected in
any way to the family or to the gallery.
Jake has been a most valued employee
even though he'd only been with us for
a short time. He came to the island last
summer. He was a capable portraitist
and very well liked by our clients. I am

terribly sorry for Virginia. She simply bloomed when she and Jake fell in love. Tonight was to have been an evening of great happiness. Instead Virginia is overcome with grief. As for this evening—I spoke with Jake about eight o'clock. His manner was normal. He appeared relaxed and in a good humor. In fact, his last words to me were to ask if I had some information about Saint Thomas. He thought it would please Virginia to go there for their honeymoon. I told him I'd get some material to him on Monday. After I left him, I found my wife and asked her to see about the band. Irene is very good at handling that kind of thing. I walked up to the tent with her, and then I was back and forth until the program began at shortly after nine. As I said, I am astounded by Jake's murder. I don't know of anything in his personal or professional life that could have led to such a dreadful at- tack. Perhaps he walked down to the point and interrupted some nefarious undertaking. There have been rumors that drugs are sold there. In any event, I am convinced the police will discover that his death was caused by someone unknown to us. Certainly all of us will cooperate in any way to help bring the killer to justice.

Annie smoothed out the sheet. Carl Neville said all the right things. Maybe that was because he was a right guy. Maybe. He sounded as though he liked Jake. But how could he have been happy about Virginia marrying him? Irene made it clear she opposed the marriage. Hmm. Probably no one else in the family was quite as forthcoming. She picked up Louise Neville's statement.

Louise Neville

Jake went out the back door of the gallery shortly before nine. He was alone. I did not see him again. I walked up to the tent and was there until summoned by Mr. Darling. Jake was a superficially charming young man with some artistic talent. Older women liked him. I was not surprised when my sister-in-law agreed to marry him. I know nothing of his personal life. I have no idea what might have prompted his murder.

Annie raised an eyebrow. Tart, succinct, and unrevealing. If Louise Neville knew anything, she had no intention of sharing it with the police. She made no claim to an alibi. In actuality, any family member could have followed Jake while claiming they'd been walking between the gallery and the tent.

Annie picked up the final two statements, belonging to Susan and Rusty Brandt. Hmm. What was that business about Max taking Rusty's dinner jacket into custody? She decided to start with him.

Rusty Brandt

I don't know anything about what happened to Jake. I decline to make any statement until I have consulted with counsel.

Annie looked at the portable phone. She was tempted to grab it and call Rusty Brandt. But if he stonewalled the police, he certainly wouldn't talk to her. She wondered if he'd summoned a lawyer this morning. Obviously—unless he was simply fractious—he had something to hide. Refusing to make a statement would attract Billy's attention faster than strolling naked on the beach. And there was the matter of that jacket. There must be bloodstains on it. She promptly envisioned Max suggesting in a cautionary tone that she hesitate before jumping to conclusions. But hey, when two plus two equals four, caution be damned. Okay. She once again held her pen over the pad, then shook her head. She'd finish the statements before she mapped out a plan. She mentally thumbed her nose at the cautionary image of Max. She wasn't impulsive. Not at all. She was, in fact, proceeding with all due diligence. She blinked, feeling muddled. Didn't due diligence have something to do with liability? That was the problem with absorbing years of legalese. After a while, the terms all sounded alike. Anyway, she was not impulsive, and she was quite capable of completing a task, even though she itched to fling herself at the telephone.

Susan Brandt

I saw Jake briefly around seven-thirty in the drawing room. He and Virginia were greeting guests. I was in and out of the kitchen most of the evening, overseeing the catering, until I went to the tent a few minutes before nine. I was surprised that Jake didn't join us there. I didn't know what had happened, but assumed there was some kind of problem when Virginia didn't announce their engagement. I can't imagine why Jake would have gone down to the point. I have no knowledge about his private affairs. He'd been with the gallery since last summer. His work was satisfactory.

"And," Annie said aloud to Agatha, "she don't know nothin' 'bout nobody. No way. Butter wouldn't melt. In public. I'd love to have been in the Brandt car when they drove home last night. Especially when she asked Rusty about his jacket."

Agatha rolled over on her back, stretched.

Annie gingerly smoothed the fur on her tummy, yanked back her hand to avoid a swiping paw. "Okay," she murmured. "Irene claims she was at the tent by eight-thirty, implies she was there most of the time, left to go find Carl. Could be true. Could be a lie. Louise says she came there a little before nine. Ditto Susan. Carl admits being back and forth. So . . ." Annie made the additions to her timetable. Sipping her coffee, she flipped to a fresh sheet, printed:

SUSPECTS/MOTIVES

1. **Chloe Martin. Jealousy over Jake's engagement to Virginia Neville.**
2. **Elaine Hasty. Another jilted lover?**
3. **Neville family members (Carl, Irene, Susan, Rusty, and Louise). To prevent Virginia from marrying Jake O'Neill and diluting their hoped-for inheritance.**

Annie thought for a minute, then wrote quickly:

4. **Tony Hasty. Anger over Jake's treatment of Elaine.**
5. **Beth Kelly, the second running woman. Near the scene but no known motive.**

Annie was pleased at her crisp summary. She reached for the coffeepot to refill her mug, and the phone rang. She scooped up the portable phone, answered "Death on Demand," and poured the strong hot coffee.

"Hi, Annie." Henny Brawley was brisk. "So what did you smuggle out of the gallery in the book bag?"

Annie was silent.

"Come on, chum." The store's best—and savviest—customer was pleasant but determined. "I haven't read mysteries from Deborah Adams to Margaret Yorke for nothing. Give."

"Last night, as you know, I was pleased to assist the minions of the law, our acting captain and his hastily appointed deputy, one Max Darling, in gathering information." Annie straightened the statements.

"Huzzah," Henny applauded.

"I was requested not to look at the statements that were produced." Annie managed to keep her tone pleasant.

"Not for the eyes of the unwashed, I take it. I'm sure you observed that stricture. Let's see," Henny mused, "you took up the statements, delivered them—unread—to Max, but . . . copy machine?"

"Sometimes you scare me." Annie wasn't altogether kidding.

"So this morning, in the comfortable confines of Death on Demand, you are perusing material that is critical to the investigation. Bully for you." Henny's tone was admiring. "Not even Miss Zukas could do better."

Annie was absurdly pleased. Jo Dereske's librarian sleuth was one of Annie's all-time favorite fictional detectives. "Okay, Henny, you got me. I promised not to read them. I didn't. Not then."

"But now . . ." There was an expectant pause.

"Right. Here's what I've got. . . ." Annie read the statements quickly, then described the crime scene and Chloe's reaction on the pier. "What do you think?"

There was a thoughtful pause. Finally, Henny sighed. "I'd say Chloe Martin's in big trouble. I'm sorry, Annie. I know you like her a lot." There was the sound of sad finality in her voice.

Annie stiffened. Henny had an instinct for crime. But this time, she was wrong. "Chloe didn't do it."

Henny's silence said more than a plethora of words.

Annie gripped the phone. "Lots of people didn't like him. Everybody in the Neville family was worried about Virginia marrying him. And evidently Elaine Hasty was upset with him. Her dad found the body, but he didn't say a word about Elaine and Jake."

"Annie"—and now Henny's voice was kind—"I understand. Chloe's your friend—"

Annie remembered the pain in Chloe's voice last night: "I thought you were my friend." And the sound of her running footsteps on the hollow wood of the pier and the way they faded to nothingness in the fog.

"—so you don't want to see what's right in front of you. But I have to tell you that I've known the Neville family for years. Susan's a good friend. A very good friend." Henny's pause spoke volumes. "About as straight a shooter as I've ever known. And those statements—everybody's up-front. Sure they were back and forth between the gallery and the tent, but nobody saw one of them heading for the point. Who walks out to the point? Jake. Who runs back from the point? Chloe. You saw her yourself. Who ran away? Chloe. Who was furious with a two-timing Lothario? Chloe. Whose stole is drenched with blood? Chloe's."

"The Nevilles didn't want him to marry

Virginia." Annie drew thick black lines beneath their names, Carl, Irene, Susan, Rusty, and Louise.

"Granted." Henny was agreeable. "I'll admit that Rusty's jacket needs explaining. I'd say he's the only hope. But the preponderance of the evidence weighs against Chloe. As Benny Cooperman so wisely observed in *Murder Sees the Light,* 'If you find kittens in the doghouse are they puppies?' "

Annie glanced toward the section of humorous mysteries. Henny loved all the books by Howard Engel. "Chloe didn't do it. You should have heard her last night. Why, for a minute she thought it might be Jake when we came to the pier. He always met her there at midnight."

Henny made a sound midway between a sniff and a snort. "Uh-huh. Pretty smart on her part. Well, I'll hope this one turns out to be murder by a person or persons unknown, the old inquest verdict. For your sake and for Chloe's."

There was an instant of quiet between them. Annie knew that her old friend was declining to be of help in this investigation. Henny was standing by her friends. Just as Annie intended to stand by Chloe.

Henny cleared her throat. Her tone was determinedly cheerful. "Oh, hey, Annie, I've got one for you. Who is the Honorable Richard Rollison?"

Annie reached back to the memory of dog-eared paperbacks belonging to her uncle that she had enjoyed in a hammock during lazy Low Country summers. "The Toff. One of John Creasey's detectives."

Henny was too good a sport to admit to disappointment. But she couldn't quite hide her surprise. "I would have thought before your time. Good going. Take care." A pause. "Try not to be too upset about Chloe."

The line buzzed. As Annie clicked off the phone, the clock struck nine. She listened to the chimes. Right now Chloe was arriving at the police station. . . .

The clouds hung so low the sky seemed to sag toward the earth. Gray sky melded into gray water. The persistent drizzle dampened Max's face. A brisk onshore breeze spun cold droplets of mist. Max was grateful for the warmth of his suede jacket.

Ben Parotti's yellow slicker glistened. He

poked back his cap, peered out at the
white-flecked water. "Chances aren't good."
A gnarled hand jabbed at the murky harbor.
"You got some currents there that can pull
flotsam all the way out to the Gulf Stream.
Yeah, if she tossed that dress from the end
of the pier . . ." He shook his head. "Anyway,
I'll round up some men, do some trawling."
Ben squinted at Max. "Pretty well signed her
arrest warrant, didn't she?" A swarm of
laughing gulls cackled overhead. Ben's derisive chuckle blended right in. " 'Course,
what choice did she have if there was blood
all over the dress."

Max jammed his hands into his pockets.
"Annie says she threw it away because she
was mad at him and knew she'd never wear
the dress again."

Ben turned up calloused palms. "Annie
may be right. No telling what a pissed-off
woman will do. His daddy should have
warned him against riling up a female. Anyway, we'll do our best to find the dress."
Ben lifted a hand in farewell and headed for
the boat slips.

Max slowly walked toward his car, his face
somber. Would it do any good to call Annie?
She was sure to be at the bookstore by now.

He glanced at his watch. Ten after nine. He'd promised Billy that he'd come back to the station after arranging the search for Chloe's missing dress. Billy might very well arrest Chloe this morning unless she came up with information to clear herself. That didn't seem likely. At the least he might hold her as a material witness while he checked out the members of the Neville family. Max knew an arrest would be a blow to Annie. Would she insist upon Chloe's innocence despite the evidence against her? Max sighed. If so, the home front was going to be chilly for a while. Annie was hurt that Billy had chosen Max to help and ignored her. In any event, an arrest would most likely mark the end of Max's service as a deputy. He hoped so because he hated shutting Annie out of anything. They were a team, the two of them together. But not this time. He was slipping behind the wheel of his Maserati when his cell phone rang.

"Hello?" His voice rose hopefully. Maybe it was Annie.

"Max, meet me at the Schmidt house." Billy was furious, his tone harsh.

Max turned on the motor. "What's wrong?"

"That girl. She didn't show up. When I

catch her"—the words dropped like boulders of ice cracking off a glacier—"she's going to be sorry she was born."

"Who could have killed him?" Annie looked into Agatha's cool eyes. The cat's gaze was eloquent of hidden mysteries, of danger, of a world perceived with clarity and icy disdain. "You don't know and you don't care. Agatha, it looks bad for Chloe. You'd care if you knew. She was lovely to you."

Annie picked up the phone, slowly put it down. Okay. It wouldn't do any good to call Chloe. She was at the police station. Surely she'd taken a lawyer with her. Or maybe she'd asked her aunt and uncle to accompany her. Annie shook her head. Chloe wasn't close to them. Chloe, in fact, had no champion. Except Annie. But what could Annie do? It was up to the police to check out the statements made last night.

The phone rang. Annie looked at the caller ID. Oh. Oh well. "Hi, Laurel."

"Annie, dear. You have been much on my mind." The husky unforgettable voice was sad and kind. "Your aura—"

Annie raised an eyebrow. Laurel often

claimed to pick up otherworldly vibrations, although Annie often felt her mother-in-law simply wrapped her own perceptions in occult trappings, the more easily to voice comments that might otherwise offend.

"—quivers with distress. I pondered your plight, and though I cannot rescue you from concern about young Chloe—"

Annie felt a prickle at the back of her neck.

"—I believe I can be most helpful by sharing with you the sustaining words from a great poet upon the high estate of friendship. As Owen Meredith observed, 'Ay, there are some good things in life, that fall not away with the rest. And, of all best things upon earth, I hold that a faithful friend is the best.' " A reverent pause, then a murmured, "I am always intrigued by the use of a pen name. I suppose Edward Robert Bulwer-Lytton did not wish to be confused with his father. Or trade upon his illustrious name. Ah well, his words ring true whatever the attribution. Dear Annie, Godspeed in your quest."

Annie refused to speculate upon the reasons for Lord Lytton's pen name. Laurel was right. It didn't matter who said it, the sentiment caught at her heart: ". . . of all best things upon earth . . ."

What did friends do for friends? With a fine disregard for mixing metaphors, Annie said sternly to Agatha, "They don't sit around and twiddle their thumbs while Rome burns. And neither will I." She grabbed her purse and headed for the door.

The Schmidt house, a one-story bungalow of pinkish stucco, nestled beneath an ancient magnolia. The drive swung around the tree to a separate garage. Parked to one side was a shabby blue Taurus. A discarded Christmas tree, festooned with limp icicles, was propped against a shabby white wooden fence. The house had a closed-in, withdrawn appearance like featureless mannequins in a forgotten store window.

As Max parked, a police cruiser with its siren wailing slewed to a stop behind him. The siren cut off in mid-blare. Billy slammed out of the car. Without regard for his crisp uniform trousers, he stalked through puddles, head forward, shoulders bunched, hands clenched, his normally pleasant face rutted by an angry frown.

The bungalow's front door opened. A middle-aged woman in a faded red velour jumpsuit stepped outside. She poked her head forward, her thin face anxious.

Billy slapped a massive hand on the sagging white gate. "She better be here." His voice was a mixture of raw fury and worried uncertainty. "And she better have a damn good explanation."

Max grabbed Billy's arm. It wouldn't do for him to charge up the walk and explode. "What's happened?"

The acting chief glowered. "I should have taken her in last night. I trusted her. And she didn't come. I've let Pete down. I've let everybody down. I blew it, Max."

"Hey, ease up." Max kept his tone light. "It's no big deal, Billy. Maybe she got cold feet. We can make sure she doesn't get off the island. Ben's got a search going for the dress. He'd know to call us if she got on the ferry."

Billy's head jerked up as if somebody had socked him. "Oh, God, I didn't think about the ferry. Max, get on the horn, alert Ben." His broad open face creased in despair. "I don't know how I could have forgot that."

Max pulled out his cell phone. "Sure. I'll

take care of it. Anyway, it'll probably turn out she's just running late. She'd be a fool to try and run away."

Billy kneaded his face with sharp knuckles. "A fool. Or guilty as hell." He glanced at the woman on the porch. "Come on."

Patches of red stained Mrs. Schmidt's cheeks. Her salt-and-pepper hair bushed in tight curls. Narrow black-rimmed glasses perched on the end of a long thin nose. When they reached the steps, she snapped, "I declare I don't know what's happening. How come you're back here this morning with your siren squealing? What are the neighbors going to think? We've never had the police at our house before. First you come in the middle of the night, and I've already had a half dozen calls this morning, people wanting to know if anything's wrong. I'll say things are wrong, the police wanting to see Miriam's girl about a murder. Miriam was always trouble, and now Chloe's even worse. We've always tried to welcome her, but she won't have anything to do with the people we know." She tossed her head like a nervous horse.

The front door squeaked. A heavyset

man stepped outside. Bulging dark eyes peered from a round face like shiny raisins protruding from thick dough. "I always told Frances that girl would come to no good end. Like mother, like daughter. Coming home last night, then going out again, that's no way to act. And she wouldn't say a word when she got home the second time, even though we'd waited up. She went into her room and locked the door, and she still hasn't come out."

"We're here to take her into custody." Billy tried to speak evenly, but he bristled with anger.

Mrs. Schmidt gasped, pressed her hands against her cheeks.

"Come now, Mother. The police got to do what they got to do." Schmidt jerked his head toward the entrance. "If you'll come this way, Officer." He bustled importantly past the living room to the right and the dining room to the left. Several doorways opened down a narrow hallway. "She hasn't even come out of her room yet. But we know she's here. Her car's still parked out there, that old blue Taurus." The four of them crowded in front of a closed bedroom door.

Billy knocked. "This is the police. Open up."

There was no response, no sound, no movement.

"Chloe, you come on out now." Frances Schmidt's voice was shrill.

Billy knocked again, a thunderous rattle that shook the door in its frame. He turned the handle.

Max frowned. He turned toward Schmidt. "Bring us a screwdriver. We'd better take down that door."

Mrs. Schmidt rushed to the doorway, flailed her hands against it. "Chloe, open up right now!"

There was no sound, no movement, no life beyond that closed door.

Schmidt brought the screwdriver, his face pale. He handed it to Billy, fingered his unshaven cheek.

Billy loosened the pins from the hinges, pulled the door free. He stepped over the threshold, his head swinging, checking the unmade, empty bed, the open closet door, the clothes strewn about.

Chloe wasn't there.

· *Seven* ·

Annie opened the driver's door of her Volvo and a note card fluttered to the floor. She retrieved it. As she settled behind the wheel, she studied the card and smiled. Stylized heads of a black Lab, massive faces upturned with a look of adoration, rimmed the border. Ornate lettering announced: "When Fortune's fickle, the faithful friend is found—Quintus Ennius."

Annie's eyes widened. The postscript in Laurel's everyday handwriting—"Across the centuries, we are touched by immortal truth. Annie, I applaud you!"—scarcely registered. Annie gave an anguished glance at the motif. A Lab. Dogs. Dog . . . She raced the motor and jolted out of the marina parking lot. Despite the wisps of fog and the sheen of damp on the blacktop, she drove fast on the winding road. She waved at the guard as she left the gated residential area. She pulled into the island's downtown gas station next to the outdoor phone kiosk. In a moment, she'd flipped to the Os in the tattered phone book. Her finger slid down the names.

"Yes!" she exclaimed. The advantages of island living were many, and chief among them was the likelihood at all times of connecting with a friend. Back in the car, she followed a familiar route, pulling up in only a few minutes at the arbor that marked the entrance to Nightingale Courts. Seven rustic cabins curved in a semicircle with a superb view of the marsh and the sound. Wisps of fog obscured the winter-brown cordgrass, hung in low patches over the gray-green water. Loons bobbed in the swells. She slammed out of the car, and shiny greenish-black grackles lifted skyward, chattering their aggravation. High in the sky, a bald eagle curved in watchful flight, most likely ready to defend its nest and baby chick.

Annie crunched up the oyster-shell path to cabin 1. Yellow curtains patterned with daisies in a deeper hue hung in the front windows. Smoke wreathed the chimney. Holly berries brightened the Christmas wreath on the door. As Annie lifted her hand to knock, the panel swung in.

Duane Webb, stocky in a blue turtleneck and baggy jeans, motioned her inside. A fiercely independent maverick, he'd spent most of his lifetime as a small-town newspaper editor, fetching up on the island in a drunken haze after the deaths of his wife and daughter in a car wreck. He'd been the driver. The drunk driver. Ingrid Jones, who managed Nightingale Courts and also worked as Annie's most valued and treasured employee, became his friend. When Ingrid disappeared and was suspected of murder, Duane pulled himself together, aware abruptly that Ingrid was not simply a friend. They'd now been married for a number of years. Duane was a committed member of AA. Sometimes he helped out at the bookstore. Mainly he ran Nightingale Courts.

Annie stayed on the doorstep. "Duane, how is Ingrid feeling?" The hip surgery had been on Wednesday. She'd come through it fine, but sometimes the days after an operation were tough.

Duane's lips curved into a wide smile. "Super. They're moving her to rehab tomorrow. I promised I'd go by the store, get her a batch of new books." He joined Annie on the steps.

She smiled in return. "You know where the key is. Go in and take a bunch. They're on the house. I just unpacked a box of the new Bill Crider title, *A Romantic Way to Die.* Ingrid loves his books. Listen, Duane, I'm here because of Jake O'Neill."

Duane squinted at her. "You a deputy, too? I hear Billy's got Max helping out."

At her look of surprise, he gave a *whuff* of laughter. "Lou Pirelli's been here to check out O'Neill's place. Told me about last night. I called Vince." Vince Ellis was the editor of *The Island Gazette.* "He filled me in. Said Billy was going to interrogate Chloe this morning." His thick gray eyebrows bristled in a frown. "Doesn't sound good for her."

Annie wasn't surprised at the spread of information. Broward's Rock was a very small island. But first things first. "Where's Jake's dog? Alexandre." That was the name of the red setter Jake had brought with him to the pier, the dog that enchanted Chloe.

"Pirelli took him. It was love at first bark."

Duane's tone was wry, but his eyes were soft.

Annie heaved a huge sigh of relief. "I was worried that no one knew about him."

"Dog's okay. How about the girl?" He was brusque, his light eyes thoughtful.

"I don't know." Annie looked at her watch. Nine-forty. Surely Billy must be almost through with his questions. "If Chloe doesn't call me pretty soon, I'll check with Billy." But as long as she was here . . . "Duane, fill me in on Jake." Duane and Ingrid weren't snoops, but they paid attention to their renters, knew when there was illness or loss of a job or sorrow, knew and tried to help.

He turned up his hands. "What's to know? A show-off. Too pretty for his own good. Ingrid liked him." Duane's tone was dry. "He was that kind of guy. Always charming to women. But Ingrid said he was cheerful and really good to his dog. That counted for a lot with her."

"Any trouble with him?" She was grasping at straws.

Duane frowned, stared off toward the marsh.

Annie scarcely dared to breathe. There

was something here, something that Duane was reluctant to tell.

Slowly he returned his gaze to Annie. He started to speak, stopped.

Annie looked deep into his eyes—skeptical, measuring, weary eyes. "Please, Duane. I'm frightened for Chloe. Right now it looks grim for her." Annie thought about the tiny window of time between Chloe's flight through the parking lot and the discovery of O'Neill's body, not more than fifteen minutes. Unless someone else could be placed at the scene after Chloe's departure, Billy would arrest Chloe. "If you know anything that could help her . . ."

Duane's face creased in indecision. "Oh, hell, Annie. I don't want to make trouble for this kid just because she was mixed up with Jake. Sure, she should have had better sense, but she's a hard-luck girl. You know the kind—good-looking and they think sex will get them what they want, but they never have the brains—or instinct or native cunning, whatever it takes—to understand that men like easy sex but when they marry, that's not the girl they pick."

Annie almost spoke, didn't.

Now his laugh was explosive. "If you

could see your face! Yes'm, I know all about modern mores. *Sex and the City* and all the rest of it. Don't think I'm an old coot stuck back in history. Sure, nice girls do—but they still do it on a selective basis. The ones with brains never get tagged as an easy lay."

"But this girl did?" How about Chloe making love with Jake on the pier in the fog when they first met? Annie pushed that thought away, hoped a jury would never hear her story.

"That's my guess. Or maybe he got tired of her. A couple of nights ago, she banged on his door, screaming that she wished he was dead. But dammit, she's a good kid. She was in one of my fishing classes at The Haven." His face was sad, remembering a child and happy summer days at the pond near the island youth recreation center.

"Chloe's a good kid, too." Annie's voice was sober. "I promise I won't involve this girl unless there's reason to think she could have been at the party last night."

Duane heaved a sigh. "Oh, hell, she was there. She works for her dad."

Annie felt a surge of excitement. "Elaine Hasty." She made it a statement, not a question.

"Yeah." His voice was flat.

"She lives here?" Annie swung a hand toward the cabins.

Slowly, Duane nodded. He pointed at the next-to-last cabin. "Number 6. Next to O'Neill. That's how they met." His face wrinkled. "Worse luck for her."

Billy paced back and forth in his office, his thick shock of hair disheveled from frequent swipes by his hand. "Okay, we got it sewed up. All boats for hire have been alerted. Ben knows to tip us if she tries to take the ferry. Is there anything else we can do?" His worried gaze implored Max.

Max folded his arms across his chest, stretched out his legs, seeking as much comfort as possible from the hard metal straight chair opposite Billy's desk. "You've got everything under control, Billy. Lou's out hunting for her."

"When we catch her"—Billy slammed a fist into his palm—"she's going straight to jail. No bail." His big square face was rock hard. "Not if I can help it." He reached the far side of the office, wheeled. "I have to find her. What will Pete think?" His voice lifted in anguish. "I got to e-mail him and tell him I've lost the major suspect in the first big case since he was called up."

Max understood Billy's chagrin and humiliation, but he wasn't going to be effective if he kept stewing about Chloe's disappearance. "Come on, Billy, let's try and figure out what she could have done. We know she's not in her car. It's parked at her aunt's house. According to her aunt, there's an old blue bicycle missing from the garage. She probably took the bike. Her aunt claims she doesn't have any friends on the island. That means she's trying to hide out on her own. We'll call the Buccaneer." The island's upscale hotel was lucky to have 30 percent occupancy this time of year. "She won't dare use a credit card, and she probably wouldn't have enough cash to stay for long. But we can make sure. Ditto the fishing lodge. Since she's on a bike, it should be easy to find her. Lou can cover all the back roads in half a day." Max frowned. Chloe should be easy to spot unless she hid in the forest preserve or found a lonely stretch of beach. "We'll get a description out to the radio stations and to the *Gazette,* asking anyone spotting her to call the police."

Billy jolted to a stop in front of Max. "How about Annie?" His voice was harsh.

A purple windsock emblazoned with two red-eyed eagles hung limp in the still air. Pine straw had drifted over the steps. Light blazed through uncurtained windows. Annie looked through the smudged panes of the bedroom at the dark-haired girl flinging clothes into a cardboard box. Elaine's royal purple sweater was molded over her breasts. Tight black slacks emphasized full hips. She looked like trouble waiting to happen. But her face drooped, and she paused every so often to gulp and rub away tears from swollen eyes.

Annie steeled herself and walked up the steps. She knocked.

Elaine wiped her hand across her face. She took a deep breath, walked to the door. When she opened it, she blinked in surprise. "What are you doing here?"

There was no good answer. Annie couldn't blurt out that she wanted to know why Elaine had screamed in the night at a man who was now lying on a slab awaiting an autopsy. Annie spoke fast, knowing the door could slam shut in her face. "I was at the party last night, Elaine. I need to talk to you. Please."

Elaine pushed back a tangle of dark hair. Her gaze slid over Annie. "Dad said you were helping the police." There was no warmth in her tone. "I saw you. Velvet dress. No back. Rhinestone straps. You looked like a princess. The straps were rhinestone, but I'll bet your earrings and necklace were diamonds." She lifted her hand, touched her neck. Her fingers closed on a gaudy red and orange ribbon with a likeness of a red setter painted on a ceramic medallion. Her face crumpled.

Annie stared at the medallion. "Did Jake paint it for you?"

Elaine turned away, stumbled back into the living room.

Annie hesitated for an instant, then pulled open the screen and stepped inside. The furniture was shabby, an old green sofa, a stained maple coffee table, a dinette that might have been new in 1950, two saggy beanbag chairs in blue vinyl, straw matting that crackled underfoot.

Elaine walked to the painted pine mantel. The fireplace held the remnants of a fire, charred wood and ash. The cabin smelled of must and old smoke. She looked up at a matted watercolor.

Annie joined her. She didn't have to ask if Jake was the artist. He'd caught a good likeness of Elaine, laughing and eager as she tossed a ball in the air for Alexandre. The dog was the focus of the painting, elegant, sturdy, straining in a high leap, glorious in his dark red beauty.

"That's who he loved." Her voice curdled in resentment. She reached up, yanked the painting from the wall. She held it in both hands and came within a breath of crushing it. Slowly, the tension eased from her arms. Her face tight and angry, she carried the stiff cardboard to the table and put it down. "I guess I'll sell it." Her voice was brittle. She swung to face Annie. "I got to get out of here. But I don't have any money. Everything takes money. I started packing, but I don't have anyplace to go." Her lips twisted. "You wouldn't know about that. You've got a rich husband."

Annie looked at her across a gulf of experience and social status and safety. Would Elaine care that Annie had waited tables in college? No. All Elaine saw were diamonds and a world far beyond her reach. "Could you go home?"

"Home?" Elaine gave a half sigh, half cry. "Go back to my dad's house? Not likely. I can work my tail off for him, but last year he told me to get out and stay out because . . . It doesn't matter. He says I'm a tramp. Like my mom." Her eyes were hurt and defiant. "He burned all her pictures, but I remember what she looked like. She was real pretty. Like me. And she wanted to have fun. Is that a crime?" She tossed her hair. "Why slave all your life if you can have nice things? See, I thought Jake would marry me. We could have a nice house. I could have helped out at the gallery. But he was lying when he said he loved me. He was going to marry Mrs. Neville, just because she's rich and owns the gallery and he would have a place for his paintings. I could have killed him."

The silence in the frowsy room grew and expanded.

Elaine pressed her fingers against her cheeks. "Somebody did. Oh, God, somebody did!" Her voice quivered. She stared at Annie, her gaze filled with misery. "I wanted to go down and look, but Dad wouldn't let me." She pulled up the sleeve of her sweater, held out her arm. Purplish bruises marked the skin above her wrist. "He said I was just one of a long line of stupid women, running after Jake."

Annie picked her words carefully. "Your dad knew about you and Jake?"

Elaine turned, looked down at the watercolor on the table, and reached out a finger to touch the dog, trace the curve of his head. "Somebody told him." Her tone was indifferent. "He laughed at me, told me nobody as high-toney as Jake was going to stick to a girl like me."

Annie stepped nearer the table, watched Elaine's profile. "So your dad wasn't mad at Jake?"

Elaine swung toward Annie. "Mad at Jake? You've got to be kidding. Dad thought Jake was good for nothing, but it's always me he's mad at. Like my mom. Dad didn't give a damn about Jake."

Annie's vision of Tony Hasty moving heavily through the fog, finding Jake O'Neill, attacking him, faded. Hasty was in the kitchen parking lot when Annie and Max hurried there, seeking Chloe. Hasty claimed he was worried about the girls who had run

through the parking lot. Would a man with
his bitter view of his wife and daughter be
so quick to hurry to the defense of girls he
didn't even know? Was his talk of protect-
ing women a smokescreen? Maybe. Maybe
not. Although he was grievously disappointed in his wife and the daughter in
whom he saw her likeness, perhaps he had
a quixotic view of women and was quick to
wish to protect those whom he thought un-
defiled. Had he headed off toward the point
because of Chloe's distress, found Jake,
quarreled with him? The picture didn't fit.
But a stubborn question remained. Why
hadn't Hasty mentioned his knowledge
about O'Neill in his statement? That answer
seemed easy. Hasty might quarrel with his
daughter. He might think her a tramp in his
vengeful anger toward her mother whom he
hated. She was still his daughter. Was he
afraid she might have followed O'Neill down
to the point?

"You saw Jake last night." Annie was
alert for hesitation, for dissembling, for too
much care and caution.

Elaine's face hardened. She threw out her
hands, the thin bracelets on her arms jan-
gling. "In his tuxedo." The jealousy still ran-

kled. "Looking like he was on top of the world. And Mrs. Neville holding on to his arm. Like he was a pet poodle. That's what I was going to tell him. . . ." She trailed off, whispered, "I had it all planned. I was going to come home and use my lipstick and write it on his door: Pet Poodle. But he went down the path and he never came back."

Annie hesitated. Maybe she should leave well enough alone, go out to her car and call Billy, tell him about Elaine. He would have to listen and come and see her. But the words were out before she could stop them. "You saw Jake go down the path?"

"Him in his fancy clothes and me with my arms in hot water up to my elbows. Oh, I saw him." Elaine's lips pouted.

"What happened when you went after him?" It never occurred to Annie that Elaine, passionate and volatile and angry, hadn't set out into the fog. What did she see? What did she know? Annie's hands tightened into fists. Chloe's fate might rest on the words of this jealous and hurt girl.

"After him?" Elaine's glance was scornful. "Do you think I could run around like I was at a party? Fat chance. The help don't dance, don't you know. I stood at the kitchen sink most of the night. I looked out the window and watched him disappear into the fog. I was still there when the sirens sounded. But I didn't know anything then. Later Dad wouldn't say much. He told me, 'Least said soonest mended,' and I was to keep quiet about Jake, not tell anybody that I'd ever known him." She gave a short laugh. "But people always know. How did you know?"

Annie brushed away the question. "Can you prove you didn't leave the kitchen be-tween a quarter to nine and"—Annie figured the time—"nine-fifteen?"

"Sure." Elaine's answer was quick and confident. "Sue Lee Harris was bringing me stuff. She can tell you. What difference does it make?"

Standing at the sink . . . Annie felt a tingle in her mind. If Elaine saw Jake, she might have seen his murderer follow him. Or the murderer might have preceded him if a meeting had been arranged.

Elaine peered at Annie. "Why are you looking so funny?"

Annie didn't even think of disguising the eagerness in her voice. "Tell me everything you saw from the window."

Elaine's dark eyes were puzzled and wary. "How come?"

"Look, you may know who killed him." Annie's voice was excited. "Don't you see? He walked down to the point. We need to know everybody who took that path. And you were watching." Of that, Annie felt certain. Stuck in the kitchen, hot, resentful, and angry, Elaine watched Jake in his finery. Of course she'd kept her eyes trained on the path.

Elaine's face was abruptly still and unreadable. "Between a quarter to nine and nine-fifteen?"

Annie felt a surge of triumph. If Billy had done his job, he'd be near the solution to the murder right this minute, but it was Annie who'd followed the clues and Annie who would oh-so-soon ring up Billy and his deputy—aka Max Darling—and inform them the case was solved. "Right. Who went down the path?" Elaine's answer could make all the difference for Chloe. Whom did Elaine see? And in what order? And when? Chloe Martin? Rusty Brandt? Maybe Beth Kelly since she too had run through the kitchen parking lot near the critical time. Elaine was a witness whose word could force the police to look at others besides Chloe.

Elaine's dark eyes flashed. "Wait a minute. Nobody's told me anything. All I know is Dad saw some girl running away and he went out to check in the gardens and found Jake. I don't even know how he died." Her gaze was insistent.

"He was found facedown on the bricked oval near the point. Someone hit him from behind." Annie didn't want to describe that massive wound. "They haven't found the weapon."

"From behind? Well"—Elaine's voice was confident—"that lets out my dad. He'd never hit anybody from behind. Besides, Dad wouldn't need a weapon to knock anybody down, especially not somebody like Jake."

Annie remembered the caterer's tough face and burly build.

Elaine shrugged. "What difference does it make who went out there? Dad said some girl in a green dress killed him." Her face twisted. "I knew Jake had found somebody new. He probably strung her along, just like me. Then she found out about Mrs. Neville."

Elaine's quick judgment was so uncannily close that Annie stared at her in surprise.

Elaine gave her a bitter look. "Oh, yeah, that's pure Jake. I kept thinking I could get him to change his mind. Jake said we could keep things going the way they were after he got married. I told him he could go to hell. But I was still seeing him until a few days ago, and all of a sudden he wouldn't let me in. I knew there was somebody." Her face looked old despite her youth, raddled by loss and anguish. "I guess he tangled with the wrong person."

"She didn't kill him, Elaine, I'm sure she didn't." Annie hoped that she could reach this angry, hurt girl. If only Annie could make Elaine understand that Chloe's life might depend upon what Elaine had seen from that window. "Yes, she went down to the point to meet Jake. You see"—Annie knew she had to be careful here—"she'd just met Jake, and she thought they were in love—"

Elaine bent her head and clasped her hands tightly together.

"—but she didn't know who he was. When she came to the party she was excited to find him. He asked her to come down to the point. He told her he was going to marry Virginia Neville. They quarreled, and she ran away. That's when your dad saw her, but Jake was alive when she left. She heard him call after her. Someone else must have been there and come up behind him and struck him down."

Elaine reached up, brushed a strand of hair from her cheek. She gazed off into the distance, her eyes narrowed. "Oh. If she didn't do it, somebody else did, somebody else who went down the path. . . ."

Annie scarcely dared to breathe. That Elaine had seen another person on the path seemed a certainty.

Elaine's head lifted. She shot Annie a cunning, triumphant look. "Yeah. Oh, sure. It makes sense."

"Who?" Annie leaned forward.

Elaine combed her fingers through her thick black hair, shook the curls away from her face. "So maybe I'm in the catbird seat. Maybe people better pay attention to me. Or I can make it hot for them." The tears had dried on her face. She looked satisfied. And dangerous.

"Elaine, no." Annie spoke sharply. "If you saw anyone, you must tell the police. Don't threaten anyone. What good would it do you?"

Elaine's dark eyes burned with contempt

and determination. "Who knows? People might be grateful not to have the police come calling. And there are those that have been so high and mighty that might have to treat me nice. That would be a change."

Annie reached out, gripped a slender arm. "Elaine, please. Chloe needs your help and—"

Elaine yanked her arm free. "Why should I care about her? A rich girl in a fancy dress thinking Jake belonged to her. Well, he didn't. I don't care what happens to her. Maybe nobody else went to the point except her and Jake. What if I told the police that? She'd be in a fix, wouldn't she?"

They stood a few feet apart, Annie beseeching, Elaine defiant.

"That isn't true and you know it." Annie would have liked to grab Elaine Hasty and shake the truth out of her. She couldn't do that. But the police had every right to demand—and get—answers from her. Annie forced herself to be calm. Maybe Elaine would listen to reason. "If you don't care about her, you'd better care about yourself. Someone who walked down that path killed Jake. You didn't see him, the blood pooling around his head—"

Elaine clapped her hands over her ears.

Annie kept talking, loud and fast. "—beaten to death. You better not try to get money—"

Elaine's eyes flared, but her gaze was unbending and rebellious.

"—for keeping quiet. I'm going to the police. You'll have to answer to them."

Elaine's hands dropped. She rushed to the door, flung it open. "Get out."

Annie tried one more time. "Elaine, please, let's talk."

"Get out." The girl pointed at the door.

Annie took one step, two, and she was through the door and down the steps.

Elaine stood in the doorway. "As for the police, I'm not talking to them. I don't have anything to say. Except maybe"—her sarcasm was evident—"I'll tell them I didn't see a thing out of that window. I'll tell them you came to my house and tried to get me to make up something to save this friend of yours."

The door slammed shut.

Billy Cameron clattered down the steps of the Broward's Rock police station. He flung words over his shoulder. "Keep after it, Max. See if you can find Annie. She's the only one in town who really knows the girl."

As Billy yanked open the door to the police cruiser, Max put out a restraining hand. "Maybe we should sketch out a plan for the investigation—"

Billy hunched over the wheel, his face set in hard, tight lines. "First thing we got to do is find that girl. I shouldn't have let her go last night. Well, I won't be fooled twice. I'm going to find her pronto. It's her fault we aren't farther ahead. We got to find out about Brandt's jacket"—the preliminary test proved positive for human blood—"and talk to the Neville family. We'll meet back here in an hour. Keep your cell phone on. I'll do the same." He pulled the door shut.

Max stepped back, and the cruiser roared away. Max watched the dust-churning car barrel down the road. Billy knew there was much to do, many avenues to explore, but everything was on hold until Chloe Martin was found. Was there anything Max could have said or done to calm Billy down? Max shook his head. The acting chief was past listening. He was too upset, still second-guessing his decision not to take Chloe Martin into custody last night. His entire focus for the moment was on capturing her. Bulletins were out to county and state law enforcement staffs. Lou Pirelli was scouring back roads. Their best guess was that Chloe was riding the old blue bike missing from her aunt's garage. Or she could have started out on the bike and now be on foot. Either way she could easily dart from a road into the woods when she heard a car. As for the rest of the investigation, the statements Annie had gathered still awaited Billy's review. Frank Saulter had already been out to the crime scene and taken a series of photos in daylight. And Frank had packaged Chloe's stained green stole and Rusty Brandt's dinner jacket to send to the state crime lab. Max's assignment was to camp out at Death on Demand in case Chloe called there. Maybe it was time to let his fingers do the walking. He pulled out his cell phone, turned it on, punched the number of Death on Demand.

"Death on Demand, the finest mystery bookstore east of Atlanta." Henny's well-modulated voice, rich and precise from years as a successful amateur actress, brimmed with welcome.

Max grinned. "Hi, Henny. Has Annie recruited you to the Let's-Save-Chloe campaign?"

"I declined. Has Annie ever seen a windmill she hasn't attacked?" Admiration mixed with bemusement. "But I felt bad that I refused to help. I called back and there was no answer so I knew she'd closed up shop and was out trying to help Chloe. I decided to come down and open the store for her."

Max frowned. "Any idea where she's gone?"

"No. But she'll be pleased. I've already sold four books, *White Shell Woman* by James Doss, *Case of the Murdered Muckraker* by Carola Dunn, *Tishomingo Blues* by Elmore Leonard, and *Death at Dartmoor* by Robin Paige." A thoughtful pause. "Your mom must have been by. There was a card slipped under the door. No signature, but I know Laurel's writing. Max, your mother is one of a kind."

Max made an indeterminate noise. It might have been acquiescence. Or resignation. Or possibly denial.

There was a scrabbling sound. Henny's voice came from a distance, grew clearer.

"Here it is. I'd propped it up by the cof-feemaker so Annie wouldn't miss it." Henny cleared her throat. " 'A faithful friend is a strong defence: and he that hath found such an one hath found a treasure—Ecclesiasticus VI, 14.' " A thoughtful pause. "And who would expect your mother to peruse the Apocrypha?"

Laurel's wide-ranging mind was a topic Max felt better left unexplored. But she was, as so often, on point. Annie defending Chloe and he defending Billy and no telling what the outcome would be. But for now, Max saw his own duty clear. "Are there any other messages?" Had Chloe called, left any hint as to her whereabouts?

"Yes." Henny was always efficient. "Two customers and I've called both. That's all."

"If Chloe Martin telephones or comes, call the station." He felt the resistance on the other end of the line. "Billy intends to take her into custody as a material wit-ness."

"I see." A hesitation. "Max, have you talked to Annie?"

"I will." His voice was firm. "I promise."

When the call ended, he stood a moment longer, frowning, then punched in the number of Annie's cell phone. After five rings, the voice mail picked up. He spoke firmly. "Annie, I need to talk to you. Chloe didn't show up this morning. She's a fugitive." He waited to let her think about that. "If she gets in touch with you—" He paused, wondering what to say and how to say it. Finally, his voice sober, he urged her, "—tell her to turn herself in. Anything else is stupid. And serious. I know this will upset you, but try not to worry. If Chloe's innocent, she'll be all right." He believed that. He wished Annie did. "Oh, by the way, Henny's manning the store. She thought you needed her. Call me on my cell as soon as you can. I'll keep it on." A pause. "Love you." He locked the keys, shoved the phone into his pocket, his face somber.

The onshore breeze rustled the palmetto fronds near the front steps of the station. The lonely sound was punctuated by the fading toot from the ferry en route to the mainland. Max pictured Frank Saulter standing at the railing, looking out toward the mainland over the choppy water, relishing the cold winter wind, holding tight to his carefully boxed evidence en route to the FedEx office. Max had a sense of isolation and uncertainty and a bone-deep conviction that Billy's investigation had to expand. Sure, Chloe Martin was suspect number one. But she wasn't the only suspect. And Billy had yet to read the statements from last night or interview the family.

Abruptly, Max swung about. He hurried into the station.

Mavis looked up from the dispatcher's desk. She tried to smile, but it wasn't a success. Her eyes were dark with worry. She knew better than anyone the strain upon Billy.

Max gestured toward the frosted door leading to the offices. "Okay if I use Billy's office?"

"Of course." She watched him open the door, called out quickly, "Let me know if you need anything. Max—"

He paused.

She shook her head. "Nothing." There was a hopeless tone in her voice.

He flashed a smile. "Don't worry. Billy can handle it." But as the door closed behind him, Max frowned. Billy would certainly look at the other evidence. He was a good law officer and a fair one. But he might easily be persuaded to charge Chloe Martin with murder. The case against her was strong. And what if Annie was right in her defense?

Max stood by Billy's desk. Frank was en route to the mainland. Lou was driving the island back roads. Billy was searching, too. That left it up to Deputy Max Darling to do his best to be sure Billy didn't make a mistake.

His gaze scanned the cluttered desk, skimming past the leather foldout with pictures of Mavis and Billy deep-sea fishing, Kevin in his Boy Scout uniform, Billy pitching to Kevin, a flushed Mavis dishing up chili at a cookout, Billy tall and solemn in his uniform accepting a commendation from Chief Garrett. There was a picture of Mavis on their wedding day, the pink of her cheeks a match for her new suit and the roses in her bouquet. A silver trophy proclaimed the championship of the island rugby team, captained by Billy Cameron. A half-eaten Snickers bar rested next to a stack of legal pads. A jar of Tums, a tin of Altoids, and—Max heaved a sigh of relief when he spotted the orange folder. He flipped it open. There they were, the statements taken by Annie last night.

Max flung himself into Billy's chair. He made notes as he read:

Check out Elaine Hasty.
Why didn't Tony Hasty mention
O'Neill's relationship with his
daughter?
Question Rusty Brandt.
Ditto Beth Kelly.

He saved Annie's statement for last.

Annie Darling

I was not personally acquainted with Jake O'Neill. He was pointed out to me during the party. I saw him talking to Mrs. Neville. I didn't see him again. Shortly after nine o'clock, I saw a figure coming along the garden path from the direction of the point. At the time I thought it might be Chloe Martin, who has been working for me over the holidays. However, it was a quick glimpse and I cannot be certain. My husband and I tried to find her, but were unsuccessful.

"Annie." Max spoke her name aloud, a chiding sigh. Talk about sins of omission. Nothing about Chloe's infatuation with

Jake, nothing about Annie's efforts to find Chloe. Max paused, added to his notes:

Chloe arrives, sees Jake, they talk— and both of them promptly disap- pear from sight.

Max nodded. The fact that Chloe and Jake were not in the gallery when Annie looked for Chloe emphasized the likelihood they'd gone together to the point. Or, if not together, slipped away to meet each other there. That made it less likely that someone else was present. "Although we can't forget Rusty Brandt and Beth Kelly. Why did Beth run?" Max murmured. He tapped his pen, scrawled:

If Rusty Brandt's jacket tests posi- tive for O'Neill's blood (a fair as- sumption since the presence of blood has been determined), Brandt was at the point. Why? To meet O'Neill? Unlikely. Did he follow O'Neill? Possibly. Why? Ah, how about Brandt spotting Jake and Chloe slipping away and going after them in hopes of discovering some-

thing compromising to report to Virginia Neville? Hmm, maybe. But where does Beth Kelly figure in?

Max raised an eyebrow. How the hell many people had been at the point? He slapped the folder shut and pushed back his chair, eager to be on his way. He was almost to the door when Billy's phone rang. Max hesitated for an instant, shrugged, reached the desk in two strides, and grabbed the receiver. "Broward's Rock Police. Darling speaking."

"Max!" Annie's voice bubbled with surprise, pleasure, and delight. Then a gasp and a quick, "Listen, I've got to go. She's coming out to her car. I thought I had time to call and tell Billy. I'm going to follow her. She knows who killed him, I'm sure of it—" And the cell phone clicked off.

Max yelled, "Annie." But it was too late.

Annie waited until the Camry flashed past. She hunkered behind the wheel of the Volvo, wished it weren't red. Had Elaine noticed her? Well, duh. She'd know the cars of the other residents. Maybe she wouldn't expect Annie to follow. Maybe she thought she was finished with Annie. The taillights of the Camry flashed briefly as the car turned right onto the dirt road leading to Sandspur Lane. Annie spurted in pursuit. She lagged back about thirty yards. Maybe Elaine would assume they were both going toward town. It was, after all, a small island.

If she could stay far enough behind, Elaine might not pay any attention. Wherever she went, it had to be connected with what she had seen from the kitchen window last night. The Camry turned onto Sand Dollar Road. Annie followed. The Camry surged forward. Annie pressed the accelerator. Forty, forty-five, fifty miles an hour. There wasn't any traffic, thanks to the island's January doldrums. But there could always be a wandering deer or a kid on a bike. Annie hunched over the wheel, her hands sweaty. She came around a curve. No sign of the tan coupe. On the right, a rustic wooden sign announced BROWARD'S ROCK NATURE PRESERVE. Dust boiled from the dirt road that plunged into the maritime forest of live oak, magnolia, and slash pine.

Annie slowed enough to make the turn into the preserve. The Volvo bucketed into deep shadows on the twisting, sandy lane. Annie drove as fast as she dared, braking occasionally to peer into offshoot lanes. There was no hint which road Elaine had taken. The preserve was a curlicue of paths that often intersected, sometimes doubled back, occasionally ended at a pond.

Annie reached the rookery, looked across winter-dull water at the rocky island, a haven for heron, wood ibis, and snowy egrets. She rolled down her window, listened for the sound of a motor, heard the chirp and wail of the birds, the sough of the high pines, a rustle in a nearby shrub.

And nothing more. She yanked up her cell phone.

Max answered on the first ring. "Annie, who are you chasing?" He didn't pause for a breath and his voice was sharp with worry. "Don't go around following people in a murder case, for God's sake."

"Elaine Hasty. Anyway, I lost her." She blew out a puff of exasperation. "She was at the kitchen window at the gallery and she saw everybody who went to the point. But she won't say who she saw. Other than Chloe."

He was silent.

"She saw somebody else," Annie insisted. "I know she did. Anyway, Billy needs to know about her, and the police have to talk to her."

"Okay." He tried to soothe. "I'll see to it he gets a full report." There was a pause, a reluctant, heavy pause. "Annie—"

She held tight to her cell phone. Whatever Max was going to say, she wasn't going to like.

"—I guess you haven't heard my message on your cell. Chloe didn't show up this morning. She's a fugitive and will be arrested as a material witness."

"Oh." Annie heard the rustle of the trees and the croon and chitter of the birds, lonely sounds. Where was Chloe? Where could she possibly be?

"Come on to Parotti's. I'll meet you for lunch. We'll see what we can come up with." There was kindness in his voice.

Annie clicked off the phone. She drove slowly, dust fluttering around the car. Once out of the preserve, she picked up speed and headed for the harbor. Chloe, a fugitive . . . Why had she run? There was nothing she could have done that would have made her predicament any worse.

Annie was almost to Parotti's parking lot when she braked and made a U-turn, then parked in front of an old two-story brick building a half block from the café. Gilt letters on the plate glass window proclaimed HASTY'S GOURMET MEALS TO GO. CATERING. FINE FOODS FAST. Light from the window spilled into the narrow yard. Annie hurried up the steps. A bell jangled as she stepped inside.

The glass of the display cases sparkled with cleanliness. Tony Hasty was pulling a dish from the case to her left. He looked up. Annie wished she had a freeze-frame of his initial expression. Had there been an instant of tenseness? Or had his rough-hewn face simply reflected its ordinary toughness?

"Hello, Tony." She walked to the counter with the register.

He stared at her for a moment, then carried the dish to a table. His steps were heavy on the wooden floor. He came to the counter, wiping his huge hands on a cloth. "Yeah, Annie. What can I do for you? Got smoked tenderloin today. Oysters and rice. Jambalaya."

"When you found the body"—she forced herself to meet his light eyes, the gaze remote and cold—"was that your second trip to the point?"

A scowl twisted his heavy face.

"Did you go down there after we talked to you? Did you find Jake? Were you—" Her words tumbled out faster and faster. She belatedly remembered that she was alone with Tony Hasty. In one great stride he could swing around the end of the counter and grab her with hands big as the kitchen mitts slung on a worktable. "—mad at the way he was treating Elaine? Did you kill him?" She began to back toward the door.

He slapped his arms across his chest. "Oh, sure. In between moving dishes, being in and out of the kitchen, seeing those women dash by. Yeah, sure. Just a little extra I forgot to mention." He gave a bark of angry laughter. "As for Elaine, she got what she deserved, panting after him, playing his game. I don't put up with men abusing women, but half the time women bring all the trouble on themselves. Elaine's just like her mother." His eyes held pain. "I didn't say anything to the police about Elaine and him because that was over. He'd dropped her. He was going for the gold. I don't know what happened to him last night. And Elaine doesn't either." He was emphatic. "Elaine was in the kitchen. I'd just come outside to the van right before that girl ran past and I can tell you that Elaine was at the sink. That girl ran past, then you and your husband came, then I was back in the kitchen and out again in time to see Beth Kelly. And Elaine was at the sink the whole damn time. You mark Elaine right off your list."

Annie's tense muscles relaxed. There was nothing to fear from Tony Hasty. Billy and Max could check to be certain, but if his story was true and he was seen both by Annie and Max and by workers in the kitchen during that critical period, he could not have made an earlier trip to the point and found and killed Jake. Tony said she could mark off Elaine as a suspect. Well, she'd already done that. Now, as Elaine had insisted, Annie marked off her father.

But she wasn't finished. "Elaine's not a suspect. I know that. But she may be an important witness."

A dull flush rose from his neck, turning his face dark as a peach pit. "Goddammit, you don't listen. I tell you, Elaine never left that kitchen. There's no damn way she could know anything about what happened at the point."

"The window, Tony." Annie flung out her

hands. "She was at the window. She saw who went to the point. She saw Jake and she saw Chloe, and I know she saw someone else. But she won't say who it was. I'm afraid she's going to try and blackmail that person."

"The hell she is." He reached back, untied his apron, pulled it off. "I'll see about that." He waved his hand at Annie. "Gotta close now. Come on, I'll lock up." He shepherded Annie ahead of him through the door.

He pulled the door shut, locked it, and ran, moving fast for a big man, to the van parked in the side drive. The motor roared to life. Oyster shells spit from beneath the wheels, and the van lurched into the street.

Annie looked at the cloud of dust and wondered what she'd unleashed.

· *Eight* ·

Cream-voiced Doris Day crooned "Sentimental Journey" on the jukebox. Annie stirred her chili, watched the mound of grated cheese soften. Hmm, steamed corn kernels and onions, too. Vidalia, of course, and as sweet as heaven. Annie loved Ben Parotti's chili even though a Texas purist would take exception to the beans. And yes, she'd had a bowl for lunch yesterday, but she could never get enough.

Even before she spoke, Annie knew it was an exaggeration, but she was determined to get Max's full attention. "Obviously Elaine knows who killed him, and she's going to try a spot of blackmail." Annie slapped the scarred wooden table of the booth for emphasis.

"That's a pretty serious accusation." He poured his beer, watched the foam rise.

"You should have heard her." Annie had a clear memory of her conversation with Elaine. "She was gloating. I think she's already counting the money in her head. Oh, Max, if only I hadn't lost her in the preserve. If I could have followed her, found out who she was going to go see or call . . ." But as her sensible Texas mother had often observed, there was no point in playing cards from the what-if deck. "Anyway, somebody's got to stop her. Maybe her dad will find her." Annie looked satisfied. "I can tell you he's going to give her an earful. But now that I've reported what she said, it's up to the police." She flicked him a glance. "You and Billy." As if it needed explanation. "When you find out what Elaine knows, Chloe will be cleared." Annie's tone was forceful, recognizing the resistance in her husband's dark blue eyes. Annie took a sustaining spoonful of chili and wished this were an ordinary Saturday, free of the omnipresent sense of impending disaster that wrapped around her denser than any fog.

Max squeezed lemon over his baked flounder, forked a piece with a scoop of spinach. "Annie, that's like spotting a raccoon with a pizza box and deciding he likes pepperoni—"

Annie frowned. The logic escaped her.

"—when all it proves is that the raccoon likes pizza. Anyway"—his words were hurried, perhaps he felt his simile lacked application—"all you can be sure of is that Elaine saw—or claims she saw—people go down the path. She doesn't know who killed Jake."

"She knows someone went to the point in addition to Chloe." Annie had no doubt that was true. "You—the police—can't ignore that."

"We won't. Billy won't." But he frowned.

Annie was afraid she understood. "Billy's mad, isn't he?"

Max added a dash of salt to his fillet, didn't meet her eyes. "He's worried. And embarrassed. He feels like he's let Pete down, made the department look foolish. He keeps saying Pete wouldn't have been dumb enough to let Chloe leave last night. He says"—Max lifted his gaze, looked at her somberly—"that innocent people don't run away."

"Chloe's scared." Annie took a gulp of iced tea. "You remember how upset she got when Billy said he was going to put her in jail."

Max spooned more tartar sauce onto his plate. "Billy's looking at all possibilities—especially Rusty Brandt—but the evidence is a lot stronger against Chloe. She's going to jail as a material witness, that's for sure. Since she ran away, there's no chance a judge will set bail. Not that she could likely make bond anyway."

"Oh, Max." Annie stared at him, misery in her eyes.

He put down his fork, reached across the table, grabbed her hand. "Chloe blew it when she ran away." His grip tightened. "If you find out where she is—if she calls you—you've got to turn her in."

Annie's face stiffened. "No." She pulled her hand away.

"That's like harboring a fugitive." His blue eyes were insistent.

They looked at each other across a divide.

"How's everything?" Ben Parotti leaned

into the booth. A chili-spattered apron only partially protected his bright green wool blazer. He glanced from one to the other, his leprechaun face concerned, and started to back away. "Not meaning to interrupt."

"It's okay, Ben." Annie managed a smile. "Don't you and Miss Jolene sometimes"— her eyes turned to Max—"agree to disagree?"

Ben rubbed his nose. "Hmm, the missus and me"—a sudden sunny smile created an angelic leprechaun—"we're boppin' to the same tune." He shuffled his shoes to a dance Annie vaguely remembered from home movies of her mother. He finished with a slap of his hands on his knees, stood straight, cleared his throat. His wrinkled face turned a rusty color. Hurriedly, he loosened his apron to search the pockets of his jacket and pulled out a folded note card. He looked at Max. "Your mama dropped by a minute ago and asked me to bring this to you. Said she thought it was something you needed." He held out the card on a calloused hand. "Both of you."

"Thank you, Ben." Annie took the card. Clasped hands rimmed the border.

Ben looked bemused. "She came and

she went with a smile and a wave of her hand and a perfume that reminds me of fields of lavender." Bemused, enchanted, and uplifted. "I don't hold with saying she's a one from without the world as we know it, but I do believe she's got a sight beyond our ken." Ben backed away, then scooted toward the kitchen.

Annie held the card where Max could read, too: "Richard Barnfield, 'Address to the Nightingale': He that is thy friend indeed, He will help thee in thy need."

In her unmistakable looping script, as if every word ended in a butterfly, Laurel had added: "Remain steadfast, Dear Children. Friendship shines with an everlasting light."

Max absently buttered a cornbread muffin. "I'm surprised she isn't holding up the boy on the burning deck as an inspiration." His eyes glinted with amusement and irritation. "Sometimes I'd like to wring her neck." Fondness warred with exasperation. "She's certainly been busy. There's another card for you at the store."

Annie raised an eyebrow.

"I called a while ago. Henny's there. She figured you needed someone to run the cash desk. She said to tell you she's sold four books. She also reported a card from Laurel." He repeated the verse from Ecclesiasticus. There was a little dimple just at the edge of his lips when he frowned. Annie wondered what he would do if she leaned across the table and kissed him there.

He caught her glance and his face brightened.

She shook her head though her eyes were soft. "Max, it's clear as clear! Laurel's been communing." Annie decided it would be unprofitable to suggest in what manner and with whom. "Anyway, she's urging us on. If you do your thing and I do mine, it will all come right." She held aloft a heaping spoonful of chili in salute.

Annie watched Max's car pull away. Maybe her brave words to Max would come true. It would certainly improve matters if Chloe came back of her own accord. Annie tapped her fingers on the steering wheel. Finding Chloe was essential. Annie pulled out her cell phone, clicked it on, called Death on Demand.

The salutation was upbeat. "Death on

Demand, the finest mystery bookstore east—"

Annie smiled. "Henny, you are a sweetheart. I appreciate your taking over."

The answer was swift, if not to the point. "The newly appointed magistrate to the Peng-lai district." Henny's voice purred like a cat surfeited with cream.

Annie's tone was equally unctuous. "Judge Dee, of course. One of his early cases, *The Chinese Gold Murders,* by Robert van Gulik."

"Humph. Very good." The accolade was gracious. "Well, everything's fine here. Not much to report. Max rang up. Oh, there was one other call for you," she said carelessly. "Some young woman."

Annie's hand tightened on the phone.

Henny was bland. "She didn't leave her name. She sounded as though she was eager to talk to you so I gave her your cell number."

If Annie had been at the store, she would have hugged her old friend. "Thanks, Henny. I'll keep my phone turned on."

"Are you making any progress?" The question was gentle.

"Yes." Annie didn't have to think about it.

"Elaine Hasty was looking out the kitchen window at the gallery last night. Max promised to find out what she saw. I'm going to the gallery now to check it out." What could Elaine see from that window?

Max eased his Maserati around a pothole just past the entrance to Nightingale Courts. Duane needed to fill that one in. Max looked toward the Webb cabin. There was no car in front. Max drove on. The tan Camry Annie had followed and lost was backed up to the front door of cabin 6, the trunk open.

A pretty dark-haired girl in a tight sweater and slacks peered over the mound of clothes clasped in her arms. She edged down the steps and flung the clothes into the trunk. She jerked around as Max slammed out of his car. Her face was wary.

"Miss Hasty?" He stopped next to the steps, looked straight into resentful eyes.

She folded her arms across her front. "What do you want?"

"Deputy Max Darling. I'm investigating the murder of Jake O'Neill." He tried a smile.

She brushed back a tangle of glossy black hair. For an instant, she looked young and sad and hopeless. The expression was gone almost before Max saw it. Her eyes flashed. "I know who you are. You aren't the police. Your wife was here, wanting to know what I saw last night. But I don't care who you are. I'll tell you and anybody who wants to know just what I told her."

Max pulled a notebook from his pocket. "I've been deputized by Chief Cameron. Whatever you observed may be helpful to his investigation."

"Maybe." Her voice was taunting. "Maybe not. Like I told your wife, I saw Jake—" She swallowed convulsively. It was a moment before she continued, her anger and jealousy clear in her bitter look. "—and he was going down the path to the point after a girl in a green dress."

"Who else did you see on that path?" Max challenged her. He held his pen over his pad.

She laughed. "Everybody wants to know, don't they?" She drawled the words. "I've got everybody's attention. Nobody cared about me yesterday. Now"—her lips curved in triumph—"everybody's listening to me. I like that."

Max felt like a bloodhound on a scent: *Everybody's listening to me.* He rapped out, "Who's listening to you?"

From the living room the telephone shrilled. She looked startled, then turned, hurried inside. The screen banged, but the door was open.

Max walked up the steps, listened.

"Hello." An impatient sigh. "Yeah, Dad." The wary tone was gone, replaced by irritation. "No. I just got back. . . . Who, me?" She half turned, glanced through the screen, saw Max. She gave him a derisive look. "Yeah. Everybody wants to know what I saw out the window. But I'm not telling. . . . Don't worry, I'm not stupid. . . . And maybe it will turn out I didn't see a thing." She gave a peal of laughter and slammed down the phone. It rang again as she moved across the living room. "I guess you heard all that. You, your wife, my dad. Hey, everybody wants to know. Well, tune in tomorrow. There may be another chapter, there may not." She tossed her head, turned away.

Max put his hand on the handle of the

screen door. "Miss Hasty, I can take you into custody as a material witness." He wasn't at all certain he could. And if he did, would Billy hold her?

She faced him, glaring, hands on her hips. "A material witness to what? I told you what I saw. That's all I'm going to say." She reached the door, slammed it shut.

Max recalled Annie's lack of success with Elaine. It looked like today the score was Elaine Hasty: 2; Darlings: 0.

Maybe Billy could change the equation.

Occasionally a shaft of sunlight pierced the thick canopy of clouds. Annie nosed the Volvo against a bulky pittosporum hedge. In summertime the hedge's tiny white blossoms smelled like ripe bananas. Today there was nothing more than the smell of damp winter air and the dankness of undergrowth beneath the darkness of the towering pines. Annie shivered and zipped her lilac jacket shut. Last night the caterer's van had been open near the walkway to the kitchen door of the gallery. She glanced at the empty parking slot where the VW had sat last night. It was the presence of the VW that had frightened Virginia Neville. Now it was gone. Had the police removed it? Max hadn't mentioned the VW, so most likely a search had revealed nothing of interest. Jake O'Neill had no knowledge when he parked his car that he would walk into the fog to his death later that night. The only cars in the lot this morning were Annie's red car and a black Mercedes sedan. The red and the black . . .

As she walked across the crunchy oyster shells, she wondered why the compartments of a roulette wheel alternated red and black. Easy to read? Danger and death? The designer's whim? Funny—perhaps chilling—to think about the difference chance makes in life. And perhaps in death. Was Elaine Hasty's sweaty job at a sink to be a determining factor in Chloe Martin's life? Maybe. Maybe not. As the wheel turned . . .

Annie knocked. No sound, no movement from within. No light shone from the kitchen windows. She bent close to the nearest window, peered inside. The kitchen was untenanted. Annie hesitated, eased open the screen door, reached for the knob. It turned in her hand. In an instant, she stood inside the long linoleum-floored room. Once, an old iron range would have stood against the wall, stovepipe grimed by smoke. Now everything was modern—two electric ranges with tempered glass cooking surfaces, two wall ovens, a massive refrigerator, and two dishwashers, everything necessary for large parties. Only the Delft tiles above the unused fireplace and an iron kettle on a tripod remained of long-ago days.

Annie's heart thudded. She had no business here. But if she'd gone to the front door and entered the gallery's public rooms, she'd have had no reasonable excuse to visit the kitchen. All she needed was a few minutes. . . .

She slipped across the floor to the double sinks and the broad window. She placed her hands on the stainless-steel rim, leaned forward—

"Hello?" The speaker's voice combined surprise, uncertainty, and a query.

Annie turned to face Carl Neville.

Carl's blue-and-gray plaid cashmere sport coat hung from his thin shoulders. He held a sheaf of papers in one hand. He pushed thin wire-rimmed glasses higher on his nose. "Oh, Annie." A faint flush rose in

his cheeks. "I thought I heard someone. . . ."

"I'm sorry, Carl. I knocked." She waved
toward the back door. "No one answered,
and when I touched the handle, I realized
the door wasn't locked. I hope you don't
mind." She managed a social smile, hoping
his innate instincts of southern hospitality
would kick in. "You see"—and she tried to
sound both confident and confiding—
"there was a question about the view out of
the window over the sink."

"Oh." He rocked back on his heels. There
was a noticeable thaw. "I know the police
have to do a lot of investigating. And you
were helping last night." He shoved a hand
through his thinning hair. "This has knocked
me for a loop. I've been boxing up the stuff
in Jake's office. Mostly odds and ends except for his paintings. I expect Virginia will
want to show them. I'll check with his family
about that. We want to do the right thing. I
talked to his mother this morning. Damn."
He took a deep breath. "The funeral's not
been set. Sometime next week. Damn."

Carl Neville was sorry about Jake and
sorry for his mother. The gallery director's
reaction, from a bewildered weariness to a

natural dislike of contact with grief, seemed utterly natural. There was no hint of fear or uneasiness.

Annie relaxed. Carl had no ulterior motives, and he wouldn't suspect them of her. "I'm sorry, Carl. If there's anything I can do to help . . ."

"Yeah, well, I guess that's what you're doing now." He gave her a shy smile. "You and Max are helping out the police."

Annie wondered how angry Billy might be if she, in effect, impersonated an officer. She said carefully, "Max is serving as a deputy, and I do what I can."

"Right." Carl waved a hand. "You say there's some question about the window?" He gave it a puzzled glance. "Well, I don't want to slow you down." He backed toward the hall. "Let me know if you need anything. I'm in my office."

As the swinging door closed, Annie scrabbled a hand through her thick blond hair, knew it probably was standing on end, and didn't care. In a stride, she was back at the sink, looking out the window.

The view encompassed part of the back porch and the steps, a broad sweep of grass crisscrossed by oyster-shell paths,

curving swaths of azaleas, which in spring-
time created a world of color unrivaled on
the island. One path, the important path,
curved in an arc to the south and was almost immediately out of view behind a
stand of loblolly pines. Annie's eyes narrowed. Last night Elaine's view would have
been even more limited by the fog and by
night. Yes, the fog thinned and thickened in
patches, growing denser near the water, but
definitely there was fog near the house,
enough that visibility was down to fifteen or
twenty feet.

Annie felt a quiver of excitement. Elaine
looked out the window, and instead of the
sweep of garden she saw a portion of the
back porch and the path. She could not, for
example, have seen the path that led
through the middle of the gardens, the most
direct route for anyone going to the point
from the tent in the north lot. Moreover, she
could not have seen the segment of path
that came from the kitchen parking lot to in-
tersect the back door path to the point.
That meant—Annie's fingers tightened on
the cold metal of the sink—everyone seen
by Elaine came out of the gallery.

Would it be possible to determine who

was in the gallery between a quarter to nine and nine-fifteen? Annie slowly shook her head. Not likely. Many of the guests began walking to the tent shortly before nine. Wait a minute. She flipped open her purse, found her notebook. There it was:

8:50 P.M. Jake goes out back door.
9 P.M. Chloe runs through kitchen parking lot.
9:10 P.M. Beth Kelly runs past Tony Hasty.
9:14 P.M. Hasty finds body.

At some time after Chloe ran through the kitchen parking lot and before Hasty found the body, Rusty Brandt must have been at the point, witness his jacket. So mark Rusty as one person seen by Elaine. Annie made a mental note to ask Max about that jacket, but she was certain it must have blood-stains. There was only one way the jacket could have been stained. Either Rusty Brandt struck down Jake or he touched the body.

Annie frowned. She plucked her cell phone from her purse, thought for a moment, then called the store.

"Death on Demand—"

Annie interrupted. "Henny, I need to talk to Doc Burford. Would you get his cell phone number from my Rolodex?" As she waited, Annie crossed her fingers. The peripatetic physician was a hard man to catch.

In a moment, Henny was on the line. "Got it." She rattled off the number, then added for good measure his home, office, and hospital numbers. "Oh, and a piece of advice: 'All detective work is sneaking. That's why only gentlemen and cads can do it.' "

Annie sniffed. "How about ladies?"

"You aren't playing the game." Henny chortled. "*The Rising of the Moon.* Gladys Mitchell." The phone clicked off.

Annie opted for the medical examiner's cell number and scored on the first try.

"Burford." He was always brusque, but his patients knew he'd fight for them for a day, a month, a year, a lifetime.

"Doc. Annie Darling." She knew better than to waste his time. "Jake O'Neill was struck from behind. Did the killer get blood spatters?"

There was a considering silence.

Annie held tight to the phone and thought about Chloe's stole and her missing dress and Rusty Brandt's jacket and the bareness of women's arms in formal gowns.

Burford cleared his throat. "Not likely. The back of his head was crushed but no gashes. Like I told Billy, somebody probably grabbed up a stout stick and whacked him. There were traces of bark in the wound. But the blows didn't break the skin. The blood that pooled on the ground came from his nose and mouth, ran mostly onto that green thingamabob. There were some smears on his face and jacket. Somebody moved the body before I got there. Anything else?"

The stains on Rusty Brandt's jacket might even prove his innocence. But if Rusty was there, he must be persuaded to tell what he'd seen. There might be something pointing away from Chloe.

Annie tried again. "Is there any indication from the position of the wound about the height of the murderer?" Rusty Brandt was almost six feet tall. Chloe was about Annie's height, around five foot five.

A snort. "Who knows? Depends how high the murderer swung his arm—or her arm—before cracking his skull. Or whether it was a sidearm swipe. Or whether the stick was long or short. I don't know. Nobody'll ever know unless you catch the killer. Well, I've got to go."

He was running out of patience. And Chloe was boxed in. There was so little time for someone else to have been there, quarreled with Jake, attacked him. Or maybe there was no argument. Maybe the killer was there and heard Jake and Chloe's angry exchange and saw her run and moved swiftly to kill, knowing Chloe would be the first suspect. The first suspect? Right now she was the only suspect.

Annie rushed to speak before Doc Burford dismissed her. "Just one more thing. How long did it take?" There was so little time. Not more than ten minutes.

"How long did what take?" Burford demanded. "To kill him? Two minutes. Maybe three. It's easy to kill." His voice was heavy with anger. "He should have had another fifty years. Goddamn, I hate killers." A weary sigh. "Tell Billy I've released the body for burial. Autopsy didn't have any surprises." He hung up.

Annie clicked off the phone. Two minutes, maybe three . . .

Fingers of sunlight poked through the clouds, turning patches of gray water to green. A brisk wind kicked up whitecaps. At the dock, *The Miss Jolene* rocked a little in a heavy swell. Despite the occasional burst of sunlight, the wind off the water was cold. Max stuffed his hands deep into the pockets of his brown suede jacket. Out on a dock, Ben Parotti lifted a hand in greeting and headed toward Max. As he waited, Max admired a formation of brown pelicans—he counted eight—as the big birds skimmed the wave tops, ready to dive-bomb for menhaden and mullet. Menhaden are too oily for human taste, but Max had a fondness for mullet roe. Annie always wrinkled her nose and declined a portion even though he pointed out that the eggs were considered a delicacy in Japan, sometimes selling for more than fifty dollars a pound. The third pelican to the left swerved and plunged. Max wished he could lean against a piling and watch the ocean and the birds. There was a black skimmer, scooting just above the water line, its lower jaw cutting through the surface. A glossy black double-breasted cormorant, Max's favorite bird, stood regally on a piling. If Max had the af-

ternoon, at some point he would see an
aquatic show, the cormorant rising a hundred feet to curve and power downward for
its prey or, even better, using strong wings
to propel itself through the water, outswim-
ming most fish. But Max didn't have a January afternoon to while away. Instead, he
listened to the sound of Ben's brisk steps
and wondered what Annie was doing and
whether Billy would agree to pick up Elaine
Hasty. He glanced at his watch. A quarter to
two. Mavis expected Billy to be back at the
station within a half hour. Max had lots to
report, might have more after he talked to
Ben.

Ben's currant-dark eyes gleamed. "I
checked with everybody. Ain't nobody had
a call from that girl, so she's not on a boat
leaving here. And I checked from the mast
to the bilge on *The Miss Jolene.* She didn't
slip on board for the morning run. She won't
get on this afternoon." He clapped his
hands together. "Tell Billy she's smack dab
on this island and I got a hundred pair of
eyes on the lookout for her." His eyes
squinted against a burst of sunlight out of
the clouds. "Oh, and that dress she said
she threw off the dock. Nobody found it.

Doesn't mean she didn't do it. It's a big ocean."

Max had known finding the dress was a long shot. He was surprised at his sharp stab of disappointment. He'd wanted that dress found. He'd wanted it for Annie, who believed in her friend. Chloe claimed the dress wasn't bloodstained. If that was so, God knew it would be better if it were found. If it weren't found . . . well, a jury would draw its own conclusions.

Max shook Ben's hand. "Thanks. I'll tell Billy."

It was a short two-block drive to the police station. As he parked, a lowering black bull of a cloud slid across the sun. The day lost all sheen, turning dull and dirty as old pewter. The bleak sky matched Max's mood as he walked into the station. Mavis looked up from her desk, her face wan and drawn, an accurate barometer of Billy's unhappiness with this case.

Max headed for the door to the offices. In the small waiting area, a young man scrambled to his feet, almost overturning the metal chair, ruffling the fern that drooped from a stand. Tall enough so that doorways would always be a challenge, he peered down at Max through wire-rimmed glasses. Thick dark hair hung almost to the frames. His thin face twisted in a frown. He almost spoke, then gave a frustrated shrug and folded down onto the chair.

Max knew that anyone waiting at a police station had a story, most likely not a happy one. Not, fortunately, Max's problem this gray afternoon. Max stepped into the corridor, closed the door behind him, strode to Billy's office. He knocked.

"Yo." Gruff as a hungry bear and possibly as dangerous.

Max stepped inside and was greeted by a burnished steel gaze and a jutting chin.

Annie allowed for walking into fog and darkness with nothing more to show the way than the tiny glow from strings of Christmas lights in the live oaks. She pretended she was Jake O'Neill hurrying from the gallery to the point. She didn't try to recreate his feelings. Who knew? There he was, his engagement to be announced within the hour, and he'd come face-to-face with a girl he'd met and loved in the night. Had he cared at all for Chloe or was she nothing more than a pretty girl who came to him too willingly? It didn't matter now. Maybe his decision to draw her far from the gallery was its own answer. He didn't want Virginia Neville to know, so he whispered to Chloe, asked her to come out into the fog and darkness to meet him, and he walked to his death.

The pine trees soughed as the wind picked up off the water, cool and damp with the smell of seawater and rotting clumps of seaweed draped over ocean-scoured boulders. Once past the pines, Annie was out of sight of the gallery. Perhaps a quarter mile ahead rose the green hump, all that remained of the earthworks that had made up Fort Loomis. Live oaks and pines and a thicket of cane obscured part of the mound.

When she reached the site, it was easy to take it all in with a glance: the oval brickwork, the steps leading down to a platform built above the crumbled rocks below the bluff, the steps on the far side of the oval leading up to the lookout point above the ruins. Wind fluttered the yellow police tape strung about the bricked pavement. Drifting pine straw had already partially covered the yellow outline that marked the location of the body.

Annie looked at her watch. It had taken her two minutes and twenty seconds to reach the point. Even if Jake or Chloe walked more slowly, it couldn't have taken more than three minutes to come from the gallery to this hidden spot. Say three minutes. They talked. Annie had glimpsed a running Chloe perhaps a moment or two before nine o'clock. Jake's body was discovered at approximately fourteen minutes after nine.

Annie felt a rush of relief. There was time for someone else to have come and gone. If only Billy could be persuaded to consider—

Her cell phone bleated.

Annie's answer was breathless and hopeful. "Hello."

"Annie." Chloe's voice sounded faint and faraway. The connection crackled with static.

"Chloe. Thank God." Annie felt such a rush of relief she realized she'd been afraid, very afraid, for Chloe. "Chloe, please, you have to come to the police station. I'll meet you there. We'll get you a lawyer—"

"No." Chloe's voice quivered with fear.

Annie held tight to the receiver. The rumble and wash of the sea slapping against the boulders, the caw of a crow, the rustle of palmetto fronds, lonely sounds all, but loneliest of all was Chloe's plaintive cry.

"Chloe, listen." Annie was brisk. She spoke with slow and careful deliberation, each word firm and distinct. "I know you didn't kill Jake. I know you weren't the only person who went to the point. Elaine Hasty—she's part of the catering staff—was standing at the kitchen window, and she saw you and Jake and someone else."

"Someone else? She saw someone else? Oh, Annie, have the police talked to that person?" The words were feverish. "Who is it? What did they say? Someone else—I didn't see anyone when I left him. I was on that path that comes out near the house."

"I'm standing on it right now." Annie looked up the path until it curved behind the pines.

"You are?" There was a note of puzzlement. "Why are you there?"

"For you, Chloe." Chloe had doubted Annie's friendship. Annie hoped now she would believe again that she had a friend she could rely on. "I'm trying to figure out what happened. You can help. Tell me precisely what you did last night, every step of the way. Start with talking to Jake in the study."

"Oh, Annie, when I first saw him in the entry hall I thought it was a dream come true. Oh, God, I was so happy. But almost at once I knew something was wrong." She sounded forlorn. "He hurried me into the study. I still thought that it was like magic, that I'd put on my prettiest dress and he was there at the party for me. But right from the start everything was wrong. He looked upset. He whispered that he had to speak to me privately and I should go down to the point, that we could be alone there. He showed me the path out the window and said to walk down there and he'd come in a few minutes. I left the study and found my way out." There was a pause, then quickly. "I pushed the wrong door and stepped into the kitchen. This girl who was at the sink—"

Annie nodded. "Elaine Hasty."

"—turned around and glared at me, like why was I coming in there. I backed out and went on down the hall and found the back door. I stopped when I was out of sight of the house, it was so dark and foggy. I was scared, but after a few minutes I kept on. He'd told me he'd be there in a little while. I waited for him on that bricked pavement. It was probably only a couple of minutes, but it seemed a long time before he came. When he got there, he took me by the elbow and led me to some wooden steps that went down to this platform above the water."

Annie looked around, decided there was no one near. She ducked under the police tape. She stayed away from the outline of Jake's body and moved to the stairway. She walked down the steps and out on the platform, the stiff onshore breeze fluffing her hair and tugging at her clothes. The smell of the sea was sharp and fresh. In daylight, the prospect was clear though bleak and wintry, flotsam beached above the tide line, old logs and tangles of seaweed and occasional shattered planks from sunken ships.

"I heard the waves splashing against the rocks and the pilings, but I couldn't see anything because of the fog. There was only a kind of soft orange glow from the light up above. That's when he told me that the party was for him and Mrs. Neville. He said he was going to marry her. He kept on talking, but I didn't hear anything. There was a roar in my head—"

Annie was thinking fast. Last night the fog had turned this small platform into a hidden cocoon. Annie turned back, climbed the steps to the shore. She looked at a clump of palmettos near the steps. Anyone could have stood there, hidden from view, and heard every word spoken on the platform.

"—and he reached out and touched my arm and said he was sorry. Sorry! I asked him how he could marry someone he didn't love. He told me she was nice and they had fun together and she could make all the difference in his career. He said he wished it could be different. I screamed at him, screamed that he was going to marry her and he didn't care about her and I hated him. Then I turned around and hurried up the steps. He grabbed at me and caught my stole. I ran across the bricks to the path. He called out for me, yelled that he loved me. But I kept on running."

Annie glanced at the outline of the body. Yes, the hands had been outflung toward the path. Jake O'Neill was struck down as he hurried after Chloe. Annie made a fist, shook it in satisfaction. Another point in

Chloe's favor. She pushed away the thought that Billy would insist that Jake left first and Chloe followed, angry at being spurned, determined he shouldn't return to the gallery and Virginia Neville.

Annie worked it out. If Jake was killed as he called out for Chloe, the murderer was there, waiting, ready. That precluded Tony Hasty as his attacker. Annie looked toward the ruins and the thicket of cane and the pines that shaded the remnants of the fort. "Chloe, did you hear anything when you came up the steps from the platform?"

A long-drawn breath. "I don't know." Her voice was uncertain. "What difference does it make?"

"Don't you see? Whoever killed him may have been hidden nearby. When you left and Jake came after you, that's when the murderer probably attacked him." Annie willed Chloe to remember. "Think. Was there anything you heard or saw? Anything at all?"

The connection crackled, buzzed. It was a long moment before she answered, and then her voice was uncertain. "There might have been a rustling sound when I came up the steps. I looked around. But it was so dark and foggy, I didn't see anything. I guess I thought maybe someone was near or I wouldn't have looked. I'm not sure. Anyway, I stopped just for an instant, then I heard him coming up the steps and I ran. He shouted. My shoes slapped on the bricks. I reached the path and the oyster shells hurt my feet through the soles of my shoes, but I didn't slow down. I came around those big pines and suddenly there were the lights of the gallery. I didn't want to see anybody. I couldn't stay there. I didn't ever want to see him again. Or that woman he was going to marry. I took a path that came out in a parking lot and some man yelled at me—"

"Was he standing by a white van?" This was corroboration for Tony Hasty.

"He was in the parking lot." Her tone was vague. "I didn't want to talk to anybody. I was crying." Her voice was hard to hear. "When he yelled, I ran faster. I got to the road in front of the house and found my car. I drove around for a long time. Finally, I went back to Aunt Frances's house. When I got to my room, I took off my dress. I hated it." Her voice quivered. "I rolled it up and threw it in the corner. But I didn't want it near me.

I put on my jeans and a sweater and went to the pier and threw the dress away. Then I just sat there in the fog. When you came, I thought maybe he'd come after me. Oh, Annie, why did someone kill him?"

Annie thought about Jake's plan to marry Virginia Neville. There were those who would not want that marriage to occur. But there was no proof. Not yet. "I don't know, Chloe. But if we keep looking"—she thought about Rusty's jacket—"we may find out why. Listen, you said you might have heard a rustling sound." Annie looked out at the wind-stirred water, whitecaps rippling as far as the eye could see. The cane rustled. The pines trembled.

Slowly she turned toward the cane. "You heard a rustle. Maybe someone hurried to get behind the cane." Annie's shoes scuffed on the bricks as she crossed to the cane. She reached out, touched a stalk. "I think it's obvious. You came down to the point." Annie rattled the cane. "Jake came." She shook the cane. "Someone followed Jake." A third time she rustled the cane. "That's the way it had to be." Her hand fell away.

For the first time, Chloe's voice was eager. "The girl at the window—Elaine Hasty? Who did she see?"

"That's the problem." Annie remembered Elaine's taunting gaze. "She won't say. But I've told the police. They'll find out."

"She won't say?" Chloe's voice rose. "Why not? Doesn't she understand? Annie, the police think I killed him. She's got to tell them who she saw." The words tumbled out, gathering momentum like rocks in a landslide. "Maybe if I call her, explain that I'm in trouble—"

"No. That won't help." Annie stopped, knew her tone was too sharp.

Silence. Then a ragged laugh. "Was she another of his girls?"

Annie was silent. The silence grew and lengthened until it was as heavy as a pall.

Chloe gave a brittle laugh. "I see. Oh, God, I was such a fool. She hates me, doesn't she? Because of him. Annie"—the cry was deep and urgent—"what am I going to do?"

"You're going to be all right." Annie wished she believed what she was saying. But Chloe could be cleared if Elaine Hasty told what she knew. At the very least, Chloe would not be the only suspect. "We'll get a lawyer, that young man who came to the store." Annie felt a surge of well-being. It was time to fight back, marshal what they knew, prod Billy to widen his investigation. "Meet me at the police station."

"They'll lock me up." Chloe's voice was high and thin, horror paring the sound to a faint, faraway cry of despair. "I'd rather die." A gasping struggle for breath bubbled over the telephone.

"Hold up." Annie's voice was loud. "Chloe, what's wrong? No one will hurt you. I know Billy Cameron. He won't hurt you. His wife, Mavis, will be there—"

"Jail . . ." Chloe was sobbing now. "They'll shut me into a cell. I can't get out. It will be like the door." The words were thin, full of pain. "The door wouldn't open and I cried and cried and cried. . . ."

Annie paced toward the edge of the bluff, looked out at the white-flecked water. "What door?" Her voice was gentle. "Chloe, tell me."

The words were interspersed with sobs and quick breaths. ". . . had to stay with her . . . Mother was sick . . . I don't know what I did . . . I don't remember . . . she locked me in the closet . . . and I cried and cried. . . ."

"Who locked you in a closet? How old were you?" Despite the cold brisk wind, Annie felt hot and sick.

"I don't know . . . maybe five. . . . Aunt Frances . . ." Chloe drew a long, ragged breath. "Don't you see, Annie? I can't bear to be locked in. I'd rather die. Maybe that's what I'll do. The water's there. I can see it. I'll walk out—"

Annie held tight to the receiver. "Chloe, stop that. Promise me you'll stay wherever you are. I'll talk to Billy. There's a way. You can wear a transmitter that will prove where you are." Annie had seen one once at a forensic demonstration, a wristband that reminded her of Dick Tracy comic strips. "Billy's reasonable." Oh, God, surely he would be. Surely Annie could make him understand. "I'll promise Billy that you will stay with us. You've got to be calm. Don't say things like that. You won't have to be locked up. I promise." Promises, promises . . .

"I won't?" Chloe sounded like a child, hoping, trusting.

"You won't. I'll take care of everything." Annie looked at her watch. "Call me at five."

Annie clicked off the phone. Five o'clock. She had less than two hours to work a miracle. All right, dammit. Billy had to listen to reason about jailing Chloe. And he had to make interrogating Elaine Hasty a priority.

A noise that differed from the susurrant sound of the wind cut through Annie's whirling thoughts. She stood still and stiff, her eyes wide. Behind her, over the rustle of the cane and the soughing of the pines and the slap of the waves, she heard footsteps on the bricks. Someone was walking toward her on this isolated, remote spit of land where a man had died, his skull crushed by an attack from behind.

· *Nine* ·

"I'm tired of being screwed over." A sullen scowl soured Billy's usually genial face. "I'm telling you, Max, Annie's gone too far this time." He picked up a tan folder, slammed it against the desktop. "She's interfering with an investigation."

Max kept his voice easy and pleasant. "Billy, the minute she got this information—and you have to admit this is important—she called you."

Billy shook his head. "I haven't talked to Annie."

"She called here." Max pointed at the phone on Billy's desk. "You were out looking for Chloe Martin. Mavis said I could use your desk. That's the only reason I happened to answer. Annie called for you." Max once again emphasized the pronoun. "She went out to Nightingale Courts because she was worried about O'Neill's dog." Billy loved dogs and had three: Gus, an old yellow Lab; Boy, a shepherd-collie mix, and Millie, an agreeable dachshund who was a lady to the tips of her toes. "Turns out Pirelli had already gotten the dog, but Annie talked to Duane and found out this girl— Elaine Hasty—lived next door to O'Neill and they'd had a fight. This is Tony Hasty's daughter, and she was right on the spot last night with the catering crew. Elaine had a box seat at the kitchen window, and I don't think she missed any of the players. Annie found out a lot, but not enough. I went out there, but I didn't get anything. It's going to be up to you, Billy. You can break the case wide open."

Billy rubbed his cheek. "So Elaine Hasty saw Chloe Martin go down the path." It was a statement, not a question. Billy looked like Gus with a bone clamped in his teeth.

"Right. But she saw someone else. I'd bet my car on it." Max slouched, seeking comfort in the hard metal straight chair in front of Billy's desk. If he'd been a felon, he might have considered confession as a route to a comfortable mattress in a cell. "In any event, when you talk to Elaine"—Max believed in taking a positive approach— "you can build your case and at the same time"—a bright smile and an easy shrug— "you can make sure we aren't missing anything." He glanced at the closed folder holding the statements from last night. "Like Rusty Brandt."

Billy made a noise deep in his throat. "I know. We got to talk to him pronto. Yeah, I got Brandt on my list to see."

Max tipped his chair upright. "We can swing by Nightingale Courts, then pay Brandt a visit." Max stood.

Billy was getting to his feet when the intercom on his desk buzzed. He shot a surly look at the intercom. "I told Mavis I'm not talking to that guy." He stood by the desk and flexed his hands, cracking the knuckles. "As if I don't have enough on my plate without having to deal with this character who's got the hots for Chloe Martin. Did you see him out there when you came in?"

Max gave a swift nod. "There was a big guy. Basketball type. He jumped up when I came in and he looked pretty unhappy when Mavis waved me through." Unhappy put it mildly. "Who is he?"

"Lawyer. Bob Winslow. I've met him at Rotary. Nice enough but now"—Billy turned his big hands palms up—"claims the Martin gal couldn't hurt anybody, not the type, sweet, kind, helps old ladies across the street. I told him she also goddamn well is a fugitive from justice and the best favor he can do for her is find her and get her here quick. Seems the aunt and uncle called him, asked if he'd seen her. I'm not wasting another minute talking to him. Like I told him, find her, then I'll talk to him."

The buzzer rasped like wasps spilling from a crushed nest.

"Dammit, Mavis ought to know better." Billy leaned over and jabbed the button. "Yeah?"

Mavis was formal. "Captain, Mr. Brandt and Ms. Kelly are here to see you. Mr. Brandt said they wish to speak to you in regard to the O'Neill case. Are you available?"

Billy's thick blond eyebrows crinkled. "Sure. Yeah. Send 'em in." He clicked off the intercom. He sat down and squared his shoulders. He was an imposing figure behind his desk. "Hey Max, speak of the devil . . ."

Annie knew a moment of terror as she turned to face the solitary figure walking toward her in heavy shadow. There had been murder here, a body sprawled only a few feet away. The winter sun slides deep into the ocean with a sudden finality. Already the shadows were lengthening. Annie strained to see.

Virginia Neville moved out of the shadow, stopped a foot away. Virginia's grief-raddled face had the lumpy and pummeled look of dirty ice on a glacier. Eyes that burned with a cold and fierce anger raked over Annie. "Why are you here?" Her voice was cold, too, icy as winter wind. Her appearance was shocking. Last night before tragedy struck she'd been an elegant and love-struck woman, her face alight with joy, diamonds sparkling above a silver dress. Now her coronet braids, tied too loose, tipped a little to one side. She wore no makeup, her skin as gray as the silk lining of a casket. She hunched toward Annie, hands deep in the pockets of her bulky wool jacket. Despite the heavy coat and billowing navy wool slacks, she looked insubstantial. She took another step, close enough so that Annie saw the lines bracketing her eyes and lips, making her look much older than her age, close enough so that Annie felt the intensity of her anger, took a step in retreat.

"I spoke with Carl." Annie pointed up toward the house. "I'm trying to work out what happened last night." Of course, Carl had no knowledge that Annie had come to the point. That didn't matter. He'd accepted her survey of the kitchen.

"Oh." The tension slowly eased out of the older woman's face. She glanced up the path that led to the gallery, nodded. "I see. I didn't know. You help the police, don't you?" Her hands came out of the pockets. She lifted one to smooth back a tendril of hair that had slipped from the braids.

Annie hoped Billy never heard of her elevation to police duty. "I'm just a citizen trying to be of assistance. There's some confusion about the timing of the attack."

Virginia looked down at the yellow tape that marked the position of the body. "I came—" She broke off, pressed her fingers against her cheeks.

Annie ached for the bereft woman. "I'm so sorry, Mrs. Neville. If there's anything I can do . . ."

Virginia's hands dropped, hung limply beside her. "Sometimes Jake and I used to bring a picnic down here. When the weather was nice." She gestured toward the cane. "There's a path from the house—"

Annie pictured the ornate Italian villa that housed the Neville family. Interesting that Virginia didn't call the villa "my" house or "our" house. It was "the" house. How welcome did she feel in Nathaniel Neville's extravagant home?

"—as well as the gallery. This was one of Jake's favorite places on the whole island. He thought it was beautiful." She looked at the uneven mound that marked the remains of the fort. "Did you know there were sixty-two guns mounted here?" Her lips trembled. "I wouldn't have known that. Jake told me." There was a wistful pride in her declaration.

Annie tried to think of something to say, anything to stem the flow of these reminiscences. "There isn't much left." Then she felt dreadful. There was nothing left for Virginia.

But Virginia was caught up in memories. ". . . such a gifted artist. He saw colors that most of us never see. He told me he wanted to paint everything, abandoned shacks and deer and owls. Once, we spent an hour watching the fiddler crabs on the mud flat. He loved to sketch me." There was a lilt of pride in her voice. "He did a lot of drawings of me. And my painting at the house . . ." She looked again at the tape outline. "I can't take it in. It seems like a nightmare that doesn't end." She rubbed the back of her hand against her cheek. "I keep thinking maybe it didn't really happen. I decided I'd come here and look"—she pointed at the place where Jake was found. "So it's true, isn't it." Her voice was dull. Suddenly her face hardened. She spit out the words, sharp as ice slivers. "If only he hadn't come down here with that girl." She looked suspiciously at Annie. "What do you mean, you're trying to figure out what happened? They know what happened. He came down here with a girl. She killed him."

Annie met her gaze without faltering. "Chloe Martin left him alive. There's evidence someone else was here."

Virginia's eyes widened. Shock sharpened her thin features. "Someone else was here? My God, nobody tells me anything. What's going on? Who was here?" She reached out and a clawlike hand clutched Annie's arm. "Who saw them?"

Even through the nylon jacket, Annie felt the sharpness of Virginia's fingernails. The desperate grip was unpleasant, and Virginia stood too near, her breath quick and uneven.

Annie wanted to jerk away but forced herself to remain still. She understood that Virginia Neville teetered on the edge of hysteria. Of course Virginia wanted to know what had happened and what the police knew. She had every right, but Annie didn't intend to identify Elaine Hasty. There was no need. "There's a witness. She was looking out of the kitchen window at the gallery. Her testimony indicates that someone other than Jake and Chloe went to the point."

"Who did this witness see?" The fierce grip tightened. "Who?" It was a cry from deep in her throat.

Annie pried the steel-hard fingers from her arm, stepped back a pace. "We don't know yet. She won't say. But the chief will arrest her as a material witness if she doesn't cooperate." Surely he would. Surely Billy understood the need to force Elaine to speak. The threat of jail time should accomplish that. Elaine wouldn't be so cocky if she found that her silence was a sure ticket to a cell.

Virginia's pale face creased in a petulant frown. "How can you know this person saw anyone if she won't say who it was? Did she see a stranger? Is that it? Did she give a description?"

The shadows from the pine were a swath of darkness across the point. Black clouds bunched in the west. The wind off the water gusted, spinning pine straw across the bricks. Annie shivered, her arms prickling with cold beneath the thin jacket. "Mrs. Neville, I wish I knew more. All I can tell you for certain is that the observer saw someone in addition to Jake and Chloe. She knows the identity of the person, but she's refusing to reveal that information. Don't worry. I'm sure she'll be made to speak. And—" Annie hesitated for an instant. She'd promised Chloe that she'd talk to Billy, make it possible for Chloe to surrender without being jailed. That was a promise— she glanced at her watch—that she had a little over an hour to make good. Now here was a distraught Virginia Neville. If Annie could say anything to lessen the dreadful strain in Virginia's face, she ought to say it. "—I'll let you know as soon as we discover the identity of the other person who followed Jake."

Virginia pressed her fingers against her temples. "I don't understand." She dropped her hands, clasped them tightly together. "Why would anyone follow Jake? You're sure she said it was Jake that was followed, not that girl?"

Annie stared at Virginia. "Yes." She answered slowly, but her thoughts were racing. It made a difference, didn't it? A big difference. Elaine saw Chloe go down the path, then Jake. Anyone who came after him was surely following Jake, not Chloe. Among those attending the reception, who cared enough about Jake O'Neill to follow him into the darkness? The faces of the Neville family drifted through Annie's mind.

Virginia's shaky voice answered the unspoken question. "I don't want to think about it. But I have to, don't I? I know who wanted Jake gone." She took a deep harsh breath. "They all hated him, Carl and Irene and Susan and Rusty. Because he was going to marry me. Louise was always polite to him. And to me. But she didn't want me to marry him." Virginia shivered. "I'm frightened. If one of them killed Jake, it was to make sure they'd get Nathaniel's money. If someone killed Jake for the money, why not kill me?" She looked wildly at Annie. "Tell that policeman he has to find out who did it or I may be next. I have to know who followed Jake. I have to protect myself." The wind gusted again, scattering the pine straw, bending the pines, pulling tendrils of hair from Virginia's braids, billowing her slacks. She brushed the hair away from her face. "When the police find out, you must call and tell me." Her querulous voice had an edge of panic.

Promises, promises . . .

"I'll call." Annie was emphatic. "Now, you'd better get home. It's getting dark and much colder."

"I know." The sound was faint, almost lost beneath the slap of the waves. "Yes. Thank you." Virginia slowly turned away. She stopped once at the stand of cane and looked back at Annie, then she curved around the stalks and was gone.

Annie looked at her watch and broke into a run.

Max brought another straight chair, placed it in front of Billy's desk. He was standing near the door when Mavis ushered Rusty Brandt and Beth Kelly into the office.

As the door closed behind Mavis, Billy stood. "Ms. Kelly. Mr. Brandt." Billy jerked his head toward Max. "Deputy Darling. I understand you wish to see me"—he looked from the quick-moving, slender woman with pain-filled eyes to the stocky, reddish-haired man with deep lines grooving his flushed face—"about the O'Neill case. Please be seated." Billy nodded toward the chairs.

Without looking at each other, Rusty and Beth sat down. Anger pulsed between them. She laced her fingers together, stared at Billy. Rusty tried for a smile, failed. "Billy, you know I want to help if I can. But I've got to know for sure"—he looked from Billy to Max and back again—"everything said here is in confidence. Right?"

"This is a murder investigation." Billy picked up a pen, nudged the tan folder. "If you have some reason to fear that public disclosure of your testimony might endanger you, we will make every effort to keep the origin of the information—"

"Billy, for Christ's sake," Rusty exploded. "It's my wife. You won't tell my wife, will you?"

Beth's lips quivered. She reached up, pressed her fingers against her mouth.

Max leaned against the wall, his gaze bleak. He'd always enjoyed playing golf with Rusty. Loud, boisterous, and profane, Rusty had a joke a minute. Max didn't think they'd ever be a foursome again. Not if Max could help it. Beth's pain flooded the room, waves of hurt and humiliation and loss. Max looked away from her face, so much older than when they'd walked through the door.

Rusty threw out his hands. "Jesus, man, is that too much to ask? Look"—he hitched his chair closer to the desk, ignoring Beth— "everything's a mess. I knew I had to straighten things out when I got that goddamn phone call this afternoon. I mean, I don't like to be hassled. If I hadn't been hassled last night"—he shot a dark look at Beth—"we wouldn't be here right now."

Beth Kelly stumbled to her feet. "Hassle?

Is that what you call it? How about all the lies you told me? You said you loved me. Sure, you'd meet me places, make love to me, stay with me in hotels in Atlanta and Charleston. But when it came down to it, you never intended to leave her, did you?" She was oblivious to Billy and Max, her entire being focused on the red-faced man who kept his gaze averted from her. "Look at me, damn you." Her voice rose, cracked.

"Oh, shit." Rusty pushed up from his chair, exasperated, embarrassed, impatient. Finally, he looked toward her. "Beth, leave it alone. Can't you think about something besides yourself for one goddamn minute?"

Beth slapped her arms across her front. "Something else? Like your wife? Like how you sure don't want your wife to know what you were up to last night? How about me? What do you think the school board will do if it gets in the papers that I was down at the point with you? What if that comes out? All you care about is Susan. You can't even think about me." She turned toward Billy. "I'm not going to say a word about anything if it's going to get into the *Gazette.*"

Billy was reassuring. "Ms. Kelly, if you didn't have anything to do with the death of

Mr. O'Neill, this office will have no reason to release any information concerning you."

"Or me?" Rusty demanded.

Beth lifted her hands in outrage. "Oh, sure, first things first. Got to keep Susan in the dark." Her lips quivered.

"Beth." Rusty spoke quietly, but the muscles ridged in his jaw. "Let's talk about this later." He took a deep breath. "God, I'm sorry, Beth." There was a note of puzzlement in his voice. "I thought we were having fun. That's all."

Billy hurried to speak before Beth could reply. "All right, Mr. Brandt. I'll hear from you one at a time. You first. Your tuxedo jacket tested positive for human blood. Now I'd better make it clear that you have a right to counsel, and anything you say . . ."

As Billy rattled off the Miranda warning, Rusty's face sagged with shock. "Jesus, you don't think I did anything to Jake?"

Billy's stolid expression remained unchanged.

"Oh, God, I never thought of being suspected. It was the hassle. Susan—" He shot a look at Beth, shook his head in exasperation. "But when I got that damn call this afternoon, I knew I had to do something. I damn sure wasn't going to pay some bitch money—"

Max pushed away from the wall, leaned forward. "Hold up, Rusty. What call? When? From whom?" He didn't look at Billy, but he hoped Billy was listening hard. Here was proof that Elaine Hasty should be picked up at once.

"Oh, hell, maybe an hour ago. I don't know who it was. She whispered. I'm pretty sure it was a woman." Anger hardened Rusty's voice. "Anyway, she said she saw me going to the point last night around the time Jake O'Neill was murdered. She demanded money, five hundred dollars in twenties. She called Beth, too, made the same pitch."

Billy pulled his notepad close. "We'll get to the calls in a minute. Blackmail's a serious offense. Murder is a capital crime. I want to know exactly what each of you did last night. And Ms. Kelly . . ." Once again, he reeled off the Miranda warning.

Beth Kelly clasped her hands tightly together. "I didn't have anything to do with murder. All I did—"

"Shut up, Beth. Nobody thinks you killed him. You probably'd never even met him.

My God, we were just at the wrong place at the wrong time." Rusty took a deep breath. "I can explain."

Billy waited, his eyes intent. "I'm listening."

Rusty flung himself into his chair. "Sit down, Beth."

She shook her head and folded her arms tight, remained standing.

His face turned even redder. "Suit yourself." He leaned back ostentatiously. "This is all a lot of trouble for nothing. That's why I didn't say anything last night. She"—he tilted his head at Beth—"was giving me trouble. She insisted we had to talk. I mean, my God, what a lousy time and place. There's Susan and the rest of the family and this stupid party. I didn't want to be there anyway. I told Susan we ought to boycott the damn thing, Virginia ramming that little creep down our throats right in front of everybody we know. Susan said we had to play along. So there I was at the damn party, and Beth comes up to me and says we have to talk. Like I can slip off with her and have a tête-à-tête without anybody noticing. She kept insisting, and finally I told her I'd meet her at the point. I mean, Je-

sus"—he gave a long-suffering sigh—
"women can be unreasonable. I went out
the back door—"

Beth's eyes burned with fury. And anguish.

Max opened his notebook. "What time
was this?"

Rusty shrugged. "I don't know. People
were starting to go up to the tent for the
program. Susan had already left the gallery.
I knew she expected me to come along
pretty soon. Must have been around nine,
maybe a few minutes after. Anyway, I went
down the path and—"

Billy held up his hand. "Take it slow here.
You walked down the path. Did you see
anyone?"

Rusty clawed at his reddish hair. "Hell,
no. Who'd be down at the point on a night
like that? That's why I picked it. Anyway, I
hurried. I knew I better get to the tent before
Susan started to wonder. I came around
that curve by the pines. I couldn't see much
because of the fog. It was cold as Green-
land. I figured the chill would cool Beth off,
get her back to the house. And then Beth
came flying up the path from the point. She
would have screamed her head off if she

could have got a breath. I grabbed her and asked her what the hell was wrong. She said—"

Billy interrupted. "Let her tell it." He turned cold eyes on Beth.

"It was awful." Her voice was husky. "I thought Rusty had gone ahead of me or I'd never have taken that path by myself. It was nine o'clock. I heard the clock—a big grandfather clock in the main hallway—striking just as I went out the back door."

Max nodded. He didn't remember seeing Beth, but it was just about then that Annie caught a glimpse of Chloe running toward the kitchen parking lot.

Beth shivered. "It was scary, the fog hiding everything. I could only see a few feet ahead."

"Did you see anyone? Hear anything?" Max asked quietly. "Take your time. You may be able to help us a lot." His tone was friendly.

She gave him a look of gratitude. Her face lost a little of its tautness. "I don't think so. Not until I got to the point. I waited near the sign to the fort. I thought"—her face squeezed in remembrance—"I heard footsteps on the path into the garden. I whirled and looked. I saw something move"—she lifted her shoulders in a shrug—"I don't know what. It was so dark and foggy. I think"—her voice was uncertain—"somebody was on that path. The other one, not the path from the gallery. I called out for Rusty, but nobody answered." She looked sick. "Maybe it was the murderer."

Billy interrupted impatiently. "Let's get this straight—"

Beth tensed.

Max drew NO on his pad in big fat capital letters. If Billy showed a little more finesse, they might learn something of critical importance.

But Billy was hewing to his own plan. "You thought maybe"—he drawled the word—"you heard something in the garden. And maybe"—again his impatience was clear—"you saw something. Let's stick to what happened."

"It was foggy." Her retort was sharp. "I didn't exactly see anything. I almost"—her shoulders hunched—"didn't find the body. But I was so cold, and it seemed like I waited and waited, and I thought maybe Rusty was blowing me off"—she shot him a bitter look—"like he is. Anyway, I started pacing back and forth and I guess I went farther than I intended toward the shore. I was close to the overlook. I saw somebody lying on the ground. I knew something bad had happened. Nobody would lay down there and not move. It was a man. I froze for a minute and he never moved. Never. I turned and ran. When I was almost to the pines, Rusty came. I told him there was somebody hurt at the point. He told me he'd go and see and I'd better go home, keep out of it."

Max was figuring on his pad:

8:50	Jake takes path.
9:00	Chloe runs through kitchen parking lot.
9:01	Beth Kelly takes path.
9:04/9:05	Beth finds body.
9:06	Beth meets Rusty on path.
9:10	Beth runs through kitchen parking lot.
9:14	Tony Hasty discovers body.

Murder must have occurred—assuming witness's account is truthful—between 8:50 and approximately 9:04. According to Chloe Martin, O'Neill was alive when she left him. That would have been about 8:58, allowing her time to reach the kitchen parking lot by 9:00. This puts the span of time during which the murder might have happened at 8:59 to 9:04.

Max looked at Rusty. "You went down to the point." The bloody jacket was proof. "You found him and left him there without doing anything?"

Rusty flushed at Max's tone. "Hell, man, there wasn't anything anybody could do. He was dead. I got down, looked. How do you think I got blood on me? I mean, I made sure. Then I thought it over. My God, what a mess. Jake dead, and what the hell could I say I was doing out there? Everybody knew I thought he was a jerk. But hey, you don't kill a guy because he's a jerk."

Max gave him a thoughtful look. "Not even when you think he's going to hijack the family fortune?"

"Hell, no." Rusty exploded. He swung toward Billy. "Look, I swear the guy was dead. It had nothing to do with me or Beth. If I'd raised the alarm my wife was going to want to know what the hell I was doing down there—"

Billy leaned back in his desk chair. "Did

you have any conversation with O'Neill at any time last night?"

Rusty flung out his hands. "Not a word. I didn't have anything to say to the creep. Anyway, why would I have Beth meet me there if I planned to kill him?"

Max's tone was casual. "It's never looked like a premeditated crime. Either Chloe Martin killed him and ran away, or she left him alive and somebody killed him after she left. Maybe you got there and heard them quarreling, and after she left, you grabbed up a heavy stick and attacked him. Beth wasn't there yet. You heard her coming and hurried off into the garden. When you got back to the gallery, you headed again for the point, and that's when Beth ran into you."

"Not bloody damn likely." Rusty's voice was strong, but beneath his bluster there was the shrillness of fear. "No way, Max. Not me. I'm not going to be a patsy for any-body. I did exactly what I said. Hell, I wouldn't dare come here and tell you about the blackmail if I was guilty. I'd have had to pay the damn money. Instead I told the blackmailer to get lost. I figured she'd call Beth, too. And she did. I told Beth we had to come and clear things up. Nope, you can't pin this on me. And I'm not paying blackmail to anybody."

Annie rushed inside the police station. She skidded to a stop in front of the counter. "Mavis, is Billy here?" Annie looked up at the clock. A quarter to five. Fifteen minutes until Chloe's call . . .

Even at the best of times Mavis never quite looked relaxed, her eyes holding the memory of old terrors despite her happy years on the island since she met and married Billy. Now her face was tired and drained. "He's got some people in there, Annie. The O'Neill case. I'll let him know you're here." She punched the intercom. "Captain, Mrs. Darling is here. She says—"

Annie leaned over the counter. "I may be able to help him find Chloe Martin, but I need to talk to him about it. As soon as possible."

"—she has information about Chloe Martin's whereabouts. There is some urgency."

Billy's voice crackled over the speaker. "Good." Surprise mingled with satisfaction.

"I can see her in a few minutes. We're finishing up. I'll buzz." The connection ended.

Billy glared at Rusty Brandt. "You should have strung her along. Said you'd pay. Then we could have fixed up a packet for you, taken it to the drop-off."

Rusty folded his arms. "I told her I didn't pay blackmail. I told her to call the cops and be damned. Then I hung up."

Billy's face creased. "So all we have is your word against hers."

"Wait a minute." Rusty held up a broad hand. "I'm not going to make a complaint. And neither is Beth."

Billy's face was about as pleasant as congealed pond scum. "Blackmail's a crime, Mr. Brandt. Your civic duty is to help the authorities. When and where was the money to be left?"

Rusty flung his hands wide. "I'd help you if I could." His voice was hearty. "But like I said, I told her it was no go and hung up. I don't know who called. I don't know where she wanted the money put."

Max's peripheral vision included Beth

Kelly. She looked sharply at Rusty, then her face smoothed into blankness.

"I just took it as a wake-up call to get over here and straighten everything out." Rusty heaved a sigh of relief. "I feel better about everything already." He pushed to his feet. "Come on, Beth."

Billy slowly stood. "You can go for now." It was a growl. "Both of you be here at nine o'clock Monday morning to make formal statements. And I'll tell you something, Mr. Brandt. You'd be in jail right this minute, but I think you're telling the truth—you and Ms. Kelly—about what happened last night. Otherwise, the blood on your jacket would be spatters, not soaked in. See you Monday."

"Mrs. Darling—" The voice was familiar.

Annie swung about, looked up and up. He was so tall, so very tall. "You came to the store yesterday. Bob Winslow." He loomed over her, shoulders hunched, his long mild face creased by worry. Young Lover Two, and Chloe had hidden from him. Annie stuck out her hand.

He grabbed her hand, crushed it, pulled

her farther from the counter before loosening his grip. He spoke in a low voice. "Mrs. Darling, do you know where Chloe is?" He poked his glasses higher on his bent nose. His dark spaniel eyes were imploring. "I heard you talking to her." He looked toward Mavis. "They say Chloe's a fugitive." He shook his head "That's crazy." His hands tightened into fists. "It's nonsense. Chloe never hurt anybody. I'm not going to let them put her in jail."

"Bob"—Annie beamed at him—"I know Chloe's innocent. She told me Jake was alive when she left the point. But she is a fugitive, and that's what has to be dealt with. I'm going to try and persuade the chief to release her to Max and me."

The door to the office corridor opened. Beth Kelly's heels clattered against the hard floor she walked so fast. Rusty Brandt hurried to catch up. "Wait a minute, Beth. Wait a damn—" The door closed behind them.

Annie gave a whoop of relief. "Billy's free." She flung hurried words toward the gangling Bob Winslow—"We'll talk when I come out"—and yanked open the door.

Mavis half rose from her chair. "Billy hasn't buzzed yet."

Annie looked up at the clock. Thirteen minutes to five. "That's okay. I'll knock." As the corridor door sighed shut behind her, Annie hurried down the hallway. Was Billy in his old office or had he taken over Pete Garrett's? It was two doors down. Light spilled from the partially open door. Yes, Pete's office. Would his unit be gone for a year? The last they'd heard he was in Kabul, interrogating terrorist prisoners. Annie lifted her hand to knock, froze like a statue when she heard Max's voice.

". . . did you see her face? Beth Kelly looked shocked as hell when Rusty claimed he hung up before the blackmailer said where the money was to be left."

Annie lowered her arm, eased close to the sliver of space between the door and jamb.

Billy was glum. "Yeah. I picked up on that. She knows he's a lying son of a bitch, but she's scared to death something will come out in public." A chair creaked, the wheels rattling against the floor. "It doesn't make any difference. If neither one will file a complaint, there's no point in our picking up Elaine Hasty. Besides, since Brandt and

Kelly came in, there's nothing more Hasty can tell us."

Annie pressed near enough to see a slice of the office. Billy stood behind his desk, one hand massaging the back of his neck.

Max's face furrowed in an intent frown. "Wait a minute, Billy." Max's tone was thoughtful. "Maybe she saw someone else."

Billy gave a hoot of disbelief. "Come on, how many people do you think went down to the point last night?" He held up his hand, flipped his fingers forward, one by one, "We got O'Neill. We got Chloe Martin. We got Beth Kelly. We got Rusty Brandt. Don't tell me you think somebody else was there!"

"Beth Kelly thought she heard something on the path into the garden." Max shrugged. "Sure, it could have been a raccoon. And she was spooked by the fog. But maybe there was somebody there. If somebody took that path, who was it? Not Chloe Martin. Annie saw her on the gallery path. I leaned on Rusty, suggested he might have gotten to the point before Beth, killed O'Neill, taken the garden path, circled around to come up the gallery path and meet Beth as she fled from the body. But I don't think there was enough time. Not if he left the gallery about nine. The murder was either committed by Chloe Martin or it occurred between Chloe's departure and Beth's arrival. Somebody else could have followed O'Neill, listened to him and Chloe, then attacked him after Chloe left. The point is that the only way this could have happened was for someone to have followed O'Neill. We know Elaine Hasty was watching out that kitchen window. We know she saw Chloe take the path to the point. Then she saw O'Neill. If anybody followed O'Neill, she knows. She saw Rusty and Beth, but they went independently. If they're telling the truth, they didn't follow O'Neill. And like you said, the stains on Rusty's jacket support his story that he was checking to see if O'Neill was still alive. We better talk to Elaine Hasty."

Billy gave a huge yawn. "Oh, we can talk to her. I'll have Lou bring her in Monday. We'll make sure she corroborates Brandt and Kelly. I don't think there's anything else there. But she's done us a good turn. Her trying a spot of blackmail on Brandt and Kelly has cleared things up considerably.

The fact that they came in pretty well clears them. Now if we can find Chloe Martin . . ."

Annie pushed through the door. She looked from Billy to Max—bless him for thinking hard, for keeping an open mind, for being her own dear wonderful Max—and back again.

"Yeah, Annie." Billy waved her inside, his eyes stern. "What have you got for me? If you know where that girl is, you got to tell me." His voice was as hard and unrelenting as a rock.

Annie gave a desperate glance at the clock. Eight minutes to five o'clock. Max always urged her to be tactful, to think before speaking, to emulate the charm and wisdom of Charlie Chan, Earl Derr Biggers's Honolulu sleuth ("The man who is about to cross the stream should not revile the crocodile's mother."—*The Black Camel*).

With a loud tick, the hand of the old-fashioned clock jerked to seven minutes before the hour.

Annie was no Charlie Chan. She was tired, upset, frantic to make Billy understand, to reach him across the towering barrier of his resentment at Chloe's escape. Annie strode across the room, her shoes clicking loudly against the tile floor. She reached his desk, leaned forward, slapped her hands against the gray metal surface.

Billy stood with his feet spread apart, arms folded, as easy to move as a mountain. He looked much older than when they'd first met, a tousle-haired giant with a rugby player's strength and a country boy's openness. His appealing cowlick now contained streaks of gray. His face was heavier, lines of fatigue and stress cutting a groove from tightly compressed lips. He'd seen the ugliest that humans can do to each other, and those sights had marked his soul.

Annie stared into blue eyes that she knew well, eyes that adored when he looked toward his wife, brightened when he played with his stepson, glowed when voices lifted in angelic praise in church, eyes that now burned with determination to do a job well for a man gone to war and for the island he loved. She looked deep into the eyes of her friend, her dear and treasured friend. Big, brave, insecure, uncertain.

Annie's face softened. She reached across the desk, placed her hand on a muscular, rigid arm. "Billy, do you remember when Mavis was frightened?"

It was like watching a kaleidoscope move, blend, reform. The elements were unchanged, the pattern utterly dissimilar. His somber face held memory of the days when Mavis had fled an abusive husband, fearing for her life and for Kevin's. It was Billy who'd found her running down a dark road, her head bloody, carrying her crying toddler. It was Billy who'd brought her to the island, helped her find a job, rented her a cabin at Nightingale Courts. All of this, his love for Mavis, his fear for her when murder came near, his devotion, looked at Annie from anguished blue eyes.

Annie's hand dropped. "Last night Chloe was scared. Do you remember what scared her? Not a murder charge, awful as that would be. Not being questioned. She was terrified of being locked up. She can scarcely bear to talk about it. You see"—Annie's tone was thin, as if the words were hard to say—"when she was little—maybe five years old—she misbehaved and her aunt locked her in a closet, a dark closet. Chloe cried and cried and cried, but she couldn't get out."

"Five years old?" Max's voice was grim.

He took two steps, stood beside Annie, slipped his arm around her shoulders.

"Five years old." For an instant the office was utterly still, quiet enough to imagine the hiccuping wails of that long-ago child. "If you lock up Chloe, it will be like dangling somebody who's afraid of heights over a canyon. Sure, maybe there's a rope, maybe there's no way to fall, but that doesn't help. Nothing helps that kind of fear. If you put Chloe in a cell, she will fall to pieces. And"—Annie's voice quivered—"she said she'd rather die, that she'd walk out into the water. Oh, Billy, I know she shouldn't have run away. But she's out there somewhere with no place to go and no one to help her, and night's coming on and it's going to rain. I know you have to question her, maybe even hold her as a material witness, but you don't have to put her in jail to do that." Annie raced ahead, talking faster and faster, the words running together, hard to understand. "She can wear an ankle monitor or wrist monitor or whatever those things are. You know, when people are under house arrest and they can't go places, they wear something that beeps or zings so you know where they are every minute. She can stay at our house. She'll have to promise to stay at our house and there won't be any way to remove the monitor—" Annie heard the tick as the minute hand on the clock moved. Three minutes to five. She plunged her hand into her purse, grabbed her cell phone. "And you can ask her all about that night, and she'll tell you how he was alive when she left the point. I'm sure Elaine Hasty saw somebody else follow Jake because I know Chloe's innocent. Billy, please!" She ended with a gulp for breath.

Billy stared down at his desktop, his face heavy with thought. And indecision. He kneaded his cheek with the knuckles of his right hand. Finally, he lifted his head, still frowning. "The evidence against her is damn strong. There's other stuff to check out, but I'm making no promises that she won't end up charged with murder. Probably second-degree. No premeditation. Still"—his tone was reasonable—"the investigation isn't over. If she turns herself in—" He looked up at the clock. It was one minute to five "—I'll agree to a twenty-four-hour monitored detention at your house, providing she agrees to be questioned."

"Oh, Billy." Annie beamed at him. "You're wonderful."

Max gave Billy a thumb's-up.

Annie smiled at them both. She yanked out the phone. "It's all going to work out. Chloe's going to call me at five o'clock." Relief pumped her voice. Annie held up the phone. She waited, her face eager. When Chloe called, Annie would explain, tell her she would be safe at Annie and Max's house. Not locked up. Never locked up.

The minute hand ticked to the hour.

Another minute passed.

Another.

The phone didn't ring.

· *Ten* ·

At five past the hour, Billy glanced at his watch. "So she promised to call." His voice was dour and cold, his gaze sardonic. "I tell you, Annie, she's acting guilty as hell. And how come you've been talking to her? Where is she?" He scooped up a small legal pad, flipped it open, waited.

"I don't know." Annie traced her fingers lightly over the buttons of the cell phone. "She didn't say. Except she could see the water . . ." Her voice trailed away. "I can't believe she hasn't called."

"If she calls again"—Billy's voice grated—"get in touch with me. Or she won't be the only one I put in jail."

Annie's chin lifted. "How about Elaine Hasty? Are you going to let her get away with hiding what she knows?"

"We know what she knows." Billy threw out an impatient hand. "You've been listening at doors, so you know Brandt and his lady friend were on the point last night. Hasty's blackmail is a flop. I can't help it if they won't make a complaint." His face flushed with resentment.

Annie's eyes flashed. "You can pick up Elaine, interrogate her—"

"What do we ask? We know what she saw. She saw Brandt and his girlfriend." Billy slammed down the pad. "You want to ask Elaine Hasty questions, you do it. Maybe you'll be lucky and find out"—heavy sarcasm weighted his voice—"that another five or six people were down on the point. Hell, maybe a baker's dozen for all I know. Of course, it's strange they didn't bump into each other. As a matter of fact we know Brandt and Kelly were there and they didn't see another soul. Nothing except a body. You can bet they would have told us if they had. Who knows? Maybe Elvis was there. I can't wait to find out. But not tonight. The only thing that interests me right now is the hunt for Chloe Martin. I've got deputies coming to the island tomorrow with dogs. We'll find her. Right now, I'm going home." He reached down, grabbed up a folder. "I got these statements to read." He took a breath, shot her a conciliatory glance. "That was good work on your part, Annie. But"— his frown returned—"this investigation's fouled up, and it's all because that girl's a runaway. I've got to talk to these people"— he rattled the folder—"on Monday as well as Hasty and Brandt and Kelly. Plus I got to keep hunting for Martin. You do what you please. In between chatting up a fugitive on your cell phone."

He moved heavily and wearily to the door.

Annie called out, "Billy—"

Max reached out a long arm, pulled her close. "Let it go, honey."

Annie looked up into sympathetic blue eyes. "Billy's not going to do anything about Elaine Hasty."

"Not right now." Max's voice was kind. And sad. "Annie, I know you're on Chloe's side, but it looks like Chloe's spun you a tale. She promised to call. She didn't. So how likely is it she's telling the truth about what happened with her and Jake? And

Billy's right. How many people could have been there?"

Annie shot back. "I heard you say that Beth thought she heard someone on the garden path. Max, somebody else could have been there."

"Maybe. It's a damn long shot." He shrugged. "There were only a few minutes between the time Chloe said she left him alive and when Beth Kelly found him dead. I don't think there was time."

"Yes, there was." Annie's tone was resolute. "I asked Doc Burford. He told me it would only take two, maybe three minutes to kill him. There was time. So we've got to find Elaine. If anyone else took the path to the point besides Rusty and Beth, Elaine saw that person."

"If you're right," he said quickly, "Elaine will have tried blackmail there, too. If she thinks she's got money coming, she won't say a word."

"Maybe we can persuade her. And"—Annie brightened—"if she won't tell us anything, that's a kind of proof right there. Then we'll follow her. If she picks up an envelope of money, well, Billy will have to pay attention to that."

"Follow her? That's a lot easier said than done. Okay." He was reassuring. "We'll give it a try. After all, Billy said you could talk to Elaine if you wanted to. We'll take my car, leave yours here for now." He grinned. "And I'm still a deputy."

As they came down the hall, angry voices rose in the waiting room. They pushed through the door. Billy stood face-to-face with a frowning Bob Winslow. The front door was wide open. Mavis stood outside on the top step, tying the belt of her raincoat, looking back worriedly at her husband and the tall young man.

Winslow blocked Billy's way. "I have a right to know what you are doing."

"I'm investigating a murder." Billy was not as tall as Winslow but he was forty pounds heavier. He leaned forward, his face stony. "You want to know more, read the *Gazette.* Or talk to them." He jerked his head toward Annie and Max. "Now"—Billy swept a big hand and the folder crackled—"everybody out. The station's closed. Out."

As the door slammed shut, Billy grabbed his wife's elbow, hustled her to the cruiser parked in the chief's slot. The engine roared.

The wind rattled the leaves in the magnolia. The air was heavy and wet with the smell of approaching rain and the salty scent from the sea. A black cloud bank hid the setting sun. Harbor lights glittered in the fading twilight like diamonds scattered on black velvet. The water, already dark as a pool of tar, surged toward shore, the slap against the harbor wall relentless, unending. Light from a lamppost spilled down over the three cars in the station parking lot—Annie's Volvo, Max's Maserati, Bob Winslow's Ford Explorer.

The taillights of Billy's cruiser diminished, disappeared.

Bob Winslow hunched against the cold breeze. "Mrs. Darling—"

"Annie. Please." She braced for his questions. She had no answers, and she was afraid, terribly afraid, for Chloe.

"Annie." Bob's voice was gruff. "You're Chloe's only friend. If she's going to ask for help from anybody, it will be from you. If she gets in touch, will you call me? Let me help? I've got a card." He pulled out his billfold, found a card. "It's got all my numbers, office, home, cell. I'll keep my cell on."

"I will. I promise." Annie shivered. She'd

made a lot of promises this day and had yet to keep a one of them.

"Yeah." Winslow stood a moment longer, then walked heavily to his car.

Annie grabbed Max's arm. "Come on, let's go."

"Faster." Annie leaned forward, straining against the seat belt, peering out into the night.

"Deer," Max said briefly. But he increased his speed. Nightingale Courts was no more than a five-minute drive from the harbor.

"I'll call Duane, see if Elaine's in her cabin." As Annie pulled her cell phone from her purse, it rang. She glanced at the illuminated number, knew it at once. "It must be Henny." A quick frown. "I wonder why she's still at the store." Death on Demand closed at five on Saturdays in the winter. Annie's voice lifted. "Maybe she's heard from Chloe." She pressed the button. "Henny, have you heard from—" she paused. Maybe she should be cautious. "—from the girl who called earlier?"

Over static, Henny spoke fast. "No. Not a word. But there has been a disturbing call."

Henny's voice was somber. "Just before closing, a man called, asked for you. I said you weren't in, could I take a message. He laughed. It was nasty. More of a giggle. Think Richard Widmark in *Kiss of Death.* A slimy voice. He said to tell you, 'People who cause trouble get trouble.' The words were slurred. I'd say he'd had too much to drink or was on drugs. After he hung up I checked caller ID, but I'd grabbed it up on the first ring, so nothing registered. Anyway, are you with Max?"

Annie looked toward her husband, his features just discernible in the glow from the dashboard. "Why, Henny"—Annie was amused—"don't tell me an old World War II pilot and Peace Corps volunteer who's been to Africa thinks a gal has to have a man around to protect her?"

Max turned an inquiring face.

Annie waved his attention back to the road, which curled among a dense stand of pines.

"My dear"—Henny's voice was acerbic—"gothics had a point. There's nothing like a white knight rushing in to save the heroine in the penultimate chapter. Or the dark and brooding master of the manse with a heart of gold, literally and figuratively." There was a slight pause, then faster than a speeding bullet, Henny snapped, "Foggy Cornish coast. Governess. Alvean."

Equally quickly, Annie retorted, "*Mistress of Mellyn,* Victoria Holt."

"Okay, okay." Henny laughed. Then she said quite seriously, "That call wasn't nice. Somebody doesn't like you—"

From her tone, Annie knew Henny was truly worried by the call.

"—so take care. Stick close to Max, independence be damned. Tell him I said so." The directive was brusque. "If you still need help at the store, I'll be glad to come in on Monday. Are you getting anywhere?"

The headlights illuminated the arched entrance to Nightingale Courts.

"Oh, Henny, we hope we're making progress." Annie added, her voice soft, "Thanks, friend."

"Friends . . ." Henny's rich contralto was thoughtful. "Another offering from Laurel. This time she quoted from *Shadows on the Rock* by Willa Cather, 'to a solitary and an exile his friends are everything.' I guess that sums it up for Chloe. Good luck, Annie."

Annie clicked off the phone. Her smile faded.

Max looked at her. The car slowed. "What's wrong?"

She reached out, touched his arm. He knew. Without being told, he knew when she was worried. She lifted her chin. She'd be damned if she'd let a slime—how well Henny had caught the sound of J. J. Brown's voice—frighten her. But—she took a breath. "Henny got a phone call threatening me. She said the voice was slimy. I'll bet anything it's that guy from Snug Harbor."

"Threatening you?" The car rolled to a stop in front of the entrance.

Annie shook his arm. "It's just a phone call. He's that kind of creep. It doesn't matter right now. Let's go." She craned to look toward the cabins.

Max hesitated, then nosed the Maserati beneath the arch at the entrance to Nightingale Courts. "Hardly anybody home." Duane and Ingrid's cabin was dark. Lights glowed in cabins 2 and 4. Cabins 3, 6, and 7 were dark.

Annie frowned. "If Elaine's there, she's sitting in the dark. Damn. Max, what can we do? How can we find her?"

The lights from the Maserati illuminated the front of Elaine's cabin as Max braked.

The front door was ajar.

Annie looked at Max, yanked the handle. She was out of her seat before he put the car in park, cut the motor. She rushed up the steps, pushed the door wider, fumbled for the light switch. There was a general air of disorder, magazines tossed carelessly on the warped coffee table, the cabinet doors wide open in the kitchenette, the wastebasket overflowing. Boxes were stacked along one wall, Elaine's belongings crammed in haphazardly.

Max was right behind Annie when she stepped into the bedroom. The drawers of the chest were open and empty, the mattress bare of cover. The closet door stood wide. Discarded hangers dangled from the rod. More boxes held clothes and shoes.

"She's all packed up to move." Annie clenched her hands into fists. "Max, this proves she saw someone besides Rusty and Beth."

Max looked bewildered. He flung out a hand. "Because she's moving out?"

"Exactly." Annie's eyes were bright. "This afternoon she said she wanted to move, but she didn't have enough money. If she's packed her stuff, it's because someone's promised to pay her off."

Max looked at the boxes. "I'd say she's going to move out tonight. We can stay here, wait for her."

Annie hurried back into the living room. Max followed. Annie shook her head. "If only we'd gotten here a little sooner. I'll bet she's gone to get money. I wonder . . ." Annie walked over to the side table that held the telephone and answering machine. The light flashed. "She called Rusty and Beth." Annie shot a quick glance at Max, then, her face determined, reached down and punched the play button.

Tony Hasty didn't mince words. "Elaine, call me. I know you're ducking around trying to avoid me. Don't be a damn fool. If you saw anything, you call the cops."

The second recording startled Annie. Chloe Martin's voice was high and distraught. "I know you're there. It won't do any good to hang up on me. You can't tell the police I was the only person you saw. You can't do that to me." The connection ended.

"Chloe called Elaine." Annie worked it

out. "Elaine answered, and when Chloe asked for help, Elaine hung up. So Chloe called back. Do you suppose Chloe came here?" Annie looked slowly around the room.

Max frowned. "Did Chloe tell you she intended to contact Elaine?"

"No." Annie had told Chloe of her conversation with Elaine to offer encouragement. Apparently Chloe had mounted her own investigation. Perhaps that's why she hadn't called Annie at five, she was busy trying to find out what Elaine knew. Where was Chloe now? Had she ridden her bike here, found this empty cabin? Or had she found Elaine? If Elaine refused to talk to Chloe, where was Chloe now?

Annie shook her head. "I don't get it. But I'm sure of one thing. Elaine wouldn't let Chloe slow her down. Elaine was determined to get money. She must be on her way right now to the drop-off spot. Max, if only we knew where it was."

Max's eyes narrowed. "Rusty claimed he didn't know where the money was to be put, but I'm sure he was lying. Elaine may be waiting there right now." Max yanked the keys out of his pocket. "There's a chance we can join the party."

The back of the Brewster Arms overlooked a swimming pool embraced by clumps of palmettos. Beyond the lighted pool lay a dark lagoon. Apartment 24 was on the second level. As they walked up the outside steps, a fine rain began to fall. Annie wished she had on her down jacket instead of her windbreaker. The cold, cheerless night matched her mood. No word from Chloe. Elaine gone. Now their hopes rested on the possibility of cajoling information from an angry woman.

Max rattled the brass knocker, a dolphin curved in a graceful arc.

The outside light flicked on as the door opened. Beth Kelly looked out. For an instant, her expression was unguarded, hope flashing like a comet before destructing into the bitterness of disappointment. "What do you want?"

"Your help." Once again Max spoke quietly. No bombast. No demand. "Annie and I are trying to find the woman who attempted to blackmail you. This won't involve you in any way. Will you talk to us for a minute?"

Annie stepped forward, edging past Max. Beth often shopped at Death on Demand. Her favorite author was Anne George, the wonderfully funny southern mystery writer whose untimely death left her fans and admirers remembering her with warmth, rereading her books to hold on to her charm. "Beth, you bought a lot of books over Christmas. Do you remember the girl who's been working for me? Chloe Martin?"

Slowly, Beth nodded. "The redhead?"

"The police think Chloe killed Jake. Chloe thought she was in love with him. He was stringing her along, but he was going to marry Virginia Neville and—"

"Stringing her along?" Beth's fingers closed around the thick gold chain that glittered on her black velour pullover. Her red lips twisted. "Join the club. You've heard about Women Who Love Too Much. I've got a better one, Women Who Pick Sorry Bastards to Love. Oh, yeah, Chloe and I can get together, talk about men—"

"Not if they put Chloe in jail." Annie reached out. "If we can find the girl who tried to blackmail you, we may be able to prove that Chloe is innocent."

Beth's tear-reddened eyes looked from Annie to Max. "I don't know who called."

"But you know where the money was to be left." Max stated it as a fact.

Beth pushed back a strand of blond hair. "If I tell, you'll keep me out of it?"

Max nodded. "All we need is a place."

She took a deep breath, held the door wide for them to enter.

The living room was small but cheerful, a Navajo rug hanging from one wall, watercolors of the beach above the fireplace, a red-and-yellow plaid sofa, two forest green easy chairs, another Navajo rug on the floor. Books filled the cases on one wall.

Beth waved them toward the easy chairs. She stood by the fireplace, her face somber. "How'd you know Rusty was lying?" She gave a harsh half laugh, half sob. "Why do I even ask? He's always lying. Okay, here's what happened. I got the call about four. Like Rusty said, she spoke in a whisper. She said she'd seen me last night going down the path after Jake O'Neill. She'd tell the police unless I paid up. I was to tape an envelope with five hundred dollars in twenties to the back of the Fort Loomis sign at the point. The envelope had to be in place by six o'clock."

She reached out to the mantel, touched the Venetian glass clock shaped like a cat. It was ten minutes to six.

The dirt road had been scoured by last week's nor'easter. Max's hands tightened on the steering wheel as the Maserati's wheels bumped in the uneven ruts. "Damn. It's a public road. Why don't they grade it?"

Annie patted his knee. Max loved his red car, and despite the rough ride and the slanting rain that splashed into puddles, turning the sand soft and slippery, he was driving as fast as he dared. The dashboard clock read 6:01. They were too late for the deadline set by the blackmailer, but as Max had pointed out, they weren't being black-mailed so it made no difference. However, if greed propelled Elaine, she was there right now, looking for her bonanza. Moreover, this was the likeliest road for Elaine to have taken. It ended at a turnaround about thirty yards from the fort and its sign.

"Almost there," he said reassuringly. He

reached out, turned off the car lights. "No point in announcing our arrival." The car slowed to a cautious crawl as it came around a curve.

"Max, look!" Annie pointed to the dark shape of a car parked in the turnaround. "I'll bet that's her car."

Max reached toward the headlight switch, changed his mind. "We'll surprise her." He eased the Maserati to a stop. Annie started to open the door.

"Wait a minute." Max turned and backed until the Maserati was sideways to the trunk of the parked car, effectively blocking the road. He took the flashlight from the car pocket. He turned it on just long enough to confirm that the car in the darkness was Elaine's tan Camry. "Okay," he whispered. "Let's move quietly. See what we can find out."

The rain pelted down. By the time they reached the graveled path that curved around the base of the ruins, Annie's hair was drenched and her clothes plastered against her. Her feet ached with cold as she splashed through puddles. She hoped Elaine Hasty was equally miserable. Where was she? Was she waiting near the sign, growing ever angrier that her hopes for quick money had come to nothing?

Rain trickled coldly down Annie's back. The physical sensation was nothing to the sudden coldness in her mind. If Elaine waited for money that hadn't come, did that mean she'd seen only Rusty and Beth, that the movement Beth had sensed on the garden path was nothing more than an inquisitive raccoon? Ahead of them the canebrake wavered in the rain.

Annie tripped over a branch. She flailed, went down, heard her own thrashing with dismay. Damn. Now Elaine would be alerted. Of course, if she was waiting to pick up a cash-stuffed envelope, she might think the noise signaled the approach of her victim. Max reached down to help her up. "I'm okay." She knew her slacks were now muddy as well as wet. She started forward, Max close behind. They reached the tall shoots of bamboo, coming ever nearer to the circular pavement of bricks and the dark hump of the ruined fort.

Max eased ahead. Annie kept a hand on his back. Abruptly, Max stiffened, stood still.

Annie bumped into him. "What's wrong?"

He didn't answer. Instead, he clicked on the flashlight. The beam poked into the wet night, insubstantial and diffused, but there was light enough to see the body of Elaine Hasty sprawled near the Fort Loomis sign, her open, sightless eyes staring skyward in the unending wash of the rain.

"Oh, Max." Annie leaned against him.

They stood, shocked and shaken, and there was nothing but the darkness of the night pressing against them and the sound of their quick breaths and the splash of rain and the wash of the waves against the rocks.

Then the silence shattered, broken by the *crack, crack, crack* of faraway gunshots, dimly heard but unmistakable.

Max grabbed Annie, held her close in a protective embrace. He bent toward the road, peered into the wet darkness.

A man shouted, distance muffling the cry.

Some of the strain eased from Max's arm. "It's that way." He gestured toward the road. "Must be up at the Neville house." He was brusque, quick. "Get to the car. Call for help. Stay there. Lock yourself in." He jammed the keys into her hand. "Anything odd, drive like hell. I'll go see."

The light from the flashlight wavered as he ran.

"Max, wait!" But he was gone. Annie never hesitated, running as fast as she could after him. As she splashed through puddles, she turned on her cell phone, fumbled to find nine-one-one, pressed. When the connection was made, she shouted, "Murder. At the point near the Neville Gallery. Gunshots at the Neville house. This is Annie Darling. Max and I will be up at the house." She clicked off the phone.

She was perhaps fifteen yards behind Max when he reached the garden behind the grandiose mansion. The ornate structure was a replica of a stuccoed villa on the Amalfi coast. Two wings extended from a central block. Two circular fountains sat on opposite sides of the tiled courtyard. Security lights glittered high in the live oak trees.

The door in the center of the main block of the house stood open. Rusty Brandt hesitated there, then bolted out into the courtyard, weaving and ducking to reach a tall stone urn. He crouched there, shouted, "Put up your hands. I've got you covered." But he remained huddled behind the protection of the urn.

Max called out, "Hey, Rusty, Max Darling here. I heard shots. What's going on?"

Rusty cautiously peered around the urn. "Hell if I know."

In the doorway behind him, Susan cried, "Rusty, keep down. Come back inside. I've called the police. Oh, my God, what's happening?"

Max took the terrace steps two at a time, thudded to a stop by the urn. He gave Rusty a quick glance and saw that he was unarmed.

Rusty reached out a shaking hand, grabbed Max's arm. "Have you seen anybody?"

Max was impatient. "Not a soul. Where's the trouble?"

A woman's voice called from a balcony on the south wing. "What's happened? I heard shots. Rusty, who's down there?" Every light in the courtyard came on, flooding the wet expanse with a sharp glare, revealing every statue, every stone bench, every huge pot, every palmetto, and the two fountains with water arching from twin dolphins.

Annie ran up the wide terrace steps. She had a jumbled impression of noises and movement, Susan Brandt edging out into the courtyard, Louise Neville remaining in the doorway, Irene Neville leaning over the balcony's edge, Rusty Brandt's shoulders hunched defensively, Carl Neville bursting out from a side door in swim trunks, clutching a thick cream-colored towel. Annie thudded to a stop next to Max.

Rusty's freckled face was pale, his eyes huge. "Somebody shot out a French door in Nat's study. See, over there." He let go of Max and pointed at the north wing and a long row of French doors on the first floor. His hand still shook.

The upper panes in one French door were splintered.

Rusty was short of breath. "How'd you get here so quick? Susan just called."

"Who shot off a gun? Who, dammit?" Irene's voice was shrill. "Wait a minute, I'm coming down," and she banged into the house from the balcony.

Shivering, pulling the towel around his shoulders, Carl slapped barefoot over the tiles toward his brother-in-law, skidding on the slick surface. "What's going on?"

"Your dad's study—" Rusty still pointed. The curtains were open and the study was as clear to see as an elegant setting on a stage. Bookcases lined every wall. Easy chairs and sofas were scattered about the large room. One sofa faced the French doors. There was movement on the floor.

"Oh, my God, is that Virginia on the floor?" Susan's voice was shrill.

Virginia lifted her head, her eyes wild. She got up on her hands and knees, scrabbled toward the French door. Shakily, she pulled herself upright. She flung open the damaged door and plunged into the courtyard, rushing toward Rusty. "Help me." Her voice was high and frantic. "Help me. Someone's shooting at me. Oh, God, help me."

"Virginia!" Carl hurried forward. He moved past her, reached the entrance to the study. He stepped inside, then cried out. He bent down, clutched at his foot.

Virginia looked wildly around. "Who shot at me?"

Max reached out, gripped a thin arm. "Are you hurt?"

She stared at him and began to cry. "Oh, I thought I was going to die." She strained to see past him. "Who's out there?"

The rain pelted against them, harder now.

Carl braced himself against the jamb of the door. "There's glass everywhere."

Virginia shuddered. "The glass broke." She sounded bewildered. "There was a terrible noise. I got down on the floor. That's how I got hurt. There was glass on the floor." She held tight to her left arm. Blood seeped between her fingers. "I didn't dare come out until I heard Rusty."

Susan splashed across the tiles. She took Virginia's elbow. "Let's go inside. Come on, Virginia. I'll take a look at your arm."

Irene stood on the top step of the terrace. She held up one hand to shield her face from the rain. Her magenta wool sweater and slacks were spotted by the rain. Everyone looked bedraggled. Rusty's shirt and slacks were drenched. Susan shivered, brushed back wet tendrils of hair. Carl's skin puckered from cold, and blood dripped from one foot. Max's suede jacket was drenched, his trousers sodden, and his sneakers waterlogged. Annie turned up the collar of her windbreaker, felt the stickiness of mud on her slacks. Only Louise, standing in the doorway, her pinched face creased in worry, was dry. She held up a blanket.

"Yeah, let's get out of the damn rain." Rusty waved his arms. "Come on, everybody. Let's take a look." He stepped toward the open French door.

"Hold up." Max's shout brought everyone to a standstill. "Not in there. We need to keep everything as it is for the police."

Rusty swung around. "Oh, sure. This way, everybody." He headed across the courtyard and up the shallow steps to the house.

Virginia ducked her head and hurried. She held her arm pressed against her blouse. Susan walked with her. As they came inside, Louise draped the blanket around Virginia's shoulders.

In the marbled hallway, the brilliant light of a chandelier revealed a motley and uneasy group. Everyone talked at once, their voices uncertain, querulous, frightened. A plump woman in an apron waited near a side door, looking about uneasily.

Outside a siren shrilled.

Annie said quietly to Max, "I called nine-one-one. They know about Elaine."

Max nodded. "If she was shot . . ." He gave a considering glance toward the courtyard.

Rusty gestured toward the front door. "It's

the police. Max, will you let them in? I'll take everybody"—he glanced at Carl's bloody foot and Virginia's arm—"to the breakfast room. Susan, can you see about some alcohol, bandages?"

Max bent toward Annie. "Keep an eye on everyone."

Annie nodded. A blackmailer's death not more than a hundred yards distant. Shots here. Cause and effect? If so, the reason was obscure. But there had to be a link. She hurried after the family members into the kitchen and breakfast room area. A rib roast sat on a platter. The succulent aroma filled the kitchen. Lids rattled atop pans on the stove. Annie glanced around the room with its bright yellow walls, shiny white table, and rattan chairs. The room's everyday appearance was marred by the strained, anxious faces and the bloody footprints left on the tile floor by Carl.

Susan bustled about, pulling out chairs for Virginia and Carl. She glanced toward the middle-aged woman with a white apron over her dark dress. "Sylvia, please bring me some alcohol and gauze and tape. Hold out your arm, Virginia." Susan's brisk tone evoked no response. Virginia slumped in a

chair, the blanket bunched behind her, her
arm resting on the table. Her eyes were
sunk in her strained face, her lips set.
Louise, her lips pressed in a tight line,
brought a decanter of whisky, poured a
good two inches into a small glass, placed
it beside Virginia.

Carl unwound the towel from his foot,
wrapped it up again. His hands were trembling. He looked anxiously at Virginia.
"What happened? I was in the pool and—"
He saw Annie's look of surprise, smiled
briefly. "Indoor pool. I was taking a swim
before dinner and I heard shots."

The housekeeper returned, carrying a
plastic bottle of alcohol, a box of gauze,
scissors, tape, and a plastic basin. She
placed everything on the table, hesitated,
then moved toward the stove, lifted lids, ad-
justed heat, glancing nervously toward the
doors that overlooked the courtyard.

Virginia shuddered. "I was in the study.
Someone shot at me." Her voice was deep
and harsh.

Susan stood with the bottle of alcohol in
one hand, the cap in the other. "At you? Oh,
no. That can't be."

"I heard the shots." Irene smoothed back

her vivid dark hair. Her lovely face was creased in a frown. "I was putting on my makeup." She lifted a hand, lightly stroked her cheek.

Louise said nothing, but her dark eyes never moved from Virginia's face.

Virginia's eyes, brilliant with anger and fear, moved to each of them in turn. "Last night someone killed Jake. Tonight someone tried to kill me."

Susan sloshed alcohol over Virginia's arm. Blood swirled into the basin.

Virginia drew her breath in sharply, briefly closed her eyes.

Rusty's head jutted forward. "That's absurd."

Louise pointed toward the door, still open to the night. "We should have searched out there."

Susan bent over Virginia's outstretched arm, frowned. "This may need stitches."

Virginia, her face a cold mask, glanced without expression at the uneven cut on the side of her forearm. "No. Cut small strips of tape, close it up. It's clean."

Annie stepped forward. "We can call Dr. Burford." He was most likely already on his way. Just like last night, the mechanics of a murder investigation were surely under way, the arrival of the forensic team, the gathering of evidence, the photographs and filming, the painstaking survey of the surroundings.

Rusty stalked across the floor, leaving more wet footprints on the cream-colored tiles. He stood beside his wife, glared down at Virginia. "Don't make things worse than they are. I don't know why anybody shot at the house. It's crazy to say they were shooting at you. Who would know you were in the study?"

Virginia pulled her arm free. She pushed back her chair and stood, the blanket sagging to the floor. She looked at each family member in turn, her lips quivering. "All of you." Her voice rose hysterically. "That's where I am every evening. Eating by myself because I'm not welcome to eat with you." Bitterness laced her voice. "All of you know that—and all of you hate me." She fingered the bandage on her arm. "There was an awful noise. Loud. The glass cracked. I threw myself to one side. I fell on the floor and crawled to hide behind the couch. I thought whoever it was would break through the door and run across the room and lean over the couch and shoot me. I lay there and waited to die." Her eyes glazed. "I waited to die." Her voice broke. "I was afraid to move. I waited and waited . . . and then I heard people outside, shouting. I crawled to the door—that's when I cut my arm—and peeked out, and everyone was there so I came out. But one of you . . ."

The lovely room with its smell of food was utterly quiet. From the front hall came the sound of men's voices and heavy footsteps. Billy strode into the breakfast room, Max close behind him. Billy's yellow slicker glistened with raindrops. Beneath the curved bill of his hat, his face was set in a hard mask.

Annie glanced toward Max. He gave an infinitesimal nod. So Billy had been down to the point, seen the sprawled body lying in the rain.

Virginia moved unsteadily toward him. She looked up, her face imploring. "You can keep them from hurting me, can't you?"

Rusty slammed his hand against a blue cupboard, rattling the dishes. "Billy, she's off her head." He glared at Virginia. "For God's sake, nobody knows who shot into the study. We all ran to see what was happening. Now that you're here, you can look it over. Whoever did it must be miles from here. Maybe you can figure out something."

"At least three shots were fired into the study," Billy announced. "But we haven't found a weapon."

Rusty threw up his hands. "Virginia thinks the shots were aimed at her. Well, the curtains weren't drawn. Whoever came up to the window could see inside. Hell, maybe they were shooting at her. I don't know. But I, for one, am damn cold and wet. I'm going to take a shower and then"—he looked toward Sylvia, holding a hot pad, her eyes flaring like a startled horse ready to bolt—"you can get our dinner ready."

"Dinner can wait." Billy pointed at a chair. "Take a seat, Brandt. Nobody's leaving this room for now."

Carl's head jerked up. "Your tone seems offensive to me." His mild face was puzzled. "We called the police because there's been an unfortunate incident. We expect to cooperate in an investigation, but your attitude is unwarranted." He leaned forward.

Susan snipped a length of gauze. "Hold still, Carl." She wound the wrapping around his foot. "Tell me if it's too tight."

Billy's voice was heavy. "An unfortunate incident. Yeah. Murder's always unfortunate." He moved around the room, staring at legs and feet, ignoring their questions. "Wet. They're all wet. It could have been any one of them." His cell phone buzzed. He unstrapped it from his belt, punched to receive, held it to his ear. His blunt face never changed. Finally, he asked, "Doc's sure?" In a moment, he clicked it off, looked at each face in turn. "Shots here. A body—shot to death—found at the point at a little after six o'clock. Nobody's leaving this room until we've searched the house."

"Someone else? Where Jake died?" Virginia Neville's voice was hollow. She reached out toward Billy. "Who? You have to tell us! Who's been killed?"

"One of the catering staff. She was working at the party last night." Billy's voice was grim. "Elaine Hasty."

"One of the catering staff . . ." Virginia swung toward Annie. "This afternoon you told me there was someone who might know who had followed Jake. You said you were going to talk to her." Tears began to edge down her face. "This girl who's dead, is she the one? Could she have told us who killed Jake?"

Each word hurt Annie. "I tried. . . ." Annie's voice faded away.

Virginia reached out imploring hands, the bandage stark against her left arm. "You promised."

Max's face was hard, his words quick. "Annie talked to Elaine. I talked to Elaine. She refused to say who she saw last night. She said people who'd never paid her any attention were listening to her now. She asked for money." His gaze was bleak. "She got murder."

"Blackmail . . ." Virginia lifted trembling fingers to her lips.

"Chief?" Frank Saulter, water dripping from his poncho, poked his head into the breakfast room. "Got something."

Billy jerked his head toward Max. "Keep 'em quiet." He walked out into the main hall, listening to the low rumble of Frank's voice. In a moment, a door slammed.

Carl brushed back a lank strand of hair. His face was slack with shock. "Elaine Hasty . . . God, that's awful." He looked down at his hands. They trembled. He clasped them tightly together.

Louise marched to the refrigerator, yanked out a container of orange juice, poured a glass. She brought it to Carl, then looked defiantly at Max. "Everything's running late. Carl's diabetic. He needs something to eat."

Carl lifted the glass with a shaky hand. His face was pale. "Thank you, Louise."

Annie glanced toward Irene. Carl's wife looked uninterested, one finger twirled in a thick tangle of lustrous dark hair. It was Louise who stood by Carl's side, watching him anxiously.

Virginia stared wildly around the room. "That girl murdered—and someone shot at me. I was supposed to die, too." She folded her arms across her front, rocked back and forth.

Annie felt pummeled by emotion. Virginia teetered on the edge of collapse. Her fear, utter and complete and overwhelming, dominated the room.

Footsteps thudded in the central hall. Billy walked into the breakfast room, Frank Saulter behind him. Billy flung a sodden heap onto the floor. Rivulets of water puddled away from the soggy mound. "We fished these out of the fountain." He used the toe of his black shoe to edge apart two canvas gardening gloves, puffed with water.

"Gardening gloves." Susan spoke quietly. "They could belong to anyone, come from anywhere."

Frank moved past Billy. He wore a surgical glove on his right hand. He held a small pistol by the tip of the barrel. "How about this, Mr. Brandt?"

But it was Susan who darted forward, bent to look at the weapon. "That looks like one of Dad's guns." She whirled toward Carl. "I thought you were going to get rid of them."

Annie was aware of them all, the bubble of panic in Susan's voice, the flaccid droop of Rusty's cheeks, the brooding frown on Louise's face, the predatory sharpness of Irene's elegant facial structure, Carl's bewildered stare, but she kept her gaze on Virginia. Virginia stared across the room at the gun as if it were a snake, horror twisting her face.

Carl pushed up from the chair, limped to stand beside his sister. He reached out for the pistol.

Frank pulled back his arm. As the barrel

dipped, drops of water spattered onto the floor. "We'll fingerprint it."

Carl's hand dropped. His face was tight and grim. "Those initials on the stock, NN. It's Dad's gun all right."

Irene's heels clattered on the floor as she hurried to her husband's side. "What does it mean?" Her sultry beauty was gone and in its place the drawn and tired look of a frightened woman. "Who put it in the fountain? How did they find Pop's gun?" Her head jerked toward the windows, her eyes wide and staring. "How did they get in?"

"Get in?" Virginia's voice rose and cracked in a hideous parody of laughter. "Oh, that's so funny. How did they get in? Nobody got in, Irene. It has to be one of you with Nathaniel's gun." She pointed at each in turn, Susan with her hands pressed against her cheeks, Carl staring at the gun in shocked disbelief, Irene plucking at the strands of a carnelian necklace, Rusty jutting his head forward pugnaciously, Louise looking like an aged, frightened crone.

Virginia swung toward Billy. "I demand protection. I want a policeman with me until I can get off the island, get away from here." She licked her lips, her breathing shallow, her eyes darting around the room to settle on Carl. "Listen, I'll sign over everything to you right now." She threw her hands wide. "The Gallery. The bank accounts. All of it. Everything. Get me some paper. I'll sign it and they"—she pointed at Annie and Max— "can witness it. The police can sign it too. I'll leave in the morning. I'll only take my clothes and enough money to get a start—"

Carl took two steps, winced as he forgot and put his weight on his injured foot. He stopped in front of Virginia, his sensitive face glacial. "Don't be an utter fool, Virginia. No one wants what belongs to you. You'll be safe here if I have to sit outside your room with a gun myself. There has to be a reasonable explanation for all of this. Like Dad's guns—one day when Jake was here, I was looking for something in Dad's desk and Jake saw them." His eyes shifted to Billy. "They were more for show than anything else. A pair of twenty-two caliber revolvers with pearl handles, both initialed. Some old friend gave them to him years ago. A bet of some kind."

"I told him guns brought death." Louise nodded like a bird over a worm. "I told him and he laughed."

Annie looked at the gun, small in Frank's gloved hand. Little but deadly. A gun didn't have to be big to kill.

Carl took a deep breath. "Jake thought they were cool and I said he could have them. I supposed he'd taken them. I didn't give them another thought."

"Jake?" Virginia shook her head. "He would have told me. I'm sure he would have told me."

Irene turned from a cabinet. She held a wineglass and a bottle. She filled the glass to the brim, drank it down, choked a little. "Would he have told you?" Her voice was sharp. "My dear Virginia, he didn't tell you everything, did he? He didn't tell you about the pretty girl he met at the point, did he? Maybe he had the guns. Maybe the girl knew about them. Maybe she got one and came here tonight—"

Annie had heard enough. "Chloe never said a word about any guns—"

"She would scarcely tell anyone, would she?" Irene challenged. She stalked to Billy. "Do we appear to be mad? I ask you. Why would one of us commit a murder, then try to shoot Virginia with a gun that belongs in the family?"

Carl came up to his wife, caught her hand in his. "Irene's right. This is crazy. None of us would shoot at Virginia." But his eyes slid back toward the gun, uncertain, worried, frightened.

Virginia's voice shook. "Carl, I've always liked you the best. You've been nice to me. But somebody shot at me. If it was that girl . . . Oh, God, I hope it was. But I don't see how she could get Nathaniel's gun. And Carl, my God, where's the other gun?"

· *Eleven* ·

"Okay, people." Billy might have been addressing marine boot camp recruits on Parris Island. "Eat your dinner. Wait here until called for an interview. Max, Annie, come with me."

They followed Billy out of the breakfast room to the huge central hallway, its black-and-white marble flooring muddied by the investigators but still incongruously cheerful beneath the glittering chandelier with tier after tier of almond-shaped globes. The door to the courtyard stood open, and the sound of the steady rain was a dismal accompaniment to Billy's heavy steps. In the center of the hallway, a Sheraton drum table held a huge jade green porcelain vase filled with spectacular blossoms, including bird of paradise with brilliant orange and blue flowers.

Billy stopped by the table, looked at them, his face grim. "How the hell did you find her?"

Max described their determination to talk to Elaine, their arrival at her cabin, the packed boxes, the messages from Elaine's father and from Chloe Martin—

Billy's eyes gleamed. "From Chloe Martin? How did she know about Elaine Hasty?"

Annie took a deep breath. She didn't want to answer, but she had no choice. "I was trying to encourage Chloe when I talked to her this afternoon. I told her about Elaine working at the party and that Elaine knew Jake. I told her Elaine saw somebody follow Jake. I wanted to make it clear that the police would talk to Elaine, find out what she'd seen." She didn't say anything about Billy dismissing that idea. But her eyes accused him.

"You talked to Hasty today. Max talked to her. We knew what she was up to." Billy was dismissive, not defensive. "I was going to interview her Monday. I didn't go after her tonight, but you did. And you missed her. We can't help it if she set herself up for trouble." He rubbed the side of his nose. "Thing about it is"—he was thinking aloud—"she didn't know Brandt and his lady friend had come to us. So she didn't know there wouldn't be a payment. She went ahead out to the point." His eyes swung toward Annie. "Maybe Martin followed her."

Annie clapped her hands on her hips. "Why would Chloe shoot Elaine? And where did Chloe get the gun? Remember, the gun came from this house."

His response was quick as a dart. "Sure, the gun was in this house originally, but O'Neill took the set. Where would he keep the guns? In his cabin. Thing about it is, Annie, you won't see the forest for the trees." Billy was patient. "Martin said she was coming to see Hasty. Who lived next door? You can bet Martin figured that out. Maybe he'd told her about the guns, said he had them at his place." Billy nodded his head at Max. "Max, go to Nightingale Courts, check out O'Neill's cabin, see if there's any trace of a search. Nothing was disturbed when

Lou looked it over earlier today. I'll bet Martin found out Hasty was another one of O'Neill's girlfriends—"

Annie pushed away her memory of Chloe's ragged sob on the telephone.

"—and that may be the whole story right there. Martin killed O'Neill because she was jealous. Tonight she decided to blow away both Elaine Hasty and Virginia Neville. Annie, you've tangled with something you don't understand."

"I understand that Elaine was trying to blackmail a killer. She saw someone besides Chloe and Rusty and Beth." Annie clenched her hands. "And I understand it was a lot easier for someone in the Neville family to get that family heirloom gun than for Chloe to search Jake's cabin and find it." She stared into Billy's stubborn eyes.

"Furthermore"—Billy was insistent—"if we're going to talk probabilities, how crazy would somebody in the family have to be to shoot Hasty at the point then trot right up here and shoot at Virginia Neville? That's nuts. The end result was to tie the crimes to this house. No, the only thing that makes sense is what we started with, a jealous woman who's out of control. Now"—he took a deep breath—"I still want to know how you got from Hasty's cabin down to the point."

Max flicked a fallen leaf from the table. "Beth Kelly. Just like we figured, Billy, Rusty lied when he said he hung up before the blackmailer specified a drop-off place."

Billy frowned. "So Hasty told Brandt and Kelly where to bring the money?"

Max was crisp. "Right. The deadline was six o'clock."

Annie could be crisp, too. "If Beth knew about the drop-off, so did Rusty. I figure at least three people knew—Beth, Rusty, and the person Elaine saw following Jake."

Billy shook his head. "Good try, Annie. Lots of luck proving it."

As she switched on the kitchen lights, Annie's eyes went immediately to the counter and the telephone caller ID. The little red light blinked rapidly, signaling a message. She didn't take time to shrug out of her jacket or to pick up Dorothy L., who paced near the sink, her meows making the point that supper was way overdue and the dry food still in her bowl was stale, thank you very much.

Annie grabbed the phone, punched the message number and the code. She kicked off her wet shoes, wriggled out of her sopping jacket, grabbed a thick dish towel and dried her hair. Tucking the receiver under her chin, she listened as she opened a can of cat food and spooned it into Dorothy L.'s bowl.

Message 1—"Annie, Henny here. I hung around until six. Mr. Giggle called again. Nastier this time, possibly drunker. I know Billy's got a full plate, but he needs to check this out. No other calls. I'll talk to you tomorrow." A pause. "Stick with Max."

Message 2—"Dear Children—As Publilius Syrus so wisely—"

Annie retained the receiver between her ear and shoulder while slapping together a sandwich. Laurel sounded in her usual good form. A smile tugged at Annie's lips.

"—exhorted, 'Do not turn back when you are just at the goal.' " A pause to encourage commitment and rededication. "When I called and there was no answer, I knew you and Max were abroad despite the inclement weather, still seeking truth. I'm sure you are making progress. As Cicero remarked, 'For how many things, which for our own sake we should never do, do we perform for the sake of our friends.' I applaud your zeal and remain ever confident that you shall prevail. Huzzah."

Annie smiled. Huzzah was surely a fetching farewell. Annie hung up and took a bite of her sandwich. The microwave pinged and she pulled out her mug of hot chocolate. She sat at the kitchen table, ate, and wished she felt as sanguine as her mother-in-law. The one call she'd hoped for had not come. Annie had almost recovered from her exposure to the cold, steady rain, but a chill touched her heart. Where was Chloe? She'd left her aunt's house on a bicycle. She was out in the cold, rainy night with no shelter. She must be sodden and miserable, chilled to the bone. Yet she hadn't called for help. There was no word from Chloe, nothing at all to explain why she hadn't called the police station as she'd promised. Annie could understand if Chloe's fear of being locked up kept her on the run. But was that the reason? Chloe had tried to contact Elaine Hasty. Everything conspired to further implicate Chloe. If Max found that Jake's cabin had been searched, Billy would be convinced the intruder was Chloe and her trophy the set of matched .22-caliber pistols. If only Chloe would call . . .

Dorothy L. jumped onto the table, oozed toward the plate, pink nose twitching.

Annie flapped her hand.

The plump white cat's paw whipped out toward the plate.

Annie jerked the plate away. "Ham is not good for cats." She bent forward until her eyes were inches from Dorothy L. "Are you laughing at me?" In fact, Dorothy L.'s round face looked amused. "What would you say if you could talk?" Annie picked up the last half of her sandwich in one hand, stroked thick fur with the other, looked deep into mesmerizing but unknowable golden eyes. "Let's see. Maybe: Cats are beautiful, people are stupid. Or possibly: Why did you come home by yourself? Or emphatically: You're okay in a pinch, but I want Max." Annie finished her sandwich, picked up the soft, sweet-smelling cat, and buried her face in Dorothy L.'s thick white ruff. "Oh, Dorothy L., so do I."

In a moment, Dorothy L. wriggled free, dropped to the floor, and waited until Annie poured fresh dry food into her blue plastic bowl. Yes, it was a bad idea to continue to feed a cat at almost midnight, setting in train who knew what unfortunate habits and importunate expectations. But Annie knew whose will was strongest, and it wasn't hers.

As she rinsed the dishes from her late supper and put them in the dishwasher, Annie felt a flicker of the old resentment. Dorothy L. was right. Max should be here. In fact, it was he who normally fixed their late night snacks. She pushed away the pang of sympathy. He'd probably not yet had a bite of dinner.

He still wasn't home when she padded downstairs a half hour later in her robe and pajamas, warmed by a hot shower. Max had dropped her off at the station to pick up her Volvo. The last she saw of him, the red taillights of the Maserati were disappearing in the gloom. So here she was, fed, comfortable in her oversize pink terrycloth robe, and fixing another mug of hot chocolate. She carried the cocoa and a notepad and pen and the portable phone—just in case— to the family room. She decided against a fire, settled on the sofa.

Dorothy L. leaped onto the sofa and wormed beneath the afghan draped over Annie's legs. Annie put the mug on the coffee table and flipped open the pad. She stared at the empty sheet. Wouldn't it be nice if automatic writing really worked, if she could close her eyes—à la Arthur Conan Doyle—and summon a useful spirit who could tell her who shot Elaine Hasty and carried the gun through the night to blast the windows of the study where Virginia Neville awaited her dinner tray.

Annie scrawled in thick black letters: Why Virginia?

She stared at the query, drew a line through it. First things first. She printed: Why Elaine Hasty?

That was easy. Whether Billy agreed or not, Elaine's death proved that she had indeed seen Jake's murderer and it was someone other than Chloe. Everyone knew Elaine had seen Chloe. She'd admitted as much to Annie, so Chloe had no reason to wish her dead. Chloe had been hurt when she realized Elaine was another of Jake's women, but she emphatically had not turned into the unreasoning and deadly figure of jealousy envisioned by Billy.

Oh, if only they'd found Elaine in time. But the result might have been the same. She'd refused to tell Annie whom she saw from the window of the gallery kitchen. She'd refused to tell Max. There was no reason to believe she would have revealed what she'd seen even if they had reached her at the point before the murderer.

Annie flipped to a fresh page, repeated her original question: Why Virginia Neville?

A white paw shot from beneath the afghan, knocked the pen from Annie's fingers. Annie lifted the soft cover, looked at bright eyes. "Are you making a cat statement? Of course, if you could talk, you'd make pithy, cogent comments encapsulating everything that mattered. Right?"

Dorothy L. purred.

Annie fished for the pen, found it. Maybe Dorothy L. had a point. Some things were obvious. Elaine Hasty tried to blackmail Jake's murderer. The price wasn't right and Elaine was killed. In fact, Elaine was shot. Moments later someone shot at Virginia Neville. So here's what mattered—

Annie wrote fast.

1. **Murder weapon and gun used to shoot into the study one of a pair that had belonged to Nathaniel Neville.**

2. Who had access to the guns? Everyone in the Neville house, plus Jake O'Neill. According to Carl Neville, Jake expressed interest in the pistols, but there was no proof Jake had taken possession of them. If Jake had the guns, it was possible, though unlikely, that Chloe Martin might have known about them and obtained them.

Annie glanced at the phone. It was too late for Chloe to call tonight. Surely she would call tomorrow . . . if she was innocent. . . .

3. Everything depended upon when Elaine Hasty was shot. If she was killed immediately prior to the shots being fired into the study, there was no time for the murderer to regain the house and dry off. If, however, Elaine was gunned down a few minutes earlier, the murderer had time to walk up to the Neville house, go inside, put away a coat and wet shoes,

and then, protected by an umbrella and perhaps bare feet— Carl Neville in his swim trunks?— step into the courtyard, fire into the study, regain the house. A quick return of an umbrella to a stand, dry feet in shoes, and there would be nothing to distinguish the murderer from the other shocked members of the family, especially after they came out into the rain to investigate the shots.

Annie sketched the courtyard. The gunman could shoot, toss the gun and gloves into the fountain, and dash into the house, ready to jettison an umbrella.

As for Chloe, why would she discard the gloves and gun? Annie could see a reason. The gun was a link to the Neville house and its occupants. How awkward for the family to try and explain its use as a murder weapon.

Annie massaged tired eyes. More than awkward actually. The gun and the shots into the study brought murder home to the Neville house. Wasn't it crazy to focus suspicion there? Until the gun was fired into the study, police suspicion had centered upon Chloe Martin. Why change that perception? What could possibly be motive enough? Granted, the members of the family had every reason to be resentful of Virginia. But was a desire to assure an inheritance worth becoming suspect in two murders? No matter how much one of the clan might want the money, not a one of them would have wanted to make so dreadfully clear and unmistakable the link between the house and the death of Elaine Hasty.

Annie could almost hear Billy's skeptical voice. "Looks like a frame to me. Nobody at the Neville house would be that dumb. No, the Martin girl got the gun somehow. . . ."

Annie finished her cocoa, put the pad on the coffee table. Yawning, she snuggled against the cushion. Her eyes began to close as she listened to the comforting purr of Dorothy L., curved against her chest.

The phone rang.

Annie flailed awake. Dorothy L. launched herself, using her claws. Annie felt the sting against her skin, blinked, came to her feet, lunged for the phone.

"Hello." She heard her voice rise, knew it

was lifted by fear. Max, was Max all right? She was enveloped by the atavistic unreasoning panic that blossoms at night in the dungeons of the mind when horror lurks behind doors that decently remain shut in sunshine.

"Annie." Lou Pirelli's voice was brisk. "Got a nine-one-one. Somebody smashed in the front of your store. I'm on my way. I caught Max at Nightingale Courts. He's on his way. I thought you should know, but you don't need to come. We'll take care of everything."

Before Lou hung up, Annie was running for the stairs, shedding her robe.

Death on Demand blazed with light. Great shards of glass poked from each corner of the front window. The glass in the front door—now standing wide open—was broken as well. Annie edged inside. The stench of gasoline was heavy.

"Oh damn, damn, damn." Two of the titles in the front window—*The House Without a Key* and *The African Poison Murders*—were very fine firsts, each worth several hundred dollars. She stepped carefully toward the window, bent near the glass-covered books, sniffed. She gave a sigh of relief. No gasoline. And the rain didn't splash far enough beneath the overhang to reach the display. She turned back toward the door. Gasoline seeped from a tin that lay on its side in the entryway. She bent toward the container, then jerked her hand back. No, there might be fingerprints. But at the very least, surely she could use something to sop up the spilling fuel.

Annie started down the central aisle. "Lou?"

The storeroom door banged open. Billy moved heavily toward her, his tired face drawn in a dark frown. That frown was directed at her. Not at the mess. Not at the intruder who'd apparently intended to set fire to her store. No, Billy's glower was aimed specifically at Annie, she had no doubt about it.

Annie stopped in surprise. Why was Billy here? Damage to her store was ugly—and she was pretty sure she knew the culprit—but vandalism was unimportant compared to murder. Why was Billy here, and why was he angry with her and not with the vandal? Then she saw Max. He came out of the storeroom. His look held love. And a question.

Annie didn't understand the hostility emanating from Billy, but she was in no mood for argument. She pointed at the front of the store. "I think I know who did this, Billy. His name is J. J. Brown. He's a big damn bully who used to work at Snug Harbor until I got him fired yesterday morning—" She heard her own word with surprise. Yesterday? It seemed an eon ago. "—for being ugly to an old lady."

Max made a fist. "By God, he's going to pay for this. Here's what happened, Billy." Quickly he sketched Annie's experience at the retirement home.

Billy flipped open his cell phone, punched numbers. "Mavis, put out a pickup for J. J. Brown—" He looked inquiringly at Annie.

"Six foot three. Sixty-two years old. A Gouda cheese face. Greasy black hair that hangs to his shoulders. Plaid shirt. Levis. Husky. A beer paunch." Annie pressed her fingertips against her temples. "Silver ring in his left ear. Brown eyes. Fat hands."

Billy repeated the description. "Last known address Snug Harbor. Wanted for vandalism, attempted arson." A pause. He kneaded a fist against his cheek. His tone was weary. "I don't know. I'll get this buttoned up. Yeah. See you when I see you." He clicked off the phone, returned his gaze to Annie, and once again his face was closed and suspicious.

Annie glanced back at the tipped-over gasoline tin. "I need to clean up the mess." She swung back to Billy. "Who can I thank for ringing up the police before Brown set fire to the place?" She didn't want to think how easy it could have been for a blaze to rage beyond control. In January no one had occasion to walk on the boardwalk of shops in the middle of the night. In summertime, lovers might stroll in the moonlight; visitors staying aboard the luxury yachts in the marina might share wine and conversation in deck chairs; even an occasional merchant might linger after hours. But this was January, the marina had no guest yachts, the one movie house was closed until spring, and the boardwalk that curved around the harbor was deserted.

Billy's eyes slitted. "A woman called. From here." He jabbed his finger at the phone sitting on the cash desk. "From this number. Screamed somebody was smashing the front glass, tossing in gasoline. She yelled for help, hung up."

"A woman?" Annie's mouth opened. Oh, dear God.

"Come back here." It was a command and a brusque one. Billy headed for the storeroom, head lowered, shoulders bunched.

Annie looked at Max. His dark blue eyes were somber. She took a deep breath, hurried to catch up with Billy.

In the storeroom, he stood on the other side of the table where they unpacked shipments of books. Three boxes sat against the wall: *Murder on the Mauretania,* Conrad Allen, St. Martin's; *Death of a Dustman,* M. C. Beaton, Warner; and *Basket Case,* Carl Hiaasen, Knopf.

Crumpled in the narrow space between the table and the wall was a moss green sleeping bag.

"So"—Billy folded his arms, demanded— "I guess you didn't have any idea somebody was spending the night here?"

"No." She stared down at the heap of bedding. Suddenly Max was beside her, his arm around her. He gave her shoulders a quick squeeze. Annie blinked back tears.

He understood. There was something infinitely sad and helpless and frightening about this uncomfortable sanctuary. Annie understood. That's why Chloe had never called. She'd been trying to get in touch with Elaine. And then the rain began. She had no place to go and she had to stay dry, but she couldn't bear to call Annie when she was using Annie's store as a hiding place. "Oh, Billy"—Annie stirred, looked toward the back door, which stood open— "where is she? Dear God, where do you suppose she is?"

Billy shoved his hat to the back of his head. "I never thought you'd do this kind of double-dealing. You lied to me, Annie." His tone was disappointed, his gaze dark with bitterness.

Annie was too tired, too frightened to resent his accusation. But Billy was right in one assumption. The sleeping bag had to belong to Chloe Martin. No one else conceivably would have chosen to spend the night in the storeroom. And as a practical matter, Chloe had a key. She'd often opened or closed the store during the Christmas season. As for why . . . it was Bob Winslow who'd looked hopefully at Annie, said that Annie was Chloe's only friend on the island, and if Chloe contacted anyone, it would be Annie. "Billy, I didn't know she was here." Annie spoke quietly. "You can believe me or not. That doesn't matter. What matters now is where she's gone, what's happened—"

There was a thud of running feet in the alleyway. Lou Pirelli burst through the doorway. "Chief, better take a look out here. Near the end of the alley . . ."

For a big man, Billy moved fast. He was out the door, following the stab of Lou's flashlight. Annie and Max hurried after them, clattering down the slippery steps. A light glowed above the back stairs of Death on Demand. None of the rear entrances of the other businesses were illuminated. Once beyond the light from Death on Demand, there was only the swath cut by Lou's flashlight. They splashed through puddles. The rain had eased to a fine drizzle. Lou stopped near the end of the alley. He held out the flashlight. Its beam traveled slowly over the blue bicycle that lay on its side, the front wheel twisted into the air. A red knapsack had tumbled out of the basket. One strap lay partially submerged in a murky pool of oil-filmed water.

"Looks to me like there was a crash. But there wasn't anything to bump into. So I kept looking and here's what I found." Lou moved the beam, sweeping it back and forth across the alley to settle on a broken piece of brick. Lou stepped closer, knelt, held the light within an inch of the fist-sized piece of brick. A tangle of red hair, perhaps three or four strands, clung to the jagged end. "That dark smear—I think it's blood."

"Move it a little to the left." Max raised the hammer.

Annie shifted the big square of plywood, wondered if he didn't have the better job. Plywood was heavy. There was still a nasty smell of gasoline even though the floor had been scrubbed and the container taken into custody last night by Lou Pirelli.

Max pounded. "Good. That gets the bottom. Now for the top . . ." He climbed the ladder, set to work nailing the protective sheet to the frame.

Annie stepped back. She'd get new plate glass installed tomorrow, but the plywood was protection against the weather until then.

The weather . . . She turned, stared out at the sweet sweep of blue sky and the glittering water. Friday's fog and Saturday's rain might never have occurred. They didn't even need a sweater on this sparkling Sunday afternoon, the kind of day that made the South Carolina seacoast a haven for winter vacationers. Golfers would pause to watch a heron in the marsh near a green, and tennis players would hear the caw of crows over the *thwock* of balls. But the forecast was for more storms, and there was a warning haze on the horizon. Annie shivered.

Max reached the ground, tossed the hammer into the tool chest, nudged it shut with his foot. "Come on, Annie, it will be okay."

"Max"—she flung out her hands—"how can Billy still think Chloe's guilty? It's simply crazy to think Jake would ever have talked to her about those guns. She didn't know where he lived—"

Max had already heard it, chapter and verse. "Annie, you have to admit she made that call to Elaine Hasty. And you know what I found last night."

She nodded. It was no help to Chloe's cause that the desk in Jake's cabin had been searched, the drawers left open. Lou Pirelli had left the cabin locked yesterday, but Elaine Hasty likely had a key. Elaine may have opened the door to retrieve a keepsake, left it ajar. For that matter, a window could have been unlocked. No one bothered much with locks on an island. Getting into Jake's cabin would have been easy for anyone. Unfortunately, that included Chloe. Annie grudgingly understood Billy's reasoning. The call made by Chloe to Elaine proved that Chloe knew where Elaine lived. It wasn't much of a leap to imagine Chloe coming to Nightingale Courts when her repeated calls went unanswered.

Annie charged into battle. "It makes a lot more sense that someone from the Neville house got those guns than Chloe." It was Virginia who understood the danger that murder had been committed with one gun of a pair and the second pistol was nowhere to be found. "Obviously Virginia's scared to death. Last night she was terrified to be in the same room with those people."

Max shrugged. "That's when she thought the gun could only have been taken by a member of the family."

Annie pounced. "Virginia insisted that Jake didn't say a word about the guns to her."

"Then who"—he was equally combative—"searched Jake's cabin?"

Annie frowned at him. "You're sure it was searched?"

"I'm sorry, honey. I wish it weren't so." His voice was kind. "Come on, let's have some coffee." He bent down to pick up the tool chest, held open the front door of Death on Demand.

Midway down the central aisle, Annie stopped to scoop Agatha into her arms. The black cat, green eyes glistening, permitted a brief squeeze, then gave a warning hiss and squirmed free.

At the coffee bar, Annie studied the collection of mugs. She chose *Unsolved* by Bruce Graeme for Max and *Where Is She Now?* by Laurence Meynell for herself. She poured the strong black Colombian, cradled her cup, and stared at the title. "Max"—her voice was small—"I'm frightened for Chloe. Why can't they find her?"

She took a gulp, welcoming the dark flavor. "And why can't they find that big jerk?" She glanced at the round-faced clock. "It's been more than twelve hours since he smashed in the window, and it looks for sure like he hurt Chloe and they haven't found a trace of either of them. Billy promised he'd call as soon as they knew anything. And there's been no word at all. Where do you suppose Brown took her?" Yesterday she'd worried that Chloe might be unjustly accused of murder. Now the fear was worse. J. J. Brown was cruel, Annie had no doubt of it, and he specialized in viciousness to those in his power. If Chloe was his prisoner . . . "He couldn't have got off island by the ferry."

Agatha jumped to the top of the coffee bar, nudged her head against Max's hand. Absently, he petted her.

Annie eyed her cat coldly. She was getting tired of being an also-ran. Dorothy L. ignored Annie if Max was present. And here was Agatha, cozying up to Max—

"Damn." Max jerked his hand so quickly he jolted the mug and coffee splashed onto the wood. A curved welt across the back of his hand welled with blood. He glared at

Agatha, who was in midair, a leap from the coffee bar to the nearest table. "Why'd she do that?" He grabbed a paper napkin, pressed it against the wound.

Annie flipped on the cold water in the sink. "Put your hand under the water for a couple of minutes." She watched the clock. Her vet had made it clear that cat bites needed plenty of cleansing. When she was satisfied the wound was clean, she reached into the cabinet and pulled out the rubbing alcohol, which was kept there for just such an eventuality. "Keep your hand over the sink."

He did. "Ow." Now the glare was for Annie. "She's your cat. Why'd she bite me?"

Annie screwed the cap back on the bottle, flung out a hand toward the front of the store. "Smashed windows. Gasoline. Pounding hammer." A smile tugged at her lips. "Who's supposed to be in charge here?"

Slowly, he responded, a small smile but a beginning. "Cat logic?"

Annie returned the alcohol to its place, made a mental note to buy another bottle. Dreadful how fast it went. She looked at Agatha, but the sleek cat was ostentatiously ignoring them, her back to the coffee bar, industriously licking one paw, applying it to her face. Cat logic . . .

"Better than some people's logic. Look, Max, this is a small island. I don't think much of our police department if—"

Max's cell phone was in his pocket, but the muffled ring shocked Annie to silence. Billy had promised to call . . .

"Here they come." Billy pointed across the whitecapped sound at the gleaming white Coast Guard cutter as it nosed toward the island, slicing through the waves. He glanced at Annie. "We'll see if you can iden- tify him for us. We picked up a palm print on the bottom of the gasoline tin. It matches prints we got from the apartment he had at Snug Harbor."

Annie was grateful for her thick pea coat. Yes, the sun shone, but a sharp cold wind tugged at her hair, whipped her slacks against her legs. She shielded her eyes against the sun. There, trailing behind the cutter, was a motorboat that might have been new fifty years ago. The original paint had long ago dimmed to a mottled coffee color.

Max shaded his eyes. "The motorboat looks empty."

"They got him." Billy's tone was confident.

Annie stood on tiptoe. "What about Chloe? Did they ask him about her? Are they hunting for her?"

"They don't have her. We'll know more when we talk to them." Billy moved toward the end of the dock.

Annie and Max hurried after him.

It didn't take long for the cutter to dock, crewmen in orange float coats securing it with heavy ropes at both bow and stern. A small metal gangway came down. An officer walked down the steps. He looked trim and fit despite the bulky orange float coat. A captain's insignia glittered on the front of his dark blue ball cap. He strode to Billy, hand outstretched. "Captain Cameron? Captain Dooley."

Billy shook hands. "Where'd you find him, Captain?"

"Adrift. Off the Fripp Island dry dock wreck." Sharp eyes looked out of a thin, sun-wrinkled face. "Apparently he ran out of gas. He's had a lot to drink, but he was sober enough to shoot off a flare. Still had some whisky. We took charge of it. He's refused to answer any questions, but we'd received the alert."

The gangway creaked as two armed law enforcement petty officers hustled a big man down the steps.

Annie pointed at the slouching, resistant figure, plaid shirt trailing over his jeans. "That's him. J. J. Brown." She moved forward toward the captain. "We think he kidnapped a girl. Is there any trace of her?"

Captain Dooley frowned. "He was alone in the motorboat."

The petty officers led Brown, his wrists manacled together, across the dock. His dark hair rippled in the wind. His round face was puffy, his eyes bloodshot. He saw Annie and planted his feet like a mule. "Dammit." The word was a rasp of hatred. "I thought it was you last night. How was I supposed to know it wasn't you? Came flying up that damn alley. Thought I'd teach you a thing or two."

Annie started forward.

Billy held up a hand. "I'll deal with him." Billy took two steps. "J. J. Brown, you are under arrest for breaking and entering and attempted arson. Further, there is a possible charge of kidnapping. Now, we can make a deal, Brown. Kidnapping is a capital crime. South Carolina has the death penalty. If you cooperate, help us find Chloe Martin, I can reduce that charge. Maybe drop it."

Annie's gaze swung to Billy. She read determination and ruthlessness in his face. He was willing to give Brown a free ride if he helped Billy capture his prime suspect for two murders. She almost objected, but Max eased to her side, gave her a tiny nudge. He bent close to whisper, "Let it go. Finding Chloe is all that matters now."

Brown licked his lips. "Goddamn, my head hurts." He struggled to lift his hands. "These damn things are too damn tight. Look, I had a little too much to drink, played a joke I shouldn't have."

Billy looked toward the captain. "Captain Dooley, your men can release him. We'll take custody of him." Billy stepped closer to Brown. "Make it easy on yourself, man. Where's the girl?"

The petty officers looked toward their commander. At Captain Dooley's nod, the handcuffs were loosed. The commander's head moved a fraction. The petty officers, one storklike thin, the other a blunt-headed giant, rested their hands on their weapons.

Brown rubbed at his wrists. His puffy face took on a look of cajolement. "Anybody can make a mistake. All I did was jump out in front of her bike. Yeah. Maybe I gave a yell. I didn't know she'd crash the bike, knock herself out."

Annie looked at Billy. How about the broken brick with its bloodied end? But Billy just nodded. "So the bike crashed?"

Brown massaged his beard-stubbled face. His high voice was smooth with satisfaction when he continued. "Yeah. That's right. I thought it was her"—he jerked his head toward Annie—"so I picked her up." He stopped, his gaze furtive.

"And then?" Billy was impatient.

Brown shifted his big body.

Annie almost shouted out that he was a liar and not a very good one, but Max gave her a reminding nudge.

Brown rubbed his neck. "Guess I was pretty drunk. I woke up and hell, I was out there on the water." He made a sweeping gesture with his soft hand. "It's kind of hard to remember. But she got knocked out, and I hauled her along with me." His eyes brightened. "Yeah, I was going to take her to a doctor. Me, I help people. Sure, I do. But I was in my boat, not a car, so I couldn't take her to the hospital. I carried her down to the marina and was putting her in the boat. When I du—set her down, her head lolled back and I saw this dark red hair. I thought that was pretty funny." He glared at Annie. "The bitch over there, she's blond."

Annie caught Max's arm, held it tight. This time it was she who gave the cautionary look. She shook her head. Slowly, Max's taut muscles relaxed, but his blue eyes burned with anger.

"Anyway, there she was. I guess I wasn't thinking too straight. I got a rowboat and tied it to my stern. I thought I'd pull the boat around close to the main harbor. See"—his voice was more confident—"I figured somebody'd find the boat and call nine-one-one."

Billy's gaze swung around the harbor. "Nobody's reported a rowboat adrift. Where did you leave the boat?"

"Yeah, well"—Brown's eyes shifted away—"that's what I was gonna do, but it was dark and I guess I lost hold of the rope somehow. I don't know where that boat is."

Captain Dooley pointed toward the captive motorboat. "There's a line trailing from the back of the motorboat. But it was cut."

Annie clapped her hands together, pressed them so hard they hurt, stared at Brown. "You took her out there"—she pointed to the water stretching as far as the eye could see—"and cut the boat loose? And she was unconscious?"

Brown looked at the ground, lifted his shoulders, let them fall. "Hell, I don't know what happened." His voice was a mumble, scarcely heard. "Didn't know who she was. The boat got away. . . ."

Dark clouds laced across the horizon, a warning smudge at the base of the blue sky. The wind gusted.

Billy looked at the commander of the cutter. "We need an all-out search."

Captain Dooley squinted against the sun. "There's two and a half, maybe three hours of daylight left. We'll call Air Station Savannah and see if we can get a C-130 deployed. We'll give it our best effort."

———

Max drove fast. Annie held the cell phone close. "Henny, listen, get on the phone. Get Pamela Potts to help and Laurel and everybody you can think of. Roust out everybody who has a boat. Chloe Martin's unconscious and adrift in a rowboat. We're searching from Betsy Ross Reef to Hunting Island Reef and everything to the west. And there's a front coming in. We're on our way to the marina. A lot of boats have already left the main harbor."

The Maserati slewed to a stop by the marina.

Annie continued talking as they ran for the steps, shouting to be heard over the clatter of their steps. "Call me if you hear that anybody finds her. We're going to head out now. Thanks, Henny."

Max led the way. As they ran along the dock, Annie fumbled in her pocket. She'd tucked Bob Winslow's card—yes, there it was. As they climbed into their speedboat and Max cast off the line, she punched in Winslow's number.

"H'lo." Short, brusque, scared.

"Bob, Annie Darling." The motor roared. Annie slapped one hand over an ear. "Bob," she yelled, "here's what's happened. . . ."

As the boat nosed out of the harbor, picked up speed, raced with a *whop-whop-whop* over the whitecaps, Annie explained, ". . . and if you have a boat . . ." Spray curled in a lace ribbon, spattering the wind-shield, misting over them. "Good. Right. We're looking, too. Right. Good luck, Bob."

Annie pulled on a slicker, steered while Max donned his. They followed a zigzag path. Annie peered through binoculars. At first they talked eagerly, excited when they spotted another boat, exchanging shouts, but time raced fast as a greyhound and the sun began its inexorable descent, lower and lower in the winter sky, until there was only a splash of scarlet above the storm clouds that bulked like a humpbacked whale on the western horizon.

Finally Annie lowered the binoculars. She didn't say anything. It was too dark to see. They could be within twenty yards of a drift-ing boat and miss it in the twilight.

Slowly Max curved the boat around, headed for home.

Annie flinched as lightning flared. When the storm struck, how high would the waves be? Out of control, the boat might easily tip and swamp. If it remained upright,

Chloe would spend the night unprotected in the open. Rain would most likely seal her fate. It wouldn't take long for hypothermia to set in.

Annie huddled within her slicker, chilled, dispirited, hopeless. Ten minutes. Twenty. Now it was utterly dark except for the brief flashes of lightning. She looked ahead. There . . . across the water, the lights of the island glowed, spelling warmth and safety and home. But not for Chloe. Was she awake, hurt, in pain? Cold, so terribly cold? She'd not been found. Annie was sure of it. Someone would have called them if—

The cell phone beeped. Annie scrambled to pick it up. Numb fingers fumbled, pressed. "Yes. Hello. Yes?"

"Annie." Static crackled, making Henny's voice wavering and indistinct. "They found her. She's still alive. The guy who has her is setting course directly to the harbor. An ambulance is waiting to take her to the hospital."

Annie beamed, turned thumb's-up to Max. "Who found her?"

"That young lawyer. He just did a new will for me. Bob . . ." Static obliterated part of her sentence. ". . . know him?"

"Bob Winslow?" It was a cheer. "Henny, that's wonderful. Bob found her." She placed the emphasis on his name, not the verb. Annie shouted again, "Bob found her. Henny, it was meant to be. We're on our way." The lights of the harbor beckoned. "Be there in a minute." She clicked off the cell phone, turned to Max. "Bob found her."

Max knew his wife. "So it's special that Bob found her?"

"Of course it is." She leaned forward in the seat, wishing they could go faster. "Because he cares. It means everything's going to be all right."

Max didn't say anything, but he shot her a quick look as he slowed to enter the harbor. The smell of creosote and seawater and coming rain mingled.

Annie waved her hands. "I know. You think that sounds like Laurel." Annie decided it might be better not to be too explicit in her comparison. "It's more than that." Annie didn't lay claim to ESP or prescience. However . . . "You'll have to read Tony Hillerman's memoir, *Seldom Disappointed.* He said every traditional Navajo understands that all things are connected, that every cause has its destined effect. You see, it was meant to be. Out of all of us searching, Bob Winslow found Chloe." There was a tone of wonder in her voice.

Max reached over, squeezed her knee through the heavy slicker, and the boat bumped against the dock.

· *Twelve* ·

The red light atop the ambulance whirled. The back door was open and light spilled out onto the dock. The big lights on their metal poles blazed, offering some illumination, but the dark sky and black sea merged, impenetrable and forbidding. The EMTs waited with a gurney near the end of the dock. Billy Cameron stood next to them in grim and determined silence. Some boat owners who'd returned from the search milled about, their voices chittery as birds settling for the night. The water slapped against the pilings, tumbled on the seawall, a harbinger of the coming storm.

Annie peered out into the darkness, felt

the sea spray on her face. "Why aren't they here yet? How far out do you suppose he was when he found her? Oh, Max, what if no one had found her?"

"But Bob did. She'll be all right now." Max's deep voice was warm and real in the darkness. She couldn't see his features clearly. The light here was more a suggestion than a reality. But she didn't need to be able to see him. Every feature was clear and distinct in her mind and in her heart and would always be. Now and forever. The phrase drifted through her mind like brightly colored beads strung on a golden chain. Maybe this was how it would be for Chloe and Bob. Please God. Let him have found her in time. Annie pulled up the hood of her slicker. She was dry and well protected against the night, but the damp wind off the water was dropping the wind chill into the twenties.

Annie looked out at the water. "It's darker than a cave. I hope Bob knows his way. And look at Billy"—her tone was angry—"all ready to pounce, standing there at the very end of the dock so he'll be the first to see them and be right at the ladder ready to arrest her."

But it was Ben Parotti, standing in the wheelhouse of his ferry, who spotted the boat. The whistle of *The Miss Jolene* suddenly shrieked and shrieked again. Ben darted out on the bridge, pointing out to sea.

Slowly the form of the motorboat took shape in the blackness, its running lights bright points of cheer. As the motorboat chugged close to the dock, a shout went up. A police cruiser eased out from the shadows and closed in behind the oncoming boat.

Annie wrapped her arms across her front, the slicker crackling in protest. "I suppose that boat's to keep Bob from turning around and speeding out of the harbor! What's Billy thinking about?" But she knew that Billy was going to be damn sure Chloe Martin didn't escape his grasp. Not now. Possibly not ever.

"Come on, Max." She headed for the end of the dock. They stopped a few feet from a flight of steps, close enough to see the motorboat pull up and moor, close enough to see the bundled figure lying motionless in the well behind the front seat, close enough to see Bob Winslow in his shirtsleeves, shaking with cold.

Annie grabbed Max's arm. "Look, he doesn't have on a coat. He used it to cover her. Oh, Max, his face . . ."

The tall, angular, too-thin rescuer shook with cold, his face pinched and bluish. As he threw a coil of rope, he shouted, "Have you got hot packs? Hurry. For God's sake hurry, she's cold as ice."

The EMTs, a husky man with a crew cut and a rangy woman in her forties, hurried down the steps, carrying a stretcher. Bob Winslow had Chloe in his arms and was stepping onto the dock as they arrived. Quickly they rolled her onto the support, covered her, and headed up the steps, the stretcher tilting as they went.

The stretcher passed within a foot of Annie and Max. Annie felt a lurch within, shocked by a glimpse of fair skin the color of Grecian marble and as lifeless. The visible swath of hair was sodden, so wet the color appeared black. A raised welt disfigured her temple, the wound stark against a purpling bruise. Bob Winslow clung to one side of the stretcher, his long legs stretching to keep up with the lope of the EMTs.

Billy Cameron blocked the path to the ambulance. "I have a warrant here for the arrest—"

"Chief"—the crew-cut EMT was brusque—"save it for the hospital. It's going to be touch and go."

A custodian sloshed the wet mop over the side of the big metal bucket. He pushed the stringy tendrils as if they were heavy as a Medusa's head in stone. Annie's nose wrinkled. One part ammonia to three parts water? Who knew? The antiseptic smell of the hospital overlay the odor from the food trays stacked in a bin and awaiting pickup. The nurses' station was a length of hall away. An occasional nurse or nurse's aide moved near the curved wooden counter. The low mumble of television flowed from nearby rooms with partially open doors. Occasionally visitors walked past.

Annie paced. Max leaned against the wall opposite room 224. Lou Pirelli sagged wearily on a hard straight chair and avoided Annie's withering gaze. Finally she stopped directly in front of him. She waited until he reluctantly met her eyes. "Does Billy think

Chloe's going to escape into the night, head wound and all?"

Lou shoved a hand through his thick tangle of black hair. "Annie, I just work here. I got my orders. She's under arrest. I'm here to make sure she doesn't go anyplace. And I got to get official word from the doc. If she's well enough, she's supposed to be moved to the jail. You got a beef, take it to the man."

"Hey, Annie." Max pushed away from the wall. "Want a Dr Pepper or a Pepsi?"

"Dr Pepper." Abruptly she hungered desperately for the bubbly tangy pop, still the most original taste in America. Max ducked into a room two doors down. The jangle of coins in a slot, a bang, another jangle and bang, and he was back with a Dr Pepper for her and orange juice for him.

Annie looked at his choice. "Canned orange juice tastes metallic. And fruit juice is just another form of sugar."

Max nodded equably. "You're right. As always." He drank, wrinkled his nose, shrugged, drank some more.

"No vitamin C in Dr Pepper," Lou observed. "Max, will you keep watch? Think I'll get a Pepsi."

Annie popped open the top, took a satis-fying sip. The sugar and the zing gave her a snap of energy. "It has to be a good sign that they moved her to a room." There had been some color in Chloe's face when she was wheeled into room 224 a few minutes earlier. A nurse's aide had deftly maneu-vered the gurney, followed by Dr. Burford and Bob Winslow. Annie had made a valiant effort. "Dr. Burford, how is—" But the door had closed. It remained shut.

The elevator midway down the hall clacked open. Billy Cameron strode down the hall. He ignored Annie and Max, planted himself in front of the door, looked around, barked, "Lou?"

Lou hurried from the snack room, Pepsi in hand. "Here, Chief."

Billy pointed at room 224. "What's the word?"

"Nothing yet. Doc Burford's in there." Lou wiped beads of cold from the can of Pepsi. "And that guy that found her."

Billy folded his arms. "I don't know that he's got any right. What's he supposed to be? A boyfriend? He's not next of kin. I don't much like that. I'll tell doc to get him out of there."

Annie bolted forward, squeezed between Billy and the door to Chloe's room, stared into stony eyes. "Okay, Max and I are invisible, right? That's fine. Ignore us. But don't think you can trample all over Chloe just because she's unconscious. Her aunt and uncle didn't even come when I called them. Bob Winslow's got every right to be there. They're"—she hesitated, then blurted—"going to get engaged." Annie was sure of it. She heard the scrape of Max's shoes behind her, carefully did not glance toward him. "Billy"—there was no more rancor in her voice—"think how Bob feels. He loves her. He thought she might be lost. Forever. He found her—and he thought she might die. Don't make him leave her."

Billy rubbed his face, a face that sagged with fatigue. "She ran away. She's not running again." He looked at Lou. "Okay, the guy stays—as long as they leave the door open enough so you can hear. We'll clear it with the doc when he comes out. But I'm going to be sure she doesn't climb out a window."

The door opened. Dr. Burford, his mane of gray hair untidy, his face stubbled with beard, his white coat stained and hanging open, stepped out. "How come you two are standing here shouting at each other outside a sick woman's door? A woman whose head throbs like a jungle drum in a B flick." He pulled the door shut.

Billy glanced at it. "Doc—"

"C'mon." Dr. Burford lumbered toward the snack room. Inside, he poked his hand around the back of the pop machine, fished out a handful of quarters, dropped in two, punched a button, and bent down to get a can of Mountain Dew. He flipped off the cap and took the one oversize easy chair. He rummaged in a pocket of his white coat and pulled out a crumpled cellophane package.

Billy planted himself in front of the chair. "Doc, what's the deal?" Annie and Max stood to one side.

"Hypothermia. Concussion. Laceration, swelling right temple." He ripped open the MoonPie wrapper, took a huge bite. "Heat packs restored body temperature. Intermittent consciousness—"

Billy leaned forward. "She said anything?"

Dr. Burford took another big bite, leaving a smear of chocolate on his chin. "Keeps muttering, 'Bob, Bob, Bob.' Not much else." He lifted the Mountain Dew and chugged a good half.

Billy jangled the coins in his pocket. "How soon do you expect her to be able to talk?"

Dr. Burford lifted his stocky shoulders, let them drop. "Tomorrow. Maybe. But it isn't going to matter." He finished the soda, shoved the rest of the candy in his mouth, heaved to his feet, mumbled over the gob of candy, "Likely she won't remember a thing. Possibly not for several days before she was injured. That's the usual way with head wounds. Short-term memory loss. Anyway, she needs quiet. Keep a guard in the hall if you want to. But she's not going anywhere." He moved toward the doorway.

Billy stepped toward him. "I want that door open."

Dr. Burford swallowed, shrugged. "Whatever. But don't bother her."

Annie stepped into his path, looked up. Her eyes implored him. "You'll keep her for several days." She made it a statement, clear and strong, a demand.

Dr. Burford squinted at her, his heavy face unreadable.

"I want her released as soon as possible.

She's going to jail." Billy's face once again had its dogged, set look.

"Dr. Burford"—Annie's voice wobbled— "Chloe was locked in a closet when she was a little girl, left there, screaming in the dark, beating her hands against the door, sobbing. She's terrified of being locked up. You can't do that to her. She's hurt, disoriented—"

"She's a murder suspect. I've already heard this sob story." Billy's tone was bitter. He stalked to Annie, his face twisted in a scowl. "She was supposed to give herself up. Instead, she stays on the run and somebody else gets killed."

"Billy"—Annie threw out her hands, palms up—"it's crazy to say that Chloe shot Elaine. Especially when we know Elaine was trying to blackmail Rusty and Beth and maybe someone else as well. Trying to blame that murder on Chloe is twisting everything to make it fit your theory. Can't you open up your mind just for a minute?"

"As soon as I get her in jail, I'll sit down and talk to you, Annie. But not a minute before then. Doc—" Billy broke off, stared at the empty doorway.

Dr. Burford was gone. Max pointed down the hall.

Billy's face flushed a rusty color. "By God, in the morning we'll see what's what. Nobody's going to screw me over. Including Doc Burford." His blue eyes blazed at Annie. "Or you either. You're trying to keep her in the hospital and out of jail. I'll bet she'll be well enough to be moved tomorrow. As for theories, Annie, why don't you open *your* mind." His sarcasm was heavy. "Look at what happened—a man struck down from behind, his head smashed. His girl-friend shot dead. Shots fired at the woman he intended to marry. Talk about a triangle, you've got one there. Connect the dots yourself. We're talking about passion, Annie, a woman beside herself with jealousy and anger. She kills him, she kills the woman he's been involved with, she shoots at the woman he was going to marry."

Annie sputtered, "Billy, she's not—"

He held up his hand like a cop directing traffic. "Hold up. Hear me out. You don't accept that she got the gun from O'Neill's cabin despite the fact his cabin was searched. But it could have happened. She called Hasty, said she was coming. Martin could have gotten that gun. Now I'll admit we didn't find the matching gun in your storeroom or in the knapsack in the bike basket. Maybe she hid it somewhere. Maybe she threw it away. Hell, she may have planted it near the Neville house."

"Oh, sure." Annie could be sarcastic, too. "She probably hid that gun in between shooting Elaine and dashing up to the Neville house to shoot at Virginia. Billy, think about it. Chloe didn't want him to marry Virginia, but there's no rhyme or reason—"

"We're not talking reason. We're talking passion." His voice was bleak. "Call it what you will. Jealousy. Selfishness. Anger."

Annie held tight to her Dr Pepper can, felt the aluminum give in her fingers. Trying to reach Billy was like tugging at a locked door. There wasn't any give, none at all. "How about a real motive? How about money? How about some member of a family that wants its money? There's a reason to kill Jake. He can't marry Virginia if he's dead. Then comes the phone call. 'I saw you.' There's a motive, self-preservation. Elaine has to die. Anyone in the Neville family could have known that Jake had those guns. Like Rusty Brandt."

Billy gave a disbelieving snort. "So he brings his girlfriend and comes and tells us about the blackmail attempt?"

"Why not? What a good boy am I. Honest Rusty. That's a perfect cover for Elaine's murder. After all, he lied about not knowing where to make the dropoff. He could have had it all planned, known where the guns were, got one and shot her. Then he hurried up to the house, and there's Virginia in the study, just like on a lighted stage. Murder's just been done. Why not another? Why not kill her? She's the cause of all the trouble."

Billy pulled some coins from his pocket, moved over to the machine, inserted two quarters, punched. He picked up a can of Dr Pepper, opened it, drank deeply. He squinted at her, a quizzical, puzzled look. "How stupid do you think they are? Rusty Brandt or Susan? Carl Neville, Irene? Louise Neville? Any of them? Virginia could be killed any time. Drown in the pool. Fall off a boat. An overdose. You can bet she's taking something to sleep. Everybody would agree she's upset, depressed. So why shoot Elaine with a gun that can be linked to the family, then run up and shoot at Virginia, tie the crimes to that house? It doesn't make any sense. No, you mark my words, Annie. There's emotion—"

Annie heard his words. Emotion. And passion. Billy kept talking about passion.

"—behind this crime, not reason. Sure the Neville family wants the money. But nobody hates Virginia. She may be in their way, but she's a nice lady. Sure, they should have inherited, but only a damn fool would have shot at Virginia and tossed that gun in the fountain. I don't see any damn fools in that house. But if you want passion, who ran away from the point sobbing? Who threw her dress in the sound? Who demanded to see Elaine? There's only one person who fits, Annie, and it's Chloe Martin."

"One person . . ." Annie spoke slowly, pressed her fingers against her temples. Her eyes widened.

"Annie?" Billy stared at her.

Max stepped near. "Annie."

It was as though their voices came from far away. She understood abruptly with a clarity that transformed her thoughts. Oh, yes, now she saw, and she was dazzled by the cleverness. A magician waves a scarlet scarf in one hand while plucking a coin from midair with the other. The coin, of course, was secreted in a sleeve masked by the rippling silk. The trick is in dazzling the eye, diverting attention.

"Billy, I know who killed him." There was utter confidence in her voice. "I know who killed Elaine. I know who shot into the study. Here's what happened. . . ."

Before she finished, Max was nodding. His eyes applauded her. He looked swiftly at Billy because there was only one opinion that counted.

Billy finished off the soda, crumpled the can. His face was crumpled, too, brow furrowed, mouth turned down. Slowly, he nodded. "I got to admit that's a possibility, but—"

Annie reached out, touched his arm, her fingers feather-soft against his sleeve. "I know. You don't believe it. But be honest, it could have happened that way. Couldn't it?"

He shrugged. "Yeah. It's clever."

"I can prove it." Annie clapped her hands together. "I know, I know, you're going to arrest Chloe. But there's an easy way to prove whether I'm right. And we can do it tomorrow while Chloe's still in the hospital."

Billy waited, face skeptical, hand squeezing the lump of aluminum.

Annie spoke over the crackling sound of the metal. "The Nevilles are a prominent family. Murder's been done—twice—close to their home and gallery, attempted a third time from their courtyard. It would be politic for the police chief to offer a report to the family members about the progress of the investigation. Here's what we can do. . . ." As she talked, she felt Max's resistance, saw his face tighten into a worried frown. He started to speak. She put a finger to her lips, shook her head.

Billy listened, his blunt head bent forward. When she finished, he stared down at his hands clasped together, his face expressionless.

Annie looked at him. Funny, she'd never noticed that Billy's face was so much heavier now. Lines splayed from his eyes, ran in a deep furrow from his lips. He had a generous mouth, so often spread in a happy grin. He lifted his head, his face filled with trouble and uncertainty, and stared into her eyes.

She didn't know what he was looking for. Maybe memories. They shared a lot of memories, she and Max and Billy. It was

Annie who'd solved a crime that threatened to engulf Mavis when she sought sanctuary on the island. If it hadn't been for Annie, Mavis might once again have fled, leaving behind the love that Billy offered. Annie and Max had helped Billy in other ways, been his supporters and friends for a long time.

And he had been their friend.

Billy looked away, lifted his arm, tossed the crumpled can in an arc to land in the wastebasket. He reached to his shirt pocket, drew out a folded square of cream note card, glanced at it with an odd half-smile. "Yeah." He turned toward Max. "I forgot to tell you when I first got here. I ran into your mom in the hospital parking lot." He reached into his pockets, pulled out a set of keys to the Maserati, tossed them to Max. "She knew you'd left your car at the marina when you and Annie set out in your boat. Somebody told her you'd docked at the main harbor after Chloe was found. Anyway, your mom knew you'd need your car. So she went by your house, got an extra set of keys, brought the car here. Henny was waiting to take her home. So your car's downstairs when you're ready to go." Billy pressed his lips together, looked at the note card, then handed it to Annie.

Max bent near and they read it together: "Pilpay—Honest men esteem and value nothing so much in this world as a real friend."

Annie reached out, clasped Billy's big warm hand. Max placed his hand over both.

Billy's mouth spread slowly in a smile. "So I guess tomorrow I'd better set up a meeting at the Neville house. . . ."

Max stood in front of the fireplace, hands jammed into the pockets of his red robe. His face was in shadow, but Annie didn't mistake the hard ridge of his jaw, knew his dark blue eyes were somber with doubt. And fear. "I don't like it." His voice was heavy.

"It's the only way." Annie spoke quietly. Her gaze moved to the glowing logs in the fireplace. Sparks suddenly showered, cheerful and comforting. A cold rain splashed against the windows, but the room was warm, filled with safety and love and layers of happiness. She sat very still. She wanted to shiver. Yes, she was scared.

But . . . She lifted her face, ran her hand through tangled hair. "I'll be all right. We've got it planned perfectly."

Max turned, picked up the poker, jabbed it roughly against the log. The wood blazed, throwing his face into clear relief, bleak, worried, foreboding. "Yeah. Well, maybe nobody will come."

If Chloe was guilty, no one would come.

But Annie was certain. Yes, the murderer would come. The murderer would have to come.

The Florentine gold of the Neville house was muted by the drizzle and the lowering sky. Lumpy black clouds piled overhead like coals heaped in a scuttle. Annie pulled up the hood of her all-weather coat, welcoming the protection from the persistent rain. The magnificent villa with its balconies and ornate stonework and red-tiled roof was still majestic, but it had a rather tatty air on this stormy January morning, a shutter hanging askew on the second floor, fronds of palmettos littering the cobbled pavement, mounds of wet leaves pressing against the front steps. Billy's mud-splashed cruiser, as out of place as a spurned lover at a wedding, was parked behind a cluster of cars, a sleek silver Mercedes, a red Porsche, a Ford SUV, a BMW sedan, a black Lexus, and a dark blue older Lincoln Continental. Annie counted. So everyone in the Neville family was there.

Carl Neville held the huge front door open. The center panes of ruby red and jade green art glass were repeated in small squares above the lintel. On a sunny day the panes would blaze like jewels in a crown. Today they were dull. Carl's long pleasant face lighted with a smile. "Good of you to come on a morning like this. Everybody's in the living room. This way." He gestured to an arch framed by painted Italian tiles.

As they entered the wide, deep room, Annie had a swift impression of understated elegance, sofas in a golden biscuit shade, deeper hues of honey from the chairs, and a brilliant splash of color from a carnelian vase on a balustrade near a starkly white pillar. She realized at once that the room with its muted colors, white tables, and expanse of white-framed mirrors had been created to showcase one person. Irene

Neville, her dark hair gleaming, her aquiline face dramatic with sharp black brows and crimson lip gloss, stood with one arm resting gracefully on a shoulder-high white marble mantel. Irene was in her element, confident, assured, imperious yet gracious. The drape of her emerald green jacket was perfect, the contrast with her cream wool slacks sensuous. There was no distress marring her lovely face this morning. She nodded regally to Annie and Max but kept her attention focused on Billy Cameron, her expression of courtesy undermined by a distinct aura of condescension.

The others were there, but they were bit players to the star. Annie and Max took empire chairs on either side of a sofa.

Carl moved to his wife, waited for her attention. His sandy hair drooped over his narrow forehead. He was unremarkable in a gray cashmere pullover, gray wool slacks, black loafers. Perhaps unknown to himself, he bent forward, shoulders bowed, hands clasped, the eternal supplicant.

Reddish face pugnacious, feet outstretched and crossed, Rusty Brandt lounged in an overstuffed chair with pebbled fabric dull as oatmeal. His faded red hair was still wet from a shower. His navy tattersall shirt looked expensive, his chinos new and crisp. He stared at Billy, his blue eyes wary above puffy pouches.

Susan Brandt smoothed back a strand of fair hair. Her chiseled features were set in a determinedly blank expression. She perched stiffly at the end of one of the big sofas, her fingers plucking at the tassels on a bulky cushion. Her navy wool dress, the somber color relieved only by bright gold buttons, made her look emaciated. She ignored her husband.

Louise Neville stood stiff as a poker in a shapeless black dress. Her wizened face was alert, like a grizzled old terrier watching strangers approach.

Virginia Neville sat to one side of the wide room on a hard straight bench near a window, clearly distanced from the others. She sat immobile, but her light blue eyes darted around the room. She'd taken pains with her hair, the coronet braids perfectly arranged, and with her makeup, a touch of pink on her cheeks, a light gloss on her lips. But no manner of artifice or care could lessen the ravages of her face, the eyes hollowed, the skin blotchy and swollen, the lips drooping. She'd chosen a burgundy silk dress, possibly in an attempt to over-shadow her paleness with the rich fabric. The effect was as garish as draping a skele-ton in scarlet. From her necklace hung a sil-ver butterfly, each wing studded with tiny diamonds. The beauty of the striking jew-elry was in stark and dreadful contrast to her stricken face.

Annie glanced at them all. It was a far dif-ferent group from last night. What a differ-ence clean, dry clothes made. Last night everyone had looked bedraggled. But more than their appearances was different. Last night fear was an unseen guest. This morn-ing even Virginia appeared calm. She no longer quivered with terror. Annie wondered if she'd had second thoughts about her of-fer to return the Neville money to her late husband's children.

". . . hope to set everyone's mind at rest." A rested Billy looked genial, his broad face pleasant. His uniform was crisp, khaki shirt ironed and starched, wrinkle-free khaki trousers creased, black shoes shiny as ob-sidian despite a glisten of raindrops. He stood at ease, arms behind his back.

Irene clapped her hands together. "It's

very good of you to take time to speak with us. It's reassuring to know that our brave officers of the law are defending us against dangerous criminals." She raised one sleek eyebrow. "I've heard the murders and the attack on Virginia were all committed by a young woman who was working in their store." She glanced toward Annie and Max. "Quite a desperado. But you've finally corralled her, I understand." There was the faintest suggestion of irony.

Carl moved restively, sent his wife a warning glance. Louise fingered the drooping collar of her dress, her hooded eyes intent.

Billy was reflected in the mirror over the mantel and in the series of decorated mirrors ranged on the opposite wall. The room seemed filled with his burly uniformed reflection. "We have had excellent cooperation from our citizens." His tone was unruffled. If offense had been meant, none had been taken.

Carl pushed his glasses higher on his nose and his tense shoulders relaxed.

Billy was, in fact, expansive. He rocked back on his heels, thumbs hooked in his belt loops. "I am happy to report that we have a suspect in custody. The young woman in question, Chloe Martin, is presently in the hospital. She's suffered a head wound and a broken leg—"

Annie thought the addition of a broken leg to Chloe's wounds was artful, and she was pleased that the imaginary injury had been her idea. No one listening to Billy would doubt that Chloe was immobilized. And helpless.

"—and she's recovering from a concussion. The leg has been set. We expect that she will be discharged perhaps tomorrow afternoon. She will then be booked and formal arraignment set."

"I suppose she's under guard?" Irene straightened a silver filigree box on the mantel.

Billy's expression was avuncular. Annie had a quick memory of Billy playing Santa Claus at the Christmas party at The Haven. "Ma'am," his voice was hearty, "there's no danger at all that she will cause any more trouble. Actually, we don't have a formal guard—our force is limited—but she is physically unable to leave her hospital bed. She will be transferred to the jail in a wheelchair. You can be assured that there is no further danger to the community or to Mrs. Neville."

Susan twined a length of a tassel around her finger. "How did she get hurt?"

Billy glanced toward Annie. "She was accosted in an alleyway down by the marina. That incident is not related to the current investigation."

"There seems to have been an uncommon amount of crime these past few days." Irene's tone was disdainful.

Susan twined two tassels together. "I'm afraid I don't understand any of it. Why did this girl kill Jake? Why did she kill Elaine Hasty and shoot at Virginia? None of it makes any sense to me."

"Here's the story as we know it." Billy was brisk. "Chloe Martin was infatuated with Jake O'Neill. She came to the reception Friday night. That's the first she knew that he was going to marry Mrs. Neville."

Virginia pressed the back of a fist against her lips. Her face looked pummeled, every bit of hope destroyed. The future Virginia had looked to, the love she had counted on, the happiness that had been within her reach, all were gone.

Billy's matter-of-fact demeanor wavered

for an instant. He looked at Virginia, his eyes dark with pity, his lips compressed. He cleared his throat. "Sorry, Mrs. Neville. I know this is hard for you. If you don't want to remain, I'll understand."

Virginia's hand dropped to her necklace. Her fingers curled tightly around the silver butterfly. "No." Her voice was faint but determined. "I have to know what happened."

"I'll be as brief as I can." Billy lifted a hand, gestured in the general direction of the point. "Martin and O'Neill made plans to meet at the point—"

Rusty's hands clamped on the side of his chair.

Billy's eyes slid over Rusty, moved to Susan. "—and we know that Elaine Hasty was looking out the window of the gallery kitchen. She saw Martin walk down that path. She saw O'Neill. She didn't realize the significance of this until Mrs. Darling spoke with her on Saturday. At that time, Hasty refused to say whether she observed anyone else on the path. As it turns out—"

Rusty's shoulders bunched.

"—two other persons are known to have visited the point. However, these individuals have been cleared of any connection to the crime. There has been some suggestion that there was yet another person at the scene, but I find that very unlikely." Billy's face hardened. "The prosecution will contend that Martin became enraged, that O'Neill gave up trying to reason with her and was leaving the point, and that Martin grabbed up a thick branch and ran up behind him and struck him down. She then fled the scene and was observed leaving the premises."

Annie jumped to her feet. She strode across the carpet, fetched up face-to-face with Billy. Her reflection joined his in the mirrors. Annie glared at him. Inside, she was focused on what she had to do and how she had to do it. There must be no suspicion that this had been prearranged. "I can't sit here and listen to you make Chloe out to be a murderer. You aren't telling the whole story. You know full well that she's been drifting in and out of consciousness and everything she says makes it clear that Jake O'Neill was alive when she ran away and that someone else came toward him. She turned to go back and she caught a glimpse of something. I was sitting with her last night and I heard it myself."

Billy folded his arms, bent his big head forward. His face was set in a furious glower. The frown and his hulking stance made him look huge and overbearing in the mirrors. "Like you said, she comes and goes. But she damn sure knows she's wanted for murder, so of course she's going to spin a tale when she's conscious. Anyway, none of what she said makes sense. No, she's going to jail as soon as she's well enough to be moved. As far as I'm concerned that will be tomorrow afternoon."

The thick canopy of the trees lessened the rain, but great dollops of water splashed down from the laden leaves. The bike tires turned the puddles on the asphalt path into geysers, but Annie felt warm and comfortable in her poncho and rubber boots. She tried to ignore the hard cold knot of fear deep within. Everything was going to be all right. Max and Billy would be hidden in an empty room next door.

"Annie." Max's shout was urgent, imperative.

She braked and her bike slewed.

Max was past her, his bike blocking the

path. He flung it down and was at her side. Two strong hands came out, gripped her arms through the plastic of the poncho. "Annie, for God's sake, that other gun." His voice was shaking.

Despite the rain-smeared gloom in the forest preserve, Annie saw the fear that turned his eyes dark with pain.

"What if the door opens and the gun goes off and there you are—" He broke off, swallowed, found it hard to breathe.

"That would be stupid." Annie didn't think this murderer was stupid. "Think of the noise. People would be out in the hall in an instant. How could there be an escape? No, this will be quiet. We can count on that." A pillow held over the face of an unconscious woman or medicine dropped into a glass and the glass held near with a soft murmur, "Drink this . . ." Not the gun.

Surely not the gun.

Max reached out, gently touched her cheek. "Have I ever"—his voice seemed to come from far away—"told you that I love you?"

The rain-drenched trees pressed close to the earth. The air was heavy with moisture, dark as evening, though there were hours yet before night. But they stood in a circle of love, bright and warm and joyful as a summer sun.

Annie took a deep breath. Her lips quivered, but her words were quick. "And I love you." She reached up, clasped his hand, gave it a squeeze, then tugged. "Come on. Race you." She nosed her bike past his, swung up to the seat, and pedaled fast, then faster. She'd made an appointment she had to keep.

The bike rack behind the hospital was empty on this sodden January afternoon. They shoved their bikes into place and walked swiftly, unidentifiable and unremarkable in their sleek ponchos, toward the basement door. It was, as arranged, unlocked. They slipped inside.

Billy was waiting, face grim, arms folded. As they shed their ponchos, slipped out of their boots, he said quietly, "Everything's ready. Chloe Martin's been moved to a room across the hall. At the desk she's still listed in 224. Bob Winslow's with her. He refuses to leave her, and he was damn suspicious about the switch. I finally had to explain." Billy cleared his throat. "He asked me to tell you thanks. He's offered to hide in the room with you. I told him we had everything taken care of." A deep-drawn breath. "Annie, I've been thinking about it. The hell of it is, you could be right. I don't think so. But if you are—"

She smiled at him. "We'll catch a murderer."

The IV taped to her arm, thankfully sans needle, felt odd, the bandage that masked one side of her face even more so, the fake cast on her leg cumbersome. The hospital gown offered little warmth in the clammy sheets. The room was quiet. Max was in the bathroom with the door ajar. He'd refused at the last minute to budge from the room, insisted he could hide in the bath or closet. She'd pointed out that there might be a quick search of the room. He'd pointed out he didn't give a damn. Now, as the minutes ticked by in silence, the quiet of the hospital oppressive, she was grateful for his presence.

The room was shadowy and dim, the only illumination a soft golden glow from the recessed light above the washbasin. The television screen, mounted on the wall opposite the bed, was quiet and dark. Annie tried to relax, but she felt stiff as a starched shirt. Max abhorred starch in his shirts, said no gentleman ever wore a starched shirt. Last week when she'd picked up the laundry and brought it to their room, he'd plucked the shirt from its plastic and stood the shirt up, pointing at it in horror. She'd returned the shirt to the laundry, but she'd kept the memory of that crisp shirt, standing on its own. Now she felt like that shirt, stiff and empty. She stared at the clock. The minute hand inched ahead with agonizing slowness. It had a little hitch. Instead of moving smoothly, the hand halted, quivered, then jerked. Slowly, so slowly, time passed. Annie strained to hear. Afternoon turned to evening. In the hallway there was the rumble of the food cart. No dinner for them. With night, the window gave onto blackness dark as asphalt. The rain pelted against the panes. The tick of the clock, the *whoosh* of rain gurgling down drainpipes, the rustle of the sheets when she moved, she heard these sounds, such homely, familiar, comfortable sounds. But not now, not in this dreadful time of waiting. She tried to turn her face toward the door. They shouldn't have put the bandage on this side. It was hard to see, the gauze puckering up near her eye. Of course, the bandage was makeshift, not intended for good vision. . . .

The door swung briskly in. A figure in white stepped inside, carrying a small plastic tray with a hypodermic syringe. As the door closed behind the nurse, Annie frowned. Damn. No wonder hospitals were always being sued for mistakes—the wrong foot amputated, the wrong medicine dispensed. This room was clearly marked empty at the nurses' station. Probably the nurse's patient was in room 222.

The nurse stood at the bedside. A competent hand firmly gripped Annie's arm. "Time for our pain medication. I'll be quick." The pleasant, well-modulated voice was the prototype of professional cheer. Despite the fringe of gauze in her line of vision, despite the dim light of the room, Annie recognized a familiar face, a face set and hard and desperate and deadly. She had time to think how easily Chloe could have been killed, and then she yanked her arm free, grabbed the wrist of the hand holding the syringe, and screamed.

For an instant the arm poised to kill was utterly still. Then abruptly the attacker pulled away, scrambling to get free. Annie's grip was broken. The door from the bathroom banged. The light flashed on. Max thudded across the room. The hall door burst in. "Stop. I've got you covered." Billy stood in the doorway, huge black gun held in both hands.

Virginia Neville's thin voice was sharp, commanding. "Drop that gun. Drop it. Stay where you are, both of you. Unless you want her to die."

Slowly loosening his grip, Billy dropped the gun. The crack of metal on the hard floor signaled Virginia's triumph.

Annie lay still as an effigy, the pressure of Virginia's gun against her temple hard and painful.

"You trapped me." Virginia's eyes flickered to each of them. "And that girl isn't even here." She jabbed the gun against Annie. "I wanted to kill her. I wanted to. Even if she hadn't seen me. I thought I heard someone on the path, but I couldn't be sure in the fog. It was all her fault. She took Jake away from me. I saw him go down the path, and there was something about his expression . . . I think I knew. When I got there, they didn't hear me. She was so angry. He told her I was—nice." The word had an ugly sound. "Nice. He'd made love to me, told me—But it doesn't matter what he said, does it? He lied to me. I hated him then, even when he sent her away, told her he'd promised me. But she wasn't even out of sight when he called after her and started to follow her. That's when I ran after him. I hit him as hard as I could. He fell down without a sound. I took the path into the garden and went to the tent. Everyone thought she'd done it, and it served her right. It was all her fault. Tonight she was going to die. Insulin can kill." Her voice was matter-of-fact.

The rain splashed against the windows. Annie wondered if Virginia had left a raincoat and hat in one of the women's restrooms, if she'd changed there into a nurse's uniform, fixed her hypodermic of death taken from Carl's supply of insulin. Annie had pushed away the hypodermic, but the gun was hard against her head. She wondered how many minutes—or seconds—re-

mained in her life. The thrust of the gun barrel was unyielding.

"Get up." The pressure increased. "Ease
to a sitting position. Yes, that's right." The
voice was hideously reminiscent of a nurse
instructing a patient. "On your feet."

Annie eased to the floor, stood a little
crookedly with one bare foot and the other
covered by the cast.

Virginia stood close behind Annie, poking
the barrel into Annie's neck, and talked fast.
"Do exactly as I say or I'll shoot. The two of
you"—clearly she meant Billy and Max—
"move over by the window and face outside. Good. That's very good. Stay where
you are. Count to ten. Don't forget, I'll
count, too. If the door opens before then,
she dies."

An iron hand gripped Annie's arm and in
an instant they were in the hall. "This way."
She pulled Annie toward the red light at the
end of the hallway, marking the stairs.
"Don't scream, don't fight, don't make a
sound, or I'll kill you."

The marble hallway was silent. The
loosely applied cast flopped, keeping Annie
off balance. The pressure of the gun barrel
was steady and hard and terrifying. They

moved quickly, despite Annie's fake cast, their shadows odd against the wall, the one shadow so near the first. At the stairs, Virginia pulled open the door. They stepped onto the landing. The stairwell was well lighted but damp and chilly.

Annie expected a command. The cold round circle of metal was withdrawn from the back of her neck. For an instant, she felt an exquisite relief and a surge of hope. She was turning to look when pain exploded in her head.

As the door into the corridor closed, Max and Billy whirled, dashed across the room. Billy lunged for the knob, but Max reached out, gripped Billy's arm. His face pale, sweat beading his skin, Max mouthed numbers—". . . four . . . five . . . six . . ."

Billy yanked free his cell phone, punched. "APB. Virginia Neville, wanted for murder, armed and dangerous, escaping from hospital. Annie Darling taken hostage. Suspect dressed as a nurse, approximately five foot six inches. . . ."

". . . eight . . ."

The sound of the gunshot was muffled by distance but unmistakable.

With a yell that came from deep inside, his face twisted by anguish, Max flung open the door and plunged into the hall, looking up and down the corridor.

At the end of the hall, the door to the stairwell was wide open. A deep voice shouted, "Help. Get help."

Max reached the doorway first. Bob Winslow, his tall, angular body bent into a tight crouch, held Annie's limp wrist in his huge hand. "There's a pulse. Oh, hey, she's moving. . . ."

Max pushed past, was on his knees, slipping an arm around Annie as she struggled to sit.

Billy stepped over them and thudded down the stairs.

"You okay?" Bob asked Annie. "Here." He dragged out a handkerchief, handed it to her.

Max gently held it against the blood welling from the back of her scalp.

Annie blinked. "Hurts." She peered up at Bob. "What happened?"

Bob's eyes were huge. "I was watching out the door of Chloe's room. After what you told us, I wanted to see what happened. I saw a nurse go into Annie's room, and then in a minute she and Annie came out, but she had a gun to the back of Annie's head. A nurse! I waited until they got to the exit and then I came after them. I got here just as that nurse"—his voice rose in astonishment—"hit Annie over the head. She had the gun by the barrel. She was getting ready to hit Annie again when I grabbed her arm. We struggled and the gun went off and she"—he looked toward the stairwell—"got away from me." His young narrow face looked stricken. "She flung herself—I don't know if she knew what she was doing—over the railing."

· *Thirteen* ·

What a difference a few weeks made. January began with heavy fog and days of drizzle and occasional heavy downpours. Now the sunny sea isle once again lived up to its balmy reputation with innocent blue skies and highs in the seventies. Golfers swung, tennis players served, and booksellers (actually Annie was the only one on the island) sold. Of course, winter might reassert its chilly dominance any day in a final February fling, but for now all was well, hey diddle diddle, and the party at Death on Demand eddied through the open front door, the overhead fans whirled, and the vigorous chatter of the guests rivaled the squawks of a migratory flock heading north.

Henny was perhaps pushing the season in her white-and-blue striped blazer and white cotton skirt. She looked the epitome of spring with a scarlet hibiscus bloom in her silver-streaked black hair. She held high the tray with the fluted glasses of champagne, caroling, "Libations for the literati," and flashing Annie a quirky, perhaps wine-induced, certainly ebullient grin. She paused, swerved toward Annie, bent close to her ear, hissed, "Who finally charmed Sergeant Ernest Heath?" Her eyes glistened and there was a distinct scent of champagne.

Annie's eyes narrowed, she gave a quick nod, hissed in return, "Philo Vance, of course." S. S. Van Dine's clever detective had eventually gained the respect of the honest but inept New York homicide officer.

Henny said, "I'm miffed. Squiffed? No, miffed. Hmm, maybe I'd better not have any more. You know, champagne is deceptive. Dyspeptic? Possibly. But definitely not déclassé. Oh, hey, as long as I can say *literati* and not lisp, I'm still the cat's meow." Her smile was beatific. "Isn't that the cat's pajamas? To be the cat's meow." She grinned, uttered a piercing and very creditable meow, then gaily swung back into the crowd, the tray at a slight tilt.

Atop the Agatha Christie stacks, the elegant black cat named in her honor lifted a sleek head and stared unwinkingly at Henny, green eyes glowing.

Annie was laughing, though she wondered if perhaps she should send Max to rescue the tray and tactfully offer Henny a comfortable chair and a cup of coffee. She almost called out to him—he was listening pleasantly to the imposing president of the Garden Club—but there was too much hubbub. Guests surged back and forth, most trying to get a glimpse of the Boston Mackey watercolors soon to be auctioned for the island literacy project.

Boston Mackey boomed, "Make way. Make way." And, of course, everyone did.

Annie grinned and climbed on a stool, the better to see. As she surveyed her kingdom, she felt a sudden rush of delight. Coming through the door, just a little hesitantly, Bob Winslow's big hand firmly on her elbow, was Chloe Martin. Though she was still pale, her glossy dark red hair shone, her narrow face looked eager. She saw Annie, gave a whoop, and held up her left hand to display a golden ring with a lovely diamond in a filigree setting.

Annie clapped her hands above her head, hopped down from the footstool, and wormed toward the front door. Behind her she heard Boston exclaim, "Ladies and gentlemen, tonight's event to benefit . . ."

Annie reached the doorway and flung her arms around Chloe. "I'm so happy for you." She turned, looked up and up and up, at Bob Winslow's long face, now a vivid cherry red. "Congratulations! I'm so happy for both of you."

Bob's big hands settled on her shoulders, gripped them tightly. "Thanks to you. And that woman almost got you. . . ."

Annie pushed away the memory of the pressure of the gun against her skin, Virginia Neville's desperate face, and her fatal plunge into the hospital stairwell.

"But she didn't." Annie was brisk.

Boston began to clap. "Let's give a cheer for our hostess, the bookseller with the mostest."

"Annie, Annie, Annie . . ." came the chant.

Startled, Annie turned.

"That's right. Bring her down here." His big face glowing, Boston stamped a foot. "No false modesty permitted. She's the lady who can tell everyone about my watercolors. You've heard about the fastest gun in the west? Well, Annie Darling's the quickest mouth in the mystery world."

Annie stopped, her face—as they used to say in Louisa May Alcott thrillers—a study. Surely Boston wasn't going to ask her to identify the paintings. . . .

"Hey there, young man," Boston shouted at Bob, "you're big enough to escort Annie. You and your girl—oh, yes, the pretty redhead. Folks, I met this young lady when I brought my watercolors to the store, and she's a delight. Any young man who has her in tow is a dandy fellow. That's right, you two, bring Annie right up here."

Laughing, Bob and Chloe each took an elbow and began to propel Annie up the central aisle.

"Annie, Annie, Annie . . ."

In an instant, Annie stood beside Boston and he was pointing at the watercolors, his face glistening with excitement. He was cheerfully and unashamedly as puffed up with pride and expectation as a papa hawk awaiting the flight of his offspring. "All right, Annie, tell the folks about my selections. These mysteries are as important as any that have ever been written. You know them."

Annie stared at the watercolors. She knew these books. Of course she did. At least the first and the second and—

Chloe's eyes widened. She exclaimed, "Boston, wait! That's not fair. Annie knows the books, but she always lets a customer identify the paintings. And I know Bob can do it." Proudly, she looked up and up and up at her fiancé.

Bob Winslow awkwardly cracked the knuckles of one hand, glanced quickly at each painting in turn. He looked diffidently at Annie. "Are you sure I'm not butting in?"

"Oh, Bob, be my guest." Annie's hands clenched. Did he know them? Would he save her from public humiliation? Even now, she could see Henny leaning forward, her gaze questioning.

"Oh, well." Bob grinned. "Sure. They are"—and he pointed them out—"*A Study in Scarlet* by Arthur Conan Doyle, *The Mysterious Affair at Styles* by Agatha Christie,

The Tower Treasure by Franklin W. Dixon, *Red Harvest* by Dashiell Hammett, and *The Secret of the Old Clock* by Carolyn Keene."

Boston's loud voice announced, "Milestones in the mystery genre and in order of their publication, as any fool would know . . ."

Annie flung herself at Bob, hugged him, pulled Chloe into their circle, and a cheer rose on the night air.